Dee Williams was born and brought up in Rotherhithe in East London where her father worked as a stevedore in Surrey Docks. Dee left school at fourteen, met her husband at sixteen and was married at twenty. After living abroad for some years Dee and her husband moved to Hampshire, close to the rest of her family. ELLIE OF ELMLEIGH SQUARE is her sixth novel set in Rotherhithe.

Also by Dee Williams

Carrie of Culver Road
Polly of Penn's Place
Annie of Albert Mews
Hannah of Hope Street
Sally of Sefton Grove
Maggie's Market

Ellie of
Elmleigh Square

Dee Williams

HEADLINE

First published in 1996
by HEADLINE BOOK PUBLISHING

First published in paperback in 1996
by HEADLINE BOOK PUBLISHING

10 9 8 7 6 5

ISBN 0 7472 5307 2

Typeset by
Letterpart Limited, Reigate, Surrey

Printed and bound in Great Britain

HEADLINE BOOK PUBLISHING
A division of Hodder Headline PLC
338 Euston Road
London NW1 3BH

I would like to dedicate this book to the memory of my very dear husband, Les. You have left a great void in my life that time will never heal.

Because he liked to like people, people liked him.

– Mark Twain

I would also like to take this opportunity to thank my son-in-law, Gez, for being so supportive to Carol, his wife, and myself through all our troubles. He has been a tower of strength. Thank you, Gez.

Chapter 1

Ellie Walsh felt, despite the pleasantness of the surroundings she worked in, apprehensive.

'Cheer up, gel,' said Peggy, rushing past waving a dustpan
and brush in the air. 'The day's nearly over.'

Ellie smiled at Peggy's retreating back. Her friend was a
slim girl, always full of energy, and, at nineteen, two years
older than Ellie. Ellie was also slim, but that was because
food had always been scarce at home. The day was nearly
over, and that was the trouble, thought Ellie; she had to go
home. Today was Friday, pay day; that would probably
bring forth more arguments from her mother about the tips
she never got. Ellie had told her many times it wasn't that
kind of tea room. Ellie sighed. If only her mother would let
her keep more than just one precious sixpence out of her
wages.

Peggy, who knew about Ellie's home life, but never
commented, began humming to herself as she swept the few
crumbs from the red stone floor into the dustpan.

Ellie smoothed the crisp white tablecloth with the flat of
her hand. Her dark eyes took on a dreamy look as she stood
back to admire the small vases of flowers on the tables she
had carefully set ready for the morning teas and coffees.
Although she'd only been working here for four weeks, she
loved her job, waiting on the tables, admiring the people it
brought her into contact with: women wearing nice frocks
and the latest cloche hats, and lots of jewellery, although

1

Peggy said most of it was made of paste and glass. The men always wore smart suits with white collars and neat ties. As the railway station was just across the road Peggy assumed most of them were on their way to and from the city. Ellie would always be grateful to Peggy for getting her the job. The Tea Room, as it was simply called, was in the better part of Rotherhithe and it was her haven; she would dream she was one of the lady customers sitting laughing and waving her long cigarette holder about. Even if she didn't smoke now, she could soon learn.

As Ellie stood and looked round the tea room with its bent-wood chairs set two to every table, she could almost imagine she was sitting there, with her legs neatly crossed at the ankles, showing off her fine silk stockings. There was only room for eight tables, but they were always busy with morning and afternoon teas. The walls were covered with red flock paper, with two long mirrors each side of the room. Near the door, on the opposite side of the counter, stood a dark wooden hatstand.

Peggy's humming brought Ellie back to herself. Although Peggy was older than her they had been to the same school, and Ellie often saw her on her way home from the tea factory where Ellie's older sisters Lizzie and Dolly worked. Her sisters had found her a job cleaning the office, but it was short-lived. Ellie had been sacked when a distant member of the boss's family wanted the job, and there hadn't seemed to be a lot of prospects left for her after that. The Depression was causing so much hardship, and so many had lost their jobs, including her father.

It was while she was out searching for work that she had bumped into Peggy. She told her she was working for Mr Jenkins, the baker who made the fancy cakes and scones at the back of the tea room. Ellie had often stood with her mouth watering as she gazed into the window at the display of lovely cakes. Peggy told her she was going to be promoted to working on the counter, as Mrs North, whose husband was very ill, was leaving. Ellie didn't know Mrs North, but was pleased when Peggy told her Mr Jenkins was looking for another girl to wait on the tables and suggested she came to see him.

Ellie worried about her scruffy clothes and kept her rough hands behind her back when she met Mr Jenkins, but he seemed pleased with her and she was given Peggy's uniform. Thankfully they were both about the same height. Over the black dress Ellie wore a white starched lacy apron. She had to wear her long dark hair tied back, and when the odd strand found its way out she had to tuck it quickly behind her ear. Her smart white headdress had a black ribbon woven through it, which made her feel important, and Peggy gave her some shoe polish, so she polished her run-down shoes till they shone.

Ellie did worry about the washing of her uniform, but Mrs Page, who made the tea and did the washing up in the back, took home all the dirty linen, including Peggy's overall and Ellie's apron. She had to change out of her black dress every evening, and Mrs Page sometimes took that home to sponge off any marks.

Mr Jenkins didn't pay a lot, only twelve shillings and sixpence a week, but Ellie didn't mind. She loved it here.

'Good job you ain't gotter get a tram home,' said Peggy, lifting a corner of the lace curtain and looking out of the window that was the other side of the door. 'Seems funny not seeing any trams.'

'I'm glad it ain't that far to walk,' said Ellie, knowing the sixpence her mother let her keep each week would never be wasted on tram fares; she was saving it to buy some new shoes.

'This General Strike's causing a lotta problems,' said Peggy, walking away from the window. 'Me old mum reckons they'll be bringing in the army soon. It's a shame, just as we seem ter be getting straight after the war, now this. Still, I feel sorry for all those poor blokes what come

3

back from the war and thought everythink would be fine.'

Ellie looked about her and asked quietly, 'You don't think we'll lose our jobs if Mr Jenkins can't get any supplies, and we don't get any customers?'

'Shouldn't think so.' Peggy smiled. 'Mr Jenkins is a kind man. I'm not so sure about his boss, Mr Cole, though.'

Ellie knew Peggy was sweet on Mr Jenkins. He was a lot older than Peggy, and Ellie knew he'd been injured during the war when he was in the army. He was a stockily built man, but his warm smile, twinkling blue eyes and slicked back dark hair made him look almost handsome.

Ellie didn't know anything about Mr Cole, although he was also her mother's landlord. Ellie had never seen him, but his name put fear into all his tenants. He owned a lot of property around Rotherhithe, including Elmleigh Square where Ellie lived, and if you got behind with your rent you were out on the streets.

'Right, that's it,' said Peggy, straightening up after brushing the last of the crumbs into the dustpan. 'I'll tell Mr Jenkins it's all tidy in here, and I'll collect your wages. I bet you wish it was Friday every day?'

Ellie nodded, as Peggy disappeared into the back of the shop.

It was a sultry May evening as Ellie made her way home. Her feet throbbed and the darn in the heel of her black lisle stockings rubbed as she trudged along Rotherhithe New Road. Ellie sighed as she pictured the scene waiting for her at home.

Her father would be sitting hunched up in his chair, upset that he hadn't found work again today. Her older sisters Lizzie and Dolly would probably be arguing about anything they could find to argue about. Baby Iris, as she was still called even though she would be fourteen this year and looking for work soon, would be sitting reading one of their sisters' penny dreadfuls. Their mother wanted her to leave school now, but Iris didn't want to go to work, and would argue with her mother about it. That would result in Ruby Walsh shouting and carrying on about everyone in the house and most of those who lived in the square, too.

With a heavy heart Ellie turned into Elmleigh Square, which was the same as always. It wasn't really a square, more of a small triangle with terraced, back-to-back houses in various states of disrepair lining two of the sides, and Fellows Road running along the other side. The whole area was run-down and dilapidated. There were just twenty houses in the square and Ellie knew only a few of the tenants, as most came and went very quickly when the tally men and rent man came knocking for their money.

Poor Mrs Collins was the last to have been chucked out, and she had five kids. Everybody had shouted at the bailiffs, but it didn't help. It had upset Ellie for days and she often wondered where they'd finished up. If only she could escape this miserable place; but her mum was always threatening her and her sisters with the workhouse, or worse still the lunatic asylum, if they ever thought about running away.

As usual Dirty Molly, as the kids in the square called her, was sitting on the rusty metal seat that surrounded the old elm tree. Some boys were climbing up the tree, completely ignoring Molly. She had become as much a part of the tree as the seat. Nobody knew how old she was; she had been sitting there for as long as Ellie could remember. Every morning she would shuffle out of the house she shared with her sister, who people hardly ever saw, and sit there till dark, unless it was raining, in which case she would be at her window watching. All day she cuddled and talked to her small scruffy dog, never saying very much to the people round about, but her sharp beady eyes constantly darted about, taking in all the comings and goings of the square. Everybody thought she and her sister were a barmy pair.

Many years ago when Ellie used to play round the tree they'd called Dirty Molly an old witch. Her red hair had seemed to sprout from her head, she'd always worn a long black coat and she'd chase the kids and have them screaming with fright, giving some of them nightmares. Over the years her hair had turned white, and she was fat now and couldn't walk very far. She was no longer a threat to the children.

As usual this evening the dusty square was full of kids running, shouting and screaming. Ellie guessed that many years ago this square was covered with grass; now it was a dust bowl in the summer and a sea of mud in the winter.

Ellie's heart missed a beat when she saw Terry Andrews come out of his house at the far end, and walk purposefully across the square. Although his jacket was torn, his trousers too short, and his boots too big, to Ellie he was tall, dark and handsome, just like the heroes in all the penny books she and her sisters read. She automatically touched her hat to make sure it was on properly, desperately wishing it was a fashionable close-fitting one. She smiled. She had been smiling at him for years, but since he left school he never spoke, only smiled back, usually accompanied by a slight nod as he said her name. She felt her face flush, but he was gone. Terry was three years older than her, and at school had always looked on her as a kid, teasing her and pulling her hair, but Ellie had always been in love with him. She remembered when she secretly cut their names into a heart in the elm tree, and put an arrow through it, although she always denied it was her when the other kids took the mickey out of them. She knew Terry didn't have a job. There was no Mr Andrews, either. Mrs Andrews let part of her house, but her lodgers never seemed to stay very long, and talk was that when she was young she'd had a lot of men friends. Although she was old, she was still slim and always had a pleasant smile. Ellie could see that she had once been very beautiful. In her dreams Ellie imagined herself looking after Terry and his mother, doing the cooking and cleaning, and being very happy.

6

Ellie pushed open the front door of number sixteen, a two-up-and-two-down with paint peeling off the door, just like all the others that fronted the square. Despite the warm weather, she shuddered as raised voices escaped from the kitchen into the passage.

Her father looked up as she walked into the kitchen. "'Allo, Ellie love, 'ad a good day?"

'Not bad.' She sat at the table and, kicking off her shoes, gently rubbed her sore heel and aching feet.

'Gonner give us the same old sob story about being overworked and underpaid,' laughed Dolly.

'Talking of being paid, come on, gel, 'and it over.' Her mother stuck her large open hand under Ellie's nose. Ruby Walsh was a sizeable woman, with thick upper arms, her threadbare floral overall bursting open across her ample bosom despite the large safety pin straining to hold the material together. Her mousy hair was always scragged back into a bun, and her darting grey eyes never missed a thing. She always wore run-down slippers with the toes cut out, even when she went to the corner shop.

'Give us a chance, I've only just got in.' Ellie picked up the black, envelope-shaped handbag she had bought for a penny at the secondhand stall in the market. She took out her wage packet and passed it to her mother.

"'Bout time you 'ad a rise, me girl,' said Mrs Walsh, turning it over before tearing it open.

'Christ, I've only been there four weeks.'

'Don't swear.'

'Well, what d'you expect?' mumbled Ellie under her breath so that her mother couldn't hear. At seventeen Ellie objected bitterly at having to give her unopened wage packet to her mother, to be given back only sixpence to last her all week. Many times at the tea factory she had tried to prise open her wage packet, but that had only ever resulted in her mother's large hand hitting her round the head. She had even given some thought to asking her new boss Mr

Jenkins to give her some cash in her hand, but she knew he was afraid of the big boss, Mr Cole, and wouldn't think of doing anything like that.

'Did yer git any tips terday?' asked her mother, counting out the twelve shillings and sixpence.

'No, course not. I keep telling you, it ain't that kind of place.'

'She wouldn't tell yer if she 'ad,' said Lizzie. She grinned as she stood admiring her short bobbed hair in the large mirror that hung over the mantelpiece.

'She'd better,' said Mrs Walsh. 'I ain't brought you lot up ter tell lies.'

If *you* went to work, thought Ellie, things might be a bit easier, but her mother had always said looking after four girls and a lazy husband was more than enough work for her.

'Well, if she tarted 'erself up a bit and made eyes at some of the old men they gits in there she might earn 'erself a few extra bob,' said Dolly, pushing Lizzie away from the mirror.

''Ere, who yer pushing?' Lizzie objected.

'Well move over, I ain't got all night waiting fer you ter finish looking at yerself.'

'Don't you two start,' said their father.

'That's it, 'ave a go at us, just 'cos you can't find work. If it wasn't fer me and Lizzie you'd all starve,' Dolly snarled.

Ned Walsh looked down and began picking at his fingers. He had a thin face, and his watery blue eyes always looked sad, his grey wiry hair never looked tidy and over the years his stoop seemed to have shrunk his stature. Once he had appeared to tower over Ellie but now they were eye to eye.

Ellie suddenly wanted to throw her arms round his neck. She knew how day after day he walked the streets looking for work, and that his boots were stuffed with cardboard to stop the rough pavements cutting his feet.

'What's fer tea, Mum?' asked Baby Iris looking up from her book.

'As it's the end of the week I could only manage a few scraps, so I've boiled 'em up with a bit o' veg.'

'That's what that 'orrible smell is,' said Dolly. 'Fought you was boiling up Dad's old socks.'

Lizzie and Baby Iris laughed with her.

Ellie didn't laugh. She knew their father didn't have any socks.

'Why don't yer start trying ter tart yerself up a bit?' said Lizzie to Ellie.

'Where would I get the money from to buy make up?' Ellie threw a dirty look at her mother.

'Like I said, flash those big brown eyes at some of the old men, and who knows what you'll get.' Dolly threw her head back and laughed.

''Ere you are, gel. This lipstick's nearly finished, you might be able to scrape a bit out of it.' Lizzie threw a black lipstick case at Ellie.

'Ow Lizzie,' yelled Baby Iris. 'You promised me the next one.'

'Well yer ain't 'aving it. Yer sister's need is more than yours. 'Sides, yer still at school.'

Baby Iris pouted. 'It ain't fair.'

Ellie looked across at her father who raised his tired eyes towards the ceiling.

'Nuffink in life's bleeding fair. Now come on you lot, clear this table, dinner's ready.' Their mother stood in the doorway between the kitchen and tiny scullery, her large frame filling the doorway. She cast her eyes towards her husband and a look of distaste filled her full face.

Ellie could never understand why her mother always spoke to her father with such venom. She must have loved him once, and it wasn't his fault he couldn't find work. But she'd never had a good word to say to him for as long as Ellie could remember, even when he was working for a while as a labourer in the docks.

Before sitting down Ellie glanced round the kitchen. Like

the outside of the house this too was in a state of disrepair. The ceiling was black from the gas lamp, and the damp seeping in under the window caused the wallpaper to hang off the wall in tired strips.

Ellie sat at the table and picked at her dinner with her fork, pushing the potatoes round the thick chipped plate – the china here was so different from the tea room's. Before she'd worked there she'd never known china could be so thin and pretty, and she was terrified of breaking it.

'Don't yer want it, gel?' asked her father, interrupting her thoughts.

'I ain't very 'ungry. We 'ad some sausage rolls left over today and Mr Jenkins let me and Peggy eat 'em.'

'Pity yer didn't fink of someone else instead of yerself for a change,' said her mother. 'We could do with a few of them. I told yer before if there's anyfink left over, bring it 'ome.'

'We don't see any of them nice cakes they 'ave in the window, do we?' said Baby Iris. 'They must 'ave some of 'em over sometimes.' She pushed her face close to Ellie's. 'I bet you eats 'em.'

'I told you, Mr Jenkins sells 'em off cheap at the end of the day.'

'So, why didn't 'e sell the sausage rolls then?' asked Dolly. 'Dunno.'

'Well if yer don't want yer dinner, then I'll 'ave it.' With that Baby Iris snatched Ellie's plate from in front of her and scraped the dinner on to hers.

Lizzie laughed. 'Christ gel, you'll never starve, yer too bloody quick.'

After they had finished their meal, their mother sent Baby Iris up to the pub for a drop of ale in a jug as usual. She reckoned it was her one treat and she deserved it. Ellie and her father went into the scullery to do the washing up, while Dolly and Lizzie finished getting ready to go out. Mrs Walsh sat in the armchair and, with her feet on the brass fender, was already beginning to doze off.

The small scullery only had a discoloured sink and wooden draining board under the window. Against the opposite wall stood an old rickety table; next to it was a cupboard that contained very little. The door led out to the yard and the lavatory.

Ellie glanced out of the window as she threw a handful of soda from the stone jar that stood on the windowsill into the chipped white enamel washing up bowl, and swirled the water round and round. 'I'll see to this and I'll do the wiping up, Dad, if you want to sit down.'

'Bin sitting down most of the day, ain't I.'

'No luck with a job then?'

'Na. This strike ain't 'elping. Mind you, there's a lot what's breaking the strike, a lot o' blacklegs about, but they're mostly the toffs what finks it's a good laugh ter drive a tram. Like a lot o' bleeding kids they are. Saw a fight this morning. They 'ad ter fetch the police. It could get very nasty if they bring the army in.'

'They won't do that, will they?'

'Well, they'll 'ave ter move the foodstuff what perishes from the docks.'

Ellie slowly rubbed the dishcloth that had been cut from an old vest round and round a plate.

'Wake up gel, yer gonner wear that plate out 'fore yer finished washing it.'

Ellie laughed, and her smile lit up her large brown eyes. 'I was miles away then. 'Ere you are, and don't drop it.' She handed her father the well washed plate. She loved her father. He was a quiet man who always tried to do the best for his family, even though it was never enough for her mother.

'You going out ternight?' asked her father.

'No. I'm saving up for a new pair of shoes, and 'sides, I ain't got no one to go out with. But I'm going to go and see that new Rudolph Valentino film when it comes to the

11

Gaumont. 'E's really handsome. D'yer know, I dream about 'im whisking me away on 'is white 'orse, and riding off with me into the sunset.' Ellie hugged herself and laughed. 'Daft, ain't it?'

Her father laughed with her. 'Don't see many sunsets round 'ere; well, not frough the 'ouses anyway.' He turned away and looked at the plate he was holding. 'There ain't no harm in dreams, gel,' he said, adding softly, almost to himself, 'we all 'ad 'em once.'

Chapter 2

Ellie went upstairs to the bedroom she shared with her three sisters.

'Thanks for the lipstick, Lizzie.'

''S'all right. I remember when I wasn't earning much and Mum took it all. As yer gets older you 'ave ter get craftier.' She grinned, pulled up her silk stockings and straightened her seams.

Ellie lay on her back on top of the bed she and Baby Iris slept in. The only other furniture in the room was the bed Lizzie and Dolly shared. Everything else had been pawned. Clothes hung from nails and hooks on the picture rail, though Dolly and Lizzie's best frocks were on coat hangers, and their coats hung behind the door.

Stretched out, and with her hands behind her head, Ellie watched Lizzie getting ready to go out. Of all her sisters she liked Lizzie the best, but they still argued. Lizzie was twenty and quite nice-looking. She had pencil-thin eyebrows, blue eyes and full Clara Bow lips. Her mousy hair was cut in a short straight bob and coloured with henna.

Dolly was nineteen but looked and acted a lot older, and she and Ellie didn't get on at all. With her short bobbed dark hair and dark eyes, Dolly also had plucked eyebrows and bow-shaped lips. She tried to look like Gloria Swanson, the siren she admired at the pictures, and she even bound a scarf round her chest when she went out, to look flat-chested like her. Both the older sisters liked to be seen in

13

the latest fashion but couldn't afford much, and spent many hours altering the secondhand clothes they got from the market. They cut out the sleeves and necks of old frocks, and shortened the skirts. They bought scarves and wound them round their dropped waists. Ellie thought they were very clever, the way they could make something out of nothing, though often rows would break out if one took something that belonged to the other.

Ellie turned on her stomach and stared at Lizzie. 'I like your new cloche hat.'

'Yer, it's nice. I was a bit worried about the colour, wasn't too sure about biscuit but the old dear on the stall said it was the latest fashion.'

'Lizzie, how can you afford so many clothes when you 'ave to give Mum all your wages?'

'I don't 'ave that many, and don't forget they all come from the secondhand stall at the market.' Her sister scooped up the contents of her handbag from off the bed and bundled them back in.

'Lizzie, do you manage to keep back some of your wages?'

'Yer, but it takes time to get in with the wages clerk.'

'But . . . how . . . ?'

'Me and Dolly told him a sob story about our mum keeping all our wages, so he give us some extra wage packets. That way we fill 'em ourselves, and keep a few bob back.'

Although Ellie nodded, she wasn't sure that she believed her.

'Right, I'm off.' Lizzie stood up and grinned. 'Got something else for you to think about.'

'What?'

'Well, I'll be glad when Sunday's 'ere.'

'Why?'

'Me and Dolly's gonner get a dressing table.'

'You are? When?' Ellie sat up.

'On Sunday morning. A bloke we know from work's

getting rid of it, so 'e's bringing it round on a barra. I don't fink it's up ter much, but at least we'll 'ave somewhere to put our few bits. I'm fed up with all me stuff being chucked in a bag.'

''As it got a mirror?' asked Ellie enthusiastically.

'Dunno.'

'Who's the bloke then?'

'Mind yer own business.'

Ellie grinned. ''E your fancy bit then?'

'Shut yer face, will yer.' Lizzie looked towards the door. 'Otherwise we'll 'ave Iris making a full song and dance about it, then Ma'll git worried in case she might be losing a pay packet.'

Ellie opened her eyes wide. 'You ain't gonner get married, are you?'

'Shh, keep your voice down. And in answer to your question, no I ain't, 'e's already married, and I wouldn't fancy him as 'usband anyway, so shut it.'

'Married?' repeated Ellie. She thought Lizzie looked ruffled, which was unusual for her.

'Yer, so shut it.'

'Where you off to ternight then?' asked Ellie, sliding to the edge of the bed. 'And what about his wife?'

'That's his problem. I'm going out.' Lizzie patted her new hat and, putting her finger to the side of her nose, said very slowly and very deliberately, 'See this?'

Ellie nodded.

'Make sure you keep yours out of my business, and yer mouth shut.'

When she left the bedroom, Ellie threw herself back on the bed and laughed.

Dolly walked in a few minutes later. 'Lizzie gorn?'

Ellie nodded.

'That bog out there stinks. You'd fink Mum would give it a clean now and again.'

'She reckons Dad should do it.'

15

'Well, she would.'

'Lizzie reckons you're getting a dressing table.'

Dolly's head shot up. 'She told yer then?'

Ellie nodded.

'Yer, well, Mum 'ad better not pawn it or sell it to the rag-and-bone man, otherwise there'll be trouble.'

'What's this bloke like?' asked Ellie.

'What bloke?'

'The bloke who's bringing the dressing table.'

''E's a bit of all right.' Dolly smiled. 'I'm going out with 'im.'

'What, tonight?' asked Ellie in amazement.

'No, 'e's got to go to 'is club.'

'Is he married?'

'What made you ask that?'

'Dunno, just curious.' Ellie giggled. 'Is 'e?'

'Course not.'

'Who's Lizzie out with tonight then?'

'I dunno, and stop asking all these bleeding questions, I'm trying ter get ready.' The front door slammed. ''Ere comes Baby Iris,' said Dolly. 'Don't say nuffink to 'er about the dressing table, she'll only go and tell Mum.'

'But what about when you get it?'

'Then we'll tell 'er, won't we?'

'What you gonner tell 'er?' said Baby Iris, walking into the bedroom, her blue eyes taking in the scene.

'Nuffink for you to worry your pretty little head about,' said Dolly, picking up her handbag and going out of the room, ruffling Iris's fair hair as she walked past.

'Oh you,' said Iris angrily, smoothing down her straight hair. 'What's she looking so pleased about?'

'Dunno.' Ellie smiled.

'Look at the state of this place. Why don't they get married and leave 'ome?'

'They've got ter find themselves a man first, and Mum won't let 'em leave 'ome as she'll be their money short,' said

Ellie, picking up one of Dolly's books.

Iris threw Lizzie's work frock from off the bed and on to the floor.

'Be careful with that, it could be mine next.'

'I hate wearing other people's left-offs. When I leave school I'm gonner find meself a good job. I ain't gonner be a skivvy like you.'

'I ain't a skivvy.'

'Yer don't get paid much though, do yer?'

'No, not yet.'

'I'm gonner get a job that pays a lot of money so I can wear some decent clothes, not old patched and darned left-offs.'

'And what if Mum takes nearly all your money; what then?'

'I won't be as daft as you and tell her what I get. I'll keep some back for meself, to buy lots of nice things.'

'She'll know if you open your pay packet.'

'I'll find a way.'

Ellie opened the book. Yes, Iris would find a way, and if she didn't Mum wouldn't tell her off as much as she did her, and she'd probably get more to spend anyway. Ellie sighed. Like her father she always felt left out. For as long as she could remember, Lizzie and Dolly hadn't had a lot of time for her, and her mother had never seemed to have a good word for her youngest daughter. Then when Baby Iris came along things got worse. Ellie had always been the one to run errands, cleaning for her mother and even chasing the coal cart to pick up any pieces of coal that fell off. Sometimes the coalman would kick it into the horse shit for a laugh, but Ellie would still have to collect it. She would do anything her mother wanted her to, anything, to get into her good books.

Ellie began thinking about her school days. She had loved them, the chance to bury herself in books and dream about different countries. When she had passed the big exam to go on to the high school she'd been very proud, but despite all the arguments she'd known she wouldn't be allowed to stay on after she was fourteen. She'd had to go out to work, and it had broken her heart. Only her father had seemed to understand how upset she was about it. But, poor Dad, there'd been nothing he could do to help, as usual.

Saturday morning in the tea room was always busy. The better-off women came in for their tea after they'd been shopping, and they didn't like to be kept waiting.

Ellie rushed up to the counter with an order. 'A pot of tea and a scone, Peg, and can you make it quick. The man said 'e's got to catch a train.'

'Good job for 'im the trains are running again then,' said Peggy, wiping her forehead with the back of her hand. 'It ain't 'alf warm in 'ere today, ain't it?' Her face was red with exertion as she hurried back and forth from the bakery to the counter.

Ellie raced off back to serve another customer.

'Miss, miss,' the man who was catching the train called her.

'Yes, sir.' Much to Ellie's relief he smiled.

'Does the scone come with butter and jam?'

'Yes, sir.'

'That's good.' He settled back with his newspaper.

'You're very busy,' he said as she set his tea before him.

Ellie smiled and nodded. She noticed he had long clean fingers, and a warm smile. He was well dressed. Ellie quickly moved away. Mr Jenkins had made it clear when she first started that she wasn't to stop and chat to the customers; not that she would know what to say, or how to speak to them.

Ellie wrote out the train man's bill and placed it on the table. When he'd finished he carefully dabbed at the corner of his mouth with the spotlessly white linen serviette, and stood up. Ellie fetched his hat and coat.

'Thank you, my dear.' He smoothed down his sandy-coloured hair. It had just a light sprinkling of grey at the temples, which made him look quite distinguished. He carefully adjusted his trilby. Ellie guessed he must have been very good-looking when he was younger. 'That was very nice. I'll call in again.'

Ellie was clearing away the dirty crocks when she noticed he'd left her sixpence. She felt like yelling out loud. A whole sixpence! Nobody had given her a tip before, well not a proper one, just the odd halfpenny from their change if she was lucky and they couldn't be bothered to pick it up. She looked round and quickly put the money in her pocket. Should she tell Peggy? Should she share it with her? For the rest of the day her mind was in a turmoil.

At six o'clock Ellie was taking off her pretty lace apron when she suddenly blurted out, 'I got a tip today.'

'Well, lucky old you,' said Peggy nonchalantly. 'How much?'

'Sixpence.'

'What?' yelled Peggy. 'A tanner! A whole tanner? Who from?'

'That old boy that had to catch a train.'

'Bloody 'ell, didn't think 'e looked all that old.'

Ellie giggled. She thought he looked about the same age as Mr Jenkins.

''Is bill only come to that,' said Peggy.

'I know. Peg, should I share it with you?'

Peggy laughed. 'No, course not. You earned it. 'Sides, yer don't 'ave ter tell yer mum about it, do yer, so you'll be able to get yer shoes a bit quicker.'

Peggy knew all about how she was saving for new shoes, and about Ellie's mother taking most of her wages.

Ellie threw her arms round Peggy's neck. 'Thanks, Peg. 'E said 'e was coming in again.'

'Don't reckon 'e'll be as generous next time,' Peggy

19

laughed. "E might make sure 'e's got some coppers in 'is change.'

Ellie looked at the sixpence in her hand and slowly turned it over. 'Peg, I'm gonner buy me dad some socks.'

'What? What about yer shoes? 'Sides, you ain't got enough.'

'I've got me pocket money, and if that man's coming back next week, 'e might leave me another tip, then I can put that towards me shoes.'

'What if 'e don't?'

Ellie shrugged. 'What I ain't 'ad, I'll never miss.'

'You're a good girl,' said Peggy with genuine affection.

At closing time Ellie's step was light as she walked from the tea room and into the small haberdashery shop.

'The cheapest I have are one and thrupence,' said the kind, whitehaired lady, taking a drawer full of socks from under the glass counter.

'I've only got a shilling,' said Ellie sadly.

'Oh dear,' said the lady, smiling. 'I'll tell you what, you take them and let me have the rest of the money next week after you've been paid. I know where you work, so you can't run off.'

'Oh I wouldn't do that.'

'I know that, dear,' she said, putting the socks in a brown paper bag.

Ellie felt elated when she walked home. If she saw Terry Andrews now, that would be her happiness complete.

When she arrived home she quickly stuffed the socks into her pocket, so that her mother wouldn't see them. She suddenly panicked. How could she explain the money when she'd told her she never got any tips? Would she stop her sixpence a week?

'All right, gel?' asked her father.

She nodded and looked around. 'Where's Mum?'

'She ain't back from the market yet.'

'It's a bit late for 'er, ain't it?'

'Yer, she said somefink about getting Baby Iris some shoes.'

'What?' Ellie exploded. 'I want new shoes. I 'elp keep this family, why won't she give *me* some money for shoes?' Ellie could have bitten off her tongue when she saw the look on her father's face. She fell to her knees and buried her head on his lap. 'Oh Dad, I'm sorry, I know you can't 'elp not 'aving a job – I didn't mean . . .'

''S'all right, love. I know that. I only wish I didn't 'ave ter rely on me gels.' He patted the top of her head. 'Yer ma ain't gitting 'er new ones, just a pair off the second'and barra.'

Ellie stood up. 'I got yer a present.'

'What? Why? It ain't me birfday.'

Ellie handed him the brown paper bag.

A warm smile swept over his face. 'Socks. Socks. Oh love, what can I say?' He suddenly looked up. ''Ere, where did yer git the money from?'

'I got a tip today. Some old man left me sixpence.'

'What?'

She smiled. 'Don't tell Mum, will yer. 'E said 'e's coming back next week.'

Her father put the socks to one side. 'Did 'e say what for?'

Ellie looked puzzled. 'Tea and scones.'

'Is that all?'

'That's all 'e 'ad this morning.'

'You wanner be careful, gel. Don't you go giving 'im any encouragement.'

'What d'yer mean, Dad? I only serve 'im tea.'

'You wanner watch old men, some of 'em can be—'

The kitchen door burst open. 'I only 'ope that bleeding kettle's on. Me feet's killing me after traipsing round that market all afternoon.'

Ned Walsh quickly put the socks and paper bag into his jacket pocket.

Ellie stood up. 'Kettle's boiling, I'll make the tea.' She

21

took the tea caddy and the brown china teapot from the sparsely filled dresser. 'Did you get yer shoes then?' she asked, walking from the scullery.

'No.' Baby Iris's face was thunderous.

Ellie stopped in the doorway. 'Why's that? Didn't they 'ave any ter fit yer then, Cinderella?'

'Don't you start,' yelled her mother. 'I've 'ad enough bloody old lip from 'er. 'Urry up with that tea.'

Ellie took the kettle from the hob and went into the scullery with a smirk on her face. She knew Baby Iris would be in a foul mood all evening.

On Sunday morning Dolly and Lizzie were up and dressed much earlier than usual. Lizzie was looking out of the window.

'What time's 'e coming?' asked Ellie sitting up.

'Who? What yer talking about?' Baby Iris pushed her feet down in the bed.

'Be careful,' yelled Ellie. 'You wanner cut your toenails, you just scratched me.'

'Shut it, you two,' said Dolly joining her sister at the window.

'What you all made up for?' asked Baby Iris looking at her two sisters. 'And what you looking out there for?'

Ellie left the bed and got herself dressed.

Downstairs in the kitchen her father was busy trying to light the fire. The large black kettle stood on the hob. 'What's all that racket in your room this morning?' He inclined his head towards the door. 'Don't usually 'ear Dolly and Lizzie awake so early.'

'You wait till you see 'em, Dad, they're dressed and got all their make up on,' said Ellie, excited at the thought of the dressing table coming today.

'They going out?'

'Don't think so.'

'Ellie, there's a pot o' dripping in the meat safe, go out

and bring it in 'ere and put it on the table.' Ruby Walsh walked in from the scullery and plonked a wooden bread board and an unevenly cut loaf of bread on the table. 'That'll do you lot fer this morning.'

'Yes Mum.' Ellie grinned to herself as she went into the yard to get the dripping. Today was going to be very interesting. She couldn't wait to see this Casanova both her sisters reckoned they were going out with. It would be fascinating to see which one he made more fuss of. Sparks might just fly – for a change!

Chapter 3

It wasn't until midday that Lizzie and Dolly raced out of the front room where they had spent all the morning gazing out of the window.

'Quick. 'E's 'ere,' yelled Dolly.

'Who?' asked their father.

'Come and see, Dad,' said Ellie dragging him up from his chair.

'There's a bloke outside with a barra,' said Baby Iris. 'And 'e's got somethink balanced on it. Can't see what it is though, it's got an old sheet over it.'

Mrs Walsh came in from the scullery wiping her hands on the bottom of her floral overall. 'What's all the racket? What's going on out 'ere?'

'Come and see, Mum,' said Ellie.

When they all arrived at the front door there was a lot of pushing and shoving to get out, but Dolly and Lizzie stood firm, blocking the way.

'Move over, gels, let the dog see the bone,' said Ned Walsh lightheartedly.

'Bloody 'ell' said his wife when a tall, good-looking fellow walked up to them. 'What yer got on that there barra?' she asked.

His smooth dark hair shone in the morning sunlight, and his thin dapper moustache gave him an air of elegance even if his shirt had a torn collar and his trousers had frayed turn-ups.

He smiled, and gave Dolly and Lizzie a wink. 'I've got a nice little dressing table for the lovely ladies of Elmleigh Square.'

'Oh yer, and where'd it come from? And how much?' asked Ruby Walsh.

'Fer you love, nuffink. Gonner give me an 'and then, Pop?'

''Ang on a minute,' said Mrs Walsh, putting a restraining hand on the man's arm. 'Whose was it, and where's it come from? And is it full o' bugs?'

'Now would I bring yer somefink like that? No, somebody I know was chucking it out, and your two lovely daughters 'ere, who I might add I work with, said they wanted a dressing table, so 'ere I am.'

Ruby Walsh looked at her daughters, and inclined her head in the young man's direction. 'What d'yer 'ave ter give 'im fer that piece a junk?'

'I told yer, missis, a smile from 'em is enough fer me.'

Ellie laughed. She could see why both her sisters fancied this bloke, he certainly had a lot of charm.

By now most of the children in the square had joined them and were jostling for position around the barrow.

'Where d'yer pinch that from, mister?' shouted one of the kids.

'We 'ad one just like that,' said a snotty-nosed little girl sidling up to the barrow. 'But ours 'ad a mirror on it,' she said cockily.

'I ain't seen that,' said another boy.

The little girl sniffed hard and wiped her nose along her sleeve. 'We ain't got it now, me dad chopped it up fer firewood.'

'Scram,' said the fellow as he manoeuvred his barrow towards their front door.

The kids quickly moved out of his way.

The Walshes stood to one side as the dressing table was ceremoniously brought into the house and taken up the narrow stairs. After a great deal of struggling, accompanied by a lot of grunts and shouts, it was finally eased through the door and deposited in the girls' room. Ellie was upset that it didn't have a mirror, though the two pieces of wood that stuck up on top showed that it must once have held one. The top was badly stained and scratched, and hadn't seen polish for years.

Dolly was fussing round it, and Baby Iris was creating a rumpus because she couldn't have a drawer to herself.

'I dunno what you're making such a fuss about, Iris,' said Ellie. 'We ain't got that much to put in 'em.'

'Not yet I ain't, but you wait till I start work, I'll get plenty of clothes then.'

'Oh, looks like we're gonner 'ave a real live fashion model in our midst then,' said Dolly, tipping the contents of a brown paper bag on to the bed.

'Well I shall need more space than 'alf a drawer, just you wait and see.'

'It's only got three drawers. Yer bloody lucky we're letting you an' Ellie 'ave one between yer,' said Dolly, carefully laying her underwear flat in the top drawer. 'Where's Lizzie?'

'Still talking to that bloke,' said Ellie.

'Is she now.' Dolly pushed up the window and, leaning out, called, 'Bye, Bob, see yer termorrer. You'd better come up, Lizzie, and sort this cow out.' She waved and smiled at Bob, then turning from the window said, 'What's she up to? 'E's my bloke, I'll kill 'er if she's trying to get 'im to take 'er out.'

Ellie laughed.

'Why? Yer going out with 'im then?' asked Baby Iris.

'Sort of,' said Dolly.

'Yer gonner marry 'im?'

'Dunno yet.'

Suddenly Lizzie's loud voice could be heard all over the house. 'You've got a bloody wicked mind.'

'Don't you talk ter me like that,' screeched their mother.

'Well don't even fink about it.' They heard Lizzie stomping up the bare wooden stairs, then she pushed open the bedroom door with such force it banged against the bottom of Ellie and Baby Iris's bed, making it shake.

'What's up?' asked Dolly.

'She's worried that we 'ad ter pay for it.'

'So, what's it to do with 'er?' Dolly nodded towards the door.

'She wants ter know where we got the money from. When I told 'er it was nuffink she wanted ter know what favours we 'ad ter give Bob for it.'

Dolly sat on the bed and laughed. 'I dunno what yer gitting upset over, chance would be a fine fing.'

'I fink she might even be finking of pawning it.'

'What?' Dolly jumped up. 'She'd better not.'

'That's what I told 'er.'

'She couldn't get it down the stairs,' said Ellie.

'She'd find a way. 'Sides, the bloke in the pawn shop would always come round with 'is barra, if 'e thought it was worth 'is while,' said Lizzie, gently running her hand over the top of the dressing table.

'What was you saying to Bob?' asked Dolly casually.

'Nuffink.'

'You know I'm going out with 'im?' said Dolly smugly.

Lizzie gaped at her. 'No I didn't know,' she said coldly. 'When did 'e ask yer?'

'Bin out with 'im a couple o' times now,' said Dolly, patting the back of her hair, relishing the situation.

'You know I've been out with 'im?'

'Yer, 'e told me.'

'And you know 'e's married?' Lizzie was getting more and more angry.

'Yer, 'e told me,' repeated Dolly.

'You just told me you was gonner marry 'im.' Baby Iris began to giggle.

'What?' yelled Lizzie.

'I was just 'aving 'er on.'

'The two-timing sod.' Lizzie slammed the drawer of the dressing table shut.

"Ere, watch it,' said Dolly. 'It might fall ter bits.'

'You wait till I get ter work termorrer, I'll give 'im a bit of me mind.'

Dolly laughed.

'I 'ate you, Dolly Walsh, when yer gets all cocky,' said Lizzie, storming out of the room.

Dolly threw herself back on the bed and, with tears streaming down her face, laughed hysterically.

'What you laughing about?' asked Ellie.

"Er. Silly cow. Dunno why she's got all upset about 'im. Everybody knows what 'e's like.'

'So why yer going out with 'im?' asked Ellie.

"Cos 'e's good fun.'

Baby Iris sat wide-eyed. 'Wait till Mum 'ears about this.'

Dolly turned on her. 'You keep yer mouth shut, d'yer 'ear? Don't you dare breathe a word or you'll feel me 'and round yer 'ead.'

With such a threat hanging over her, Ellie knew Baby Iris would keep quiet.

Monday evening Ellie raced up the stairs when she got home from work to find out what had happened to Lizzie and Dolly, and the cheeky Bob. To her surprise both her sisters were sitting on the bed laughing.

'Well?' she asked, looking from one to the other. 'What did you say to 'im?'

'Who?' asked Lizzie.

'Bob.'

'Oh 'im. Not a lot. Me and Dolly decided to go along with 'im thinking 'e was being very clever.

'We both made a date with 'im. 'E'll be all in a stew 'bout which one ter stand up, but 'e'll be the one wot's stood up,

29

'cos we're going orf ter the pictures on our own.'

'That'll teach 'im,' said Dolly.

'But Dolly, I thought that you was . . .'

'Well yer fought wrong. Come on, let's get downstairs before Mum starts yelling.'

'But I thought . . .'

Lizzie looked at Ellie and smiled. 'You don't wanner worry about it, gel. All blokes are the same, only interested in one thing, getting inside yer drawers.'

Ellie couldn't believe the casual way Lizzie was accepting that this bloke had been two-timing them. 'But I thought you liked him.'

'I did, 'e was good fun, but that sort always gets their comeuppance in the end. 'Sides,' said Lizzie grinning, ''e don't know his wife come up the factory and warned us off. I'm not 'avin' that. Now come on, let's get downstairs.'

All week the dressing table was the most important thing the girls had to talk about and Bob was forgotten. By Saturday Ellie was eagerly looking forward to seeing the train man again, and wondering if she would get another big tip.

''E's gonner miss his train if 'e don't hurry up and come in soon,' said Ellie to Peggy as she collected yet another tray of tea and cakes.

'I told yer, you shouldn't bank on him coming back.'

But she had, and at the end of the day was very disappointed he hadn't been in.

'Bet you wish you hadn't bought those socks for yer Dad now, don't yer?'

'No, course not; you should 'ave seen his face.' Ellie smiled. 'I wish I could buy 'im lots of nice things.'

'Pr'aps you will one day if yer ends up marrying a toff.' Peggy laughed. 'Right, come on, home you go.'

But Ellie couldn't help feeling dejected when, as she took her week's sixpence into the haberdashery to pay off the threepence she owed on the socks, her shoes seemed to be getting further and further away.

After the day's disappointment Ellie was thrilled when she turned into Elmleigh and almost bumped into Terry Andrews. They stood on the pavement staring at each other for a few moments. Ellie felt her face flush, and smiled so much her mouth hurt.

''Allo Terry,' she managed to blurt out. 'Don't see much of you these days.'

He lowered his head. 'Well, I don't go out much. Mum ain't ser good.'

'Oh, I'm sorry.'

He stood kicking his overlarge boots against the wall. Ellie wanted him to say something, but he remained silent.

'Couldn't we go out for a walk sometime? I could buy you a cup of tea.' As soon as she spoke Ellie felt she could have bitten off her tongue. Girls didn't ask boys out. But then, she was desperate for his company.

Terry looked up, his dark brown eyes full of feeling. 'I'd like to Ellie, but well, you know how it is.'

She nodded.

'I'd better be off.' He hurried away.

Ellie stood for a few minutes watching him, feeling ashamed at what she'd said. When he turned the corner she suddenly realized that almost every Saturday night when she came home from work about this time, she saw him. Did he have a job? No, he couldn't have, he looked too scruffy. Unless he wore a uniform like her. Next Saturday she would ask him outright why he didn't want to go out with her.

Ellie walked on across the square, and was surprised when Dirty Molly called her and beckoned her over.

'Sit yerself down, Ellie.' She patted the iron seat. 'Yer turning out ter be a nice-looking gel. I've seen all the shenanigans what goes on round 'ere, but you've always behaved yerself.'

Ellie smiled and thought to herself, She wouldn't think so

if she'd just heard me trying to get Terry to take me out. She sat next to her. 'What do you want, Molly?'

Molly looked around cautiously, then back to her dog, and began fondling his head. 'Don't let yer muvver see yer talking to 'im.' She inclined her head in the direction Terry had taken.

'Why?'

'She ain't got no time for his muvver, had a big row they did, some years back; well, it was more of a fight. Nasty, don't 'old with women fighting. Right 'ere, it was.' She pointed to the ground. 'Yer muvver was carrying on like a raving loony, kicking and shouting. Reckon that's what made Mrs Andrews—' Molly quickly looked at Ellie.

Ellie was suddenly intrigued. 'My mum and Mrs Andrews? What over?'

'It 'appened many years ago. Shouldn't 'ave mentioned it.' Dirty Molly looked uncomfortable.

'What was it about?'

'Dunno, you'd better ask yer muvver.'

'I bet you do. Anyway if it 'appened years ago, what's that got to do with me talking to Terry?' Ellie was beginning to get annoyed.

'Just telling yer, gel. Just be careful.' She paused. 'See yer got a nice piece o' furniture last Sunday. Let's hope yer mum don't git rid of it like she 'as everyfink else.'

'We 'ad to eat when we was little.' Ellie knew she had to defend her mother, but her mind was still on what Molly had said.

'Yer, I know, gel. The way that Lizzie was flaunting 'erself at that bloke, she should be ashamed of 'erself. And as fer wearing those short skirts, well I dread ter fink what 'er and your Dolly gits up to. Wasn't like that in my young days.'

'Lizzie and Dolly are very fashionable.'

'That's as may be, but it ain't right young gels showing orf their legs like that, gives a man all sorts o' ideas.'

'Is that all you've got to say?' Ellie stood up.

'Remember what I said. I don't fink yer mum would like yer ter go out with young Terry, yer know.'

'What? I ain't going out with 'im.' Ellie knew her face was going red again.

'Not yet you ain't, but . . .'

''Sides, it ain't none of your business what I do.' She moved away.

'Just be careful, gel.' Dirty Molly held her dog closer. 'Seen it all, ain't we Ben?'

Ellie walked away, flustered. Silly old fool, what was she on about? Still, she would have to try and find out what the fight was about. Perhaps her dad would tell her. Did Terry know?

As Ellie pushed open the front door, she realized it was unusually quiet. Lizzie, who was sitting at the top of the stairs, beckoned to Ellie, and putting her finger to her bright red lips, pursed them into a silent shh. But Ellie had only got one foot on the first wooden stair when the kitchen door flew open and her mother's loud voice yelled out.

'Where d'yer fink you're going? Get in 'ere at once, yer lying little cow!'

Ellie was bewildered. What had she done? Had she been seen talking to Dirty Molly? But surely that wouldn't bring this about; and she couldn't have been seen talking to Terry. Besides, what was wrong with that? She had known him all her life. Her mind was racing as she walked along the passage to the kitchen.

Her father was sitting with his head in his hands. He looked up. 'I'm sorry, love.' It was a sad, pathetic little voice.

Ellie's dark eyes flashed from her mother to her father. In a split second she noticed the empty beer jug in the hearth. Suddenly her mother brought out of her overall pocket the pair of socks.

'Well?' The socks were pushed into Ellie's face.

'I bought 'em for Dad, 'cos 'e didn't 'ave any.' Ellie tried to sound grown up and confident, but she was physically shaking.

'And where did the money come from?'

'Some man gave me a tip.' Ellie's voice was barely above a whisper.

'So, yer bin telling me lies all these weeks?'

'No.'

'How many more tips yer 'ad and not told me about?'

'None, honest, that was the first one.' Ellie could have bitten off her tongue. Why didn't she say she'd saved up for them. Had her father told her mother about the tip?

'Oh yer, I should coco. Honest? Yer don't know the bloody meaning of the word. So yer reckon it was the first one? How much did 'e give yer?'

'Sixpence.'

'A tanner, and yer reckon yer bought yer dad some socks fer a tanner?'

'I put some of my money with it.'

'Oh very nice. Pull the other one, it's got bells on it,' she said sarcastically. 'Seems I'm giving yer too much spending money, if yer got it ter waste on socks fer 'im.' She jerked her thumb towards her husband.

Ellie hung her head. What was the use? She knew her mother would never believe her. Why didn't her dad say something to defend her?

'Right, 'and over what yer got terday.'

Ellie's head shot up. 'I didn't get any.'

'Don't tell me lies.' A hand flew out and struck Ellie a mighty blow round the head. Her teeth rattled.

'I said 'and it over.' Mrs Walsh grabbed Ellie's long dark hair and pulled it back till tears filled her eyes.

'Ruby, stop it.' Her father was on his feet.

Mrs Walsh pushed him back in the chair. 'You can sit down, yer worthless bit o' flesh.'

The kitchen door burst open and out of the corner of her eye Ellie saw her three sisters standing in the doorway, their faces drained of colour. Ellie couldn't move her head as her mother was still hanging on to her hair. Tears ran down her face.

'Stop it, Mum. Ellie ain't got no money.' Lizzie moved closer.

'O yer, and how d'you know?'

'She would tell yer.'

'Like she told me last week?' Mrs Walsh flung Ellie across the room. 'You're all the bleeding same. I 'ave ter work 'ard to keep this place, find the rent and coal money and feed yer. No wonder I took any bits worth anyfink up the pawn shop. D'yer fink I enjoyed it? Do yer? As fer you, yer miserable bit of shit – even the army didn't want yer. And when you did 'ave a job and a few bob you used ter come and go as yer pleased, out with any old tom while I 'ad ter stay 'ome and look after this lot.' She waved her arm at the girls, who were standing open-mouthed. 'Now you lotter earning a bit I fink I'm entitled to it, and if yer don't like it, then sod off, the lot of yer.'

The door slammed so hard when she left the room that Ellie thought it would fall off its hinges.

'Now look what you've done. More bloody trouble. What d'yer wanner go and buy 'im socks for, yer silly cow?' shouted Lizzie.

'I wanted to,' sobbed Ellie.

Lizzie turned angrily on her father. 'And it wouldn't 'ave hurt you to 'ave got off yer arse and helped 'er.'

'I'm sorry, gel. I . . .'

'Sorry, sorry, you ain't sorry, only for yourself.' Lizzie's blue eyes were flashing with anger.

'What's Ma bin on?' asked Dolly flippantly.

Their father picked up the empty beer jug. ''Ave yer got a couple o' pence ter get this filled up again? It might calm 'er down.'

'I ain't got any,' said Dolly.

'And don't look at me,' said Lizzie.

'I 'ave,' said Ellie. 'I didn't get any tips,' she added quickly. 'It's the sixpence Mum let me keep yesterday. I'll go up and get it.'

Ellie felt utterly miserable. This was all her fault. Why hadn't she realized how hard it had been for their mother to bring them up? She had been so busy feeling sorry for herself. Ellie remembered how when she was small, and before Baby Iris was born, her mother had sat night after night darning and altering her sisters' clothes by the dim gaslight. Her dad never seemed to be in regular work. If only their mother had told them how hard things had been; talked to them. Dolly and Lizzie always said it was because she liked a drink or two that she pawned anything she could get her hands on, but that hadn't always been true.

In the bedroom Ellie sat on the bed. Should she go and say she was sorry? Would it help? And what did her mother mean when she said their dad was out with any old tom? Perhaps it was because she was angry with all of them that she said those sort of things. Ellie took one of the sixpences she kept wrapped in paper, from an old wage packet that now sat in her half of the drawer, and took it downstairs. The least she could do was use her money to buy her mother a drink; it might help to heal the rift. She would have to wait a while longer for her new shoes.

Chapter 4

Sunday was miserable. Everybody was frightened to talk, and made sure they kept out of their mother's way as much as possible. All day Ellie tried hard to say something nice to her mother, but she wouldn't listen; even when Ellie was doing her best to apologize she was pushed away. Her father just sat in his armchair and looked dejected. Ellie couldn't understand; if he had stood up for himself all those years ago, what had happened to make him change so much? Was it because he had been out of work for so long that he'd lost heart? When Ellie looked at the faded photograph of their wedding, so long ago, they seemed happy enough. What had gone wrong?

But at least Ellie's sisters didn't blame her for their mother's outburst, although they made it clear she had been daft to spend her money on the socks. That evening all four girls sat in their bedroom discussing it.

'How did yer reckon 'e was gonner wash 'em without Mum knowing?' asked Lizzie.

'What makes yer fink 'e'd ever wash 'em?' laughed Dolly.

'I didn't think about that,' said Ellie.

'Well you wouldn't would yer, yer daft cow,' said Dolly, filing her nails.

'Now pr'aps you'll learn ter use yer loaf a bit more. I told yer, yer gotter be crafty.' Lizzie sat on the bed next to her sister. 'Lend us yer nailfile, Dol.'

'No, get yer own.'

'You two still seeing that Bob?' Baby Iris suddenly asked her sisters.

'Course, we work with 'im, daft cow,' said Lizzie. 'The two-timing sod.'

Dolly said nothing.

'What about you, Dolly?' Baby Iris wasn't going to let it rest.

'Not since I found out 'e was married. Ain't no future in that.' Dolly didn't sound very convincing.

Baby Iris laughed out loud. 'That was a laugh, 'im going out with the both of you at the same time. You must be daft.'

'Leave it out, Iris,' said Lizzie.

'I reckon that's very funny. You wouldn't catch me going out with me sister's bloke.'

'Lizzie said leave it out. Now turn out the gas lamp and let's get some sleep,' said Dolly angrily.

'I ain't gitting out o' bed,' said Baby Iris, snuggling down under the thin blanket.

'I'll do it.' Ellie padded across the bare floorboards. When she turned out the light, the pop still made her jump. As she lay on her back next to Baby Iris she couldn't help thinking what a miserable weekend it had been. She'd be glad to get back to work tomorrow.

It was early on Monday morning before the Tea Room opened, and while Ellie was busy polishing the silver cruets she told Peggy in a hushed voice about her mother, and the saga of the socks.

'See, I told yer you should 'ave kept that money.'

'Honest, Peg, I didn't realize the trouble it was gonner start. I wish that man hadn't come in.'

'Shouldn't think you'll 'ave that problem again. Don't reckon 'e'll be in again.' Peggy was cleaning the glass cabinet the fancy cakes would go in. She looked at the door behind the counter that led to the bakery, and lowering her voice said, 'I went to the music hall Saturday night with Mr Jenkins.'

'You didn't?' Ellie opened her big brown eyes wide with curiosity. 'You didn't say you was . . .'

'It wasn't till we were leaving 'e asked me.' Peggy had a smug look on her face.

Ellie grinned. 'Was it all right?'

'Yer, we saw these dancers and—'

'No, I mean was it all right being with Mr Jenkins?'

'Yer, 'e's ever so nice and considerate.'

'He's a bit old, though, ain't 'e?'

'He ain't that old. We're going again next Sat'day.'

'I'm really pleased for you, Peg, if that's what you want. I only wish I had someone to take me out.'

'I'm surprised you don't go out with your sisters sometimes.'

'No, they don't want me, they only want blokes to take 'em so they don't have to pay. 'Sides, where would we go?'

'You could always go for a walk round the park and listen to the band, that's free.'

'S'pose I could. Be better still if I could get Terry Andrews to come with me though.'

Peggy laughed. 'You're not still in love with 'im, are yer?'

Ellie blushed. 'No, silly, but it would be nice to go out with 'im.'

'Ain't seen 'im fer years. 'E still spotty and lanky?'

'No.'

'I remember the time 'e 'ad impetigo, and 'ad that mauve stuff all over 'is face, 'e didn't 'alf look a sight.'

'A lot of us caught it,' said Ellie, quietly thinking back on the embarrassment those painful days had caused her. ''E looks very nice now.' Ellie wasn't going to let on he didn't have any decent clothes. ''E ain't at work and 'e looks after 'is mum.'

'They still 'ave lodgers?'

'Sometimes.'

'My mum reckons she was a bit of a girl in her young days, and that 'er lodgers were, well . . . you know? And talk was that young Terry was born the wrong side of the blanket.' She nodded knowingly. 'You know what I mean. Don't ever see or 'ear anyfink of a Mr Andrews, do we?' asked Peggy pointedly.

Ellie looked aghast. 'I didn't know that. She always said she was a widow. D'you think that's why 'e don't say much and keeps 'imself to 'imself?'

''E never used to.'

'No,' said Ellie thoughtfully, thinking on what Dirty Molly had said. But then if Terry was illegitimate Molly would have taken great joy in telling her. 'Pr'aps 'e's only just found out,' added Ellie.

'Could be.' Then as if reading her thoughts Peggy asked, 'Does Dirty Molly still sit under the tree?'

'Yer. Think she's part of it be now.' Ellie laughed. 'When I was little I used to wonder why that tree never got too big for the bench. Maybe Molly put a spell on it.'

'She used to frighten the life out of me when I had to cross the square to get to school. That bright red hair sticking out from under that old black hat.' Peggy shuddered.

'She's nearly all grey now, and she don't run like she did, she's too old.'

'Does she still live with her sister?'

'Yes.'

'Thought she'd be dead by now.'

Mr Jenkins pushed open the door at the back of the counter, and the warm baking smell drifted out. 'Right girls, put these cakes out, and be careful with them, they're still warm.' He gave Peggy a beaming smile. 'Everything all right?'

'Yes Mr Jenkins,' they said together.

The summer was long and hot. Everything in the Walsh household remained the same, and neither the socks nor the sixpence was ever mentioned again, although her mother still didn't believe Ellie when she told her she didn't get any tips.

At the end of August 1926 Ellie was devastated when her hero died. Dolly and Lizzie also cried when they heard that their idol Rudolph Valentino had passed away. The news reel showed pictures of his funeral, and women throwing themselves at his coffin. Baby Iris thought they were all daft.

Every Saturday night Ellie would deliberately dawdle home hoping to see Terry Andrews – but somehow she always seemed to miss him. She wondered if he was trying to avoid her after that time she had suggested they might go out. She often thought of asking Dirty Molly about his father, but thought better of it. She still wondered about the fight their mothers were supposed to have had. When she asked Dolly and Lizzie they said they knew nothing about it, and reckoned Dirty Molly had made it up, so she was none the wiser. Now, with her head down, Ellie hurried past her.

Saturday evening was a big night out for Dolly and Lizzie. Ellie and Baby Iris sat on the bed watching Lizzie getting ready.

'Who's Dolly gone out with?' asked Baby Iris.

'Don't know, and don't care. I've got a nice bloke now,' said Lizzie, smugly.

'What's this one like?' asked Ellie.

'A right darling.' Lizzie powdered her face. She peered into her compact mirror and pursed her red lips. She then took a small, dark blue bottle with a silver top from her handbag and dabbed the perfume behind her ears. 'This ought ter get 'im going.' The smell of Evening in Paris scent filled the air.

Ellie coughed and waved her hands about. ''E married?' she asked.

'No 'e ain't, and 'e's got a few bob. Taking me to the music 'all, and out fer a meal after.'

'Wow, lucky old you,' said Baby Iris, hanging on to every word.

'Peggy at work goes to the music hall with Mr Jenkins,' said Ellie.

'She's got 'er 'ead screwed on right enough, that one 'as, going out with the boss.' Lizzie picked up her handbag.

'When we gonner see this 'ere bloke then?' asked Iris.

'When I'm good and ready,' said Lizzie. She stood at the door and, waving her finger at them both, said, 'I'll be late ternight, so don't start making a racket when I gets in, I don't want Mum ter know. Savvy?'

They both nodded, and giggled.

Peggy was now going to the music hall every Saturday night with Mr Jenkins, and tomorrow, Sunday, she told Ellie, he was going to have tea with her and her mother.

As she took off her coat and donned her apron she said excitedly, 'D'yer know, 'e's baking some extra cakes to bring with 'im tomorrow.'

'I'm really pleased for you, Peg,' said Ellie. 'When we gonner hear wedding bells then?'

Peggy blushed. 'Don't talk daft, we ain't walking out or anyfink like that, it's just that we both like the music 'all, and it's nice to go with someone.'

Ellie nodded, and grinned. 'Well we could be busy today, so let's get started.'

All the morning weary women came in for tea. Ellie was rushed off her feet, and noticed with envy when some of the women sneakingly slipped off their winklepicker shoes and, after wriggling their silk-clad feet, put them on the cold, red-tiled floor.

'Won't be sorry when today's over,' said Peggy red-faced, as she went back and forth to the kitchen where on a Saturday deaf old Mrs Page made the tea and washed up.

At half past one there was a slight lull, with only two

customers, women who sat at the far table talking in hushed voices. As Ellie got on with clearing the crocks away and bagging up the dirty linen ready for Mrs Page to take home to wash, the little silver bell over the door tinkled. Ellie looked up to see the train man. Unconsciously she gave him a big smile as she took his hat.

'Thank you, my dear, it's so nice to see such a happy face. I'll have a pot of tea and a scone, if you please.'

Peggy gave Ellie a grin and a knowing nod when she gave her the order. 'Let's 'ope 'e ain't got much change,' Peggy whispered.

'Not so busy today, I see,' said the train man.

'It was earlier on.' Ellie went to walk away.

'Have you got a minute?'

Ellie looked about her anxiously. 'Mr Jenkins don't really like us talking to the customers.'

He smiled and Ellie noticed it was a warm, pleasant smile. She wondered what kind of work he did. She decided it was probably in an office or a shop.

'I was just wondering if you could do me up a small box of cakes.'

Ellie felt foolishly deflated. For some unknown reason she had thought he was going to ask her something far more exciting. 'Yes, yes of course. Is there anythink in particular you like?'

'No, not really, they're for a young lady and I know she has a sweet tooth.'

Ellie nodded politely and went up to the counter.

'You was 'aving quite a chat with 'im,' said Peggy eagerly.

''E wants a box of cakes, for 'is girlfriend.' Ellie grinned. 'She's got a sweet tooth.'

'Lucky old 'er, having someone to buy 'er nice cakes. I wonder how old she is.' She glanced over her shoulder. ''E don't look like a dirty old man.'

Before Ellie took him the fancy box, with a neat ribbon tied round it, she paused. The thought running through her head was how nice it must be to have someone buy you nice things.

'Thank you,' said the train man as she put the box on the table. 'I've been invited to a friend's daughter's birthday tea. And after we're all taking her to see that new Rudolph Valentino film, *The Sheik*.'

'Oh, she's ever so lucky. I'd love ter see it. I think 'e was wonderful, and I was ever so upset when 'e died.'

'Yes, that was a shame, such a good-looking young man with everything to live for. Do you like the cinema?'

'Oh yes. I think it's wonderful.' Ellie quickly regained her composure. 'Sorry,' she said looking around, terrified some one might be waiting, or that Mr Jenkins might see her talking.

'No need to be sorry, my dear. I'm glad you've got a moment to spare.'

'Miss, miss,' called one of the women in the corner.

Ellie gave a little curtsey and hurried to the back of the room.

When he had finished his tea, the train man took his hat from the hatstand and left. Ellie swiftly moved over to his table. He had left her another sixpence. She quickly put it in her pocket. This one she was going to keep, and not tell a soul about it. Well, perhaps just Peggy.

On Monday morning Ellie was eager to know how Sunday's tea went with Mr Jenkins.

''E's ever so nice, ever so different away from work,' whispered Peggy, her eyes sparkling. 'Him and Mum got on like an 'ouse on fire.'

Ellie envied Peggy her relationship with her mother. They could talk and laugh together.

'Mum's asked 'im to come round again, I fink it was the cakes what did it.'

The door behind the counter opened, and the usual warm, sweet-smelling draught of air came from the bakery.

'Good morning, Ellie,' said Mr Jenkins, wiping flour from his face with the bottom of his apron. 'Did you have a nice weekend?'

'Yes thank you.' She couldn't tell him it was the same as any other boring old Sunday.

He smiled. 'Now come along, girls, no more standing around gossiping, it's back to work.'

'Yes Mr Jenkins,' they said together.

Chapter 5

The summer and autumn of 1926 continued to be almost uneventful for Ellie. She hadn't seen Terry for ages, and it didn't matter if she dawdled or hurried home, she seemed to miss him. Her only highlight was once a month when 'her train man', as Peggy called him, came in to the tea room. If she wasn't too busy he liked a little chat. He didn't say much about himself, or his work, it was mostly about the weather or the latest films. He was pleasant-looking, clean shaven, and his vivid blue eyes followed her round the room, lighting up when she smiled at him. He was well spoken and seemed a kind man. He always wore a dark grey suit with a matching trilby and carried a small briefcase. Ellie noted his shoes were always well polished, and his hands clean. She and Peggy by now reckoned that he must definitely work in an office, but why he only came into the tea room once a month, and on a Saturday, was a mystery. But to Ellie, the important thing was that he always left her sixpence.

Baby Iris had left school and was now working in the dress department of a small family-run store in Rotherhithe New Road. There had been many arguments about it, but as usual Baby Iris had got her own way, and Ellie was never sure if she gave her mother her unopened pay packet.

Ellie now had her new t-bar black shoes of which she was very proud. They made her feel very grown up. Every night, much to all her sisters' amusement, Ellie stuffed them with paper in case they lost their shape. She was also saving for Christmas, but had to be very careful about what she bought, otherwise her mother would know she'd been given more sixpences.

Lizzie had been going out with her new boyfriend for months now, and when she did talk about Ernie, Ellie noted it was with a lot of feeling.

'What's 'e like, Dolly?' asked Baby Iris one night after Lizzie had gone out and the three of them were lazing about in their bedroom.

'A nice bloke.'

'You've met him then?' asked Ellie.

'We went out for a drink a couple of times.'

'Who's we?' asked Ellie, pouncing on any information she could.

'Only a mate of his. Don't ask so many questions.'

'What's 'e look like?' asked Iris.

'Who?'

'Lizzie's bloke.'

'Tall, got dark 'air.'

Ellie, who was lying on the bed, turned over on to her stomach. 'Lizzie said 'e works in the print.'

'Yer,' said Dolly. 'Got a good job, by all accounts.'

'Does 'e look like that Bob?' asked Baby Iris.

'What Bob?'

'That bloke at your work.'

Dolly laughed. 'Na, 'e's better looking than 'im.'

'Wow, 'e must be a smasher then, I think that Bob was really gorgeous. Wouldn't mind going out with 'im meself.'

It was Ellie's turn to laugh. 'You've been reading too many books.'

'I reckon our Lizzie's in love,' said Iris.

'Could be,' said Dolly with a smirk.

''Ere, she ain't getting married is she?'

'Dunno,' came the reply.

That night when Lizzie came home she woke Dolly getting into bed.

'Your feet're like bloody lumps of ice,' whispered Dolly angrily. 'And get over, I ain't warming you up.'

'Be quiet you two,' said Iris.

'I can't sleep. I'm too excited.'

All three girls sat up.

'Why?' asked Iris.

'No reason.' Lizzie snuggled down.

'You can be so bloody infuriating at times, Liz,' said Dolly.

'Just lay down and go to sleep.'

Ellie grinned to herself. She guessed Lizzie had a secret.

At the beginning of December it was Lizzie's twenty-first birthday, and on the Friday she'd asked them if they would like to come to the pub on Saturday night to meet Ernie for a drink to celebrate her birthday.

Ellie couldn't believe it. For the first time they were going out as a family. There was plenty of excitement and activity as they began to get ready.

'I'm really looking forward ter meeting 'im. What's 'e like?' asked Baby Iris standing in front of the mirror and combing her hair for the third time. 'Is 'e really good-looking, Lizzie?'

'I fink so,' Lizzie replied.

'I told yer. You ain't going, you ain't old enough,' said her mother, edging Baby Iris away from the mirror and pushing a large hatpin into her old, battered, black felt hat.

'Oh Mum.'

'Don't you oh Mum me.'

Baby Iris slumped in the chair with a scowl. 'I ain't too young to go to work or go up the pub and git yer a jug o' beer every day though, am I?'

'Don't you talk ter me like that.'

An answer like that would have earned me a clip round

49

the ear, Ellie thought. 'Well Lizzie?' she said, hoping to defuse the situation. 'What is 'e like?'

'I keep telling yer, 'e's a smashing bloke,' said Lizzie lightheartedly as she and Dolly crowded in front of the mirror.

'Well I dunno why 'e's asked us lot ter come out with yer,' said Ned Walsh.

''E wants ter celebrate me birfday, and ter meet yer all, that's why. Blimey, I never fought it would cause so much bloody trouble. I'm sorry I said anyfink.'

'If 'e's that keen ter see us, you could bring 'im round 'ere.'

Their mother and father didn't see the way Dolly shook her head and screwed up her nose at that remark.

'Oh Dad, don't be such a moaner,' said Ellie. 'I think it's very nice of 'im ter ask us all out.'

Mrs Walsh eyed her eldest daughter suspiciously. 'Hummh. You'd fink 'e'd 'ave somefink better ter do with 'is money than spend it on booze.'

They looked at their mother in disbelief.

''E 'as got a bob or two,' said Dolly.

Lizzie smiled and looked pleased at that comment.

'You've met 'im then?' asked their father.

'Yer, a couple of times.'

'You sure it ain't 'cos yer got somefink ter say? You ain't finking of leaving 'ome, are yer?' asked their mother, looking at Lizzie with some distrust.

Lizzie carried on brushing her hair and, wetting her finger, curled it round the hair that rested on her cheek.

'I asked you, you ain't finking of leaving 'ome, are yer?' Their mother's voice was harsh.

Lizzie threw her hairbrush on the table. 'I don't believe this. It's me birfday, fer Christ's sake, all the fuss it's causing, I'm bloody sorry I said anyfink.'

'I won't let yer leave 'ome yer know. I ain't gonner be your money short.'

'Mum, I'm twenty-one now. Why don't yer just shut up and come and 'ave a drink with us?'

Ellie was shocked when her father suddenly announced, 'Well I ain't going.'

'What?' yelled Mrs Walsh. 'Why?'

'We look too scruffy to go out with them.' He waved his hand at Lizzie and Dolly. ''Sides, where we got money ter buy 'im a drink?'

'Please yerself,' said Lizzie. 'I've 'ad enough of this. I ain't getting on me 'ands and knees ter beg yer ter come. You ready, Doll?'

Dolly nodded, picked up her handbag and, linking her arm through Lizzie's, went out.

Ellie stood open-mouthed. 'They didn't ask me to go with 'em,' she whispered.

Baby Iris laughed. 'Now yer know what it's like ter be left out.'

'It's all your bloody fault,' shouted Mrs Walsh, pointing her finger at her husband. 'We coulder gone out and 'ad a nice quiet drink with 'em instead of sitting 'ere night after night. Yer bloody miserable sod.' Mrs Walsh slammed the kitchen door as she left the room.

'I'm sorry, gel,' said Ellie's father. 'But I ain't got no money ter spend on drink, and I ain't taking charity from no one. If I can't pay me way, then I'd rather not go.'

Ellie sat at the table and gently rubbed her hand over the faded oilcloth. She ran her fingers along the band of faded flowers that had once formed a garland in the middle but over the years had been scrubbed away. 'I could 'ave given you some money if that was all that stopped you.'

'You bin getting more tips then?' asked Iris quickly. 'You'll 'ave Mum after yer if she finds out.'

'Shut up, Iris, and mind yer own business.' He sounded irate. 'What Ellie does with 'er money is 'er affair. She gives yer mother more than enough as it is.'

Ellie sat back amazed. She'd never heard her father talk to

51

anyone like that before. Suddenly she too was filled with anger.

'I'll tell Mum you shouted at me,' sniffed Baby Iris, peering resentfully at her father.

'I've got some money 'cos I've been saving up, that's why, and don't you dare tell Mum otherwise I'll kill yer.' Ellie jumped up from her chair, her eyes flashing.

Baby Iris looked up at Ellie. Fear filled her face. It was the first time she'd seen her sister like this. 'All right. Don't worry. I won't tell Mum,' she muttered.

''Sides, you've been at work a few months now, so you should 'ave a few bob saved.'

Iris didn't answer.

'D'yer think our Lizzie might be thinking of gitting married?' asked their father.

'Dunno,' said Ellie, calming down.

'I reckon that's why yer mother wanted ter go, ter try and put 'im off.'

'Oh Dad, that ain't a nice thing ter say. She wouldn't do that, would she?'

'Yer mother'll go mad if she 'as ter lose a pay packet every week.'

'But what about Lizzie?' asked Baby Iris. 'What's she gonner say?'

'She ain't gonner be none too pleased. Now up ter bed with yer.'

'She's over twenty-one now, Dad,' said Ellie. 'And she can please herself.'

'Yer, that's true enough.'

They sat staring into the fire.

Ellie toyed with the poker, desperately wishing she'd been able to go with her two sisters. Just to go out and see a bit of life. Would her lot ever change? Would she ever find someone to take her out? What did the future hold?

'Fink I'll go on up now,' said her father. 'Let's 'ope yer mother's asleep, I don't fancy any more lectures ternight.'

Ellie smiled. 'Goodnight, Dad, I'll put the gas out.'

Ellie reached up to turn out the gaslight, when her father came racing back into the room. 'She's gorn.'

'Who?' asked Ellie.

'Yer mother.'

Baby Iris walked in. 'What's up?'

'Yer mother's gorn.'

'What, left 'ome?'

'Dunno.' Mr Walsh slumped in the chair.

'What we gonner do?' asked Ellie.

'Did she take 'er coat?' asked Baby Iris.

'Dunno. It's freezing out there, she must of.'

Ellie ran up the passage. ''Er coat's gone,' she shouted hysterically, and hurried back into the kitchen. 'Dad, you don't think she's gone up the pub?'

His head shot up. 'Iris, quick, gel, put yer coat on and run up and find out.'

'I'll go,' said Ellie pulling on her coat.

Ellie stood outside the pub. She had never been inside; only to the off licence for her mother's ale before it became Baby Iris's job. The sound of a piano being played badly and a lot of noisy singing, mixed with the smell of warm stale beer and tobacco, wafted out when the door was opened. Ellie took a step back when a large elderly man staggered out.

'What's a pretty little gel like you doing waiting outside a pub?' he asked, swaying uneasily, when he caught sight of Ellie standing near the doorway.

'I'm waiting for someone.'

He moved closer and put his arm round her shoulders. ''As yer boyfriend let yer down then, love?'

She quickly pulled away. 'No. I'm looking for me mum.'

'Yer mum, cor bugger me. Don't worry about yer mum, gel, come and 'ave a drink with me.'

'No thank you.' His beery and onion breath made her feel sick.

He lurched forward. 'Come on, love. Just 'ave a little 'un.'

'Get away from me,' she yelled, looking round for help.

'All right, all right. Keep yer 'air on.' He moved back and straightened up. 'Please yerself. But I could show yer a good time.' He pushed open the door. 'Yer going in then?' he asked harshly.

Ellie quickly stepped round him and peered through the open door. To her surprise, she saw her mother dancing in the middle of the floor with a woman she'd seen but whose name she didn't know. Her mother was panting and staring out with glazed eyes, her face bright red.

Ellie looked around for Dolly and Lizzie, but they weren't anywhere to be seen.

Ellie ventured in. 'Mum, Mum,' she called trying to make herself heard above the din. 'Come on, Mum, come home.'

''Ere,' shrieked the other woman. ''Ere's your Ellie. Come ter take yer ma 'ome then, gel?'

'I ain't going nowhere,' said Mrs Walsh, quickly pulling her arm away from her friend. 'Me other gels 'ave buggered orf and left me, so now I'm gonner enjoy meself. Go on, sod orf 'ome.' She flapped her hands at Ellie.

Reluctantly Ellie left the pub. She knew there was no use in making a fuss. But why had Dolly and Lizzie left her there? She would have to wait till morning for the answers.

Her father wasn't very pleased when he heard what had happened, but told Ellie he had no intention of making a fool of himself by going to get her.

But it wasn't morning when the racket woke Ellie.

'What's that noise?' asked Baby Iris, sitting up in bed.

'It's Mum,' said Ellie, slipping out of bed. She put on her coat that had been on the bed to help keep them warm. 'I'll give 'er an 'and to get up the stairs.'

Her father was at the bottom of the stairs trying to get his wife to move. 'Come on, love.'

'Leave me be. I ain't doing what you want, I've 'ad a

bloody good time ternight, 'ad lots o' drinks bought me.'

Baby Iris had joined Ellie, and Ned Walsh looked up at his two daughters. 'Go back ter bed, I'll see ter yer mother.'

'Where's that cow Lizzie, and Dolly, they 'ome yet?' yelled their mother.

'No, not yet,' said Ellie.

'I'm gonner chuck 'er out when she gits 'ome, leaving me on me own. D'yer know she left me, left me sitting in the pub all on me own, just 'cos I told 'er la-di-da boyfriend what I fought of 'im.'

Ellie shuddered. There was going to be another almighty row in the morning. 'Come on, Mum, let's 'elp Dad put you to bed.'

'Sod off.'

'Go on, love, I'll see to 'er.' Her father looked very sad.

'Wow,' said Baby Iris as they settled down in the warm bed once again. 'Can't wait till morning.'

Ellie hoped morning wouldn't come too soon.

Very slowly Ellie opened her eyes. It took a few moments to adjust to the early morning gloom. She looked across at her sisters' bed. There was only one lump. She lifted her head and could just about make out Dolly's head on the pillow. Where was Lizzie?

'Stop fidgeting,' moaned Baby Iris.

'I ain't fidgeting,' said Ellie.

'You are. Now you've taken all the covers, and yer talking and waking me up.'

'I ain't.'

'Fer Christ's sake shut up, the pair o' yer.' Dolly's grumpy voice, thick with sleep, came from under the coat that had been thrown over the thin blankets.

'Dolly, where's Lizzie?' asked Ellie.

'Shut up.'

Ellie got out of bed.

Baby Iris sat up. 'Didn't Lizzie come 'ome last night?'

'I told yer ter shut it.' Dolly turned over.

When Ellie got downstairs, she found her father lighting the fire.

'Dad, I don't think Lizzie come home last night.'

He sat back on his hunkers. 'That's all we need. Does Dolly know where she's gone?'

'Dunno, she ain't talking.'

He stood up. 'Fill the kettle up, gel. I'll make yer mum a cuppa, she don't feel very well.'

Ellie grinned. 'I ain't surprised.'

It was almost dinner time when Dolly finally got up. Ellie and Baby Iris had spent the morning getting the dinner ready; their mother was still in bed.

'Where's Ma?' asked Dolly, walking into the kitchen, scratching her head and yawning.

'In bed, she ain't well,' said her father.

Dolly sat at the table. 'I ain't surprised. You should 'ave seen 'er last night. Gawd only knows what she'd 'ad ter drink. I tell yer, me and Lizzie was ashamed of 'er – we buggered off.'

'I know, I went looking for yer,' said Ellie.

'You did?'

'You'd gone.'

'Did you bring Mum 'ome?'

'No, she wouldn't come.'

'Dolly, where's our Lizzie?' Her father's voice was forceful.

'She's gorn.'

'What?'

'She's gorn, left 'ome.'

'What? Where?'

'She's gorn ter live with 'er bloke.'

'What? She can't 'ave.' Ned Walsh sat at the table. 'This'll kill yer mother.'

'She don't care about us,' said Dolly aggressively. 'We're only a pay packet that comes in every week.' She stood up.

'And I tell yer if I 'ad 'alf a chance and somewhere ter go, I'd be off as well.'

'What about all Lizzie's fings?' asked Baby Iris.

'I'm taking 'em ter work termorrer.'

'Wow. That means I can 'ave a drawer in the dressing table all to meself.'

'That's all you bloody well fink of, is yerself.' Dolly left the kitchen, and the three of them sat silent with their mouths open.

The kettle's lid bobbing on the hob brought them quickly back.

'I'll make some more tea,' said Ellie jumping up.

'You gonner tell Mum?' Baby Iris asked Ellie.

Ellie shook her head and looked at her father.

'I'll do it,' he said, taking a cup from the dresser and pouring out the tea.

Ellie and Baby Iris sat quietly listening when their father took up the tea. They waited for – something, but no sound came.

'Did yer tell 'er?' Baby Iris asked her father when he finally came into the kitchen.

He nodded.

'Well?' asked Ellie.

'She reckons she'll be back termorrer.'

'Is that it? Is that all?'

'Yer. She's gitting up, so lay the table.'

Ellie felt a little deflated. It wasn't the sort of reaction she had expected.

For the rest of the day Ellie tried to keep out of her mother's way as much as possible. Nothing was said about Lizzie leaving home, or Ellie seeing her in the pub, and Ellie wasn't going to mention it.

That evening Dolly was in the bedroom busy packing Lizzie's few things in bags.

'Mum reckons she'll be back tomorrow,' said Ellie, lying on the bed watching her.

'She won't.'
'How can you be sure?'
'I just know.'

Two weeks before Christmas Mr Jenkins and Peggy stayed behind to put up the tea room's decorations. When Ellie walked in the following morning she couldn't contain her excitement at the thought of her first Christmas working here.

'It looks really lovely,' said Ellie, turning in a complete circle as she looked up at the pretty coloured paperchains hanging in loops from the high ceiling.

'Next we're gonner put some holly round the mirrors,' said Peggy.

'I wish I could stay 'ere all over Christmas.'

Peggy laughed. 'Yer wouldn't get any dinner.'

'I'm sure I'd find something.'

'Is it that bad at 'ome?' asked Peggy, her voice full of concern.

'No, not really.' Ellie busied herself with the cutlery. She didn't want Peggy to feel sorry for her, but she knew this Christmas was going to be awful without Lizzie.

''Ave you 'eard from yer sister?'

'No, but Dolly works with 'er, and she seems to be all right.'

'That's good. She gonner marry this bloke?'

'Dunno. You seeing Mr Jenkins over Christmas?'

'I expect so.' Peggy looked over her shoulder at the door to the bakery and whispered, 'I've bought Mr Jenkins a shaving mug for Christmas.'

Ellie looked surprised. 'Should I get 'im somethink?'

'No, course not, silly. What yer gonner get yer sisters?'

'Dunno.' Ellie wasn't going to tell Peggy they never gave presents.

'Me mum makes scarves and mittens; she'd only charge yer for the wool if yer fancied getting 'em somethink like that.'

'That could be a good idea, but . . .'

'You might find yer'll get a few tips this week,' said Peggy quickly changing the subject. 'People get a bit generous this time o' year.'

'That'd be nice.'

As the week went on Peggy was right, Ellie did get the odd penny or tuppence left over from the customers' change and one lady even gave her a bright new shiny silver thrupenny bit.

'There you are my dear,' she said, ceremoniously putting it into her hand. 'When your mother's making her Christmas pudding put this in and make a wish.'

Ellie didn't have the heart to tell her she'd never tasted Christmas pudding, let alone stirred it and made a wish.

It was a cold Saturday night as Ellie walked home; the wind was catching the rubbish and blowing it round her feet. Next Saturday was Christmas Day. Her bent head was full of what the lady had said about making a wish. At this moment she didn't know what she wished for most; for Lizzie to come back home, or Terry to come along and ask her out.

The gas lamp hissed as she walked past. As a child that noise had terrified her, but not now. Her eyes strayed to the tree. Normally it stood proud in the middle of the square, but tonight, in the dark, it looked eerie as its naked branches waved back and forth like clutching fingers. Ellie guessed it had even been too cold for Dirty Molly to be in her usual seat, but Ellie knew she would be sitting in her window, and could almost feel her eyes following her, watching and looking at everything that went on. I bet she knows all about Lizzie, she thought, and pulled the scarf Peggy had given her a while back tighter round her neck.

She felt sad. There wouldn't be any bright Christmas decorations at their house. Her mother wouldn't let them waste money on things like that, not now she didn't have

Lizzie's money coming in. What sort of Christmas would they have this year? Their mother was still very angry.

What sort of Christmas would Lizzie have? Ellie knew Dolly knew where she was but she wasn't telling. If only she would come home. Over the past few years things had got a little easier with the three wages coming in, and now they even had Iris's bit as well. They could have had some treats. But there had always been rows, even on Christmas Day.

Did Lizzie and Dolly get presents before she was born, when their dad was working? Ellie remembered when she was a small child and how the other children at school had proudly boasted of what they'd had for Christmas. She had never had the thrill of finding a stocking at the foot of her bed, never had the thrill of feeling the lumps in the dark and trying to guess what they were. When she asked why they didn't get presents she was told they didn't have enough money to waste on such things. Sometimes after Christmas they might get a small present from the market, if they were very cheap, but it wasn't the same. She sighed and hurried on. How she used to envy the other girls. How she still did.

Chapter 6

Ellie turned over and opened her eyes. The sunlight shining through the thin bedroom curtains made her blink. It was Christmas morning. She lay on her back thinking about last night. She had gone home with Peggy to collect the presents Peggy's mum had knitted for her to give to the family. They had laughed and talked all evening as they wrapped them. Ellie could see they were very close and, despite not having a lot of money, very happy. Mrs Swan was lucky; she received a small pension from her late husband's firm. Peggy said her mother was always cooking and making things, which pleased Ellie, as all her presents had come from her, and they only cost a few pence for the wool.

The two rooms where Peggy lived were small, but warm and cosy; everywhere were signs of the work from Mrs Swan's nimble fingers. It was a clean, bright home. Ellie had wished she'd been going back to a happy house, and had been very reluctant to leave.

She sat up and, putting her hand under the bed, fished around for the shopping bag she had carefully placed there last night.

Would Baby Iris and her dad like the mittens she'd got them? And would her mother and Dolly be pleased with their scarves?

'Ellie. Keep still,' moaned Iris.

Dolly groaned and turned over. 'Will you two be quiet.'

Baby Iris sat up. 'You awake? Did yer go and see Lizzie last night?'

Ellie thought about the scarf in the bag for Lizzie. She would dearly love to give it to her sister herself.

'Merry Christmas,' said Ellie cheerfully.

'O yer. Merry Christmas.' Dolly's thick tones came from the other bed.

'Dunno what's ser merry about it,' said Baby Iris. 'Mum still ain't in a good mood over Lizzie. I think Lizzie's very mean going orf like that, leaving us ter put up with Mum's bad temper. We ain't got no paperchains, or—'

'Fer Christ's sake shut it, Iris,' growled Dolly.

'I bet Lizzie's gonner 'ave a better time than us.'

Dolly sat up. 'I said give it a rest, Iris.' She held her head in her hands. 'I've got a thick 'ead.'

'Did you have a nice time last night?' Ellie asked cautiously.

'Yer. And you're right, Iris, Lizzie is gonner 'ave a good time terday, and termorrer, and every day for the rest of 'er life.'

Baby Iris scowled and slowly slid back down under the covers.

Ellie brought the bag up on to the bed. 'I've got you a little present,' she said.

Baby Iris sat up. 'What, me?'

Ellie nodded, and smiling broadly handed her a small package.

Iris tore at the paper. 'Cor, did you make these?' she asked, ramming her hand in a mitten and turning it this way and that.

'No, Peggy's mum did. D'yer like 'em?'

'Yer, fanks. It'll be nice to 'ave warm 'ands fer a change.' She leant over and kissed Ellie's cheek.

Ellie touched her cheek; she felt strange. None of her sisters had done that for years, not since they had grown up. She remembered the way they used to cower together in a corner when their parents had one of their many rows, often throwing things at one another. Lizzie would hold her tight and give her a kiss. But that had been many years ago. Now she and Dolly seemed as hard as their mother. 'I've got somethink for you as well,' said Ellie to Dolly, throwing a packet onto her bed.

Dolly pushed down the bedcovers. All round her sunken eyes was smudged mascara. When she opened them wide to peer at her sister Ellie wanted to laugh because she reminded her of Bela Lugosi when he played a vampire in a film she'd seen. 'Fer me?' Dolly sat up and carefully opened her parcel. 'Fanks, Ellie. This is really nice o' yer.'

Ellie felt a warm glow. 'Peggy's mum makes some nice things.' She wished she had plenty of money, so she could buy all of them lots of good presents. Then perhaps they could have Christmases like other families.

Baby Iris sat up and looked at Dolly.

'What yer looking at me for, I ain't got yer nuffink. Didn't fink there'd be any point. It ain't like Christmas in this 'ouse. We've never 'ad presents before.'

Baby Iris got out of bed and went to her drawer. 'I know I'm at work, but Mum don't let me 'ave much money, and I wasn't sure if . . . They give presents at work. The boss gave us an extra shilling, and Miss Jackson gave me an embroidered handkerchief, and, well, I couldn't give them anything.'

Ellie felt sad for Iris. She didn't talk much about her job, and although she said she liked it she didn't seem to make any friends.

'I made these when I was at school,' she said softly, handing both Dolly and Ellie a green felt bookmark. 'That's all the school would let me 'ave fer free, and I saved them for Christmas. I've got one fer Lizzie as well.'

'Thank you, Iris, this is really nice.' Ellie could have cried. She had kept them all this time; she had thought of them all that while ago. Had being at work made her realize how other people lived?

Even Dolly looked sad. 'I didn't fink . . . I ain't got anybody . . .'

'Don't worry,' said Ellie cheerfully.

'I'll 'ave a look in me drawer later ter see what I can find yer.'

'That'll be nice, won't it?' said Ellie to Iris.

'Yer,' said Baby Iris, obviously very upset about it.

'Dolly, did Mum and Dad give you and Lizzie presents before we was born?' asked Ellie.

'I can't really remember, but I fink so.' Dolly pulled her knees up and sat hugging them.

'What makes Mum like she is?' asked Ellie.

'Dunno. They've always been at each other's throats.'

'I wish we was like other families,' said Baby Iris, slipping back down under the bedclothes.

Dolly looked guilty. 'Iris, I'll find yer a nice scarf later on, and what about a bracelet?'

'That'd be nice,' said Iris halfheartedly.

'I wish we was more like Peggy and 'er mum. They ain't got much money, but they do things tergether. 'As it really always been like this?' asked Ellie.

'Yer, but it's got worse since Dad's been out o' work. Mind you, I reckon he could try and do sumfink. Lizzie reckons 'e suffers from lazyitis.'

Ellie sat looking at her bookmark. 'This is very nice, Iris.'

'Well everybody at school was making leaving presents, so I fought I'd better, and it was free.'

Ellie smiled, that was just like Iris, she didn't want to be left out.

As usual their father was already downstairs lighting the fire when Ellie walked into the kitchen.

'Merry Christmas, Dad,' she said, kissing his cheek and handing him his present.

'Fer me? Thanks, love.' He looked sad as he sat at the

table and turned the parcel over and over. 'I ain't got anybody . . .'

'Don't worry about it, pr'aps next year you'll 'ave a job and then . . .' Ellie didn't really know what to say. 'Open yer present then. I'll make the tea when the kettle boils.' Ellie's mind was racing. This could be the time to find out why things were like they were. After all, Christmas should be a time for peace on earth, so why not in the Walshes' household?

'Thanks, Ellie,' he said, trying on his mittens. 'These're nice. I could really do with these.'

Ellie sat at the table. 'Dad?' she said in a soft voice. 'What 'appened between you and Mum ter make 'er so angry?'

He looked embarrassed, and said quickly, 'It was Lizzie going what—'

'No,' interrupted Ellie. 'I mean before that, even when we was little. She's always been angry with us.' Ellie looked down. 'And even with Mrs Andrews,' she whispered.

He shot her a glance. 'Who told yer that?'

'Dirty Molly.'

'Yer don't wanner believe what that silly old fool goes on about. She's a bit . . . you know.' He put his finger to his forehead, then, picking up the wrapping paper, carefully folded it. 'Better not throw it away, paper's always useful, yer never know when it might come in 'andy. Kettle's boiling.'

Ellie filled the teapot and sat back at the table. 'Why won't you tell me?'

'Ain't nuffink ter tell.'

Ellie was suddenly getting resentful. 'You're always making excuses for the way we live, and I think we've got the right to know what started it. After all, I help keep this family as well, which is more than—'

Baby Iris pushed open the door. 'Merry Christmas, Dad.' She handed him a bookmark. 'I know yer don't read, but you might one day.'

Ellie choked back a tear and began clattering the cups. She was angry. Why didn't he make some kind of effort? He could have made Baby Iris something, anything, out of an old box. After all, she had made him a bookmark. Ellie was suddenly seeing him in a different light. Perhaps Lizzie was right, perhaps he did suffer from lazyitis; and with four daughters and a lazy husband no wonder her mother was angry. 'You gonner take this tea up ter Mum?' she said aggressively.

'Yes love.' He stood up.

'What was yer going on at Dad about?' asked Iris.

'Nuffink,' said Ellie. 'I'll go and look in the safe to see what we've got for dinner.'

Out in the yard she opened the meat safe and sighed. There wasn't any chicken like Peggy and her mum were having, just a plate with some minced meat on, and a few lamb chops. They wouldn't be hunting for a bright shiny silver thrupenny piece in a Christmas pudding. She took the chops out. At least they could be roasted, and that had to be better than cottage pie.

After dinner they sat round the fire, and had a sandwich for tea. Baby Iris, Dolly and Ellie played cards for a while, then Christmas was all over.

'I'll be out fer tea,' said Dolly when they finished the cottage pie the following dinner time.

'Where're yer going?' asked her mother.

'Just out.'

'Yer got a boyfriend then?' asked Baby Iris.

'Mind yer own business. And if you must know I'm going out with a mate from work.'

'Christ, she only asked,' said Mrs Walsh.

'I know.' Dolly left the room.

''Ere, you ain't seeing that cow Lizzie, are you?' shouted Mrs Walsh.

'No I ain't,' yelled Dolly from the passage. 'She's got 'er

boyfriend, she don't want me hanging round 'em.'

After a while Ellie followed her upstairs. 'Dolly, you seeing Lizzie at work termorrer?'

Dolly looked taken aback. 'Yer. Course. Why?'

'I've got somethink for 'er, for Christmas. It's a scarf like yours. I'd like you to give it to 'er.'

Dolly sat on the bed. 'You're a funny one. Look, don't tell Mum, but that's where I'm going for tea.'

Ellie sat beside her, her eyes lighting up. 'But you said—'

'I know.'

'Good, that means you can give 'er 'er present terday.' She took the last packet from the bag and gently fondled it. 'I wish I was going with you. I'd like ter see Lizzie again,' she said wistfully.

Dolly fiddled with her nails. 'I might stay overnight.'

'Oh,' said Ellie, any thoughts she had of hoping Dolly would take her with her quickly dashed.

'Mum'll think you're staying with your boyfriend, then there'll be a row.'

Dolly laughed. 'She can fink what she likes.'

'Would you take Lizzie 'er scarf?'

'Course.' They sat quiet for a while then Dolly said softly, 'Ellie?'

Ellie quickly looked up at Dolly's tone. 'Yer, what's wrong?'

'I know you can keep a secret.'

Ellie opened her eyes wide.

'We ain't going ter work termorrer, 'cos our Lizzie's gitting married.'

Ellie's mouth fell open.

'Well, ain't yer pleased for 'er?'

Slowly Ellie nodded her head.

'That's why I'm staying the night. I'm gonner be a sort o' bridesmaid.'

Ellie didn't know why, but a tear ran down her cheek. 'But it'll be on a Monday. Ain't she 'aving a big wedding and a long white frock?' she asked.

'Na, it ain't in church, and it's only gonner be me and Tom, a bloke from Ern's work.'

'What about 'is mum and dad?'

'They live miles away.'

'What about us? Ain't we invited?'

'Lizzie's worried about Mum. That's why she ain't said nuffink.'

'I'd like ter see 'er married.'

'Well, don't tell Baby, or Dad, but if you can get out and be at the town 'all at twelve, who knows?' Dolly smiled.

'I will, I will,' Ellie said excitedly. 'I'm sure Mr Jenkins will let me slip out, we ain't very busy on Mondays. This is the best thing that's ever 'appened ter this family.'

Dolly looked towards the door, and keeping her voice low, said, 'Fer Christ's sake, don't breathe a word o' this ter anyone. Lizzie will 'ave my guts fer garters if Mum turns up.'

'Especially after what 'appened in the pub.'

'Yer, that was a bit of a fiasco.'

Ellie was almost beside herself with excitement. 'I won't tell, I promise.' She stopped. 'Our Lizzie ain't 'aving a baby, is she?'

'Na.'

'That's good. What you wearing?'

'I've got a new brown coat with a fur collar, it's ever so nice. Didn't want Mum ter see it so I've kept it over at Lizzie's.'

'What's 'e like?'

'Who? Ern?'

Ellie nodded.

'Very nice. 'E's got a couple o' rooms, not too far from work, they're living there. 'E works in the City, 'e's got a good job.'

Ellie pulled her knees up and hugged them. ''E still in the print?'

'Yer, 'e gets good money.'

'How did Lizzie meet 'im?'

'In a pub. Cor blimey, any more questions?'

'How old is 'e?'

'I dunno.'

'I'd like ter see Lizzie.'

Dolly sat studying her nails. 'Would yer like ter come with me this afternoon? Lizzie won't mind giving yer a bit o' tea, but you'll 'ave ter come 'ome on yer own, and fer Gawd's sake, don't tell Mum.'

Ellie thought she would burst with joy. 'Could I? Could I? I promise I won't eat much.'

Dolly laughed. 'Daft 'aporth.'

Ellie and Dolly sat for a while trying to think of a way to get out of the house without anyone guessing they were going out together.

'I know,' said Ellie jumping up. 'I'll go out and wait under the arches in Green Street. You can come round a bit later on.'

'What'll yer tell Mum?'

'I'll tell 'er I'm going round ter see Peggy, and when I get back I can say she asked me ter stop fer tea.'

'OK. You go orf now, and I'll see yer later.'

Ellie walked into the kitchen. 'Think I'll just go round and see Peggy,' she said nonchalantly.

'Why?' asked her mother.

'No reason, just feel like going out.'

'Can I come?' asked Baby Iris.

'No you can't,' said Ellie quickly.

'Oow,' said her young sister. 'Why not?'

''Cos she might not be in, and 'er mum might not want anybody round there.'

'Hummh,' said their mother. 'She didn't say that when yer went round ter pay 'er some money.'

'That was for the presents she'd made me.'

'Why can't I come?' moaned Iris.

'I don't want you.'

Baby Iris sat up. 'Why's that?' She looked across at Ellie and said smugly, 'I bet you're gonner meet that Terry Andrews.'

'Who?' yelled their mother.

'Ellie's always bin keen on Terry. I've seen 'is and 'er names scratched on the tree. I bet yer going out with 'im, ain't yer?'

'What?' Ellie felt herself blushing with anger and embarrassment. 'No I ain't.'

'You ain't going nowhere with 'im, young lady, so you can take yer 'at and coat orf and sit down.' Ruby Walsh's face was full of fury.

'What?' Ellie couldn't believe this conversation.

'Why can't she go out with 'im, Mum?' asked Iris.

''Cos I say so. 'Is old woman ain't nuffink but a dirty old tramp. She always said she was a widder woman when she moved 'ere, but I've got me doubts, all those so-called lodgers she 'as in that 'ouse. I don't want any gel o' mine mixed up with 'im, 'cos I reckon 'e's tarred wiv the same brush.' She glared at her husband. 'Ain't that right?'

Ned Walsh sat staring into the fire.

Mrs Walsh leaned over and poked him with her long sausage-like finger. 'I was talking ter you.'

He didn't answer.

Ellie sat at the table, her face full of disbelief. 'Why do you hate 'er so?'

'None of yer business.'

'Dirty Molly said you 'ad a big row once.'

'Did she now, well she ought ter learn ter keep 'er trap shut. But you still ain't going out, my gel.'

'I ain't going out with 'im, honest.' Ellie scowled at Baby Iris. 'It's a pity you don't mind yer own business.' What had happened to the caring Iris of yesterday?

'Well, who yer gonner see then?' asked Iris cockily.

'I told you, Peggy.'

Dolly walked into the kitchen. 'I fought you was going out?' she said to Ellie.

'She ain't going nowhere,' said their mother. 'Fought she could slink orf wiv that Andrews kid. Well I soon put a stop ter that.'

'What?' Dolly's face was full of surprise. 'Who told yer that?'

''Er,' said Ellie pointing aggressively at Baby Iris.

Dolly suddenly began laughing. 'So, what's wrong with 'er wanting ter go out with Terry then?'

Ned Walsh stood up. 'I'm going out for a jimmy.'

'Well I said she ain't. She ain't mixing with trash like that. She'd 'ave 'er move in over there if she 'ad 'alf a chance, and I ain't losing anuvver wage packet. Bad enough Lizzie going orf like that.'

'Mum, she's only going round to 'er mate Peggy. I dunno what all the fuss is about.' Dolly peered in the mirror and adjusted her hat.

'And I don't want you finking you can bugger orf any time either, 'cos if you do, I'll 'ave the law after yer.'

Dolly turned and looked long and hard at her mother. 'Better make the most of me then, 'cos as soon as I'm twenty-one I'll be orf, and there won't be a fing you can do about it.' She picked up her handbag and left the room, slamming the front door behind her.

Ellie could have cried. She wouldn't be seeing Lizzie today after all; but worst of all, she would have to live here for another four years, till she too was twenty-one, and couldn't be brought back by the police and put in the workhouse.

Chapter 7

It was early the following morning, and still dark, when Ellie opened her eyes. The only light that filtered through the thin curtains came from the flickering gas lamp in the square. She lay for a few moments letting her eyes get accustomed to the gloom before looking over at Dolly's bed. She knew it was empty, but couldn't help hoping Dolly had come home silently, so as not to disturb them.

Ellie slipped out of bed, moving about the bedroom and dressing as quietly as she could, not wanting to wake Baby Iris, or be around when her mother discovered Dolly hadn't been home all night. Last night Ellie had thought of sleeping in Dolly's bed herself, but Iris would have suspected something, and asked questions.

Ellie, downstairs before her father, shuddered in the cold kitchen, and decided not to hang around for a cup of tea.

Thankfully the day was dry but very cold. She walked to work with her thoughts full of Lizzie. What sort of weather would they have today? She desperately hoped the sun would shine for her. She prayed Mr Jenkins would let her go to the town hall at twelve to see her sister married. If only Lizzie could have had a proper wedding; a nice ceremony with a long white frock and bridesmaids, like the ones she'd seen outside the church on a Saturday before she was working. 'That's what I want,' she said out loud.

As she was early, she had time to gaze in the pawn broker's window, which was as usual full of a mishmash of objects. This was where most of the objects that had once been in their home finished up, including the clothes they had all grown out of. Ellie smiled; the old man that owned the shop must be a soft touch to take in that load of tat.

She put her hand on the dirty window and peered in. For weeks she had looked longingly at a coat hanging at the back of the overcrowded window. It had gone. She had never managed to find the courage to go in and ask how much it was. Not that she could afford anything else just yet; and in any case the secondhand stall at the market was a lot cheaper. She continued on her way, her thoughts full of what Lizzie would be wearing for her wedding.

'Christ, Ellie, yer frightened the daylights out o' me,' said Peggy putting her hand on her chest when Ellie tapped her on the shoulder. 'What yer doing round 'ere this time o' morning? 'Ere, yer mum ain't chucked yer out, 'as she?' she asked in alarm.

Ellie laughed. 'No, course not. I got up early and thought I'd come and meet you. I didn't mean ter frighten you.'

'Well I didn't expect you of all people to jump out on me. Look at me, I'm all of a flutter.' She held out her hand and shook it.

Ellie linked her arm through Peggy's. 'Don't talk daft. Come on.'

'Anyway, did yer 'ave a nice Christmas?' said Peggy when she finally settled down.

'Christmas!' Ellie had almost forgotten about Christmas with so many other things on her mind. 'No, not really.'

'Oh that's a shame. Why didn't yer try and come round to us? Mr Jenkins came to tea on Boxing Day, and after we played charades. Mum didn't half enjoy 'erself.'

'I was going to, but Mum made me stop in.'

'Why was that?'

'Baby Iris said I was going out with Terry Andrews and Mum kicked up a stink about it and wouldn't let me out.'

Peggy looked at her. 'And was you?'

'No, worse luck.'

'It's a pity yer didn't come round.'

'Peggy, d'yer think Mr Jenkins would let me go out at twelve?'

'Dunno, is it important?

Ellie nodded. 'Yes.'

'Well if it is really important I don't see why not. It ain't as though it's market day, and we shouldn't be all that busy, not just after the holiday. I could cover for you.'

'Would you?'

'Just as long as you won't be too long. Where you gotter go?'

Ellie smiled. 'The town hall.'

'Town 'all? What for?'

'Our Lizzie's getting married,' said Ellie smugly.

'What? Who to?'

'Dunno, ain't ever seen 'im. His name's Ernie.'

'Christ, what did yer mum say about that?'

'She don't know. She has met 'im though, in the pub on Lizzie's birthday. They had a row.'

Peggy laughed. 'There's never a dull moment in your 'ouse, is there? So who told yer about Lizzie?'

'Dolly, she's gonner be a sorta bridesmaid.'

'What yer mean, sorta? Ain't she 'aving a big wedding? 'Ere – Lizzie ain't, you know, up the spout?' Peggy nudged Ellie's arm.

'Dolly said she ain't.' Ellie laughed.

'Does Baby Iris know?'

'No, we don't tell 'er much, she always blurts it out ter Mum. Mum'll be livid when she finds out Lizzie got married.'

'Well I wouldn't like ter be in your 'ouse when she does.'

Ellie shuddered. That was something she too was worried about.

'By the way, how's Iris getting on at her job? She's been there a few weeks now, ain't she?'

'She likes it, but she's only in the back room at the moment. She don't say that much. I think she's only a skivvy really, you know, picking up pins when the dressmakers do alterations, and getting the tea and that.'

'I was surprised your mum let 'er go there. I don't think they pay much.'

'Well, you know Iris, I don't think she made much effort to get anywhere else, and she'll whine and get round Mum somehow.'

Peggy looked at the bakery door. 'We'd better get on.'

Mr Jenkins very kindly let Ellie have half an hour off to see her sister married.

She was very excited as she hurried to the town hall. Although it was cold, she was pleased it wasn't raining. She stood outside waiting for her sister.

Two men laughing and joking stood near the door. They were both tall and good-looking, and wearing white flowers in their buttonholes. One caught sight of Ellie and came over to her.

'Excuse me, but you wouldn't be Ellie Walsh, by any chance?' he asked.

Ellie blushed. 'Yes, yes I am.'

He held out his hand. 'Hello. Dolly said you might be here. I'm Ernie, I'm marrying your sister today.'

Ellie looked at him. How did Lizzie find such a good-looking and well spoken bloke?

'And this is my mate and best man, Tom.'

Tom smiled at Ellie. 'Hallo there.'

Ernie continued, 'So far, none of you Walsh girls look alike. I've only got to meet Baby Iris, then that's the lot.' He grinned. 'Unless you've got another one hiding in a cupboard somewhere.'

'No, no we ain't, haven't,' Ellie quickly corrected herself.

He laughed. 'You'll have to come round and visit us one day.'

'I'd like that, I'd like that very much. I miss Lizzie. Look,' she said pointing across the road, ''ere she comes. Cor, don't she look smashing.'

Ellie could have cried. Lizzie and Dolly looked so smart. Dolly wore her brown coat with its fur collar and a matching cloche hat. Lizzie was wearing a beige coat that tapered to her knees and fastened with a large single button; it had a big dark brown fur collar and cuffs, and her hat matched her coat. It was lovely, just like one Ellie had seen and envied in a shop window. They were both laughing as they tripped daintily across the road in their beige court shoes.

''Allo Ellie,' said Lizzie. 'Dolly said you might be 'ere.' She seemed genuinely pleased to see her, as she kissed Ellie's cheek.

'Lizzie, you look very nice.' Ellie's eyes shone with sheer delight.

'Thanks. You've met my Ern then?'

'Yes, I 'ave.'

'Come on Liz, we'd better get going.' Ernie looked at his watch before taking her arm and leading her into the town hall. Tom took Dolly's arm.

Ellie had never been inside this building before and was amazed at the opulence of it. She gasped at the panelled walls, with large framed pictures of serious-looking, bushy-browed gentlemen frowning down on her, and at the painted ceiling held up by thick pillars.

'This way,' said Ernie.

Ellie followed them up the magnificent staircase and into a small plain room that had just a few chairs and a table with a bowl of flowers and a large open book on it. A narrow-faced man wearing thick-rimmed glasses stood behind the table. Another man closed the door behind them. The thin-faced man mumbled a few words, then Lizzie and Ernie said a few words. Ernie put a ring on Lizzie's finger, they signed the big book and kissed, then Dolly and Tom signed the book. They all shook hands with the man behind the table, and it was over. Ellie was amazed at how quick it all was.

Then, arm-in-arm and laughing, they walked out into the weak midday sunshine. Dolly threw a handful of confetti over her sister and Ernie. Ellie was sorry she hadn't got any. Lizzie kissed Dolly and Ellie, and so did Ernie.

"'Ave yer got time to come to the pub?' Lizzie asked Ellie.

'No, sorry, I've got to get back to work.'

'That's a pity,' said Ernie. 'Never mind. Look, why don't you come to tea on Sunday?'

'I'd like that. Where d'yer live?'

Lizzie quickly looked at her new husband, then turning to Ellie said, 'Dolly'll tell yer, but don't you dare let on ter Mum.'

'Course I won't. I must go. Lizzie, I wish you and Ernie all the best luck in the world.' She sniffed. 'Sorry I ain't got yer a present.'

'That's all right.' Lizzie turned to Dolly. 'Come on, gel, let's get a drink before I freeze ter death out 'ere.'

All four crossed the road and, laughing loudly, walked away.

Ellie stood for a few moments watching them. She wanted to cry. This wasn't right. This wasn't how you should get married. She wanted to dress up, and everybody to enjoy themselves.

As soon as she took her coat off Peggy was asking her all about Lizzie's wedding, and her new husband. Between customers, and keeping her eye out for Mr Jenkins, Ellie managed to give her all the details.

Ellie was eager to get home; she was dying to ask Dolly lots of questions. But it was Ellie who faced a barrage of questions as soon as she opened the kitchen door.

'You bloody well slunk orf a bit sharpish this morning didn't yer?' Her mother was sitting in the armchair in front of the fire, her feet resting on the fender, and one of her big toes was poking its way through a hole in her thick lisle stockings. Her skirt was pulled up, showing the elastic garters she wore below her knees. 'What d'yer know about that cow Dolly staying out all night? What's she told yer?'

'Ruby, give 'er a chance ter git 'er 'at and coat orf.'

She gave her husband a withering look, and he visibly shrank down in his chair.

'I'm talking ter you.'

Ellie glanced at Baby Iris who was sitting at the table. She had her head buried in a book and was busy writing. 'I didn't know till I woke up,' said Ellie firmly crossing her fingers behind her back. She didn't like telling lies.

'So, why d'yer slope orf, then, and not tell any one?'

'I didn't want a row, and be late fer work.'

'D'yer know where Dolly finished up last night?'

Ellie turned away and began taking her hat and coat off. 'No.' She wasn't going to tell them that Lizzie had been married today.

'Well just you wait till she gets in. If she's bin out all night with a bloke—' Ruby Walsh stopped. 'It ain't that snotty nose sod I saw at the pub with Lizzie's bloke, is it?'

'I don't know,' said Ellie getting cross.

'If it is, she's gonner feel the back of me 'and. I ain't 'aving it, d'yer 'ear?' Bending down she put on her worn-out slippers and went into the scullery. 'And that goes fer you two as well,' she yelled through the open doorway.

Ned Walsh quickly shook his head when Ellie made as if to speak. His eyes were full of fear.

Everyone was very quiet over dinner. Ellie felt guilty; she wanted to tell them her news, but knew it was more than she dared do.

'I'd like ter know what that Dolly's up ter,' said their mother, looking straight at Ellie. 'She said anyfink to you about a bloke?'

Ellie shook her head.

'You just wait till she gits in.'

'What if she don't come back, like Lizzie?' Baby Iris asked.

'She'd better. I'll 'ave the law after 'er, can git 'er locked up yer know. Baby Iris, go and git me beer.'

'Yes Mum.' Iris quickly grabbed the jug from the dresser and left.

'You look pleased with yerself,' said her mother to Ellie. 'Did yer ask fer that rise?'

'No. I told yer I should be getting one next month, on me birthday.'

'Yer better, or else I'll be down ter see old Jenkins meself.'

Ellie shuddered. That was something she couldn't even bear to think about.

Dolly still wasn't home when Ellie went to bed. Were they having a party? Would she stay out again tonight? No, she had to go to work tomorrow. She lay on her back, dreading the row that was sure to come.

'Ellie, you awake?' asked Iris.

'Yes, why?'

'You know where Dolly is, don't yer?'

Ellie didn't answer.

Baby Iris propped herself up on one elbow. 'I reckon she's gone ter live with Lizzie.'

'I don't know. She might 'ave. But you 'eard what Mum said, she'll 'ave the police bring 'er back.'

'Can they?'

'Dunno. She's under age.'

'Yer, I know, but they gotter find 'er first.'

Ellie smiled. 'Yer, that's right. Now turn over and go ter sleep, you'll hear soon enough if and when Dolly does come home.'

Ellie was just drifting off, when suddenly the silence was broken. Raised voices, shouting and screams came from downstairs in the passage. Dolly was home, and from the sound of their voices, both their mother and Dolly were very drunk.

Chapter 8

'Ellie, I'm frightened,' said Baby Iris, cuddling up to her. 'Mum'll kill Dolly.'

The screams, shouts and yelling also frightened Ellie. 'I'm gonner go down and look.'

'No, no, don't leave me.' Baby Iris clung to her.

'I must, I've gotter stop 'em.'

'Let Dad do it.'

'You know Dad, 'e's more frightened of Mum than we are. Now let me go.'

Reluctantly Iris released her grip, and Ellie crept out of bed. She didn't stop to put her coat on over her petticoat – she didn't have a nightie. She opened the door; Iris was right behind her.

The gaslight in the passage was still alight but had been turned down very low. In the gloom Ellie could see Dolly lying on the floor near the front door. Her mother, who had her back to them, was standing astride Dolly.

'Mum, Mum, don't,' yelled Ellie, almost falling down the stairs in her hurry to reach them.

'Leave 'em, Ellie,' said her father, appearing from the kitchen end of the passage, holding a towel to his nose. It was covered with blood.

Ellie was bewildered. 'Dad, what 'appened? You've gotter 'elp me – we've gotter stop 'er, she'll kill Dolly.'

Ruby Walsh turned around. Her face was bright red, some of her hair had fallen from its bun and hung limply round her face, and her eyes blazed with anger. She lurched forward and almost lost her footing; grabbing the post at the bottom of the stairs to steady herself, she looked up. 'I ain't gonner kill 'er,' she slurred. 'Just gonner show 'er who's boss in this 'ere 'ouse.'

Dolly lay very still. Ellie could have cried when she saw the state of her new coat; she had been sick over the fur collar. Her new hat was squashed in the corner, and her lovely shoes had been kicked to one side. She rushed down the few remaining stairs and, pushing her mother, who lashed out at Ellie but missed, to one side, knelt beside Dolly.

Ruby Walsh sat glassy-eyed at the bottom of the stairs. 'She's drunk.'

Ellie looked at her mother and gathered the unconscious Dolly in her arms.

'She fell over when she come in and I was trying ter pick 'er up. When 'e come down, I was waving me arms about and caught 'im on the nose.' She began laughing.

'Iris, go and get me a basin full o' water.' Ellie turned to her mother. 'She didn't get this bruise, or this cut on 'er 'ead, just by you trying ter pick 'er up,' she said accusingly.

'She's 'eavy. I dropped 'er.'

'Look, she's bleeding all over me petticoat,' said Ellie in alarm.

'Leave 'er, she'll be all right be the morning. 'Sides, that'll teach 'er ter come 'ome at a respectable time, and not stay out all night in some bloke's bed. Dirty little cow. Look at these clothes.' She kicked Dolly's shoes against the door. 'They must o' cost 'er, or 'im, a pretty penny or two. And what's she all dolled up for, that's what I wanner know. She should 'ave bin at work.'

Dolly moaned and opened her eyes. Her face, streaked with the day's make up, was bloody and bruised. She slowly raised her head. 'What 'appened?'

'You fell over,' said her mother.

Dolly eased herself up and, still in a sitting position, held her head in her hands. Suddenly, as if just remembering, she lifted her head and yelled, 'No I didn't. You wicked cow. You 'it me and knocked me down.' She put her hand up to the back of her head and looked at her fingers. 'I'm bleeding, look, I'm bleeding. She pushed me down the stairs. Ellie, 'elp me git up.'

'No, stay 'ere for a bit, I'm gonner bathe your 'ead when Iris gets 'ere with the water.'

'No, 'elp me up,' sniffed Dolly, trying to struggle to her feet. 'I'm gonner give you a bloody 'iding,' she said to her mother.

'Dolly.' Their father's voice was forceful, and it caused her and Ellie to look up. 'Pack it in.'

'But Dad,' whined Dolly, still sitting on the floor.

'Do as Dad says,' said Ellie. 'Iris, put the water down 'ere.'

Iris carefully put the pudding basin on the floor.

'Dolly, why didn't you come 'ome last night?' asked their father.

'I ain't gonner tell yer.'

'See, I told yer, she's a tramp, just like 'er sister. Must run in the family,' said Ruby Walsh with a smug look.

'Is that what you was then, a tramp? It takes one ter know one.' Dolly gave her a lopsided grin.

'You saucy cow. Don't you talk ter me like that.' Her mother lunged forward.

But before her mother could reach her, Dolly picked up the basin and threw the contents over her.

Ellie and Baby Iris gasped in amazement.

Ruby Walsh sank back on the stairs, spluttering and fighting for breath. Water was dripping from her nose and chin.

'Dolly,' said Baby Iris quietly, her voice full of alarm, 'yer shouldn't 'ave done that.'

'Come on Dolly,' said Ellie shivering, 'it's cold down 'ere. Let's get you up to bed.'

Dolly began struggling onto her knees.

'Give me an 'and ter git yer mother up ter bed,' said Ned Walsh to Baby Iris.

Ruby Walsh quickly pushed his helping hand away. 'Leave me be.' She stood up and with one swift movement hit Dolly round the head, sending her crashing to the floor again.

Ellie and Baby Iris both screamed and fell to their knees beside Dolly. She was out cold.

'You've killed 'er,' cried Baby Iris, her eyes full of fear.

Ellie sat crying. 'Why do you hate us so much?' she asked her mother, who was sitting on the stairs humming to herself.

'She don't 'ate yer. Do you, love?' said their father, squatting down and putting his arm round Ellie.

There was no reply.

Ellie quickly pushed his arm away. 'Yes she does. She only lets us stay 'ere 'cos she wants our money, otherwise we'd be in the workhouse.'

'Don't talk daft.'

'I ain't talking daft. And why don't you stick up for us, and yourself? What hold's she got over you?'

'Come on now Ellie, you're upset.'

'She won't let us do anythink,' sobbed Ellie. 'I couldn't go to high school, I can't go out when I like, or buy what I like.' She wiped her nose and eyes on the bottom of her bloodied petticoat. 'Look at me petticoat. I can't afford a new one. She keeps nearly all me money.'

'You know we couldn't afford ter send yer ter that posh school, love,' said her father. 'And yer knows we need yer money.'

'Then why don't you find work?'

'You know I would if I could. Do you think I don't try?'

'I'm sure you could find something to do.'

'You ain't seen the blokes standing outside the labour

exchange, waiting around in all weathers, 'oping for some work.'

Ruby Walsh's singing was getting louder.

Ellie sniffed. 'As soon as I'm twenty-one I'm gonner leave 'ome, and I ain't never ever coming back 'ere again.'

'Don't say that, love.'

'Why? 'Cos yer frightened you'll be my money short? I'd go now if I didn't know she'd send the police after me and have them put me away.'

'Ellie, calm down,' said Iris, her young face etched with worry and concern.

'I ain't calming down. I wanner know why our own mother hates us so,' said Ellie again.

'She don't 'ate yer, love,' said Ned Walsh. 'Do yer, gel?'

'I'm going up ter bed,' said Ruby Walsh ignoring the question and, pushing the wet strands of hair back from her face, walked very unsteadily up the stairs.

Ellie sat on the floor holding Dolly's head, and cried bitter tears. All the pent-up frustration and anger spilled from her eyes.

Iris put her arm round her shoulder and cried with her.

Their father stood looking at the sad trio, but made no attempt to comfort them. He didn't say a word.

Ellie knew that only he knew what made his wife so sullen, bitter and angry. And he wasn't about to spill the beans.

Dolly moaned.

"S'll right, Dolly.' Iris held her hand. 'Me and Ellie's 'ere.'

Dolly wearily sat up. She looked up the stairs and shouted, 'I'm gonner git out this 'ouse. I'm going first thing termorrer. She's a wicked old cow, and I ain't staying 'ere any longer.'

'Where will yer go?' asked Baby Iris.

'I'll go and stay with our Lizzie.' Again she attempted to get up. 'Look at me best silk stockings,' she wailed. 'And me 'at.' Tears ran down her face. 'Just look at me best coat, only wore it terday for the first time.' She sank to her knees and cried.

Ellie gently eased her sister up. 'I'll help you clean it up termorrer. Come on now, let's get you up to bed.'

Ellie lay on her back wide awake. Dolly was mumbling in her sleep as she turned over; she was very restless. Ellie knew sleep wasn't going to come easy tonight. It wasn't fair. Now Dolly was going away, that would only leave Ellie and Iris bringing money in, and even with the rise she would get on her birthday, fifteen shillings a week wasn't going to go far after the five bob rent money had been taken out; there was money needed for coal, and food . . .

Ellie choked back a sob. Things were going to get very hard. Where would it all end? Baby Iris would have to try to get promoted, or find another job. What about their father? He would have to make much more of an effort to find work. There must be something he could do. All these thoughts were racing round and round Ellie's head. She wanted morning to come, so that she could go to work and get out of this place for a few hours.

Today had been Lizzie's wedding day. Ellie and Dolly would never forget it. Ellie suddenly panicked. She must get Lizzie's address before Dolly left, otherwise she might never see either of her sisters again. Despite the problems they had had over the years, they were still sisters after all.

'Ellie,' whispered Baby Iris. 'Was Dolly out with a bloke?'

'How should I know?'

'Why didn't she go ter work?'

'I dunno. Turn over and go to sleep.'

'That was a smashing coat. Yer know, I reckon she's been off out somewhere.'

'Maybe. Ask 'er termorrer.'

Ellie wasn't going to let on. If Dolly wanted to tell them about Lizzie, then that was up to her.

★ ★ ★

Once again shouting woke Ellie up. What time was it? It was dark outside but someone had lit the bedroom gaslight. She sat up bewildered and blinking, and asked, 'What's 'appened? What's the matter?'

'Where's me clothes?' yelled Dolly.

Baby Iris sat up. 'What's wrong?'

'Me clothes, all me clothes 'ave gorn.' Dolly was frantically searching the drawers of the dressing table. 'Me frocks an' all, look.' She waved her arms round the empty walls.

'I dunno, I ain't seen 'em,' said Ellie.

Baby Iris shrugged her shoulders. 'Don't look at me. They was here last night.'

Dolly plonked herself back on the bed, tears rolling down her cheeks. Her lips were swollen and the bruises had taken on a different hue. 'I bet she's got 'em.' She looked towards the bedroom door, and hatred filled her eyes. She stood up.

Ellie leapt from the bed and flattened herself against the door. 'No, don't.'

'Git out the way. I mean it, I'm gonner kill 'er.'

'Dad,' screamed Iris jumping up and down on the bed. 'Quick, Dad, come in 'ere.'

Ned Walsh didn't need a lot of strength to push open the bedroom door. Ellie fell against the end of the bed. He stood in the doorway. 'Dolly, I fink yer better clear orf. I fink you've upset yer mother enough.'

Ellie stood open-mouthed.

'What? *I've* upset '*er*? You mean you're chucking me out?' asked Dolly in surprise.

'Not me, love, it's yer—'

'Well I ain't going till she gives me back me clothes.' Dolly sat on the bed.

Their father looked uncomfortable. 'She said she ain't got 'em.'

Dolly eyes were blazing. 'What? Where are they then?'

He looked down at his hands. 'Ellie, and you, Iris, go

downstairs. The kettle's boiling. Go down and make a cuppa.'

'In a minute.'

'I said now.'

Baby Iris and Ellie quickly did as they were told.

In the kitchen they waited for the shouting, but the bedroom door must have been shut, as only muffled, slightly raised voices floated down the stairs to the kitchen. Suddenly the loud clatter of Dolly's shoes on the bare boards as she rushed downstairs caused Ellie and Baby Iris to look up. They expected her to burst into the kitchen; instead the front door slammed shut.

'No, no,' cried Ellie. 'Dolly. Dolly, wait,' she yelled, running up the passage. She flung the front door wide open and rushed out into the cold early morning air. It had been snowing and the bitter wind took her breath, her stockinged feet quickly became wet through. She looked across the square; Dolly was nowhere in sight.

Dejected, she turned and walked back in.

'You'll see Dolly when she gets 'ome from work,' said Baby Iris.

'I don't fink so,' said their father, walking into the kitchen. 'She ain't coming back.'

Ellie slumped in a chair at the table, and with her head on her hands wept.

'What 'appened to 'er clothes, Dad?' asked Iris.

'Under our bed. Yer mother reckons she's gonner pawn 'em.'

'She can't,' cried Ellie.

'You gonner stop 'er then, gel?'

Ellie slowly shook her head. 'When did she get 'em?'

'Last night when you was down 'ere. Did yer know our Lizzie got married yesterday?'

'Wow,' said Iris.

Ellie quickly looked up. 'Who told you?'

'Dolly. That's where she was, out with Lizzie and 'er

'usband. Well, I can tell yer, that didn't go down too well with yer mother.' He sat in a chair. 'Pour us out a cuppa, gel.'

Baby Iris did as he asked. 'I would 'ave liked ter see Lizzie married. I wonder if she 'ad a long white frock?'

Ellie wasn't going to let on she knew. She looked at her father; he didn't seem worried that his family was breaking up. Ellie sighed. Her biggest problem now was finding out where Lizzie, and now Dolly, lived.

Chapter 9

Ellie, her head down against the wind, hurried to work. Her mind was in turmoil. She couldn't wait to get to her only haven, her job. She loved it; it was warm and friendly and she wished she could stay there for ever.

'Christ, Ellie, you looks like you've 'ad a night on the tiles,' said Peggy.

Ellie knew her eyes were swollen and bloodshot through lack of sleep and crying.

'You 'ad a bad time then? What did yer mother say when she found out Lizzie got married?'

Ellie sat at a table. 'I dunno. Peg, Dolly's gone now.'

Peggy sat opposite her. 'No,' she said, wide-eyed. 'Why?'

'She stayed out all night, and when she got home Mum went for her. They had a fight.'

'No,' said Peggy again. 'Poor old Dolly. Did she stay with that bloke you was telling me about?'

'Dunno, I didn't get a chance to ask 'er, and I didn't find out Lizzie's address.' She leant across the table, tears filling her eyes. 'I might never see 'em again.'

'Don't talk daft. Course yer will. You know where they work.'

'I know, but they finish before me.' Ellie dabbed at her eyes.

Peggy also leant across the table but it was to pat Ellie's hand. 'Now come on, dry those big brown eyes.' She looked over her shoulder. 'Pr'aps Mr Jenkins will let you go a bit earlier one night when we're not too busy, then you can go and meet 'em at the factory.'

'D'you think e' would?'

Peggy nodded. 'Should think so.'

'D'you think 'e would let me go this week?'

'Dunno. We could ask. Mind you, you'll 'ave a job finding them in that crowd. It's pitch black down that alley, and when that lot come flooding out through those gates you'd probably miss 'em.'

'S'pose so.' Ellie knew Peggy was right.

''Sides,' said Peggy, 'they might come in 'ere one day. They know where you work, and it ain't so cold as hanging round outside the factory gates in this weather.'

Ellie cheered up. 'You're right. I reckon they'll come here to see me.'

'Right. Let's get on with some work.'

Ellie smiled. Peggy was such a nice person, and always so practical, no wonder Mr Jenkins was sweet on her.

The tea shop wasn't very busy all day and the snow continued falling steadily. Ellie watched it pile up against the kerbs, and grew anxious about spoiling her shoes on her way home. She wondered if she should spend some of her money to get the tram.

It was almost four o'clock and very dark outside when the door was pushed open hard, banging against the wall and causing the silver bell over the door to ring ferociously. Ellie and Peggy looked up.

Peggy gasped. 'Mr Cole,' she said, almost curtseying. 'I'll get Mr Jenkins.'

'No hurry, I'll have a cup o' tea first.' He stamped his feet hard to dislodge the snow, which quickly turned into a puddle on the floor. 'Not too good out there.'

Mr Cole, a tall, well-built man, took off his black overcoat and handed it to Ellie. Ellie noted its weight before shaking the snow from it and hanging it on the hatstand. After handing Ellie his black trilby, he smoothed down his thick dark hair, sprinkled with grey, with both hands. Ellie guessed he must be in his early fifties. He then put two fingers into the small pockets each side of his flowery waistcoat, causing his thick gold watch chain to be pulled tight across his portly figure, and took a leisurely stroll round the empty room, his deepset eyes darting about, not missing a thing. He looked a man of great confidence and wealth. Ellie was pleased everything was clean and sparkling.

When he seemed satisfied he smiled and eased himself into a chair. Ellie hurried to take his order, her hand shaking as she wrote down: one pot of tea. 'Did you want a cake, sir?' she spluttered. She too felt she should curtsey, but didn't know why; she had never met this man before, but his name seemed to put fear into everyone who knew him.

'No thanks. You're new here; ain't never seen you before.'

'I've been 'ere a few months now,' she whispered.

'Have you now, I'll have to come in more often. Who else has Jenkins got hiding out there?' He laughed. 'D'you live round these parts?'

'Not too far away, sir.' She wasn't going to tell him she lived in one of his houses.

'Well I hope not, otherwise you might have a job to get home in this weather.'

Peggy came from the back room with the tray of tea. 'Mr Jenkins will be out when you've finished yer tea, sir,' she said putting the silver tray on the table.

'Thanks.'

As Ellie busied herself at the far end of the room, she could feel Mr Cole's eyes following her, and was grateful when Mr Jenkins came bustling out, wiping his floury hands on the bottom of his apron, and spoke to him. Mr Cole beckoned him to sit, and very soon they were deep in conversation.

Mr Cole finished his tea and talk with Mr Jenkins and

stood up to go. Ellie rushed over, helped him on with his coat, and handed him his hat.

'Thank you, my dear,' he said, brushing imaginary dust from the rim. 'It's so nice to see a fresh pretty face in one of my establishments.' He left without paying.

Ellie began clearing the crockery away and was surprised to see a silver thrupenny bit under the saucer. She smiled and, clutching it in her hand, walked over to Peggy.

'Guess what I've got?'

''E ain't left yer a tip?'

Ellie nodded and held out her open palm.

'You're the first ever.' Peggy stood back and looked Ellie up and down. 'You know, you ain't bad looking, and I reckon 'e's taken a fancy to you.'

Ellie laughed. 'Yer, and I can just see him waiting outside to take me out.'

Peggy raised her eyebrows. ''E ain't, is 'e?' She went over to the window.

'Daft. Could you just see it?'

'Dunno. 'E's got a bit of a reputation for being a ladies' man, and I've 'eard 'e likes 'em young and pretty, so you'd better watch out.'

Ellie laughed. 'Is 'e rich?'

'I should say so.'

'Well, that's it then.' Ellie threw open her arms. 'I'm his.'

Peggy gave her a knowing look. 'Shouldn't joke about things like that.'

'Oh come on, Peg, you've gotter be mad to fancy an old bloke like that.'

'Or desperate,' came Peggy's remark.

Ellie was still smiling. Again she opened her hand and looked at the thrupenny bit. 'You gave him his tea, so be rights you should 'ave half.'

'No, that's all right.'

'Thanks, Peg. Well at least I can get the tram home now.'

★ ★ ★

Ellie sat on the tram staring out of the window. Although she was out of the bad weather the tram was taking her home a lot faster than she wanted it to, and as she would be home early, she would tell her mother Peggy had given her the money for her fare, to avoid arguments. She was dreading going home. Would there be more rows?

Her father was sitting in his usual armchair when Ellie pushed open the kitchen door. 'Did yer git very wet, gel?' he asked.

'Not too bad,' replied Ellie, quickly glancing round the room. The table had the knives and forks on, and part of a loaf of bread, and an appetizing smell came from the pot gently bubbling on the stove. 'Peggy lent me the fare for the tram home. Where's Mum?'

Baby Iris looked up from her book. 'In the lav.'

Ellie took off her coat and hung it on the nail behind the door. 'Been looking for work then, Dad?'

'Ain't much doing this weather.'

'Dinner smells good.'

'Yer, yer mother got a few bob fer Dolly's clothes.'

Ellie sat at the table. She suddenly felt sad; she didn't want to eat now she knew where the money for dinner had came from. Poor Dolly. Over the years she had scrimped and saved for her clothes, and worked hard sewing and altering. Now they had finished up in the pawn shop. Ellie had an idea. Perhaps she could get the ticket and redeem them. But she quickly dismissed that thought; her mother would never give her the ticket. Besides, where would she get the money from to get them out of pawn?

'We've got stew ternight,' said their mother coming into the kitchen. 'Smells good, don't it?'

Ellie couldn't believe this was the same woman who had behaved like a mad person last night. They sat down to dinner, and not a word was said about Dolly or Lizzie.

The weather remained cold and miserable, and Ellie didn't

have the chance to leave work early and go and meet Dolly and Lizzie from the factory. Their names were never mentioned in the house. The only good thing about them going away was that Baby Iris and Ellie managed to get some of their bedclothes before they were pawned. They didn't sleep in separate beds, as it was far warmer when they slept together. Gradually their sisters' bed was stripped. First the blanket, then the pillows and feather mattress. One day when Ellie came home from work, the few bits she and Iris had had in the drawers of the dressing table were strewn over her bed whilst her elder sisters' bed, and the dressing table, had gone. She sat down and cried. Everything of her sisters had disappeared; it was as though they had never existed.

Downstairs she asked her father about the bed and dressing table.

'The means test man came this morning and told yer mother ter git rid of 'em, then she might be entitled to a few shillings relief.'

Ellie sat in the chair. They were now on relief. So much for her father not wanting to take charity from any one.

Why didn't he really try to get a job? It was almost as if he'd given up. What about those poor men that stood on street corners selling bootlaces and matches? They must have pride when it came to feeding their families. Now they, the Walshes, were on relief.

At the end of the month Mr Jenkins said Ellie could leave half an hour earlier to go and see her sisters.

She ran all the way to the factory, only to find it was closed. A notice pinned to the railings told her that it was closed for the day owing to the funeral of the owner. She couldn't believe how unlucky she'd been. Why did it have to be today of all days?

On Saturday Ellie eagerly waited for her train man to appear, only to be disappointed. Crestfallen she told Peggy she was worried about him.

'We ain't seen him for weeks.'

'Wouldn't be surprised if 'e ain't got this 'ere flu what's going round,' said Peggy. 'Me Mum was saying people are dropping like flies. I told Mr Jenkins 'e's gotter look after 'imself.'

'Don't know why you don't marry 'im. You'd be able to look after 'im properly then,' said Ellie grinning.

Peggy blushed. 'I wouldn't mind, but 'e finks 'e's too old for me.'

Ellie was stunned. 'You asked 'im?'

'Well, no, not really. But we talked about people getting married after your Lizzie, and 'e said everybody should marry people about their own age.'

'But Lizzie did.'

'I know,' Peggy grinned. 'But I told 'im 'e was a lot older, just ter see what 'e said.'

Ellie laughed. 'And yer soon found out. You didn't tell me.'

'No I know,' Peggy said jauntily, 'you might 'ave fought I was being a bit fast.'

Ellie looked at her friend, and giggled. Somehow Peggy always managed to look on the bright side, and make things turn out right.

February 18 was Ellie's birthday. As soon as she arrived at work Peggy wished her happy birthday and gave her a present. Ellie was so thrilled with the small shiny gold powder compact, her eyes sparkled as she turned it over and over. She choked back a sob and kissed Peggy's cheek. She couldn't remember when she had last had a birthday present.

'Thanks ever so much, but you shouldn't have.'

'It's from me and Mr Jenkins,' said Peggy smugly. 'What did yer mum and dad give yer?'

'I was up before 'em,' said Ellie quickly, moving away. 'Better get going. It's market day terday and I expect we'll be busy.'

'Pr'aps your sisters will be in tonight to wish you happy birthday.'

'That'd be nice,' said Ellie, knowing deep down that they wouldn't remember it was her birthday.

At the end of the day Mr Jenkins locked the shop door, and turning to Ellie said, 'I've got something for you before you go.'

'What is it?' said Ellie softly to Peggy who was grinning fit to burst. She didn't answer.

Mr Jenkins came out of the bakery carrying a small cake with candles blazing on top.

'Happy birthday, Ellie,' said Mr Jenkins and Peggy together as he presented her with the cake.

Tears welled up in her eyes. 'I ain't ever had a cake before. Thank you ever so much.'

'Blow the candles out then,' said Peggy eagerly. 'And don't ferget ter make a wish.'

'Sorry it ain't big enough to put all eighteen on,' laughed Mr Jenkins.

'I don't care. Eight's enough for my little puff. Thank you ever so much.'

'Did yer make a wish?' asked Peggy.

Ellie nodded vigorously.

They sat laughing and eating the cake, and the piece that was left over Ellie took home. The family wished her happy birthday and quickly finished it off. The only other comments were from her mother asking about her rise.

It was another month before Ellie had a chance to ask Mr Jenkins again if she could go half an hour earlier; she desperately wanted to see her sisters, and was very disappointed that they had never bothered to get in touch with her.

She left the tea room, and ran all the way. The hooter went just as Ellie arrived breathlessly at the factory gates, and a stream of men, women and girls spilled out. Ellie jumped up and down trying to catch sight of Lizzie or

Dolly. Suddenly she recognized Nell who worked with them. She shouted, and frantically waved her arms.

''Allo gel, whatcher doing round 'ere? Ain't seen yer fer ages,' said Nell, coming up to her. 'D'yer like yer new job? Gotter be better than cleaning in there.' She jerked her thumb behind her.

'Is Lizzie and Dolly still working with you?' asked Ellie, her eyes still scanning the crowd of workers.

Nell looked surprised. 'No. Don't yer know?'

Ellie took a step back, her face full of fear. 'Know? Know what? What's 'appened to them?'

Nell put her shopping bag on the ground and pulled her coat tighter around herself. 'I'm surprised yer didn't know. Didn't they tell yer?'

Ellie shook her head.

'They've gorn. Moved away.'

Ellie felt as if she had been punched in the stomach. She wanted to collapse, and held on to the railings for support. 'When?' she whispered.

Nell looked vague. 'Must be a couple o' months now.'

'Do you know where they went?'

'Fink Lizzie said over the water somewhere. North London I fink. 'Er old man's job moved, and they got an 'ouse with it.'

'What about Dolly?'

Nell looked flabbergasted. 'Ain't yer seen 'em? Don't yer know?'

'No.'

'Your Dolly's living with Lizzie.' She nudged Ellie's arm and grinned. 'Wouldn't be surprised ter be 'earing wedding bells from that one soon. She's going out with Lizzie's old man's mate. Thought they would 'ave had the decency to let yer know, full of it for weeks they was.'

Ellie was devastated. She had lost her two sisters. Would she ever see them again? Why didn't they write, or come to see her at the tea room?

Nell interrupted her thoughts. 'Best be orf, gotter git the old man's tea. Nice ter see yer again, Ellie.' She picked up her shopping bag. 'Bye.'

'Bye,' said Ellie halfheartedly.

The factory yard had emptied. Ellie was alone. She turned and slowly walked away. What was she going to do? She didn't know where Ernie worked. She felt so helpless and so low.

Ellie passed some of the factory girls, laughing and giggling at the tram stop. She didn't know them. As she trudged on her head was full of thoughts. How could she find out about Dolly and Lizzie? All the years they had argued, but they were still sisters. Where were they working? Where did Ernie work? She turned into Rotherhithe New Road.

'Miss? Miss, is that you?'

She looked up.

'I thought it was you. Do you live round this way?'

Ellie stared astonished at her train man.

'Are you all right?'

Suddenly her tears fell.

'My dear, whatever is the matter?'

Ellie buried her head in her hands. 'I'm sorry. I'm all right.'

He gently took her arm. 'I don't think so. Look, there's a café near here, come and have a cup of tea.'

She suddenly stopped and looked up at him horrified. 'I can't. I can't have tea with you, you're a customer.'

'But you're not at work now.' He took her arm again.

'I know,' she sniffed. 'But what would Mr Jenkins say if 'e found out?'

'Who's going to tell him?'

Ellie let a slight smile lift her tearstained face.

'That's better. You've got a lovely smile.'

Ellie let herself be led along.

The train man sat her at a table and brought two cups of tea over.

Ellie sat staring into her cup, slowly stirring her tea. She began to giggle, a shy nervous giggle. She looked up. 'I should be waiting on you.'

'No, this is my treat. Do you want to talk about what's making you so unhappy? Is it boyfriend trouble?'

Ellie shook her head. She wanted to tell someone, but this man was a stranger. You don't tell strangers all your business.

'Please yourself. But I don't like to see you so sad. You are normally such a happy young lady.'

'D'you live round 'ere?' Ellie asked on the spur of the moment.

'No, I live over the river, near the West End. But I teach at the high school three times a week.'

'I nearly went to the high school.'

'Why didn't you?'

Ellie was quickly on her guard. 'Er, family matters.'

'Oh I see.'

'But school ain't open on a Saturday,' she suddenly said.

'No, I give private lessons on a Saturday, and once a month it's only in the mornings, which is how I can get to your little tea shop.'

'You're a schoolteacher. What d'you teach?'

He laughed, making the lines round his twinkling blue eyes crinkle. 'No, I'm not a teacher as such, I'm a pianist by profession. At night I work in a club. I play in a dance band.'

Ellie sat entranced. She thought he looked too old to play in a dance band, but he definitely looked like a teacher. She stared at his long, clean, tapering fingers. 'How wonderful, a dance band. Do you play all the latest tunes? My sisters tell me all about the new dances.'

'Do you dance?'

She shook her head. 'It must be really lovely to be talented and good at somethink.'

'I suppose it is. Can't say I've ever really thought about it in that way.' He leaned forward. 'Teaching is my first love, but, well, dance bands pay quite well.' He smiled and sat back. 'Would you like another cup of tea?'

'No thank you. I best be going, me mum will wonder where I've got to. Thanks for the tea.'

'It's my pleasure. By the way, my name's Leonard Kent.'

'I'm Ellie. Ellie Walsh.'

'Pleased to meet you, Ellie Walsh.' He held out his hand. She smiled, and took it.

He gently curled his long, cool, soft fingers round hers, and politely shook her hand. She wanted to giggle. Nobody had ever done that to her before.

Chapter 10

When they left the café, Leonard Kent asked Ellie, 'Are you on your way home?'

'Yes.'

'Where do you live?'

'Rotherhithe.'

'That's on the way to the station,' he smiled. 'We can walk together.'

Ellie felt scruffy; her coat was well worn, and she knew the hem was hanging down, but at least she had her new shoes on. 'I'd better not.'

'Why not?'

'Well . . .'

'I won't take no for an answer. Now come along, otherwise I'll be late for work.'

She felt so proud that this well dressed man didn't mind being seen with her.

As they approached the station, he looked at his watch. 'Sorry, but I must hurry.'

'Thank you ever so much for the tea.'

'It was my pleasure. It's my Saturday afternoon off this week, so I'll be in for tea and scones as usual.' He laughed. 'It's lovely to see you smile again. Take care now.' He ran into the station.

Ellie gave him a beaming smile as she waved him goodbye. He was such a pleasant man, and although she hadn't told him what was worrying her she felt happy and looked forward to telling Peggy all about him.

Despite being upset about Lizzie and Dolly, Ellie's step had a spring in it, and as she turned into Elmleigh, she almost felt like giving Dirty Molly a wave. But Dirty Molly was one jump ahead, and beckoned Ellie over.

'See yer muvver's got shot of the dressing table then, and a bed.' She sat back and folded her arms across her chest, squashing her dog against her. She had a smug look on her face. 'So, what's 'appened ter young Lizzie and Dolly then? Ain't seen 'em around fer a while.'

Ellie grinned. 'Our Lizzie's got married, and Dolly's left 'ome. So now you know all our business. Bye.' Ellie couldn't hide her delight at Molly, sitting with her mouth open as she watched Ellie walk away laughing.

'Saucy cow,' shouted Molly just as Terry Andrews turned into the square.

'Terry,' called Ellie. 'Just a minute.' At this moment she felt confident, and it was so long since she'd seen him she wasn't going to waste this opportunity.

He stopped. ''Allo Ellie. You look 'appy.' He grinned. 'What yer been saying to Dirty Molly?'

'I'm not too bad. Just told 'er about our Lizzie getting married and Dolly leaving 'ome,' she said, getting closer to him.

'So you're the breadwinner now then, just like me.'

She wanted to touch him, hold him, kiss him. Instead she asked as casually as she could, 'How's yer mum?'

'A lot better, thanks.'

'That's good. Ain't seen very much of you lately. So you're working then?'

'Just a bit o' casual. Got to go.' He went to walk away but she put out her hand to stop him.

'Terry, I was wondering . . .' She hesitated, she mustn't make a fool of herself again.

'Yer. What is it?'

'Oh it doesn't matter,' she said hastily.

'I'd better go, Mum's waiting.'

'Oh yes, course. Bye.'

'Bye Ellie.'

She turned to see Dirty Molly wagging her finger at her and laughing.

Dirty Molly always seemed to have the last laugh, and Ellie had never found out any more about the row between her mother and Mrs Andrews. Perhaps Terry might know; she'd ask next time she saw him.

Peggy was upset when Ellie told her about her sisters moving away.

'Why didn't they come and tell you?'

'Dunno.'

'It wouldn't 'ave hurt 'em. Well I reckon that was real mean of 'em. After all, they know where you work.'

'I was a bit upset when I found out. Peggy, I met me train man as I was coming home, and he took me for a cup of tea.'

'What?' Peggy quickly looked round in case Mr Jenkins caught them gossiping. 'No. What'd 'e do that for?'

Ellie told her all about their meeting.

'That was kind of him,' said Peggy. 'But fancy 'im being a teacher, and playing in a band. Did 'e say where?'

'In a club somewhere. I didn't like to ask.'

'Be nice if 'e give you an invite.'

Ellie laughed. 'I could just see me going off to some posh place. The only decent thing I've got ter wear is me uniform.'

The following Saturday afternoon Ellie was very busy when Leonard Kent came into the tea room, so she couldn't talk to him. He didn't mention their meeting, but to Ellie, the smile he gave her, and the sixpence he left, was more than enough.

Spring gave way to summer. Ellie loved the long light

evenings and, as she was never in any great hurry to get home, would dawdle and dream. Her thoughts often went to Lizzie and Dolly. She wondered how they were getting on. Would Dolly be getting married next January, when she was twenty-one? Was Lizzie having a baby yet? If only she could see them again. She was upset they hadn't tried to contact her; she kept hoping they would write or come to the tea room. Ellie did worry that if they wrote to her at home she might never see the letter. Their names were still never mentioned.

One evening as Ellie was walking home, her head full of thoughts as usual, she saw Dirty Molly sitting as always watching the kids larking about round the tree. She spotted Ellie and called her over.

''Allo gel. You look like yer lorst a tanner and found 'apenny. Come and sit down fer a bit.' She patted the dirty wrought-iron seat.

Ellie did as she was told. 'Ain't got nothink to tell you,' she said, eyeing Molly suspiciously.

'How's yer mother managing?'

Ellie had been waiting for some caustic remark. 'Not too bad,' she said, taken aback by Molly's apparent concern.

'See you've 'ad the means test man round. Yer mum on relief, then?'

Ellie was cross and didn't answer. Why did everybody have to know their business?

Molly continued, 'That's a shame. She's gotter make sure she pays the rent, that Cole can be a right sod when 'e likes. I see it all, sitting 'ere. Got very upset when that poor Mrs Collins got chucked out. I wonder what workhouse she finished up in. It's the kids I feel sorry for.'

Ellie was surprised at the tender way Molly spoke. 'I reckon it's mean of the landlord doing that,' she agreed.

'They wasn't the first, me girl, and I don't suppose they'll be the last. See Baby Iris found 'erself a job. I gather yer dad's still 'ome. 'E don't look too well if yer ask me.'

Molly was in full flow again and Ellie wasn't going to interrupt.

'Young Terry Andrews only doing a bit 'ere and there, be all accounts. Shame about 'is mum, still she still manages ter get a lodger now and then. Mind you she has had some rough 'uns in 'er time.'

Ellie had to ask her. 'Molly, what 'appened between me mum and Terry's?'

'I told yer, they 'ad a fight.'

'What over?'

Dirty Molly looked behind her. 'Well, I reckon yer old enough now to hear about this. Mind you, I don't know if I should be telling yer.' She bent her head nearer to Ellie. 'Promise me yer won't breathe a word o' it to anyone round 'ere, especially yer mother.'

Ellie opened her eyes wide and shook her head.

Suddenly Ruby Walsh's harsh voice screamed out across the square. 'Ellie, git yer arse in 'ere.'

Ellie looked up.

'Yer better go, gel,' said Molly.

As Ellie walked past her mother she got a clip round the ear. 'I've told yer before, don't sit listening to that silly old cow's stories. She talks a load o' old cods wallop. Now git indoors.'

Ellie felt like a small kid again, being dragged in off the street. She wanted to yell out and answer back, but knew that would only mean another swipe, and the next one might be harder. Would she ever find out what Dirty Molly was on about?

The summer continued long and hot. Ellie never got another chance to talk to Dirty Molly, who was always surrounded by kids or neighbours.

Despite the lack of money the Walshes seemed to be struggling on. Baby Iris was hoping to get moved out of the alteration room and on to the shop floor, which would mean more money. She was full of her ambitions to go into the dress department, but they didn't seem to materialize as fast as she'd hoped.

When one day Ellie suggested her mother took in washing to help out with the money, it started such a row that she fled from the room.

Her father now appeared to have given up all hope of a job – he said going out to work would stop them from getting relief – and spent his days wandering round the market picking up any odd bits of fruit and veg he found lying about. Ellie was beginning to wonder if Lizzie was right, and he was just lazy.

All their clothes were secondhand, and many nights Ellie sat and sewed, darned, and unpicked jumpers to make things fit. Peggy sometimes gave her something she said she'd grown out of, but Ellie knew that wasn't true.

Just once a month Leonard Kent came into the tea room and Ellie found she looked forward more and more to seeing him. His warm smile brightened her day.

After one of his visits Peggy gave her a funny look. 'Left yer another tanner then?'

Ellie nodded. 'I wish 'e came in every week.'

'Yer wanner be careful about these musicians, I've 'eard they can be a wild bunch.'

Ellie laughed. 'Mr Kent's a bit old to be a wild one. 'Sides, 'e's a teacher, and only plays in a band to give him extra money.'

'Yer I know, so yer told me.' Peggy sounded bored. 'But 'e didn't tell yer if 'e was married or not though, did 'e?'

Ellie was upset at Peggy's attitude towards him, and couldn't understand her change of heart. 'Why should that matter to me? Don't you like 'im?' she asked.

Peggy shrugged. 'Don't know him, do I, but I don't wanner see yer hurt,' came the quick reply.

Ellie laughed. 'He only comes in for tea.'

Peggy busied herself wiping the counter. 'I'm just warning

yer, that's all. And don't go relying on ''is tip every month.'

'I don't,' said Ellie, knowing deep down she did. But because she couldn't spend it without her mother finding out, every month she hid it in the tea room, so it was well away from Baby Iris's prying eyes. She was saving for when she left home in three years' time; at the moment she had the grand total of three shillings.

The following Sunday morning Ellie woke to a bright warm day. She felt she had to get out. Since her sisters had gone the house seemed dead; after dinner it was the same old routine – her mother asleep in one armchair, while her father sat dozing in the other. Baby Iris sat at the table reading and writing.

'Fancy coming fer a walk round the park, Iris?' Ellie asked after they had finished dinner. Today it had been a greasy piece of bacon, more fat than meat.

'No fanks,' came the curt reply.

'Well I'm going.'

'Don't slam the door as yer go out,' said Ned Walsh, drowsily.

Ellie put on her hat and coat, and as she closed the front door, smiled to herself. She was pleased Baby Iris didn't want to come, and as she fingered the penny in her pocket, thought how she was going to treat herself to an ice cream.

In the park the band on the stand looked resplendent in their uniforms, their instruments glistening in the afternoon sunlight. They were playing a march and people were lying back in the striped deckchairs listening, many with their eyes closed. Children were playing all sorts of games and the air was filled with the sound of balls hitting bats, and children and grown ups running and shouting. Some of the boys, along with their fathers, were quietly sailing boats on the pond. It was a happy, carefree scene. Ellie went over to the ice cream man who had a box on the front of his bike and was shouting, 'Stop me and buy one.'

After making her choice, she walked along sucking her ice

cream without a care in the world. If only this could go on for ever. If only every day could be like this. She sat on the grass. A couple walked past hand in hand. If only she could find someone to love, and know that he loved her. She had always loved Terry Andrews, but he didn't love her. She felt lonely, but it had been like that all her life, even with three sisters. Lizzie and Dolly had always had each other to go out with, but she was the odd one out. How she would love to go to a dance, to be held in someone's arms. She sighed. She even went to the pictures on her own. That was her one expensive escape – it was sixpence to go in the cheapest seats, but she could sit in the dark, dreaming. She imagined she was Pearl White being held by the villains till the tall dark hero came and saved her.

After a while she decided to walk slowly, the long way home. It would take her past the lunatic asylum, which as a child she had been terrified of, mainly because their mother frequently threatened to have them locked away in there if they didn't behave.

The asylum was set in its own grounds, which people said had been part of the park many years ago. It had once belonged to a rich family, and when the man went mad they'd given it away. Now tall trees hid most of the house from inquisitive eyes, but Ellie could just about make out some of the small, barred windows, and today the large redbrick imposing building didn't look so frightening in the bright sunlight.

She passed the huge black wrought-iron gates that fronted the road and casually glanced in. She gasped. To her surprise Terry Andrews was inside, walking along the gravel path, coming towards her. He looked a little smarter than she'd seen him of late. He was wearing a cap, but kept his head down, and was walking very slowly towards the tall majestic gates as if deep in thought. Ellie quickly hid round the corner. She heard the hinges creaking as the gate was opened.

What was Terry doing here? Did he work here? Ellie, intrigued, stood and watched him come into the road. He stopped, looked around, then walked away in the opposite direction to where Ellie was hiding. She wanted to run after him, stop him and talk, but decided against that. Perhaps he didn't want anyone to know he worked here?

All the way home her head was full of questions. If Terry did work there, why had she seen him on a Saturday night coming from a different direction? Perhaps he had two jobs. She would ask him the next time she saw him, or perhaps, she smiled, she'd meet him here next Sunday. But would he be angry if he found her standing outside waiting for him? She would have to be crafty and make it look like a casual meeting.

All week Terry was on Ellie's mind. She wanted to tell Peggy, but decided not to. When she woke on Sunday morning it was to the rain beating on her window. Now she would have to wait another week, as her mother would know she was meeting someone if she went out for a walk in the rain.

When Sunday came round again Ellie was relieved to find the sun shining, and found it hard to control her excitement. She had made up her mind to approach Terry in the park, so that she could talk to him without Dirty Molly listening and watching all the time. She carefully went over and over what she would say. All through dinner she tried to remain calm.

'I'm going out after dinner,' she said casually as they sat at the table.

'What, again?' asked her mother. 'Yer went out the other Sunday. Who yer meeting?'

'Nobody. It's ever so nice in the park, I sat listening ter the band.' She crossed her fingers behind her back. 'D'you want ter come with me, Iris?'

'No thank you, sounds boring.'

Ellie almost sighed with relief.

A few hours later she was standing outside the asylum gates, full of anticipation.

She felt her heart miss a beat when she caught sight of Terry. All the things she had planned to say to him had completely gone out of her head.

She hurried along the road and turned round, trying to look as if she just happened to be strolling along that particular spot at that time.

As the gate opened her heart pounded. She attempted to say his name but her mouth went dry and the words stuck in her throat.

'Ellie, Ellie Walsh, what you doing 'ere?' Terry quickly closed the gate behind him.

'Terry. What a surprise.' She smiled and, looking over his shoulder, inclined her head towards the redbrick building. 'You working in there?'

'No, I mean yes. What you doing round 'ere?' He suddenly looked angry. ''Ave you been following me?'

'No. No, course not. I've just come out for a walk in the park, ain't nothink wrong in that, is there?'

'No.'

'What's it like working in the loony bin?'

'They ain't all loonies. Some of the patients are . . .' He stopped.

Ellie was taken aback. 'D'you see 'em?' she asked, wide-eyed.

'Course.' Terry began to walk away.

Ellie put her hand on his arm to stop him. 'Let's walk through the park.'

'Sorry Ellie, got ter get 'ome, Mum's waiting.'

Ellie stood in front of him. She was angry. He was always walking away from her. 'What's the matter with me, Terry Andrews? Am I so ugly that you don't like ter be seen talking to me?'

He stood still. 'No Ellie. It ain't nothink like that. You're very pretty.' He lowered his gaze and kicked a stone.

'Well, what is it, then?'

A couple walked past and smiled at them.

'I'm going 'ome. You coming?' he growled.

Ellie was elated. In a way, he was asking her to walk along with him.

They continued in silence. Ellie smiled up at him and was busy churning over in her mind what she wanted to say, but didn't know how to start. Suddenly she burst out, 'Terry, why don't you like me? You used to at school.'

He stopped. 'Look, Ellie. I do like yer. I like you a lot, but, well . . . How can I ask yer out? I've got no money, and I've got me mum to worry about.'

He said he liked her! Why was he so worried about money? 'We don't 'ave to go anywhere that costs money. I just need someone to . . .' She turned her head. How could she tell him she needed someone to love and to talk to?

'I'm sorry, Ellie, but I couldn't ask you out if I couldn't pay.'

'But I don't mind,' she whispered.

Terry walked on.

Ellie hung back. He didn't turn round and call her. She had to let him go. There was no point now. The clouds darkened the sky. She shivered. It was as though the sunlight had gone from her life. Terry had made it very clear: he didn't want any commitment.

Chapter 11

Over the past few months Peggy and Mr Jenkins had been going out together every Saturday evening. They would go to the music hall or the pictures, or sometimes they'd just spend the evening at Peggy's house. Mr Jenkins was a bachelor, and lived alone. As Peggy lived quite close to him, she would often wait behind till Mr Jenkins finished in the bakery, then they would walk home together. When Ellie asked her if he'd changed his mind about them walking out, Peggy blushed and said they enjoyed each other's company. Ellie could see he was very fond of Peggy, and was surprised when Peggy told her he was thirty-six, eighteen years older than Ellie. Peggy looked older than her nineteen years, so perhaps the big age difference didn't matter to her.

Life at home was very much the same, just poverty and all the misery that brought. Ellie couldn't see where her life was going.

At the end of October the buses and trams were carrying pictures of Al Jolson, advertizing his film *The Jazz Singer*. They told of how for the first time he was singing and talking. Ellie was enthralled.

'I'd love to go and see it,' she said to Peggy. 'Just think, he really talks.'

'Harry—' Peggy quickly corrected herself— 'Mr Jenkins said there was ever such long queues outside.'

'I know. It must be really exciting though.'

Ellie went to the pictures as often as she could afford it. Like her job it was her escape from home life, sitting in the dark and falling in love with the hero, crying with the heroine.

Today was Leonard Kent's Saturday, and Ellie eagerly awaited his arrival. She brushed nonexistent crumbs from the table she knew he liked to sit at, and as soon as he pushed open the door she was at his side taking his grey trilby hat. He did his usual habit of smoothing down his hair.

'Good morning, Mr Kent,' she said, smiling and looking up at him.

'Hallo, my dear,' he said, smiling in return, taking the seat she offered. 'I'll have my usual.'

Ellie hurried over to Peggy. 'Tea and a scone please.'

As she put the tray on the table, he asked, 'Have you seen the new Al Jolson film everybody's talking about yet?'

She shook her head.

'Miss, can I have my bill?' the woman at the next table asked.

Ellie didn't have any time to talk to Mr Kent, and was disappointed when he too asked for his bill.

'What time do you finish?' he asked.

'Six o'clock.'

'You have a very long day.'

'I don't mind, I like my job,' she said, handing him his hat.

'I can see that. Bye.'

'Bye, Mr Kent,' she said softly as he went out of the door.

'Got yer sixpence?' asked Peggy.

'Yes,' said Ellie, putting it in her pocket. Somehow, although she didn't know why, Ellie had been expecting something more.

At six, when she left the tea room, Ellie shivered and pulled her scarf tighter against the keen wind.

'Ellie. Ellie Walsh.'

She turned. 'Mr Kent, what are you doing here?'

'I'm waiting for you.'

'Me, what for?'

He took her arm and gently eased her along the road away from the tea room. 'I didn't like to say anything while I was inside, but I know how much you like the pictures, and I was wondering if perhaps next Monday, on my night off, you would like to go and see *The Jazz Singer*, you know, the new Al Jolson film?'

Ellie stopped dead. 'What, me?'

He laughed. 'Yes, you.'

'But why?'

'They say the songs are terrific, and I can get complimentary tickets, and I thought that perhaps you would like to come along.'

'But why me?'

'I like your company, and I like your smile.'

Ellie suddenly felt silly. This man was offering to take her out, and she didn't know how to behave. 'I don't know.'

'I thought you liked going to the cinema.'

'Oh yes, I do.'

'Well then, what's the problem?'

'I don't . . .' She stopped. She knew what the problem was, she didn't have anything decent to wear, and what would her mother say if . . .

'Look, Ellie. You don't mind me calling you Ellie, do you?'

She shook her head.

'I'll be outside the tea room at six. That's when you finish, isn't it?'

She nodded.

'I'll be discreet, if you don't want Miss Swan to know. I'll go round the corner.'

Ellie stood, her mind going over and over. 'What about your wife, what will she say?' she finally whispered.

He laughed out loud. 'I'm not married. Besides it isn't as

though I'm—' He stopped. 'Good heavens. I'm not asking . . . I just wanted you to see this film, I'm sure you'll love it. If you'd rather, I'll get the tickets and you could go on your own, or take Miss Swan.'

'She's going with Mr Jenkins,' Ellie said, though she didn't know for sure.

'I'll be outside at six on Monday, that gives you time to make up your mind.' He raised his hat. 'Bye.'

Ellie was stunned. He was asking her out. She couldn't go, not with her scruffy coat. She desperately wanted to ask Peggy what she should do, but then realized that would be silly. Peggy thought Mr Kent was an old man, although Ellie didn't think he was much older than Mr Jenkins. But he said he only wanted to take her to the pictures. Was he feeling sorry for her? Despite the cold wind, she glowed, and ambled along, hugging her thoughts to herself in delight.

All day Sunday her mind kept returning to Mr Kent's offer. In the kitchen she tried to clean the stains off her coat. If it had been Terry she would have been more enthusiastic. But he couldn't take her to the pictures; he didn't even seem to want to walk along the street with her. But Mr Kent was a customer, and a man that must have plenty of girlfriends, so why did he ask her out? He said it was because he got complimentary tickets, and she did so want to see that film, and this way it wouldn't cost her anything. She smiled to herself. Going out with Mr Kent had to be the best thing that had ever happened to her.

'What yer doing?' asked Baby Iris.

'This 'as got ter last me all winter, so I'd better try and clean it up,' said Ellie, rubbing at her coat. 'Don't know who 'ad it last, but they must 'ave been mucky devils.'

'You know the hem hangs down at the back,' said Baby Iris.

Ellie nodded. 'I'll 'ave ter fix that. Don't bother about any tea for me termorrer night, Mum, I'm going to the pictures straight from work,' she said casually.

'Don't make a noise when yer gets in then.'

Ellie was surprised there were no other comments.

'What yer gonner see?' asked Baby Iris.

'Dunno yet.'

'Wish I had money fer the pictures.'

'You might be able to go when you get your rise,' said Ellie pointedly, looking at her mother.

'Well I ain't giving her any,' said their mother, and turning to Ellie added, 'and I reckon you shouldn't be wasting yer money on it either, not if yer wants clothes as well.'

'Christ, Mum, I only go now and again as it is,' said Ellie, glaring at Iris. She grabbed her coat from the wooden draining board and quickly left the scullery. She stomped up the bare wooden stairs, terrified Iris might persuade their mother to give her money to go to the pictures with her.

Ellie sat on the bed and sighed, her thoughts full of Mr Kent. Should I go? He knows I ain't got any decent clothes, but that didn't put him off when he took me in that café for a cup of tea. She threw her coat beside her. What harm would it do? She desperately wanted to see this film. And at least her shoes were nice.

'You look smug,' said Peggy as they finished tidying up the tea room on Monday evening.

Ellie glanced at the clock. 'I think I'll try and see that Al Jolson film ternight.'

'You'll be lucky,' said Peggy. 'Who yer going with?'

'Meself. Why?' asked Ellie abruptly.

'Christ, I only asked. Wouldn't mind seeing it meself.'

'Thought you'd go with Mr Jenkins.'

'I expect we will.'

At six Ellie hurried out. 'Bye,' she shouted behind her, closing the tea room door.

Leonard Kent was waiting round the corner as promised.

Ellie hesitated. He looked so smart.

'Hallo Ellie,' he said, striding towards her. 'Well, are you coming with me, or is it just you and Miss Swan?'

'I'm coming with you, if that's all right,' she replied quietly.

He took her arm. 'I wouldn't have asked you if it wasn't all right, now would I?'

Ellie shook her head.

At the cinema, Ellie couldn't believe it – they went upstairs. She had only ever sat right at the front in the cheapest seats. And he bought her a box of chocolates. Excitedly she sat on the edge of her seat, and in the dark she absentmindedly clutched at Mr Kent's arm when Al Jolson began to sing. She was thrilled, not only at the wonderful talking film and the music, but at the thought that she was with someone.

'Well, what did you think of it?' asked Leonard Kent as they bustled their way through the crowds towards the underground.

Ellie looked up at him, her eyes shining. 'It was lovely, thank you, thank you ever so much. When 'e sang – I couldn't believe it.' She clasped her hands. 'I'll remember this day for ever and ever.'

He laughed. 'You're a funny little thing. You like music, don't you?'

'Yes.'

'Do you sing along with the wireless?'

'We don't 'ave a wireless.'

'Oh. How would you like to come along to the club I work in one night?'

'Oh, I couldn't.'

'Why's that?'

'Me mum's a bit strict.'

'Surely she would let you come one evening. You wouldn't have to stay to the end, if you didn't mind going home on your own.'

Ellie suddenly panicked and stopped at the station's

entrance. 'Where're you going? I thought you said you lived in the West End.'

'I do, but I can't let you go home alone. That wouldn't be very gentlemanly.'

'You can't, you can't take me home.'

'Why not?'

''Cos . . . 'cos you can't.' She began to walk away.

'Ellie, I'm sorry.' He held up his hands. 'If that's what you want. But look, here's your fare.'

'I can't take that.'

'Yes you can. If you'd let me take you home I would have paid. Besides, I know you don't earn a lot, and I have enjoyed your company tonight.' He held out a shilling.

Ellie desperately wanted to take it. 'I've enjoyed being with you, but I can't take that.'

'Come on now, I insist.' He took Ellie's hand and put the shilling in it.

'Thank you, Mr Kent, for such a lovely time, and I'll give you the change.'

He laughed. 'Don't worry about it, and thank *you*, Ellie, you are a delightful young lady, and I'd like to take you out again one night.'

'I don't know about that.'

'We'll discuss it more next month. You go down on to that platform,' he said, pointing to the sign. 'Bye, Ellie Walsh.' He smiled.

'Bye.' She walked away on a cloud. He was so nice.

'Did you manage to get in?' asked Peggy the following morning.

'Yes,' said Ellie, dewy-eyed.

'You look all soppy, was it that good?'

'It was really wonderful. To hear Al Jolson singing, and talking, and . . .' She stopped. How could she tell Peggy she went with Leonard Kent, and it was the best night of her life? 'You must go and see it.'

Ellie wished the following month away. If only Mr Kent would come in more often. If only she could find a way of going to his club. Should she tell Peggy all about it? What would she say?

At last it was Leonard Kent's Saturday and Ellie could hardly contain herself.

'What yer keep looking at the door for?' asked Peggy.

'Nothink,' said Ellie, busying herself dusting crumbs from empty tables, moving the flowers round and generally trying to keep occupied.

When the bell rang she looked up once again. Her eyes lit up; he was standing in the doorway, dripping wet.

'It's filthy weather out there,' he said, shaking his umbrella and handing it to Ellie.

She smiled. She wanted to throw her arms round his neck and thank him over and over, again and again.

He didn't say a lot and, when he finished his tea, left.

Ellie was devastated. She was hoping he would have asked her out to his club, or the pictures again. She put the usual sixpence in her pocket and began clearing away the crocks. Under the plate was a note. Ellie quickly looked across at Peggy; fortunately she was busy with a customer. Ellie hastily put the note in her pocket.

It seemed forever before she had a chance to go out to the lav. She sat on the seat, and read her note.

Dear Ellie,

I thought it better this way than to ask you out in front of Miss Swan. I would like you to come to the club next Saturday. I will be outside the tea room on Saturday at six. Don't let me down.

Yours affectionately,

Leonard.

Ellie read it four times before it really sank in. She couldn't believe he was asking her out. What could she do? She would desperately love to go, but what could she wear? And would her mother let her stay out late? Slowly Ellie put the note back in her pocket. This could have been the most wonderful night of her life, even better than the pictures. A tear slowly trickled down her cheek. She brushed it away. Peggy had sharp eyes and didn't miss much. She mustn't see her upset.

It wasn't fair, why did they have to be so poor? And why was she so afraid of her mother? She knew why; she didn't want to finish up in a home, or the workhouse. She thought about Mrs Collins who with her five kids used to live next door to Dirty Molly. Although it was many years ago, Ellie could still remember the bailiffs banging on the door after her husband died. The poor woman had shouted and screamed that she didn't want to go, as the men threw her few tatty belongings out of the house. The kids were crying and the little one had stood in the square and peed himself. Everybody came out of their houses to watch and offer their sympathy, but nobody could help, as money was always tight in this community. Ellie shuddered. The workhouse must be a terrible place, and she would never give her mother any reason to send her there.

Chapter 12

All day Sunday Ellie's mind was turning over, trying to think of ways and means of going out next Saturday without her mother knowing where she was going. But as soon as she came up with one solution, the problem of what she could wear would override everything else. 'Even if I did have something to wear, how could I get dressed up and made up here? I'll just have to forget it,' she mumbled to herself as she settled down to sleep. 'It's no good trying to be something I'm not.'

The following morning as Ellie walked to work she had to pass the pawn brokers as usual. Normally she just casually glanced at the window. Amongst all the everyday bric-à-brac, pictures in large ugly frames were stacked at the side, and there was always a pile of boots and shoes in the front of the messy, overcrowded window. Lately something else had made her look in enviously, for hanging on a piece of rope at the back of the window were two lovely beaded frocks, with colourful boas made of fine feathers draped over them. For weeks she had drooled over them, but guessed they would be out of her price range. Besides, where would she wear such lovely creations? But this morning she stopped and looked closer. Now she had somewhere exciting to go, she could ask the price. Then something else caught her eye.

There, hanging on the line beside the frocks, was a coat just like Dolly's. Although it was partly hidden Ellie was sure it was the lovely brown one with a fur collar, the one she'd had for Lizzie's wedding almost a year ago.

Ellie pressed her nose against the glass, turning this way and that. The shop was dark and the window very dirty, so it was hard to see in properly, but it looked very much like Dolly's. Was Dolly living round this way? Ellie felt excited at that thought. She would try and find her. But why would she pawn her lovely coat? Was she that hard up? And what about Lizzie? Where was she? She wanted to rush into the shop and ask the owner who it belonged to, but she knew he wouldn't tell her. Besides it was Monday, and it was just her luck that he didn't open till later on Mondays. She stopped. Was Dolly wearing her coat when she left home? Then Ellie suddenly realized this was where her mother would have brought it. Could it be Dolly's? The pawn shop only kept goods for so long, then sold them. She couldn't see how much it was. Ellie felt sad. Were all Dolly's clothes for sale in there? The hurt of losing her sisters was beginning to lessen, but now to see Dolly's coat hanging in a pawn shop window brought it all back again.

Ellie slowly moved away. If only she could see her sisters again; but they'd never bothered about her, or even tried to get in touch. They knew where she worked, they could have made the effort, just once. She began to get angry, her thoughts churning. Perhaps if Dolly's frocks were in there, and not too expensive, she could use her savings to buy one. That could be the answer to her prayers, and after all it was better than a stranger wearing it.

Ellie continued to the tea room almost lightheaded. On Saturday she could be going to Mr Kent's club in the West End. She felt dizzy with excitement, but sobered when the thought returned that there was still the problem of getting ready.

'You look pleased with yerself,' said Peggy when Ellie walked in.

'Guess what? I think I've just seen Dolly's coat in the pawn shop.'

'Well that's a turn up for the book. So, do you reckon she's living round this way?'

'Dunno. I didn't see if she had it on when she left. If she didn't then it could be that Mum pawned it.'

'Well in that case you can't tell 'er about it, can you? I think it's rotten of 'em not telling you where they live.'

'So do I.' Ellie knew she just had to tell Peggy all about Mr Kent, she couldn't keep it to herself any longer. 'Peggy. Before we start work, could we 'ave a little talk?'

Peggy looked surprised. 'What about?' She quickly sat at one of the tables. 'Here, yer mum ain't been giving yer 'ard time again, 'as she?' she asked with genuine affection.

'No, nothing like that, in fact it ain't been that bad at home lately, and even Baby Iris is bringing in a bit more now she's been moved onto the shop floor. Mind you, I'd still like to know how much Mum lets her keep.'

'Well, what is it you want to talk about then?' Peggy was beginning to sound a little impatient.

Ellie sat opposite her and began to tell her all about how Mr Kent had taken her to the pictures, and now she'd got this invitation to his club.

Peggy didn't interrupt, and her eyes and mouth were wide open.

'So you see,' continued Ellie, 'I would love to go with him on Saturday; but even if I did get one of Dolly's frocks, how could I get dressed up in it at home and then get back in late? Me mum'd kill me.'

Peggy sat back. 'Well I'll be . . . I'll tell you this, Ellie Walsh, when yer gets yerself a problem, it's a great big one. Do you really want to go out with 'im?'

Ellie nodded.

'But 'e's old.'

'So, what about you and Mr Jenkins? I think 'e's about the same age as Mr Jenkins.'

'Well, I know 'im. You don't know anythink about this Mr Kent.'

''E ain't married,' added Ellie hastily.

Peggy looked smug. 'That's what 'e tells you.'

'Why should 'e tell me lies?'

'Well, girl, if you don't know, then there's no hope for you.'

'Peg, what should I do? I dearly want to go. Just to see how other people live. It's a chance in a lifetime for me.'

Peggy smiled. 'Yer, you 'ave 'ad it pretty rough.'

The door at the back of the counter opened. 'Come along girls, what do you think you're doing, sitting chatting? I ain't paying you to sit around. Now get on with your work.'

'Yes Mr Jenkins,' they said in chorus.

For the rest of the day, every time Ellie looked at Peggy, she grinned. It was almost six before they had a chance to speak quietly together.

'Ellie, Mr Jenkins 'as to go and see Mr Cole ternight, that's why 'e ain't very 'appy.'

Ellie looked alarmed. 'Why? What's wrong?'

'It ain't nothink, but what if you come 'ome with me ternight, then perhaps we could work somethink out for you next Sat'day.'

Ellie wanted to throw her arms round Peggy. Why did she ever doubt that she would go out of her way to help her?

Later, sitting in Mrs Swan's comfortable little kitchen, Ellie relaxed.

Mrs Swan put a tray of tea things on the table. 'So how you gonner get this 'ere frock then?' she asked, after hearing the story.

'I've got my savings 'ere.' She patted her handbag. 'I only 'ope it's not more than five shillings, 'cos that's all I've got.'

'It shouldn't be as much as that,' said Mrs Swan, pouring out the tea. 'When yer go in there don't look too eager, 'cos the crafty old bugger'll put up the price. Look at somethink else, then work yer way to what you really want.'

'She don't know if any of Dolly's frocks are still in there yet, Mum.'

'I'll go in the morning. But how am I going to get ready to go out? I can't do it at home. And what can I tell Mum?'

'You can tell yer mum you're spending the evening with us.' Peggy laughed. 'Just as long as you ain't too late home, Cinderella.'

'I should be able to creep up the stairs all right, but what about . . .?'

Peggy must have anticipated Ellie's next question, as she said, 'I'll 'ave a word with Mr Jenkins. Can't say 'e'll approve, mind, but I'm sure 'e'll let you get ready in the back of the shop.'

Ellie thought she was going to burst with excitement.

Mrs Swan smiled. 'It's good ter see you looking so 'appy, Ellie, but be careful, love.'

'What about?' asked Ellie.

'Men.'

Ellie frowned. 'But 'e's ever such a nice man.'

'They all seem nice till you get to know 'em. I'm surprised 'e ain't got a girlfriend, 'im playing in a band like that. Would 'ave thought they 'ad plenty of gay young things 'anging round 'em.' Mrs Swan gathered up the cups and saucers and put them back on the tray.

'I think 'e feels sorry for our Ellie,' said Peggy. 'And 'e just wants to show 'er a good time. And I love a bit of intrigue.' She laughed.

Ellie also laughed, but it was with less enthusiasm. She stood up. 'I'll 'ave to go. Thanks for the tea, Mrs Swan.'

'My pleasure, love, enjoy yourself on Sat'day, and try and come round Sunday to tell us all about it.'

'I'll try. See you in the morning, Peg.'

All the way home Ellie pondered on what had been said. Did Leonard Kent feel sorry for her? Peggy and Mrs Swan had put some doubts in her mind. He *was* old, a bit like an uncle really, and why did he want to take her out when he must have the pick from all sorts of girls? Posh, well dressed girls. Well, she'd find out on Saturday. Her first problem was to get the frock.

'You're late,' yelled her mother when Ellie walked into the kitchen. 'Where the bloody hell yer been? I s'pose yer know yer dinner's spoiled be now?'

'I'm ever so sorry, Mum.' Ellie quickly crossed her fingers behind her back. 'I had to take Peggy home, she wasn't feeling very well.' She suddenly thought, Lizzie was right all that while back; living here did make you crafty and devious.

'Couldn't that Mr Jenkins take 'er? From what you've told us 'e's taken a shine to 'er.'

'He had to go out.'

Her mother looked at her suspiciously. 'Yer dinner's in the oven, it's a bit dried up be now.'

Ellie looked at her father. Since Dolly had gone and they had been on relief, he had looked old and worn out, and had shrunk deeper into his shell and was quieter than ever. It seemed as though all the fight had gone out of him. 'Been out today, Dad?' she asked cheerfully, knowing what the answer would be.

'Only round the market.'

'No job then?'

'No. Ain't a lot o' point looking these days, not with the long queues at the labour exchange, and this cold goes right through me when yer standing about.'

Her mother tutted and tossed her head in the air.

Ellie took the unappetizing meal from the oven and screwed up her nose. What was once gravy was now a dried brown stain round the edge of the thick, chipped plate. The potatoes looked grey and lumpy, and some yellowed, watery greens was all that was on the plate.

'Didn't 'ave no money fer meat,' said her mother. 'At least he,' she jerked her thumb at her husband, 'managed ter get these bits o' veg from the market.'

Ellie made no comment and forced herself to tuck into her dinner to avoid more rows.

When she woke early on Tuesday morning, Ellie slid her hand under her pillow, just to make sure her handbag was still there, out of the way of Baby Iris's prying eyes. She smiled to herself as she quickly got dressed; she knew the pawn shop would be open early this morning to catch any workers who wanted to pawn something to see them through the rest of the week till pay day.

She felt very apprehensive as she approached the shop. What if there weren't any of Dolly's frocks in there? What if it was only her coat? What if there wasn't anything in her price range? Fear gripped her. First she looked in the window. The coat was still there.

As she pushed open the door, the clang of a large bell made her jump.

'Good morning, young lady, and what can I do for you?' A grey-haired old man stood behind a glass counter and peered at her over his hornrimmed spectacles.

It was a dingy, cluttered shop and a musty, damp, dank smell, mixed with mothballs, sweaty shoes and clothes, filled her nostrils. 'Can I 'ave a quick look round?' she asked.

'What yer got to sell then, love?'

'Nothink.'

He grinned. 'Don't be shy.'

'I ain't got nothink to sell – I might even want to buy somethink.'

'Oh yes, and what would that be?'

Ellie looked round. There was no sign of any of Dolly's frocks, just her coat. 'How much d'you want for that?' She pointed to Dolly's coat.

'Seven and six.'

'That's a bit much.' Ellie wondered, if it had been her

mother that pawned it, how much he had given her.

He laughed. 'It's a good coat, pure wool, and the latest fashion. What you got ter spend? Did you want a coat? Got some more over 'ere.' He came from behind the counter to a pile of what looked like rags. He began sorting through them. 'This ain't bad, could let you 'ave it for a couple o' bob.' He held up a brown tweed coat that in its day must have been good quality, but the collar was torn, and the buttons missing.

'No, that's not what I'm looking for.' Ellie began turning the pile over.

'Please yerself.'

The doorbell clanged again. Ellie looked up; a man with his cloth cap pulled well down over his eyes came in with a bag full of something.

''Allo Fred,' said the shopkeeper, shuffling back to the counter. 'Brought the sheets in again then? They'd better be clean.'

The man put the bag on the counter without looking round. The shopkeeper took some money out of a box on a shelf behind him and gave it to the man. He left without saying a word.

'Have you got any other frocks?' asked Ellie, casually glancing around.

'Thought you wanted a coat?'

'Dunno, I might want a frock.' Ellie was beginning to get worried. What if she didn't see anything she liked, or could afford?

'What about that?' He pointed to a blue beaded one.

'How much?' asked Ellie.

'Nine and six.'

Ellie laughed, it was a false laugh. 'Can't afford that, 'sides, where would I go to wear something like that?'

The old man picked up the bag with the sheets in, and sniffed them. 'Don't like to open too early on a Monday morning just in case the old dears bring 'em in without washing 'em. Makes the place stink to high heaven with dried piddle.' He climbed up some rickety steps and threw the bag onto a shelf. ''Ere, I've just remembered, the old dear that brought that nice coat in had a couple of frocks as well. I've got 'em here somewhere, they're right at the back.' He fished behind a pile of bundles that looked like washing. 'She ain't come to redeem 'em, so I'm in me rights to sell 'em.' He pulled out a mass of screwed up material.

Ellie's hopes that Dolly might be living round this way were quickly dashed when she immediately recognized her frocks. Her heart was pounding. He shouldn't want a lot of money for them. 'What, those? They look a bit of a mess, but let's 'ave a look at 'em,' she said as nonchalantly as she could.

One by one Ellie held them up. There was the lovely blue dropped-waist one she'd always admired. It was very creased, but that would be just perfect for Saturday. She quickly put it to one side when she caught sight of the old man looking at her, and sorted through the others. If only I could have them all, she thought to herself. 'How much for any of these?'

'Can let you 'ave two for five bob.'

'What about for one?'

'Humm,' he stroked his chin. 'You ain't a regular. Could let you 'ave one for three and six.'

Ellie's brain was working overtime. Should she give him all her savings and have two frocks, or should she just have the one for three and six? 'I'll think about it.' She went to walk away.

'OK, you can 'ave one for three bob.'

Clutching the paper bag, Ellie walked out of the shop on a cloud, after telling the man she might be back for more later.

At the tea room Peggy thought the frock would do just perfectly, and promised to take it home to iron, and to look out a chiffon scarf she had to see if it would match.

For the rest of the week Ellie thought of nothing else but her night out. Peggy was getting almost as excited as Ellie, and would come up with all sorts of offers. After the scarf, it was a thick, white bone bracelet.

'What if you tie the scarf round yer 'ead, like the girls in this book, look.'

Ellie quickly glanced at the book Peggy had under the counter. 'It looks good. Peg, don't let Mr Jenkins catch you, I'd hate for you to lose your job.'

'Don't worry about it.' Peggy put the book away. 'There shouldn't be any fear of that, not now anyway.'

'Why? What d'you mean? You're not going to marry him, are you?'

Peggy laughed. 'Get on with the clearing up.'

Ellie wanted to say, but he's an old man, but then she thought about Mr Kent. She had so much on her mind that her head was in a whirl, but the most important thing was that she did so want to look nice for him on Saturday.

Chapter 13

Not even the cold, drizzly November morning could dampen Ellie's spirits as she walked to work on Saturday. Ellie had told her mother she was spending the evening with Peggy, and Peggy had asked Mr Jenkins if Ellie could get changed at the tea room.

'All right then?' asked Peggy when Ellie walked in. 'Looking forward to ternight?'

Ellie grinned and nodded. 'What do you think?'

All through the day, every time Peggy gave her a knowing look Ellie felt her stomach churn, and her mind went over and over. What would the place be like? Would what she was wearing look right? Would she feel out of place? What if he didn't turn up . . . Ellie wished the day would soon end.

Dolly's frock was hanging behind the door in the lav. Ellie had tried it on, and it fitted perfectly. She felt so proud and grown up in it; it was the only nice frock she'd ever had. Peggy had ironed it and made it look really smart. How should she wear the pale blue chiffon scarf Peggy had lent her? Should she tie it round her head like she'd seen in the magazines, or should she push Peggy's thick bone bangle up her arm and drape it through it? If only she'd had her hair cut in the new short bob that was all the fashion.

'At six you had better go and tell Mr Kent to come inside,' said Mr Jenkins when he came into the tea room towards the end of the day. 'Don't want him to think we don't appreciate his custom.' He stopped at the bakery door, and turned. 'Mind you, Miss Walsh, this is the first and last time. I'm not going to encourage this sort of thing, after all this is a business, and I dread to think what Mr Cole would say if he came in.'

'Thank you, Mr Jenkins,' said Ellie nervously. 'I'm sure it won't happen again.'

'I hope not.'

Peggy grinned at Ellie, and as soon as he closed the door, rushed over to her. 'Don't worry about it. If 'e does ask you out again, we'll work somethink out.'

'Thanks, Peg.'

Ellie stood patiently waiting for the minute hand to touch twelve. At long last it was six o'clock. Without bothering to put on her coat Ellie ran round the corner to tell Mr Kent to come and wait in the tea room while she got ready.

She stopped. He wasn't there. She ran to the other corner and looked up the road; although it was dark the street lamps helped her to see there was no sign of him. She shivered and thought she was going to be sick. Why had he said he wanted to take her to his club? He wouldn't let her down, would he? Perhaps he was ill. Perhaps his train was late. Slowly Ellie turned and walked back to the tea room. She would never know if he was ill.

'Well,' said Peggy eagerly. ''E outside?'

Ellie shook her head. A tear ran down her face. 'He ain't there. I've spent me savings on a frock I can't wear. Oh Peg, why did 'e say that . . .' Her lip trembled and she couldn't speak.

Peggy came round from behind the counter and put her arm round Ellie's heaving shoulders. 'You don't think 'e's been leading you on, do yer?'

Ellie shrugged. 'I don't think so. Why should 'e?' Her voice was caught on a sob.

''E'll get a bit of me mind if 'e 'as, upsetting you like this. The sod. Fancy stringing you along like that. How could 'e be so heartless?' Peggy led Ellie to a chair.

'I don't think he's like that.'

Peggy tossed her head. 'Hummh, we'll see. Just as long as 'e wasn't doing it for a laugh.'

'He wouldn't, would he?'

'Some old men 'ave got some very funny ideas about young girls.'

'Oh Peg, you make him sound awful.'

'I'll get you a cup o' tea.'

Ellie put her hand out to stop her moving away. 'Don't tell Mr Jenkins.'

'Course not.' She disappeared into the bakery.

Ellie put her head on her hands and wept. Was Mr Kent leading her on? She didn't think he was like that, and why should he? No, he was nice, there had to be something wrong.

Peggy came out with a tray of tea. She turned and glanced at the bakery door. 'I told Mr Jenkins we'll be a little while.'

'D'you think somethink could 'ave happened to Mr Kent?' asked Ellie looking up, her big brown eyes full of tears.

'Dunno.'

''E's such a nice man,' sniffed Ellie. 'I'm sure there must be something wrong.'

Peggy slowly stirred the tea in the pot. 'What can I say?'

Ellie dried her eyes on her handkerchief and sipped her tea. 'What am I gonner do? I can't go 'ome, Mum thinks I'm going round your 'ouse.'

Peggy looked guilty. 'I'd ask yer round, but, well, Mr Jenkins is coming to tea tonight, and we thought we'd stay in.'

Ellie gave her a faint smile. 'That's all right, I wouldn't want to play gooseberry.'

'Daft, me mum'll be there. Seriously though, what you gonner do?'

'I could always go to the pictures, I suppose.' Ellie played with the spoon. 'It'll 'ave ter be in the sixpennies this time.'

'If you've finished I'll take these tea things away,' said Peggy, clearing the table. 'I'm always terrified Mr Cole'll come in and catch us doing somethink we shouldn't. I'd hate for Mr Jenkins to get into trouble over us.' She took the tray out.

With her back to the door Ellie sat with her thoughts. When the bell over the door tinkled, Ellie quickly wiped her eyes and jumped to her feet expecting Mr Cole to walk in.

The sight of Leonard Kent standing in the doorway filled her with happiness, even though he was looking flustered.

'My dear Ellie, I'm so sorry I'm late.' He rushed towards her and took hold of her hand. 'I was worried that you might not wait.'

Ellie couldn't speak.

'Are you ready to go? I'll explain everything to you on the way.'

Peggy came out from the bakery. 'Mr Kent?' she said in amazement.

'Miss Swan. I was just apologizing to Ellie here.'

Ellie was still standing looking at him.

'We don't have to be at the club till eight, so we'll have plenty of time to get ready.'

'But . . .'

'Don't stand looking at 'im, Ellie, just get going. I'll get yer frock.'

'Thanks Peg.'

Peggy quickly returned and, carefully folding the frock, placed it in a paper bag.

As they went out of the door, Peggy called, ''Ave a good time.'

'I will. Thanks.' Ellie waved.

Outside she suddenly felt on air again. 'Where're we going?'

'We'll go to my place first, then you can get changed.'

Ellie froze. He was asking her to go to his house. She didn't know what to say; she had never been in this situation in her life before. Why did he want to take her home? Mrs Swan's warning was going over and over in her head. She looked up at him; he was taller than her. He was smart and good-looking, and she was a scruffy waitress. Why did he want to take her out? She didn't know what was in store for her, but she thrust her doubts to the back of her mind, determined to enjoy this new experience. He smiled at her and she smiled back. For some unknown reason, the only thing running through her mind was that, if she was going to get changed at his place, thank goodness last night was Friday and she'd had a bath and put on a clean vest and knickers! Except, of course, they weren't very posh . . .

When they were settled on the train he told her that one of his pupils was going through a bad patch, and he'd stayed on to help her. 'She has this very hard exam coming up. It's a difficult piece she's having trouble with.'

Ellie felt so proud to be with this caring man.

'So I do apologize for being late.'

'That's all right,' she said, smiling and trying to look knowledgeable. 'I thought it might be something like that.'

When he stopped outside one of the tall, well-lit terraced houses, Ellie went to walk up the stairs, but Leonard Kent caught her arm and guided her to the steps leading down to the basement.

'The flats down here are a lot cheaper to rent,' he said, opening the door. 'Stand still while I light the gas.'

The pop made Ellie jump, and as the room was flooded with light she looked all around her. 'This is a lovely room,' she exclaimed.

On the floor in front of the fire and covering the brown lino, was a green rug; the grate was still full of last night's cinders. Ellie smiled to herself at the mantelpiece, cluttered with a mishmash of papers. She could see a black sock hiding amongst them. On one side of the room was a small dark green leather sofa with newspapers popping out from under the seat. Green satin cushions were resting against the back, a black tie was thrown over the arm. A small round table covered with a lace tablecloth stood in the middle, a pipe lay in the glass ashtray, with a tin of tobacco at the side. An upright piano was against the other wall. Papers and sheet music were strewn over the floor and Leonard Kent hurriedly gathered them up and put them in the lid of the padded piano stool.

'Sorry about the mess, but I had to find some music for my student and I overslept this morning.'

Ellie smiled and nodded slightly, not knowing what to say, in awe at being alone in this man's home.

'Please, sit down Ellie. The club's not far, only round the corner. That's another reason I like living here, it's not far to fall into bed when I've finished. Are you cold? I could light the fire, but it takes a while to warm the place up.'

'No, I'm all right thank you.'

'Would you like a cup of tea?'

She nodded.

He disappeared through the only other door.

Ellie moved round the room. This didn't look as if a man lived here alone; it was too comfortable.

'I have a bathroom you can get ready in,' he said, poking his head round the door. 'It's this way.'

'A bathroom,' said Ellie eagerly, following him along a small narrow passage that had a red carpet runner on the floor.

'In there.' He pushed open a door with thick golden-coloured glass at the top. 'That's my bedroom.' He pointed to another door. 'And down there is my tiny kitchenette. It's hardly big enough to swing a cat round, but it suits me. I have a Mrs Tomms come in three times a week, she keeps the place clean and does my bit of washing. So that's it, you've now done a whirlwind tour of my humble home, and know all about my domestic arrangements.' He bowed.

Ellie laughed.

'I love to see you happy. You have such a lovely smile.' He quickly kissed her cheek. 'Now for the tea.'

Ellie blushed and touched her face. 'Can I . . .?' she looked towards the bathroom door.

'Of course. I'll take the tea into the lounge.'

Ellie closed the door. An inside lav. A sink and a bath – a proper bath! She peered into it, amazed. She had never seen a proper one before. A white bath with taps and a drain hole, it stood on iron feet and wasn't like the old tin bath at home that had to be filled and emptied by hand. She looked anxiously towards the door, then quickly turned on the tap. The water ran over her fingers, making her giggle. She wiped them on the towel and then, her hands at her sides in case she knocked something over, she twirled round and round. She picked up his shaving brush and looked inside his shaving mug. Everything was very clean. There was no sign of any woman staying here. She sat on the scrubbed wooden lavatory seat and swung her legs. I could be happy living here, she thought. I could be happy with Mr Kent. I would love to do his cooking and cleaning. He ain't that old, and he does like me. She touched her cheek again. He'd kissed her, the first man ever.

Ellie could hear Leonard Kent whistling in his kitchen when she returned to the lounge, as he had called it. She grinned. The Walshes would have called it the front room, nothing so posh as a lounge. She sat nervously on the edge of the sofa. What would her mother say if she could see her now? This was a different world. This was the sort of world she would like to live in. But Ellie was worried. How could she fit into this kind of world? How should she behave? Suddenly she was full of doubts.

'What's that frown on your face for?' asked Leonard Kent as he walked in and placed the tray on the table. He sat beside her. 'What's wrong, Ellie?'

'Mr Kent—'

He laughed. 'Please. Don't call me mister. Call me Leonard, all my friends do, and I regard you as a friend.'

'Leonard.' Ellie hesitated. 'Why did you ask me here?' She was very precise about the way she was speaking, being very careful not to drop her aitches.

He leant forward, put the tea strainer in the cup and began pouring out the tea. 'I'll be frank with you, my dear. I think you are a very charming young lady. You're like a breath of fresh air, and I shall really enjoy your company.'

'But I'm just a—'

'I know, just a child. But I'm sure we could get on together.'

'I'm not a child, I'm nearly nineteen,' she said tossing her head indignantly.

He laughed. 'And I'm nearly thirty-nine.'

'That ain't all that old.'

He leant forward and patted her hand. 'Thanks. That's what I like to hear. Now, about tonight.' Leonard took his pipe from the ashtray and settled back on the sofa. 'I won't be able to sit with you, but I'll get you a seat near the band and you can let me know when you're ready to go, and if you like it – well, you can come again. Now, when you've finished your tea you can go along to the bathroom and get ready.'

Ellie finished her tea, took her frock and did as she was told.

When she returned to the lounge she felt very shy and uneasy. Leonard was busy in front of the mirror that hung over the fireplace, tying his black bow tie.

Ellie shuffled awkwardly. The frock was sleeveless and she was aware of her thin, white, bare arms and didn't know what to do with them. Suddenly they felt long and gangling. Even the pale blue scarf draped through the bangle she had pushed up her arm didn't seem to help.

'You look very nice,' he said looking at her in the mirror. 'That's a pretty frock.'

'It was me sister's,' she croaked. 'What do the women wear at your club?' she asked suddenly, wishing she could go home and forget all about going out.

'Can't say I take a lot of notice. Ready?' He helped her on with her coat.

Ellie nodded and fidgeted with the brown paper bag that held her day frock, screwing it up and then unravelling it. Her coat felt old and shapeless, and she now wished, in some ways, that she wasn't going.

Leonard Kent pulled on his coat and picked up his door key. 'Right then, Miss Walsh, off we go.'

Chapter 14

Ellie clutched Leonard Kent's hand as they hurried up the steps and entered the wide bright doorway of the club.

'You're shaking; are you cold?' he asked, looking down at her as they went through the doors and into the foyer.

'A bit,' she replied. But it was really with excitement and apprehension. The noise and laughter coming from the other side of the thick red velvet curtain was almost frightening. What had she let herself in for?

'You'll be all right when we get inside. Hello Ben,' said Leonard Kent to a man wearing a top hat and a long black overcoat with gold braid on his epaulettes.

'Evening, Mr Kent, a bit parky out there ternight.' Ben gave Ellie a nod. 'Evening, miss.'

A curtain was pulled aside as a couple went in. The smoke, bright lights and noise made Ellie gasp.

'This way,' said Leonard, taking her hand.

They went along a passage. 'This is where the band hang out.' He pushed open a door. 'Give me your coat.'

Ellie quickly took it off and, standing in the doorway, watched him put it and her paper bag on a chair. This room was also full of cigarette smoke, but only men's deep voices and laughter came from within.

'Be back in a mo,' Leonard shouted into the room. Then taking Ellie's hand again, he led her through another door and out into the club.

Ellie thought she would faint with elation. This was just

like she'd seen at the pictures, but she was here, in this large, dimly lit room. She stood for a moment and looked around, trying to take it all in. Small tables were dotted about, most taken by couples, some of whom were laughing loudly while others sat looking into each other's eyes and quietly talking. In the middle of every table was a white bulbous stand that had an electric light and a frilly red shade on top. The air was thick with smoke. The laughter and chatter was loud. This was a different world.

Leonard smiled at her. 'This way.' He took her hand and led her to an empty table next to the stage. There was a tiny polished wood dance floor in front of her, and potted palm trees to the side.

'I'm up there at the piano. I'll be able to keep an eye on you. Order yourself a drink.' He kissed her cheek again and disappeared back behind the stage.

Ellie sat on the edge of the gilt and red plush chair. She ran her fingers over the crisp white tablecloth. She wanted to touch the lampshade, it was so beautiful. A real electric light! Her face was beginning to ache with grinning so wide. Had she died and gone to heaven?

'Would you like a drink, miss?' A very smart waiter wearing a short white jacket and black trousers stood before her with a silver tray in his hand.

She wanted to giggle; this was usually her job. 'Yes please,' she said eagerly, then suddenly felt embarrassed when realizing she hadn't got a lot of money. 'Sorry. I mean no thank you.'

As if reading her thoughts the waiter looked down his nose and said in a condescending manner, 'Mr Kent is looking after the bill.'

Ellie glanced around. On every table were tall, elegant glasses and she could just about make out bottles standing in silver containers at the sides of the tables. The waiter coughed, he was making ner uneasy. What should she ask for? She had only tasted beer, and she didn't really like that.

'Can I have a ginger beer please?'

A few minutes later a tall glass of ginger beer was silently placed in front of her. 'Thank you,' she said to the back of the waiter as he walked away.

The small door at the side of the stage opened and some men came out carrying musical instruments. There was a polite ripple of applause as they took their seats, Leonard at the piano. Soon they were playing and Ellie could hardly keep her feet still.

Couples began dancing. A lot of the women were wearing long evening dresses and they looked very beautiful. Nearly all of them had the new short bobbed hair, and some wore glittery cloche hats. A few women sitting on the high bar stools wore short frocks and were unashamedly showing their knees. Although Ellie didn't want this evening to end, she was also aware of how dowdy and old-fashioned she looked. She touched her long hair. It would have to go.

She would have so much to tell Peggy on Monday. How Baby Iris would love to be here – but she would never let on to her about this. Ellie's feet were tapping. If only she could dance, she thought excitedly, although she was secretly thankful no one came to ask her.

When the band had an interval Leonard came and sat with her. 'Enjoying yourself?'

Her face was flushed and her eyes sparkled. 'This is the most wonderful night of my life. I can never thank you enough.'

He laughed.

'I see you're cradle snatching again then, Len.' A tall slim man with dark curly hair and a thin moustache leant across the table and flicked his cigar ash into the ashtray. He was wearing a black evening suit like Leonard's, but Ellie hadn't seen him in the band.

'None of your business, Curly.'

He smirked and walked away.

'Who was that?' asked Ellie.

'Just one of the boys, nothing for you to worry your pretty little head about. Well, what do you think of the place?'

Ellie hunched up her shoulders. 'Wonderful. Everything is wonderful. Thank you, thank you, thank you.'

Leonard laughed. 'It does me good to see life through your eyes.' He looked at the stage when the band returned and settled themselves down again. 'Look, sorry, but I must go.'

Ellie sat starry-eyed as she watched Leonard play the piano. To her he was the only man on the stage. He smiled at her and her heart missed a beat. She didn't care if he was old, she knew she could love him.

At the next interval he hurried over and sat next to her.

'Ellie, it's after midnight, what—'

'What?' she jumped to her feet. 'Me mum'll kill me. I'll 'ave to go.' She suddenly panicked. She had to get home!

Leonard looked around. He leaned forward and pulled her back down into her seat. 'You could stay at my place tonight if you didn't want to go home just yet,' he whispered. 'We don't finish till two.'

Ellie looked shocked. 'I can't stay out all night, me mum'll go mad.' She was thinking with dread of the rows there had been when her sisters had stayed out all night.

'How will you get home?' Leonard looked anxiously at the band, who were returning to the stage.

'The tube's still running. I'll be all right.'

'Len,' one of the band called out, 'come on, we're waiting.'

'Look Ellie,' he pleaded, 'I have to go. Please wait.'

'I can't.' She stood up.

'Please, Ellie. I'll get you a taxi.'

'Come on, Len.'

'They're calling you,' said Ellie.

'Your coat, I'll get your coat.'

'No, don't worry, I'll get it. Bye.' She half ran away.

'Bye, Ellie,' he said softly.

Ellie went quickly to the band's room and, grabbing her coat and her paper bag, ran down the corridor towards the exit.

As she rushed into the foyer two large, laughing elderly men, accompanied by two very made-up young women, were blocking the corridor. She was trying to push past them when she suddenly realized she recognized one of the men. It was Mr Cole! She held back, appalled. He must have been inside. Had he seen her?

'My car's round the corner,' the other man called out. 'Come on girls, we'll show you what a good time is.'

Ellie followed them at a safe distance.

'D'yer want a taxi, miss?' shouted the doorman after her.

A taxi. She had no money for a taxi. She should have waited for Leonard after all. He should have mentioned earlier that he was going to have to leave so late. He knew she had to get home. Suddenly tears were streaming down her face, she felt so miserable. Now she knew how Cinderella must have felt – but the Prince came after *her*, and *she* had a coach to get her home. Ellie just about had enough for the train, but even then she'd have a long walk home. Why did it all have to end? And had Leonard really wanted her to spend the night with him? He must have known he would be working till two. Or was springing this surprise just a ploy to get her to stay? Why hadn't he asked her before? Part of her wished she'd had the courage to stay; but what about her mother? As she stood shivering on the platform waiting for her train, she wondered what she'd have said if he'd asked her outright to sleep with him. Despite her misery, Ellie began to smile to herself. She could have told her mother she was going to sleep at Peggy's . . .

On the train a crowd of drunks were pushing each other through the sliding doors, laughing and forcing them to open again. Ellie moved away. The last thing she wanted was to be near them. Now she'd calmed down a little, she just wanted to be alone with her thoughts and memories of the best night of her life.

The church clock chimed one when, very gently, and as quietly as she could, Ellie pulled the key through the letter box and opened the front door, terrified her mother was waiting for her on the other side, just as she had been when she waited for Dolly. Ellie carefully closed the door and stood very still, listening for any unfamiliar noise other than the usual barking dogs and fighting cats.

She took off her shoes and carefully made her way up the stairs, hardly daring to breathe, scared stiff one of the steps would creak.

She knew the bedroom door squeaked, and pondered on whether to open it quickly or slowly. Taking a deep breath she pushed it open just wide enough to get through. To her the noise was deafening. She stood still. Her heart was beating so loudly she thought that it would wake them all up, and she couldn't stop the paper bag from rustling in her shaking hands.

All remained quiet. Baby Iris moaned and turned over.

Ellie slipped out of Dolly's frock and panic filled her. What would happen in the morning if Iris found the frock? She would be sure to recognize it; and what about the bangle and the scarf? How could she hide them? She stood rooted to the spot, her mind racing.

She couldn't put them under the feather mattress for fear of rolling Baby Iris over. If she put them in the paper bag, Iris would certainly find them. The room was so bare that anything different stood out. She'd put it under the bed now, and in the morning push it right underneath. Ellie hoped and prayed Iris wouldn't see it first.

She took off the frock and snuggled down under the flimsy blanket. At least Iris had warmed the bed, but Ellie was careful not to touch her with her cold hands and feet, otherwise her sister would jump out of her skin.

Ellie lay very still. Sleep wouldn't come. A smile filled her face and her thoughts were on Leonard, the club, his lovely home, his way of life. She would love to be part of it. She was dreaming of being whisked around the dance floor in his arms, of him kissing her lips and telling her he loved her. She knew for sure she could learn to love him.

Ellie waited until Baby Iris had gone downstairs before she got out of bed, then quickly fished under the bed for the paper bag. After taking out the scarf and bangle and putting them in her handbag she screwed the paper bag with the frock in into a tight ball and put it under her half of the mattress. Iris never helped her make the bed so she wouldn't see it, and tomorrow morning she would put it in her handbag, to take to work.

Her father was clearing out the ashes when she walked into the kitchen.

'Any tea?' she asked, sitting at the table.

'Just made a pot.'

'And what time did you waltz yer arse in last night, young lady?' asked her mother, walking into the kitchen from the scullery. She plonked the teapot on the table.

'I don't know, me and Peg just got carried away talking.'

'It must o' bin late, so just don't you go making an 'abit of it, and don't think you're going out today, 'cos you ain't. I've got some patching for you to do.' Ruby Walsh poured out a cup of tea, and although Ellie was disappointed that she wouldn't be seeing Peggy till tomorrow, much to her relief nothing more was said. Even Iris didn't make any comment. For once, Ellie couldn't believe her luck.

'Well?' asked Peggy as soon as she clapped eyes on Ellie. 'What was it like?'

'Sorry I couldn't get round yesterday.'

'That's all right. Well?'

Ellie hugged herself. After having to keep it to herself all day Sunday, at long last she could talk about her night out. 'Oh Peg. It was wonderful. 'E's got ever such a nice place, and a proper bathroom.'

Peggy perched herself on a table, and opened her eyes wide. 'A bathroom. D'yer know, that's somethink I've always wanted. What about the club? Was it good?'

Ellie nodded excitedly. 'More than good.' Ellie became dreamy-eyed. 'Oh Peg, it was wonderful, truly wonderful, just like in the pictures. I only hope he asks me out again.'

'What did yer frock look like?'

'Great. I've brought it here with me. I was worried sick in case our Iris found it, that would have caused an almighty row, and I wouldn't know what to tell 'em. Would you keep it at your house for me?'

'Course. Now tell me all about Saturday.'

'The women there are ever so fashionable, and I've made up me mind I'm gonner have me hair cut like them.'

'That'll cost yer, and it'll be a bit of a shock for yer mum.' Peggy quickly stood up when the bakery door opened and Mr Jenkins' arrival put a stop to the friends' gossip.

As the day wore on, however, Ellie managed to pass snippets of information to Peggy. She told her about Leonard's flat, and the club, and how grown up she felt in Dolly's frock.

Peggy did ask if Leonard Kent tried to do anything when they were alone in his flat, but Ellie was able to put her mind at rest on that score.

'Fancy old Mr Cole being there,' said Peggy when Ellie told her.

'And he was with a young flighty girl, you should have seen 'em, loads of make up on.'

'Good job he didn't see you.'

'Why?'

'He might have thought Mr Jenkins was paying you too much wages if you could afford to go to a place like that.'

Ellie giggled. 'I hadn't thought about that. I would love to go there again.'

'Pr'aps you will one day.'

Ellie sighed. 'I've got to wait another two weeks before I see Leonard again.'

''Ere, hark at you calling him Leonard. Don't you go getting all silly over 'im.' Peggy grinned. ''Sides, I thought it was Terry Andrews you was keen on and wanted to marry.'

Ellie looked wistful. 'He don't want me, and he ain't got nothink to offer me, so I might as well stop thinking about him,' she said sadly.

'Yer, that's all very well, but this Leonard's an old man,' said Peggy.

'He's thirty-eight,' Ellie said loftily. 'Not that much older than Mr Jenkins.'

Peggy blushed. 'Mr Jenkins ain't that old, 'sides, what's this Leonard's intentions?'

'I don't know. What about Mr Jenkins?'

Peggy walked away. 'I've gotter finish clearing up.'

Ellie smiled. Did Peggy have a secret about her relationship with Mr Jenkins? Was there more to tell than she was letting on?

Chapter 15

'Good morning,' said Ellie as she walked purposefully across the tea room on Friday morning.

Peggy gasped when Ellie took off her hat. 'Christ. What did yer mother say when she saw that?'

'She don't know. Me and Iris did it this morning 'fore she got up. Well?' said Ellie twirling round. 'What d'you think?'

'Dunno. It makes you look ever so grown up.'

'Good. Baby Iris said all the girls in the frock department have got this new short hair. She's even thinking about cutting hers.'

'How does she like 'er new job?'

'She reckons it's great. She has to try and talk a bit posh now, and Mum's still has a bit of a go about her not going in a factory.'

'What d'yer dad 'ave to say about it?'

'Not a lot.' Ellie sighed. 'In fact 'e don't 'ave a lot to say about anythink these days.'

''E's still not got a job then?'

'No. I think 'e's given up looking, all 'e ever does is sit slumped in 'is chair with 'is eyes closed. Mum won't give 'im any money for his tobacco.'

'It's a bloody shame. Still it must be hard to get a job with so many people out of work.'

Ellie shrugged her shoulders. 'S'pose so.'

'Ain't you gonner give 'im money for 'is baccy?'

'You must be joking. After all the fuss with the socks, it's more than I dare do. Anyway, what d'you think of it?' She touched her hair.

'What's yer mum gonner say about it?'

'Dunno. Can't put it back now though, can I?' She laughed. ''Sides, she ain't got nothink to hang on to now if she fancies giving me a good hiding.'

'She won't, will she?'

'Dunno.'

'Is this fer, you know? 'Im?' asked Peggy knowingly.

Ellie smiled and nodded.

'Mind you, it does look nice,' said Peggy. 'And you've made a good job of it. Let's see if Mr Jenkins notices the difference.'

Ellie patted the back of her short bobbed hair. 'Feels a bit cold.'

All day Ellie felt proud of her new hairdo, and even Mr Jenkins commented on it, but deep down she was dreading what her mother would say.

It was cold and dark as she hurried home. When she turned into the square the wind was making the elm tree's branches sway and creak ominously. Ellie shuddered. Her thoughts went to Leonard Kent's flat; it was warm and cosy. She looked at Terry Andrews' house. She knew deep down if Terry wanted to take her out and to love her she would willingly go. But Leonard was kind and could offer her so much more, and if the chance ever came . . . She grinned to herself; here she was, daydreaming again. She pushed open her front door.

Her mother dropped the plate with a clatter when Ellie walked in and took her hat off. 'What the bloody 'ell yer done with yer hair?'

'I cut it.'

'I can see that. When d'yer do that, yer silly cow?'

'This morning. What d'you think?' Ellie was trying hard to put on a brave act.

'Well I don't like it, never liked short hair.'

'What about you, Dad?' Ellie twirled round in front of her father.

He looked up. 'How much that cost yer?'

'Nothink, me and Iris did it this morning.'

Her father sank back in his chair.

'You all right, Dad?' she asked.

'Course 'e's all right.' Her mother banged the bread board on the table.

Ellie looked at her father. He didn't look well. His eyes had lost any sparkle they once had, and he was painfully thin. Perhaps he was ill. If he was, there was no way her mother would pay two and six for him to see a doctor. Ellie suddenly felt guilty. Should she take the money out of her savings and give it to him? What if something happened to him? She would never forgive herself.

When Baby Iris came home from work she grinned and commented on Ellie's hair. 'It looks really great. Could you do mine tonight?' she asked Ellie.

Ellie glanced at her mother.

'Don't look at me. I ain't got no say in the matter.'

Ellie smiled. Was she losing control of her daughters, more so since Iris started work? 'OK.'

After dinner, Baby Iris, who loved her job in the big store, chattered away endlessly about the girls, the fashions and Miss Jackson, the lady boss of the new department she now worked in, who she didn't get on with, all the while Ellie was cutting her hair.

'You wanner watch yourself, me girl,' said her mother. 'You'll end up getting the sack.'

Iris laughed. 'I don't think so. I've met Mr Massy, the owner, and he likes me.'

Ellie grinned as she snipped away. Knowing Iris she'd have him wrapped round her finger before long.

'Well?' asked Ellie. 'What d'you think?'

Iris studied herself in the mirror. 'It looks good. This'll give 'em all somethink to talk about tomorrow.' She patted her short hair. 'By the way, Mum, I'm saving up for a new frock.'

'What? And who says so?'

'I can't go ter work looking like a ragbag.'

'You wear a uniform.'

'I still 'ave ter go and come back, and all the other girls look smart.'

Ellie was sure Iris didn't give her mother her unopened wage packet, but as much as she moaned about it, it didn't get Ellie anywhere. Iris was more assertive than Ellie and wasn't as frightened of their mother as she was; perhaps that was because she'd never been on the end of one of her clouts. Ellie smiled; she had guessed things would change when Iris started work, but never dreamt it would happen so quickly. Was it because their mother was frightened of losing the last two wage packets?

'What yer gonner do with all this hair?' asked their mother.

'Put it in the fire. Why?' asked Ellie.

'I reckon you could get a few bob for it.'

Ellie laughed. 'Who'd buy it?'

'Dunno. Someone who makes cushions. Ned, put it in a bag, and in the morning see what you can sell it for. What did you do with yours?' she asked Ellie.

'Put it on the fire.'

'Silly cow, don't yer never fink of no one but yerself?'

The following week seemed endless for Ellie. It was Leonard's Saturday, and it couldn't come quick enough. She was desperate to see him again, to thank him for her wonderful night out, and to get his reaction on her new hairdo. All morning she eagerly looked for him.

She wanted to run into his arms when he walked through the door, but instead simply took his hat and coat.

'Your favourite table's empty,' she said courteously.

'Thank you, Miss Walsh.'

He touched her hand and she felt a tingle. Would he ask her out again?

'I'll have my usual, please.' It was all very polite and proper, till he winked at her and said softly, 'And I like your new hairdo.'

'Thank you.' She blushed and beamed.

When she put his tea and scone on the table he smiled and whispered, 'You got home safely?'

She nodded.

'Miss, my bill please.'

Ellie hurried to her customer.

All the while Leonard was there she was busy coming and going, and to her annoyance there wasn't any time to linger.

Leonard finally stood up. He was going; panic filled Ellie. She looked round at Peggy, who was with a customer. Ellie gave Leonard his coat and hat. She smiled. 'Thank you for taking me out,' she whispered.

He leaned forward. 'We must do it again sometime.' He straightened up. 'Bye, Miss Walsh,' he said pointedly.

'Bye, Mr Kent,' said Ellie sadly.

She cleared away his crocks, hoping a note would be under the plate. Even his sixpence didn't thrill her so much now. She just wanted to go out with him again. Why didn't he ask her? Had she made a fool of herself? Was it because she wasn't well dressed and he was ashamed of her? Had she had her hair cut for nothing?

'Cheer up, girl,' said Peggy. 'Ain't 'e left you a tip?'

Ellie put on the smile she kept for the customers. 'Course 'e has.'

It was two weeks before Christmas and Peggy was telling Ellie how she was staying behind to help Mr Jenkins put up the decorations.

'Would you like me to help?'

'No, it's all right, we can manage. By the way, Mum said she's finished making those things for you. You can leave it till Christmas Eve if you like, to pick 'em up.'

'Thanks.' Ellie continued to clean the silver cruet. Was it only a year ago Lizzie had left home and got married? She let her thoughts drift on. Was Dolly married? Were they both happy? Was she an auntie perhaps? If only they had come to see her. If only she knew where they lived, she could go and see them. Whenever she met any of the women who used to work with her sisters, Ellie asked if they'd heard from them, but the answer was always the same. This was going to be yet another bleak and boring Christmas. Even Leonard Kent wouldn't be coming in till after the holiday. Ellie sighed. Suddenly the door of the tea room was opened with a rush and the little bell above it tinkled madly.

'Mr Cole,' said Peggy, looking up from polishing the inside of the glass counter. 'I'll get Mr Jenkins.' She rushed through the bakery door and almost at once Mr Jenkins came into the tea room wiping his hands on the bottom of his apron.

'Good evening, sir. Everything to your liking?' he said, almost bowing.

Mr Cole didn't attempt to remove his hat or coat. He walked round the room picking up first an ashtray which he examined in great depth, then a pepper pot. 'I think so, Jenkins. I see you still have the same staff, good, good. Customers like to see the same faces.'

'Would you like some tea?' asked Mr Jenkins.

All three were standing to attention.

'No. I was just passing and I thought I'd drop in. Everything all right with you, Jenkins?'

'Yes, sir.' Mr Jenkins gave Peggy a quick glance.

Ellie noted Peggy looked flustered.

Mr Cole frowned and looked Ellie up and down. 'Didn't I see you . . .?' He gave a little cough. 'I see you've had your hair cut, it looks very nice.'

Ellie was speechless. He *must* have seen her at the club.

He walked over to the door. 'Could be in for a white Christmas.' He went out as fast as he'd come in.

'Well I never,' said Mr Jenkins sitting in a chair. He wiped his face with his handkerchief. 'I wonder what he wanted?'

'Dunno,' said Peggy, looking serious. 'You don't think . . .?' Mr Jenkins quickly shook his head at the flustered Peggy and she changed the subject. 'Fancy 'im noticing your hair,' she added, grinning. 'Always said 'e fancied you.'

'Miss Swan, watch what you say.'

'Sorry Mr Jenkins.'

'I'd still like to know why he came in.' Mr Jenkins was still shaking his head as he walked back to the bakery.

'Well it wasn't to tell us about the weather,' said Peggy when he closed the door.

'I wonder if we will have a white Christmas,' said Ellie wistfully.

'If we do at least the streets will look clean for a change,' said Peggy. 'By the way, if you'd like to come round Christmas afternoon it'll be all right, you could stop for a bit of tea.'

'Thanks, I'd like that. Peggy, what did you mean, when Mr Cole came—'

'Don't worry about it,' interrupted Peggy.

But Ellie did worry about it, and wondered if they had anything to hide.

'I reckon he did see you that night,' said Peggy quickly, changing the subject. 'But he couldn't place you.'

'Well he never expected someone like me to be at that posh place. And I don't reckon he would want his wife to know too much about what he gets up to.'

'Should think she already knows.'

'Have you met her?'

'Only once, a quiet woman. Come on, it's time for you to go home.'

Once again the tea room looked bright and Christmassy

with all the lovely decorations Peggy and Mr Jenkins had put up. And as last year, people were also a little generous with their tips.

'How much you got in yer box now, Ellie?' asked Peggy.

'Seven shillings.'

'Seven shillings. Wow, that's almost a king's ransom. How come you've managed to save that much?'

Ellie laughed. 'I ain't spent much, and I did get a few tips this week. Mind you, I'd blow the lot on a frock and shoes if I thought Leonard would ask me out again.'

'Well it won't be before Christmas; 'e ain't due in till the week after, is 'e?'

'No, worse luck. Anyway, next Saturday's Christmas Eve. I bet they have a good time at that club.'

They finished clearing up and pulled down the blind at the window.

'It's bitter cold out there,' said Peggy.

'I'm gonner get a tram, I can't walk all the way home in this cold, it goes right through this coat.'

'You should use some of yer money to get another one. What about Dolly's? That old man in the pawn shop still got it?'

'Don't think so, ain't seen it in 'is window. 'Sides, I couldn't let Mum see it. Good job I've got me scarf your mum made.'

Peggy smiled. 'Yer, she ain't a bad old stick. If only . . .' Peggy stopped.

'What?' Ellie jumped on the half-finished sentence.

'Oh nothink. Go on, be orf with yer.' Peggy undid the door. 'Goodnight, see you Monday.'

Ellie pulled her collar up round her ears. She missed her hair. Perhaps Peggy was right, she should get herself a warmer coat.

The sound of someone running behind her caused her to stop and look round.

'Ellie. Ellie, thank goodness I caught you.'

'Leonard,' breathed Ellie, her breath forming a cloud in front of her. 'Leonard, what you doing round here?'

'I wanted to see you. I thought I might miss you. Ellie, I'd like you to come to the Christmas Eve dance at the club. Will you?'

Ellie was ecstatic. 'Oh Leonard, do you really mean it?'

He laughed. 'Wouldn't be standing out here in the cold if I didn't, now would I?'

She laughed with joy. He wanted to take her out again. He wasn't ashamed of her.

'I'll pick you up from the tea room when you finish at six. You can get ready at my place. Look, I'm sorry I can't stay, I have to get back. You'll be all right, won't you? Here, take this and get a tram home.' He put a coin in her gloved hand. 'See you on Saturday.' He held her shoulders and pulled her to him, kissed her cheek and was gone.

Ellie stood rooted to the spot. She didn't even feel the cold. She was going to his club on Christmas Eve. She opened her hand. He had given her a shilling, and her fare was only tuppence. He was such a generous man.

She glowed with excitement all the way home, till she suddenly realized her problems. Her mind started racing. What would she wear? She would definitely spend her savings on a new frock now; perhaps Peggy would go shopping with her after work on Friday. But how would she get home if the dance went on till two? She pushed open the front door. She had all week to worry about that.

Chapter 16

'What's the latest fashion?' Ellie casually asked Baby Iris that evening as they sat around the table.

Iris laughed. 'Why? Got yerself a fancy man and you wanner dress up for 'im?'

Ellie laughed with her. 'Chance would be a fine thing.'

'It's short, of course.' Iris's voice took on a different tone, almost as if she was speaking to a customer. 'And for evenings it's these new floaty frocks with handkerchief skirts.'

'What's that when it's out?' asked their mother who was taking an interest in their conversation.

'They go up and down like they've bin made out of handkerchief squares. Gonner see a lot of 'em at Christmas do's.'

'Sounds very nice,' said Ellie.

'They are if you've got somewhere posh to go to.'

'Sounds a right mess if you ask me,' said Mrs Walsh putting her jug of beer on the fender. 'Don't like hems what go up and down.'

'What do they cost?' asked Ellie.

'A few bob, I can tell you, but they're smashing.'

Ellie would have dearly loved to know the price, but she knew she dare not pursue it any longer in case they got suspicious.

'Some of the women who come in look really lovely in 'em.' Iris sat forward. 'We 'ave this really super one, it's different shades of pink floral and all floaty. I'd love it, but where would I wear a thing like that?' She sat back and began fiddling with the faded oilcloth tablecloth, first folding it then straightening it out.

'You couldn't afford it?' asked Ellie, hoping she would be told the price.

'No I know, but at least we get ten per cent off all stock, so that's always useful. If we ever got the chance to go out that is.' Iris looked sullen. 'A lot of the girls are going to a dance on Christmas Eve. They asked me to go with 'em, but I told 'em I couldn't go 'cos of problems at 'ome.'

''Ere, what you bin telling 'em?' asked their mother. 'I 'ope you ain't bin talking about our business.' She filled her mug with beer.

Iris held up her head. 'I told 'em I 'ad to look after me invalid mother. That way they felt sorry for me.'

'You saucy cow.'

'Well I couldn't tell 'em we was on relief and I 'ad to 'and every penny over to you.' She stood up and pushed back her chair aggressively.

''Ere, I 'ope you ain't getting above your station, young lady. Just remember where you comes from.'

'As if I could ever forget.' She left the room and went stomping up the stairs.

'You should 'ave gone into a factory like your sisters,' her mother shouted after her. 'Always knew that job would give 'er high and mighty ideas.'

All the while their father sat silently with his head in his hands.

Ellie felt sorry for Iris. She had certainly grown up since she'd been out to work. Now she knew what it was like to be with other girls who had a few shillings to spend.

Ellie sat at the table and held her breath. Should she go to Iris and let her into her secret? If she did, perhaps Iris could get her a frock with ten per cent off. But would she tell their mother? Should she try and say something later; or perhaps it would be better to wait till Monday and ask Peggy's opinion? Suddenly, a week didn't seem long to work things out.

'What d'you think, Peggy?' asked Ellie on Monday morning after she'd told Peggy that Leonard Kent had seen her and wanted to take her to the club on Christmas Eve. 'Should I ask Iris about a frock?'

'Dunno.'

'Is that it? Is that all you've got to say?'

'What else can I say? You've made up your mind to go with 'im. What about getting 'ome after? You should be more worried about that than a new frock, especially on Christmas Eve.'

Ellie cast her eyes down. 'S'pose I should.'

'What if you can't get 'ome?'

'I'll have to make sure I leave in time, won't I?'

'That's all right then. Ellie, I don't . . .'

'Don't what?'

'It ain't none of my business really, but I don't want to see you get hurt. What if 'e asks you to stay the night?'

'Course 'e won't, he's too much of a gentleman to ask that.'

'Yer, but 'e's also a lot older than you, and a lot wiser, and it could be just a ploy to get you into his bed.'

Ellie laughed. 'You make him sound like one of those wicked villains in the films.' She looked around her, and sidling up to Peggy said fiendishly, 'He rolled his moustache as the heroine cried, "Unhand me at once." '

Peggy laughed. 'Daft 'aporth.'

But what Ellie hadn't told Peggy was that if Leonard did ask her to stay the night she was going to say yes. All weekend she had given it a lot of thought, and had decided she was going to tell her mother she was staying the night with Peggy. 'I'm still going with 'im, so would you come out with me after work and help me choose a new frock?'

'I'd like that. What if we went over Brick Lane? Those Jew boys get some good stuff over there, and cheap. We could go Wednesday straight from work.'

On Wednesday evening Ellie and Peggy made their way to the East End, and Peggy was right, they did have some lovely frocks, and all the latest fashion. Ellie picked out one of the floaty floral handkerchief ones Iris had told her about. She held it against her and asked the owner the price.

He rubbed his chin and smiled. 'To you, my dear, nine and eleven. Should 'ave another three farthings added on, but you'll look so pretty in it I'll just 'ave to forfeit me profits so you can look like a princess.'

Ellie laughed. 'Sorry, I can't afford that.' She placed it back on the rail. 'Let's go, Peg.'

The man stood in the doorway blocking their exit. 'Now then, my love, don't let's be too hasty. What if I say nine bob?'

Peggy piped up. 'Seven.'

The shopkeeper held his head. 'On my life, my wife and kids'll starve. Eight bob and it's yours.'

Ellie looked anxiously at Peggy, who nodded her head. 'But Peg, I ain't got eight shillings,' she whispered.

'Don't worry,' grinned Peggy. 'We'll take it,' she said to the shop owner.

They walked down the road laughing. 'Thanks Peg, I couldn't 'ave done that without you. I'm so excited. Do you like it?'

'It's lovely.'

'Just think, this is me first ever brand new frock. I've never had anythink that didn't smell of mothballs and belong to someone else before.'

Peggy took her arm. 'You deserve something nice, and I only 'ope Mr Kent will appreciate it.'

'He will, I know 'e will. Now I've got to worry about

paying you back and getting some shoes.'

'You can pay me back after Christmas.'

'Thanks. I'll go and see what the pawn shop's got.' She grinned. 'Roll on Saturday.'

Friday night Ellie told her mother that tomorrow she was going round Peggy's straight from work, and staying the night.

'But it's Christmas Eve,' said Iris.

'So,' said Ellie nonchalantly.

'Thought you would 'ave stayed in on Christmas Eve.'

'Why? Ain't nothink 'appening. 'Sides, I'll be staying in all over Christmas, so I don't see what difference one night's gonner make.'

Her mother gave her a funny look, but didn't make any comment.

That night when they were in bed Iris asked, 'Ellie, you gonner see Lizzie and Dolly tomorrow night?'

'No, whatever made you ask that?'

'Dunno. You looked a bit guilty about somethink, and me and Mum thought you was going to see them.'

Ellie was taken aback, she hadn't thought about that. 'What did Mum say?'

'Nothing really. I think she'll wait till you've been, then give you the third degree about 'em. I think in a way she misses 'em.'

Ellie laughed. 'Misses their money, more like it. I only wish I did know where they lived.'

'I was gonner ask you to take me to see 'em. D'you know, I really miss 'em too.'

'I s'pose Mum'll give me another clout even if I say I ain't seen 'em.'

'She ain't hit you for a long while.'

'That's only because I make sure I do as I'm told.'

Ellie was stunned. Iris wanted to see her sisters, and her mother hadn't made a fuss about her staying out all night.

There were a lot of changes going on in this household.

'Are you really gonner stay with Peggy?'

'Course I am. Turn over and go to sleep.'

Ellie lay thinking about tomorrow night. Wouldn't they have a fit if they saw her new frock and the silver shoes she'd got from the pawn shop for a shilling? Peggy was a real good friend, lending her two shillings. What would they say if they knew she was going with a man to his club . . . and staying at his flat all night? But what if he didn't ask her to stay? She smiled, but she knew he would. She wanted to giggle and shout about it out loud. It was all so very exciting.

All day Saturday Ellie was on cloud nine. All the customers were cheerful despite the freezing cold weather.

'Don't like the look of it out there,' said Peggy as they began clearing the tables and folding the tablecloths. ''Ope Mr Kent's not gonner be late.'

'Don't say that, Peggy, I'll go out and kill meself if 'e is,' laughed Ellie. 'Thanks for looking after me frock, and for bringing in the presents your mum made. Do you think Leonard will like his scarf?'

Peggy grinned. 'I should think so. Wonder what 'e's bought you?'

'He might not have bought me nothink. I think you and Mr Jenkins are ever so kind to buy me a brush and comb set. It's lovely. I only wish we had a really nice dressing table to put it on.'

'You will one day.' Peggy quickly looked about her. 'Ellie, I know it ain't none of my business, but you won't leave it too late to get 'ome, will you?'

'Course not.' Ellie laughed. 'You sound just like me mum.' She left it at that. She had it all sorted out. She had told Peggy she was going home, and her mother she was staying with Peggy. But at the back of her mind was the little niggle that Leonard might not ask her to stay; then she'd have to get the underground, and walk home. Ellie smiled, she wasn't going to let that worry her. 'This could be the best Christmas I've ever had,' she said out loud.

'I 'ope so,' said Peggy.

At five minutes to six Leonard Kent pushed open the tea room door. 'I'm not late this time,' he said cheerfully, removing his hat and sitting at a table.

Ellie blushed. His hat had ruffled his hair and he looked younger.

Mr Jenkins came out of the bakery, folding his apron. 'Good evening, Mr Kent,' he said, struggling into the jacket Peggy was holding for him. 'Thank you, my dear,' he said to her and, turning to Leonard, added, 'The weather don't look too good out there.'

'Looks like we're going to have a white Christmas. Have you far to go, Mr Jenkins?' asked Leonard.

'No, not too far. Are you ready, Miss Walsh?'

Ellie nodded.

'Off you go then. Merry Christmas to you both.'

'And to you, Mr Jenkins, and you Peggy,' said Ellie.

Leonard held the door open. 'Merry Christmas both,' he said as they went out into the cold.

Once more Ellie was in Leonard's flat, but this time she didn't feel so self-conscious.

'Would you like a cup of tea?' Leonard asked as soon as they walked in.

'Yes please.' Ellie held her hands out in front of the warming fire.

'Cold?'

'Only me hands.'

He came over and gently rubbed them. She shivered. 'You are cold.'

Ellie didn't like to tell him she was shaking with anticipation. She was worried she was going to make a fool of herself and say or do something silly. 'If you show me where everything is I'll make the tea,' she said, to try and dispel the anxiety of the situation.

'Right, follow me.'

In the tiny kitchenette, as Leonard called it, Ellie was shown where everything was. She was in her element. This was like being in paradise. She was so happy she wanted to cry.

Leonard looked amazed as a tear slowly trickled down her cheek. 'What is it? What's wrong?'

'I'm so happy being here with you,' she sniffed.

He laughed. 'Oh my dear Ellie, you are such a charming child. How can anyone be happy at being in a kitchen?'

The weeks of anticipation and wondering if he would ask her out again had got to her, and she suddenly burst into tears.

'My dear Ellie, please don't cry.' He held her close. 'There, there.' He gently rocked her, and kissed her forehead.

She felt warm and cosy in his arms and her tears subsided.

'Now come on, dry those tears, you can't go out with red eyes. You go along to the bathroom and get yourself ready, I'll make the tea.' He smiled. 'Can't have you crying in the teacups, can we. You'll make the tea salty.'

Ellie smiled. 'I'm sorry.'

'You don't have to be sorry. I'm very touched. You are a lovely, sensitive girl. Don't ever change.' He turned and filled the kettle.

When Ellie returned to the lounge Leonard let out a low whistle. 'You look sensational. That's a very beautiful dress. It goes so well with your new hairdo.'

Ellie twirled round in front of him. 'It is nice, ain't it? I feel ever so grand.'

'It certainly is, and I shall be the envy of the band tonight.'

Ellie smiled. 'I've got you a Christmas present.'

'Oh Ellie, you shouldn't have, you can't earn much, and

you shouldn't waste your money on me.'

Ellie felt a fool. What had she done? Was she being a bit pushy? 'It ain't much,' she said sadly, handing him a small parcel.

'Thank you. I'm sorry, that was very bad-mannered of me. This is so kind of you.'

'It don't matter if you ain't got me one, I don't expect you . . .' She stopped. She was being silly and childish again.

'As a matter of fact I have got you a present, but I won't be giving it to you till tonight, after twelve, on Christmas Day.'

'You'd better open yours now,' she said, trying not to think about what he was going to give her.

'This is lovely,' he said, admiring the scarf. 'Thank you, did you make it?'

She shook her head.

He wrapped the scarf round his throat and admired it in the mirror. 'With this weather closing in, it's just what I'll need. Thank you.' He kissed her cheek. 'Now if you're ready I think we should be off.'

Once again they were climbing the steps to the club. Although still very excited, this time Ellie felt a little more self-assured. She smiled at the doorman when he greeted them. Leonard took her along to the band room, and then into the club.

They moved towards the table she had sat at before, but this time she wasn't going to be alone; there were two other young women sitting there.

'This is Ellie,' said Leonard. 'Sorry, must dash. I'll leave you to do the introductions. I'll see you during the interval.'

'Hallo,' said a dark-haired girl who must have been in her late twenties. 'Sit yourself down.' She carried on talking to the other girl, a blonde who looked older.

When the dark-haired girl had finished talking the blonde

turned to Ellie and said, 'Hallo Ellie. My name's Greta, and this is May. Before you ask, I'm with Harry, who's on drums, and May here is with Barney, he's the vocalist.' She then ignored Ellie and carried on with the conversation she was having with May.

Ellie was in awe. These two looked so beautiful. Greta was wearing a very daring, figure-hugging pink frock that was held up by tiny thin straps. It was covered with fringe, and with every move she made the frock seemed to ripple. Round her head was a silver band that held a tall pink feather at the side.

May's frock was also pink, but not so daring. It was covered with silvery threads and beads that glittered with every turn. She wore a large sparkling clip in her dark hair; very elegant.

Ellie tried hard not to stare. If only she could look like them. If only she had half their confidence. She suddenly felt very young and very insecure.

She looked around. This time the club was decorated for Christmas. A huge tree with bright twinkling lights stood in one corner. Coloured lanterns were strung round the room. A net high up on the ceiling was full of balloons and paper hats. Everything looked so beautiful, and despite her anxieties she was very happy to be here.

'Would you like a drink, miss?'

The waiter who had made Ellie feel inferior before was standing in front of her again. She looked at the glasses in front of Greta and May. What should she ask for?

'Just bring another glass,' said May. She turned to Ellie. 'You might as well have some of our champagne, after all it is on the house.'

'Thank you,' said Ellie as the glass was quickly placed in front of her. May poured her a drink, and she carefully watched Greta pick up her drink and swallow a large quantity. As Ellie brought her glass up, the bubbles tickled her nose and she wanted to laugh. She took a sip and shuddered.

'I know, it's not the best, but it is free,' said Greta.

'Have you known Len long?' asked May.

'A little while,' replied Ellie.

'Haven't seen you in here before. Have you been to the club?'

'Yes, once.'

'Must have been when our boys were playing away,' said Greta. 'Do you work?'

'Yes,' said Ellie. She was being very guarded as she didn't want them to know all her business. 'Do you?'

Greta threw her head back and laughed. 'I should say not, not while I've got old Harry to keep me.'

May held out her left hand; there was a huge diamond ring on the third finger. 'I'm married to Barney, so in a way I work.'

'They must earn very good money in the band,' said Ellie in amazement.

'It does help if they come from the right family,' said Greta, finishing her drink. She reached for the bottle resting in a bucket filled with ice that stood on long spindly legs next to the table. 'Paul,' she shouted. 'This is empty.' She waved the bottle at the waiter.

Paul the waiter soon arrived at the table with another bottle.

Ellie was pleased when the band came onto the stage and began playing, and the questioning had to stop.

Several men asked Greta and May to dance. Everybody knew them, and they seemed to be very popular, laughing and talking loudly. Ellie was dreading anybody asking her to dance, as she didn't know how to, and her shoes were beginning to pinch.

Champagne appeared to be drunk at every opportunity, and Ellie's glass was continually being topped up. The dimly lit club was crowded, and the loud laughter of people enjoying themselves came from all around the room. The music, the noise, the smoke and the drink were having a wonderful effect on Ellie. She was happy and relaxed, and didn't want this evening ever to end.

In the first interval Leonard came and sat with her.

She took hold of his hand and looked up into his blue eyes. 'I'm having such a lovely time. I'll never be able to thank you.'

He smiled. 'You look so happy.' He nodded in the direction of Greta and May, who were talking with Harry and Barney. 'How are you getting on with the girls?'

'All right. Did you know May was married to Barney?'

'Yes.'

'And did you know Greta was living with Harry?' She giggled and put her hand over her mouth.

'I think you've had a little too much champagne, my dear.'

Ellie sat up. 'You're not cross with me, are you?'

He laughed. 'No, of course not. Just you enjoy yourself. Look, I must go, but I'll be back later.' He kissed her cheek and went back to the stage.

Ellie gently touched the spot where his lips had been. She was so happy. She loved him. She knew she loved him.

Ellie listened to the music and watched people dancing. Despite her sore feet she was now longing to have a dance. She stood up to go to the ladies, but had to hold on to the table to steady herself. She wanted to giggle; she had never felt like this before, lightheaded.

She was very surprised when just after she returned the announcer told everyone to get ready; she hadn't realized the time had gone so fast.

He looked at his watch and began to count down: 'Five, four, three, two, one. Merry Christmas everyone!'

The crush on the dance floor was unbelievable as balloons and hats fell from the ceiling. People were blowing hooters and kissing everybody, the band was playing loudly and couples were doing the Charleston. May had told Ellie this was the very latest dance craze, and she should learn how to do it. To Ellie it was magic, she felt she was in fairyland, and didn't want it to end.

After they had played the national anthem, the band left the stage, and gradually couples began to leave. A loud laugh made Ellie look up. She sat back down on her chair almost too frightened to move. Among a group of people swaggering and swaying across the dance floor was Mr Cole. He was wearing a silly paper hat and blowing a hooter, and he had his arm round a young girl who wasn't much older than Ellie. She quickly bent down and pretended to see to her shoes, so she was half hidden under the table. She didn't want him to see her.

'Ellie. Ellie, are you all right?' Greta was leaning over her. 'We're going on to a party at May and Harry's, are you and Len coming with us?'

She slowly straightened up and looked around. 'I don't know.' She could just make out Mr Cole's party going out of the door. 'I don't think so.'

'Well, please yourself. You all right?'

Ellie nodded.

'We'll probably see you here New Year's Eve then. Bye.'

Leonard came over to her. 'Ellie, here's your coat and shoes. Are you ready?'

She nodded, but made no attempt to stand up. She looked around at the mess over the floor. 'I ought to stop behind and help them clear up.'

'What?' laughed Leonard. 'They pay people to do that. Come on, my little Ellie, I think you've had just a bit too much champagne.' He helped her change her shoes and pulled her to her feet.

Outside the cold night air quickly cleared her head. She shuddered. 'Are we going to May and Harry's party?' she asked.

'No, not tonight. They have plenty, so perhaps we'll go to the next one. It's cold out here. Good job I don't live too far away.' He tucked her arm through his and marched her along.

'What time is it?'

'It's one o'clock.'

She giggled. 'I've missed me bus.'

'Everything has stopped. It's Christmas Day. Merry Christmas, Ellie Walsh.' Leonard stopped and, taking her in his arms, kissed her full on the mouth. 'You do want to stay the night, don't you?'

Ellie nodded. Suddenly her dream of staying with him was going to become a reality. At this moment, as thoughts of her mother came into her head, she wasn't quite sure if she was doing the right thing.

Leonard put his arm round her waist and hugged her. 'I'm so pleased,' he said, kissing her again.

All thoughts of her mother disappeared.

Chapter 17

The snow was coming down thick and fast, and lay inches deep. The driving wind was causing it to drift against the walls, making the kerbs disappear. It clung to Ellie's long lashes, and stung her eyes, and she shivered in her thin coat as they battled against the swirling blizzard.

The warmth of Leonard's flat hit them when they walked in.

'Get your wet shoes and stockings off while I make some coffee. I think you'd better have black,' said Leonard glancing over his shoulder as he poked the fire, bringing it to life.

Ellie sat on the sofa watching the flames dance, without making any attempt to take off her coat. She found she was having trouble keeping her eyes open, and in focus.

'I've put the kettle on. Right, let me take your coat.'

Ellie stood up and let Leonard take her coat. He softly kissed the back of her neck. 'You are very lovely.'

She closed her eyes. A warm contented feeling came over her. She had never been told she was lovely before. She fell back down on the sofa.

Leonard bent and removed her shoes. 'My, we are a tired little girl. I'll get the coffee, then you can get to bed.'

Ellie quickly opened her eyes. 'Where will I . . .?'

'In my bed of course,' said Leonard, walking back into the kitchenette.

Suddenly Ellie was wide awake. This is what she had

wanted to happen, but would he . . .? What would happen? Now she was here, was she beginning to have doubts?

Leonard returned and handed her a cup of coffee. 'Ellie,' he said softly. 'That is all right, isn't it? You did want to stay?'

She nodded.

He smiled, and all her doubts disappeared.

'That's good. Did you enjoy yourself tonight?' he asked.

Ellie held the cup with both hands, and gently sipped the hot sweet liquid. 'It was wonderful, even better than the last time.' She suddenly felt wide awake, and grinned. 'And I like champagne.'

'I gathered that. Do you feel better now?' he asked, sitting next to her.

She giggled. 'Yes thank you.'

'Good.'

'Leonard. You knew I wouldn't be going home tonight, didn't you?'

He put his cup on the table. 'I must confess that was at the back of my mind. Do you mind?'

She shook her head.

'You have to be sure about this, Ellie.'

'I am sure,' she whispered.

'You have told your mother you'll be out all night?'

Ellie nodded.

'Ellie, I'm very fond of you, and I was hoping you'd . . .' He quickly stood up. 'I'll give you your Christmas present now.' He went into the bedroom and returned holding a flat box. 'Merry Christmas.' He kissed her cheek. 'I hope you like it.'

Ellie took the box and very carefully undid the fancy string. She gasped and held up a shimmering white nightgown. 'Leonard, it's beautiful,' she said excitedly, and gently ran her hands over the satin. 'It's the most beautiful thing I've ever seen,' she whispered.

'I'm glad you like it.'

Ellie put the nightgown back in its box and covered it with the tissue paper. 'I'm sorry, but I can't accept it.'

'Why? Don't you like it?'

'It's lovely, but . . .'

'I'm sorry. I was stupid.' He ran his hands through his hair. 'I should have realized it's far too personal. Please accept it, Ellie. It would mean such a lot to me.'

Ellie looked down at the box. 'It is very nice.'

Leonard took her hand and kissed it. 'Please, Ellie.'

She tingled when he kissed her hand.

'I know you like pretty things and guessed you wouldn't have one exactly like that.'

'No, no I haven't.' Ellie didn't have the heart to tell him she had never ever owned a nightie. Once again she took it from the box. This time she held it close to her chest and, casting her eyes down, said softly, 'I didn't bring a night-gown with me, so can I wear it tonight?'

'Of course; after all it is Christmas Day. Ellie – you are sure about wanting to stay?'

She nodded and went to pick up the coffee cups. Leonard took her hand. 'Leave those, I'll see to them.'

Ellie nervously picked up her nightie and made her way to the bathroom.

She closed the door and stood still. She was going to sleep in his bed, with him. Everything that happened in the tales she'd heard from her sisters and other girls was really going to happen to her, tonight. She was a little apprehensive. He was a lot older than her, and must be very experienced, but he had told her he was very fond of her. She knew she could love him, and she mustn't be silly and childish. She smiled and held the lovely nightgown to her cheek. 'I'll be a woman in every sense after tonight,' she said to her reflection in the mirror.

Ellie took off her clothes, carefully folding her new frock and placing it on the chair before slipping the nightie over her head. Two brand new things in one day. Had she died and gone to heaven? She ran her hands down her thighs, over the smooth satin. It felt like nothing she had ever known. Ellie touched her hair and gave a little giggle. She'd better take her vest off; the white satin made it look very grey. She could hardly believe she was going to be so daring as to go to bed without wearing a vest, but it didn't look quite right underneath her lovely nightie. She walked round the small room. She felt like a queen with a long flowing frock. She was so happy and knew that this was what she wanted.

'I'm so sorry, Ellie,' panted Leonard, falling back on the pillow. 'I didn't realize I was the first.'

Ellie quickly turned her head.

Leonard took her head in his hands, turning her to face him. 'Ellie I'm sorry, did I hurt you?'

She bit her lip to stop the tears.

'I'm so sorry, my dear.' He buried his head in her neck. 'I wouldn't hurt you for the world.'

'It ain't that,' she sniffed. 'It's because . . . It's 'cos you thought I'd done it before. I ain't that sorta girl.' She was upset, and all the careful attention she had given to trying to talk properly, went.

Leonard gathered her up in his arms. 'Oh Ellie. Oh Ellie,' he moaned. 'I don't think that of you. It's just, it was a surprise.' He propped himself up on his elbow. 'You didn't mind, did you?'

She shook her head and smiled weakly. 'I'm glad it was you.'

'So am I.'

Ellie lay on her back and began reflecting on all that had happened earlier.

She had been marvelling at the well decorated room and at being in a soft bed with sheets and pillowcases when Leonard had come into the bedroom. She slid further under the clothes, too scared to look at him. She knew what he was going to do, and at first had been frightened. But when Leonard had put his arms round her and held her close and kissed her mouth long and passionately, she'd wanted to scream out with pleasure. When he'd slipped the lovely nightie from her shoulders and gently moved his soft hands over her body, she'd wanted to die. She didn't mind the pain, she desperately wanted him to love her.

Leonard now also lay on his back. He eased his arm round her shoulders and she snuggled against him.

He was a wonderful, gentle and kind man and she was so lucky to be here with him. She felt grown up at last. Would Terry have been so kind? With him it probably would have been a quick fumble in the park. She was surprised that Terry Andrews had suddenly come into her thoughts. Would Terry want her now . . .? She squeezed her eyes shut to stem the tears of happiness that were ready to fall. At this moment Elmleigh Square was a lifetime away.

'Good morning, my dear.' Leonard Kent was standing at the bottom of the bed holding a tray. 'I trust you slept well?'

Ellie made to sit up. She quickly put her hand to her head and lay back down again. 'Me head's killing me,' she groaned.

Leonard laughed. 'It's what they call a hangover. You had just a little too much champagne last night.'

Very slowly Ellie lifted her head and sat up. She suddenly realized she was naked and quickly grabbed a sheet to cover her bare breasts. Her face turned scarlet; nobody had seen her bare body before. 'I've only ever tasted beer before. What time is it?'

'It's ten o'clock.'

'Ten. Christ, I've gotter get 'ome.'

'But I thought you were going to stay.' Leonard looked puzzled.

'Only the night, not all Christmas Day.'

'But I've got a chicken and . . .'

'I'm sorry, but I gotter go.' Ellie was wondering how she was going to get out of bed and into her clothes, which were at the other side of the room.

'And how do you intend to do that? Remember it's Christmas Day and there aren't any trains or trams, and it's thick snow out there.'

Ellie lay back down again. 'I didn't think about that. What am I going to do? Me mum'll kill me.'

Leonard sat on the bed. 'Ellie, I thought you said your mother knew you weren't going home last night?' His face was full of concern.

Ellie nodded. 'Yes, but she thought I was going to stay with Peggy from work, and I'd be able to walk home from there.' She chewed her lip with anxiety.

'Please don't upset yourself. I didn't think . . . I'm so sorry. I thought you would have told her.'

Ellie half smiled. 'You don't know me mum.'

'Well, we'll have to find some way of getting you home. Get dressed while I go upstairs.'

Ellie heard the front door close, and quickly jumped out of bed and got into her day clothes. She took a great deal of care not to crumple her new frock, or her lovely nightgown, as she placed them in her paper bag.

After taking the tray into the kitchen and washing up she sat in the lounge waiting for Leonard to return.

What if she couldn't get home? It was a long way to walk, and the snow was very thick. Ellie was worried. She remembered last year and the rows with Dolly, and knew what she would have to face when she got home. Would her mother have her put away? She felt very down. Why had she been so stupid? But she knew why. It was because she wanted some excitement in her life. Well, now she would have to face the consequences.

'I'm sorry, Ellie,' said Leonard. 'I was hoping Mr Brown who lives upstairs might be able to help us out; he has a car. Unfortunately he's at his sisters', out Essex way.'

'What am I gonner do?' Ellie's eyes filled with tears.

'I'm afraid there's nothing we can do.'

'Can we walk?'

'Ellie, it's miles away, and in this weather. No, I'm sorry, but that's impossible.'

Ellie sat on the sofa. 'Me mum'll kill me. I'm ever so afraid.' Ellie let her tears fall.

'Oh Ellie. I should have told you about the buses, but I thought you were going to stay.' Leonard sat beside her and put his arms round her. 'I never realized this would cause you so much pain. I'm so selfish.' He gently rocked her.

'No you ain't. It's my fault as well. I should have gone home last night.'

'Does your mother know about me?'

Ellie sniffed and wiped her nose on the handkerchief Leonard offered. She shook her head. 'She'd have a fit if she knew.'

'We'll have to try and think of something,' said Leonard patting her hand.

A slight smile suddenly lifted the corners of Ellie's sad mouth. 'I could always tell her I went to see me sisters and couldn't get home. I'll still get a clout, but it won't be as bad as telling her I stayed out all night with a man.'

Leonard looked shocked. 'Your mother hits you?'

'Not quite so much now. As I've got older I've learnt to keep me mouth shut.'

'Your mother hits you,' he repeated. 'Ellie, what can I say?'

'Don't worry about it. In fact, I quite like the idea of being here all day with you. We don't have much of a Christmas at home.'

'My dear, dear Ellie, I mean about your mother hitting you.'

'As I said. Don't worry about it.'

'Doesn't your father stop her?'

Ellie laughed. 'You don't know me dad.'

'I've so much to learn about you, and as we are going to be here all day I think I'll get us something to eat now, and you can tell me all about yourself. That's of course if you want to?'

'There ain't much to tell really.'

'I expect there is.'

Ellie stood in the doorway of the kitchenette watching him prepare a meal. She looked surprised. 'Was you gonner be all on your own at Christmas?'

'Yes, but I was hoping you would be here. Now I'm going to have a wonderful Christmas.'

'Was you gonner eat all that on your own?' Her big brown eyes were wide open with amazement.

He licked his fingers. 'Yes, if you hadn't been here to share it with me. It's only a small chicken.'

Ellie laughed. 'I ain't ever tasted chicken.'

He came over and put his arms around her. 'We'll pull the wishbone together.'

'This is gonner be the best Christmas I've ever had.'

'Sorry we haven't got a tree, but I have a bottle of port, and we can sit and talk to our hearts' content.'

Ellie smiled. Her heart was so full of love for this man she just wanted to stay with him, and not worry about tomorrow, or what pain it might bring.

All afternoon they sat and talked. Ellie told him about where she lived, her sisters and her parents. Leonard was enchanted, just asking enough questions to clarify any of her stories he couldn't quite believe, such as the socks incident.

'And I love me job,' Ellie went on. 'Mr Jenkins and Peggy have been ever so kind.'

'Everybody should be kind to you.'

She laughed. 'Why? I ain't nothink special.'

'Oh but you are.'

'What about you. 'Ave you got any secrets?'

'Not really. Let me see. I'm thirty-eight, a bachelor, a

music teacher, and I play in a dance band. There you have it in a nutshell.'

'What about your mum and dad? You must 'ave a mum and dad somewhere, and what about brothers and sisters?'

'My parents lived in Germany, and as you know we were at war with them.'

'Germany. That's a long way away. I ain't even been to the seaside.'

He laughed. 'I'll have to take you one day.'

'That'd be nice. I'd like that.' But Ellie was still intrigued about his parents and asked, 'Do your mum and dad live over here now?'

He took a cigarette from the packet on the table and lit it. 'No, and I haven't heard from them since the war.'

'Was you in the war?'

'Seems I was unfit.' He tapped the end of his cigarette into the ashtray. 'Another cup of tea?'

Ellie shook her head. 'No thanks. Did you ever live in Germany?'

'Yes, many years ago.'

'Ain't you ever wanted to go back and find out about your mum and dad?'

'Many times. But something has always prevented me.'

'Ain't you worried about them?'

'Yes.'

'Do you write to them?'

'Since the war my letters have been returned.' He took a long drag on his cigarette. 'Perhaps one day I'll go back.'

Ellie could see this was a painful subject. 'What about a wife? Have you got one hidden away somewhere?' she asked softly, almost dreading the answer.

He laughed. 'No. Not even a girlfriend – unless you'd like to be my girlfriend.'

Ellie giggled with relief. 'Why did you ask me out?'

'You are beautiful and so refreshingly different from all the young women I meet. They are either silly schoolgirls, most of whom haven't any idea about music, or girls like Greta and May who are only after what they can get from any man.'

Ellie sat back. 'Do you earn a lot in a band?'

'My, you are full of questions.'

'I'm sorry, I didn't mean to be nosy, but everything is so different to what I know, and seeing how nice Greta and May looked, I thought they must have a lot of money.'

He laughed. 'Both Harry and Barney have parents who are comfortable; they're with the band for something to do, and of course because they love music.'

'You love music, don't you?'

'Yes. Yes I do.' He sat back and looked relaxed.

'Play somethink for me.'

'OK.' He smiled and sat at the piano. Very softly he began playing 'Silent Night'.

Ellie sat entranced as she watched his long tapering fingers delicately run over the keys. She was being carried away on a sea of joy. Nothing was going to break this wonderful spell.

That evening, after the delicious chicken dinner, they laughed and talked. Leonard played the piano and she leant over his shoulder and sang along with him from the sheet music. In the evening they sat on the floor in front of the roaring fire watching the flames cast interesting shadows around the room. They toasted each other with the port. It was the best Christmas Ellie could imagine, and she wished it could last for ever.

Leonard kissed her long and hard. 'Time for bed. Remember, we've got to get you back home tomorrow.'

Ellie held on to him. 'I don't want tomorrow to come. I don't want to go back to Rotherhithe,' she whispered.

'You must. Your mother will wonder what's happened to you.'

Ellie sat back. Why did he have to go and spoil it? Why

did he have to mention home?

He held her close. 'Come on, my darling, don't look so sad. Let's make the most of our time together.'

She smiled.

'Off you go.'

Once more Ellie eagerly slipped on her nightie. She settled down between the sheets. She knew what was in store for her this time, and she was going to enjoy every minute of it, and let all thoughts of tomorrow, her mother, and the consequences, disappear.

Chapter 18

Ellie lay very still, reluctant to break the spell. Leonard, with his arm round her, was softly breathing. She didn't want this moment to end.

What a lot she had to tell Peggy; not the details of what she and Leonard had done, but about the club and what a wonderful time she had had. She would tell her what the women wore, and about the balloons and champagne, and seeing Mr Cole there again. Her thoughts suddenly went back to what would be in store for her today. It didn't matter how many times her mother hit her, nothing could take yesterday away from her. She snuggled against Leonard, causing him to stir. She didn't want to leave him. She didn't want to return to her life in Elmleigh. A tear slowly trickled from her eye into her ear. Leonard turned over.

'You're awake.' His voice was thick with sleep.

Ellie quickly brushed the tear away. '*I'll* make *you* tea this morning.' She grabbed her nightie and jumped out of bed.

She stood shivering in the tiny kitchenette watching the blue flame from the gas ring dance around the kettle. She was terrified at the thought of going home.

'You look frozen. Put the tray on the bedside table and come back to bed,' said Leonard as she entered the bedroom. He sat up and pulled back the bedclothes for her. 'You are cold,' he said, putting his arms round her and cuddling her close.

She nestled against his bare chest. He had a strong, firm body.

'Leonard, I don't have to go to work today, so would you mind very much if I stayed here, just for today?' She didn't look at him.

'But what about your mother? Won't she be worried about you?'

'Don't know. Shouldn't think so.'

'If you don't face her today you will have to tomorrow. You can't put it off for ever.'

Ellie made a move to get out of bed.

'Where are you going?'

'To get dressed.'

'But Ellie . . .'

'If you don't want me to stay, I'd better be off then.' She almost fell off the bed in her eagerness to get away from him.

'Come back here. I didn't say that.'

'You didn't have to.' She was upset and angry. He hadn't asked her to stay. He didn't ask her to move in with him. If he was that fond of her he wouldn't want to see her after her mother had finished with her. He was spoiling what had been the most wonderful time of her life, a dream come true. Now it seemed he couldn't get rid of her quick enough. Perhaps he had someone coming and he didn't want . . . She knew she was being silly and unreasonable but it didn't stop her saying under her breath as she stormed off into the lounge, 'I thought you was s'posed to be upset when you knew me mum hit me.'

Leonard Kent was right behind her. He grabbed her arm.

'Stop it, you're hurting me,' she cried.

He quickly let go. 'Oh Ellie, my dear, dear Ellie. I wouldn't hurt you for the world.' He held her close. 'Of course I don't want you to go.' He kissed her mouth.

She responded.

'Come back to bed,' he whispered.

She took his hand. She couldn't say no to him, not now.

★ ★ ★

All day they laughed, sang and talked about almost every subject. She wanted to know more about him when he was a child, but he told her he didn't want to talk about that.

She laughed. 'Have you got a dark secret then?'

'No, of course not, it's just not very interesting, that's all.'

She couldn't believe that; everything about him was interesting. But then she supposed she didn't want to talk about her life, either, determined as she was not to let any thoughts of her mother spoil their day.

That night Ellie lay quietly beside him. She was blissfully happy, but knew this had to end. She didn't want tomorrow to come. Her life would never be the same now.

This is what she wanted, wasn't it, to live here? All day she had been waiting for Leonard to say something about her moving in with him, but nothing had been mentioned. They came from such different backgrounds, and he was a lot older than her. That didn't matter to her, she loved him and wanted to be with him, but did it worry him? Did he see her as a child? She certainly wasn't a child when they made love, though she was still under twenty-one and could be made to go back home. Tomorrow she would go straight to work, she decided. She would put off seeing her mother for as long as possible. She shuddered at the thought. Leonard's arms pulled her close. Yes, this was where she wanted to be, this was where she felt safe.

The snow was still lying in thick drifts, and the wind made it difficult to walk. Ellie pulled her scarf tighter at her throat. 'Bet you're glad you've got a new scarf,' she said as they struggled along.

'It's lovely and warm. Ellie, I wish you would let me take you home,' he said hanging on to her arm.

'I'll be all right, honest.'

'But what about tonight? Let me meet you from the tea

room and come home with you. At least let me try to explain to your mother.'

Ellie laughed. 'I don't think that's such a good idea. No, I'll tell her I was at Lizzie's. I'll tell her she lives over the water; she can see I couldn't get home with no buses and all this snow. Besides, she can't kill me.' But Ellie knew she could finish up very close to dead if her mother discovered she'd been with a man. 'Let's hope the underground's running.'

As they trudged on, Ellie couldn't help feeling confused. Although Leonard wanted to take her home to explain to her mother, he'd also said she should take her nightie with her. Did this mean she wouldn't be invited to his flat again? Did he want to see her again?

But at the station he kissed her lovingly, dispelling most, if not all, of her fears.

'Did you 'ave a nice Christmas?' asked Peggy as soon as Ellie walked in. Without waiting for an answer she went on, 'Bloody awful weather, ain't it, shouldn't think anybody will come out today, not if they've got any sense that is. What was the thingy like, you know, the club? What did 'e give you for Christmas?'

Ellie took her hat and coat off. 'I've got such a lot to tell you,' she said enthusiastically, looking anxiously at the bakery door.

'Grab a cloth,' said Peggy, 'and we'll pretend to be seeing to the tables, that way we can chat at the same time.'

As they dusted and polished Ellie went into great detail about the club, how lovely it looked; then she went on about Greta and May and what they were wearing.

'What did your frock look like?'

'Smashing. Oh Peg, I was ever so proud. And I drank champagne.'

'No!' said Peggy. 'You're really living it up with the nobs now then. What was it like?'

'Fizzy, quite nice really.'

Peggy was amazed. 'Did you get drunk?'

'No, course not. And guess what, Mr Cole was there again.'

'No. Who with?'

'Some young girl, don't think it was his wife.'

'No, she's quite old. He's a dirty old bugger. Did he see you?'

'No,' Ellie laughed. 'I dodged down under the table.'

'He must be a member of that club. You wanner watch out he don't take a fancy to you.'

'He probably wouldn't know who I was even if he did see me. Well, not without me uniform on anyway.'

'No, pr'aps not. I'm glad you had a nice time. How did you manage to get 'ome?'

Ellie looked down and continued to polish the salt pot. She knew she had to tell Peggy the truth. 'I didn't go home,' she said softly.

'What?' exploded Peggy.

'Shh. You'll 'ave Mr Jenkins out.'

'But where . . .? You didn't stay at 'is place, did you?'

Ellie nodded.

Peggy straightened up. 'No. I don't believe it. You stayed at 'is place, all night?' She looked towards the bakery door. 'I 'ope it wasn't in his bed?'

Ellie didn't answer.

'Was it in 'is bed? With him?' she whispered.

Again Ellie only nodded.

Peggy sat on a chair. 'Did 'e . . .? You know, 'ave his wicked way?'

'Yes,' came the faint reply. 'You won't tell your mum, will you?'

'Well I'll be . . .' Peggy began to laugh. 'No, I won't tell me mum. Did you mind, or was you too drunk to know about it?'

'I told you, I wasn't drunk.'

'What did your mum 'ave to say about it when you got

'ome yesterday? You ain't got no bruises – any that show, that is.'

'I ain't been 'ome yet.'

'What?' exploded Peggy again. 'You ain't been 'ome since before Christmas? What you gonner tell 'er when you do get 'ome?'

'I was gonner say I went to see Lizzie, and couldn't get home 'cos of the snow.'

'D'you think she'll believe you?'

'I don't know.'

Peggy stood up. 'Well I wouldn't like to be in your shoes tonight.'

'Can't say I'm looking forward to it. Can I leave me new frock and silver shoes here?'

'Course.'

'And me Christmas present?'

'Yer. You didn't tell me what he bought you.'

'I'll show you.' Ellie took the lovely nightdress from the paper bag.

'Bloody hell. That's really smashing. No wonder you jumped into his bed after him buying you something like that. Did you wear it?'

Ellie nodded and quickly put it back in the bag.

'Ellie, when you seeing 'im again?'

'I don't know. We didn't make any arrangements.'

'Look, I know it ain't any of my business, but—'

The bakery door opened and they quickly made themselves look busy.

'I haven't made too many cakes and things this morning, as I don't expect many customers. You all right, Miss Walsh? Did you have a nice Christmas?'

'Yes thank you, Mr Jenkins.'

'Good.' He gave Peggy a beaming smile as he disappeared back into the bakery.

'Did you have a nice Christmas?' Ellie asked Peggy, eager to change the subject.

'Yes.'

'Did you see Mr Jenkins at all?'

'He spent most of the time with us.'

Ellie laughed. 'He really is getting his feet under the table then?'

'Yes, 'e is,' said Peggy.

'You don't sound too pleased about it.'

'Well, it does create problems.'

'In what way?'

Peggy looked sheepish. 'Ellie, what was it like? You know, with Mr Kent?'

Ellie felt embarrassed. She didn't want to answer. 'Well it's all right. Can't really say.' She didn't want to tell Peggy it was the most wonderful feeling in the world being in the arms of the man you love, letting him kiss you and make love to you. Instead she asked, 'Here, you're not worried about, you know? Doing it with Mr Jenkins, are you?'

'No, course not. Here, what if you end up up the spout? Will he marry you?'

'Don't know. But he makes sure it's all right.'

'Well, I wouldn't even think of it till we was married.'

Ellie's mouth fell open. 'You gonner marry 'im?'

'Don't know.'

'Has he asked you?'

'Course not.' Peggy was blushing.

Ellie laughed. 'He has, ain't 'e?' She was pleased she was now no longer the main topic of their conversation. 'When did 'e ask you?'

''E didn't really ask outright. Mum said she thought 'e was asking in a roundabout way. For a long while now 'e's been talking about how 'e would like to open a tea shop in the country. And over Christmas 'e asked me what I thought about it. I told 'im to be careful. If Mr Cole ever found out, 'e'd be out on 'is ear.'

It was Ellie's turn to sit down. She was stunned. 'You mean you might leave here?'

'Na. It's all talk. 'Sides, where would 'e get the money from to buy a tea shop? And I told 'im I wouldn't move anywhere without me mum.'

Ellie looked thoughtful. Was this what they were worried about all those weeks back when Mr Cole came in? 'What does your mum say about all this?'

'She reckons she'll not move till she's carried out in her box.'

'So you've been talking about this for a long while then?'

Peggy laughed. 'Well, a little while, but it's only pipe dreams and it don't hurt to have dreams, now does it?'

Ellie shook her head. 'No.' She knew all about having dreams. 'I hope you don't go away. I might lose me job if you do.'

'Don't talk daft. I told you, we ain't going nowhere.'

Ellie didn't think she sounded very convincing.

'Now about this Mr Kent.'

'Why don't you call him Leonard?'

'Oh I couldn't, he's a customer.'

'Don't be daft, Peg.'

'Well, all right then. Anyway, what about him? Did you find out much about him? Is he married?'

'No. Besides he wouldn't tell me if he was, now would he?'

Peggy shook her head. 'No, s'pose not. But does his flat look like a woman lives there?'

Ellie sighed. She was getting fed up with all these questions. 'He has a woman who comes in a couple of times a week to clean for him. Satisfied?'

'Don't get on your high horse with me. I only asked.'

'Sorry. All I know is that he told me he wasn't married and his parents live in Germany—'

'What? They must be old,' interrupted Peggy.

'I think they're dead.'

'Oh,' said Peggy. 'And he's a German? Don't let Mr Jenkins hear about that, he can't stand the Germans, not after being in the war.'

Ellie laughed. 'He ain't German. 'Sides, he said he wasn't fit to fight in the war.'

'On whose side?'

'Oh Peg, you do keep on.'

'Well I worry about you.'

'Thanks, it's nice to know somebody does.'

'Well anyway, when you seeing 'im again?'

'I told you, I don't know, we didn't make any plans.'

'I would 'ave thought that after 'im 'aving—' She suddenly stopped. 'Sorry Ellie. I shouldn't 'ave said that. Does 'e want to see you again?'

'Don't know, but he did say he liked me.' Ellie looked a little sad.

'Don't worry about it. I reckon we'll 'ave 'im poking 'is head round the door one afternoon. 'Ere, what about New Year's Eve? You going to 'is club then?'

'Dunno. I've got to get tonight over first.'

'Oh yer, I forgot.'

As the day wore on Ellie got more and more nervous over what was in store for her when she got home.

'Good luck,' said Peggy as Ellie left.

Ellie smiled. She was going to need more than good luck.

Outside Ellie eagerly looked for Leonard. Although she had told him not to come, she was dearly hoping he would be there to take her home, to give her some kind of support. As she trudged home, walking through the snow and the slush seemed to be proving difficult; or was that because she dreaded what would happen when she reached her journey's end?

Chapter 19

Ellie took a deep breath before pushing the front door open. The thought of Dolly lying on the floor in the passage a year ago quickly filled her mind. She smiled bravely. Whatever the outcome, her two days with Leonard had been more than worth it.

Baby Iris's head shot up, her eyes filled with fear, as Ellie walked purposely into the kitchen. Her father was slumped in his chair and seemed thinner and more drawn than ever. He looked up and was about to speak but Ellie beat him to it.

''Allo Dad,' she said breezily to hide her feelings; inside she was quaking.

'Where yer bin?' he asked.

Ellie slowly took her hat and coat off. 'Where's Mum?' she asked casually.

'In the lav,' said Iris, her eyes wide and staring. 'I wouldn't like to be in your shoes.'

'Ellie, I asked you a question. Where yer bin?' asked her father again.

'At work.'

'I mean over Christmas.'

'Why? Didn't think you was that worried about me, or interested in where I've been.' She was trying very hard to put on a confident face.

Suddenly the scullery door flew open. Ruby Walsh filled the doorway. Ellie stood, fixed to the spot, although she dearly wanted to run away.

'So yer back then?' Her face was gradually turning scarlet with anger. 'Thought I heard your voice.' Her mother came slowly towards her. 'You've got a bloody cheek to come waltzing yer arse in 'ere like nothink's 'appened.'

Ellie heard Baby Iris quickly take in her breath, as she braced herself for the first blow.

'Well, come on, out with it. Where yer been? I know you ain't just been round to that Peggy's. Yer know you spoilt our Christmas, don't yer, you selfish cow.'

Ellie crossed her fingers behind her back. She wanted to laugh and ask what sort of Christmas they ever had that she could have spoiled, but instead she took a deep breath. 'Been to see Lizzie,' she said softly. 'And I couldn't get back 'cos of the snow.'

Ruby Walsh, her hands resting on her wide hips, stood in front of Ellie. They were the same height and their faces were very close. Ellie could feel her mother's hot breath on her face, and see the fury mounting in her mother's darting eyes.

'I knew it. I bloody well knew it.' She turned to Ned. 'Told yer all along she knew where those cows lived, didn't I?' She turned back to Ellie. 'You've kept very quiet about it. Well, where d'they live?'

'Over the water.' Ellie knew it was her speaking but the voice sounded far away.

'I asked you where they lived.' The vein on Ruby Walsh's neck stood out as her temper rose.

'Tell her!' screamed Iris. 'For Gawd's sake tell her!'

Ellie moved back to face Iris. 'Lizzie's married, and they don't want to see you, or come back to this—'

The first blow caught Ellie on the side of the head. She quickly held on to the table to regain her balance. She looked at her mother, whose eyes were blazing with anger.

'When I ask you a question I expect a proper answer,' she shrieked. 'Now, give me 'er address.'

Tears began to fill Ellie's eyes. 'No, I won't. She don't

want to see you.' Ellie put her hands above her head to try to stem the blows that quickly fell.

Ellie could hear Iris shouting, 'Don't, Mum, no, don't,' as she fell against the table.

'I'll get an answer, yer cow, even if I 'ave ter beat it out o' yer,' yelled her mother.

The blows continued to fall. Pain filled her head, and a warm sticky liquid, which she knew must be blood, trickled down the side of her face.

More punches, and she was falling to the floor. She could hear screaming, but was it her? Something hit her ribs and filled her with excruciating pain. She tried to think of Leonard. She should have let him come with her, he wouldn't have allowed this to happen. Was that her father's voice, was he trying to stop her mother? She could hear yelling and shouting. Who was it? Was it her? There was a loud crash, then silence, and Ellie drifted away.

Ellie tried to open her eyes. She could hear voices; was one of them her mother's? She sounded calm. Ellie couldn't see. What had happened? Panic filled her. Why did she hurt so much? Where was she? Suddenly a small chink of light filtered through her half-open eyes. She was in the kitchen, lying on the floor. She moaned, as all that had happened flashed through her mind.

'Ellie. Ellie. It's me, Iris.'

Ellie felt a soft hand on her cheek.

'Ellie, can you hear me?' Iris's tears fell wet and warm onto Ellie's face.

Ellie tried to move her head.

'Just lay still. I'll see to you in a minute.'

Ellie could hear more voices, but couldn't see what was happening. 'Iris,' she tried to call, but only a gurgling sound left her lips. She tried to lever herself up, but pain made her fall back again. Noises and blackness filled her head. What was happening to her? She was floating, being lifted high in the air and carried away.

★ ★ ★

Ellie lay very still, too frightened to move. Her head was throbbing, her eyes felt large and puffy, her mouth swollen. Very slowly, and with a lot of concentration, she managed to open her eyes. Where was she? She could only move her eyes and everywhere was white. Was she dead? If so, why did she hurt so much?

A lady wearing a spotless white overall and a large white hat leaned over her. 'I see you're awake now. How are you feeling?' She gave Ellie a warm smile.

'I . . . I don't know. Where am I?'

'In St Olaf's Hospital.'

'Hospital? How? But . . .' Ellie tried to move.

'Just lie still.' The lady gently patted her shoulder. Ellie could feel her smoothing down the bedclothes. 'I expect your sister will be in this evening. You should be feeling a little better by then.'

Ellie made to speak but the lady glided away.

Gradually as Ellie took in her surroundings she began to remember what had happened. But how did she get to hospital? And just how badly injured was she? What about her mother? She wouldn't pay for her to stay in hospital. Why was she so wicked? She had to get away from her. Slowly and very carefully she ran her hands over her face. It felt unnatural, puffy and tender. Her lips were swollen and sore, her throbbing head was bandaged. Her whole body ached and felt limp. She would never go back home again.

All day she drifted in and out of sleep. She was aware of other people in the ward as she was fed, washed and generally made comfortable.

It was when people who were wrapped up against the cold began drifting in that Ellie guessed it was visiting time, and wanted to cry when she saw Iris walking towards her bed.

Iris kissed her cheek. 'How d'yer feel?'

'Iris, what happened? How did I finish up here?'

Iris sat on the chair at the side of her bed and took a handkerchief from her handbag. 'Ellie.' Tears ran down her cheeks. 'Oh Ellie it was awful. If only you'd told Mum . . .' She blew her nose. 'Ellie, I don't know . . . There ain't no easy way . . .'

'Please, Iris,' said Ellie, struggling further up the pillows, 'just tell me what happened. And who brought me here to the hospital.'

'The police.'

'What?' The sudden movement made Ellie fall back into the pillow; her head was pounding. 'The police,' she whispered. 'But . . . how . . .?'

Iris took hold of her sister's hand. 'Ellie, I don't know how to say this, it ain't easy.'

Ellie looked at the baby of the family, and could see her eyes were red and swollen with tears, her face full of worry.

'Ellie. Dad's dead.'

Ellie thought her head was going to explode. It was suddenly full of questions. How? Why? When? Her dad was dead. It must have been her fault. She was dimly aware that the shock was making her groan out loud.

Ellie could hear Iris sobbing. It sounded a long way off. Someone was gently wiping her brow. 'There, there, my dear. It's a great shock. Would you like a cup of tea, Miss Walsh?' asked the lady in white.

Ellie opened her eyes. Screens had been put round her bed. Iris had tears streaming down her face.

'I'm sorry Ellie. I didn't know how to tell you.'

Ellie stared at her and asked quietly, 'What happened?'

'It was Mum.' Iris blew her nose. 'When she started hitting you. It was like she went into some sort of frenzy, like a mad woman. Her eyes were blazing, Ellie, it was awful. Me and Dad tried to pull her off you.' Iris dabbed at her eyes. 'She seemed to have a lot of strength. You fell to the floor, your face and head was bleeding. When Mum started kicking you, Dad went to get between you and

Mum, and she . . .' Iris had to stop again to wipe her eyes. She gave a deep sob and twisted her soggy handkerchief round and round her fingers. 'Mum pushed him out of the way, and he hit his head on the fender. The doctor said it killed him outright.'

Ellie's eyes were wide open now. She swallowed hard. This was too much to take in. Her dad was dead. 'Mum killed Dad? Our mum killed our dad,' she whispered. Her head was going round and round. She closed her eyes and gripped the sheets. This was just a nightmare, she would wake up soon, she must. When Ellie opened her eyes, Iris was still crying into her wet handkerchief.

'What happened then?' whispered Ellie, knowing it wasn't a bad dream.

'I didn't know what to do. I just ran from the house screaming. It was like it was all happening to someone else. Dirty Molly must 'ave been sitting in her window because she saw me running round and round the elm tree like a wild thing. She came out and took me back indoors. I didn't want to go in. When we did you were still unconscious and Dad was dead. Mum had sat him back in his chair and she was calmly drinking a cup of tea. She said she'd offered Dad one, but he didn't want it. Ellie, she's really gone barmy this time. Dirty Molly sent a kid to get a policeman. You should 'ave heard Mum screaming and shouting when they took her away and brought you into hospital.'

Ellie was still staring at Iris. 'This is all my fault. If I hadn't stayed away over Christmas this would never 'ave happened, and Dad would still be alive,' she whispered.

'You mustn't blame yourself. I think it was only a matter of time before Mum . . .'

'Where did they take her?'

'I don't know. I ain't 'ad a chance to go to the police station yet to find out. I still 'ave to go to work.'

Ellie began to cry, quietly at first, then as the real horror began to sink in the tears ran down her swollen face in great torrents.

Iris threw her arms round Ellie and wept with her.

The next morning every bone in Ellie's body ached. She had to get home. Poor Iris; she shouldn't be on her own at a time like this. There was so much to do. Slowly she sat up, and very carefully eased her legs over the side of the bed.

'Miss Walsh. Miss Walsh, what are you doing?' A young nurse came swiftly down the ward towards her.

'I've got to go home.'

'You can't go anywhere, not with your injuries,' she said anxiously.

'I ain't broke nothink. I'll be all right.'

'You must stay here.'

'I can't, I've got to go home. Help me out of bed.'

'I'll get Sister.' The nurse quickly moved away.

A tall woman wearing a navy blue long-sleeved frock and a crisp, well-starched white apron that rustled, came striding down the ward, a small white hat perched on her head. Ellie noted that the other patients quickly sat up and straightened their bedclothes. She reached Ellie's bed.

'What's all this nonsense about wanting to leave?'

'I've got to get home. I can't leave me young sister to sort out everything.'

'Don't you have anyone else who can do that?'

'No.' Ellie nervously wound the stiff white sheet round her fingers.

'You are in no fit state to go home. Especially in this terrible weather.'

'But I must, please let me go.' Tears began to fill Ellie's eyes.

'This isn't a prison, young lady. You can walk out any time you wish. But you don't even have a coat; you do know that of course?'

Ellie felt like screaming at her, how do I know I haven't

got a coat, I was unconscious when I came in here, but decided against it. She sank back on the bed, exhausted. 'I'll wait till me sister comes in tonight, she might bring me coat in with her.'

'Very sensible.' Sister swiftly walked away.

All day Ellie let her mind wander over and over what had happened in such a short time. Her dad was dead and her mother had been put away – and it was all her fault. If only she hadn't stayed with Leonard. If only she had never met him. She was selfish, just as her mother had said. She only thought of herself and having a good time; but that was all over now she had Iris to look after. What about Lizzie and Dolly? They would have to be told. But how? Where were they? Ellie had cried so much she didn't think she had any more tears left, but still they fell, and guilt was beginning to hang very heavily on her shoulders.

'Did you bring me coat in?' asked Ellie as soon as she saw Baby Iris.

'No. Why, you coming home?'

'I can't stay 'ere, we can't afford it.'

'Well you'll 'ave to wait till tomorrow.'

'How you managing?'

'Not bad. The girls at work 'ave been ever so good.'

'What did you tell 'em?' interrupted Ellie.

'I said me dad's died and me mum's in hospital. I didn't tell 'em it was you I was comin' to see.'

'Suppose that's the best thing to say.'

'Miss Jackson said I mustn't worry about 'aving some time off for . . .' She stopped and took her handkerchief from her handbag.

'I thought Miss Jackson was a bit of a tartar.'

'So did I, but she's being really kind. Ellie, I'm worried about the money I'm spending on fares.'

'Ain't you got any?'

'No.'

'Has Mum?'

208

'I don't know.' She blew her nose. 'I don't like to go down Mum's things.'

'You'll have to.' Ellie lay back. 'Iris, I'm ever so sorry. I've made such a mess up of so many lives.' She sobbed.

'It wasn't your fault. Well, yes, I suppose it was in a way. Why didn't you give Mum Lizzie's address?'

Ellie didn't answer.

'If you give it to me I'll write and tell her what's happened. Her and Dolly will surely want to come to Dad's funeral. Fancy her being married. I would 'ave liked to 'ave gone to the wedding. Did she show you any photos? Is Dolly married yet?'

Ellie turned her head away.

The bell rang for the visitors to leave.

'I'll write to them when I get home. You won't forget my coat, will you, and my scarf and gloves?'

Iris stood up. 'No, and I'll find you some clean drawers as well.'

The nurse rang the bell again, this time with more vigour.

Iris kissed Ellie's cheek. 'See you tomorrow.'

Ellie watched her walk down the ward. Iris turned and gave her a little wave.

Ellie put her head back on the pillow. How was she going to tell her she didn't know where Lizzie lived? And what would Iris say when she found out where Ellie had really been? She began to think about Leonard. She couldn't even think of leaving home now; Iris would need her. That was another letter she would have to write. She panicked; she knew where he lived but didn't know his address. Her mind was flitting from one random thought to another, half filled with grief and guilt, while the other half was trying to be practical. What about her mother – she had to find out where she was. Then she had to arrange her father's funeral. What did you do? Who would tell her? Ellie's head was filled with pain and questions. Finally she closed her eyes and let sleep take over.

Chapter 20

'It's ever so good to 'ave you back home,' said Iris.

Ellie hung back apprehensively as she watched her young sister pull the key through the letter box.

Iris, who suddenly appeared very grown up, seemed to sense how she felt. 'Come on,' she said, smiling. 'It's all right.'

'Wasn't you frightened at being here on your own?' asked Ellie as they stepped inside the dark passage.

'A bit, specially that first night.' Iris moved on to the kitchen and lit the gaslight. It popped, making Ellie jump.

'I kept the gas alight all night in our bedroom 'cos I didn't want to sleep in the dark. It's ever so cold and eerie being on your own. Ellie, are we still gonner sleep in one bed?'

'Dunno. I ain't really thought about that.'

'I don't think we should.'

'Why?'

'Well I was really shocked when I was helping you get dressed in the hospital and saw all those bruises on your back. What if I turn over in the night and hurt you?'

'Dunno. Can't say I fancy sleeping in Mum and Dad's bed, though.'

'That was really wicked of Mum to do that to you.'

Ellie shivered. 'It was really wicked of Mum to kill Dad.'

Iris nodded. 'But she didn't mean to, it was an accident.'

For the first time Ellie caught sight of her reflection in the mirror. 'Look at me face,' she cried. 'Why did she do this to me? Why did she hate me so much?' Tears ran down her face.

'Come on now, sit yourself down. It'll get better.' Iris plumped up the cushion on their father's armchair and gently eased Ellie on to the chair.

'Yes, but how long will it take?'

Iris didn't answer that question. 'Keep your coat on for a bit, I ain't 'ad time to light the fire so it's perishing in 'ere. I'll get some wood and get it started.'

Ellie pulled her scarf tighter at her throat and very carefully sat back. The tram journey home had been long, cold and bumpy, and every part of her body hurt. But the physical pain wasn't as bad as what she felt when she looked in the mirror. Would she ever be the same again? Ellie shuddered and looked around. The house seemed strangely quiet, dark and sinister.

'When the fire's alight we'll 'ave a bit of toast,' said Iris, pushing the wood on top of the paper and setting light to it. 'I'll get a bit of coal. The bread's stale, but that don't matter,' she said, bustling in and out of the kitchen.

Ellie was amazed that in just a few short days Iris was suddenly in charge, and had become very domesticated. She sat back and closed her eyes.

'We've got a lot to talk about,' said Iris, sitting at the table.

'I know. We'll wait till after we've had tea.' Ellie wanted Iris's full attention when she told her all about Leonard.

The fire was glowing and the room became warm. Ellie began to relax.

'More tea?' asked Iris.

Ellie shook her head. 'I've got such a lot to tell you, and I'm afraid you might hate me afterwards.'

'But why . . .?'

'Don't stop me. First of all we've got to find out where Mum is.'

'I can't do that, I'm at work.'

'I know. I can't go to work looking like this, so I'll go

along to see Mr Jenkins and explain to him what happened. He is very kind and with a bit of luck he might keep me job open; we ain't very busy at this time of year.'

'God, I hope so. I dunno how we're gonner manage the rent on our wages.'

'Mum did.'

'I know, but she was also on relief. We can't go on relief, we're both working. And what about food?'

Ellie could feel herself growing agitated again. 'Let's get one problem over at a time.'

'Don't you start getting rattled with me, it's your fault all this happened,' Iris said angrily. Tears sprang to her eyes. 'If you'd given Mum Lizzie's address when she asked for it, none of this would 'ave happened. You'd better write to her as soon as we know where Dad's gonner be buried. You know it'll 'ave to be a pauper's grave, we can't afford a proper funeral.'

'I'll go along to the police station tomorrow and find out what we've got to do.' Ellie was trying to stay calm.

'Lizzie and Dolly might help us.'

'Iris, I don't know where Lizzie lives.'

Iris didn't speak. Her eyes were wide open and she sat staring at Ellie. It was probably only for a few seconds, but to Ellie it seemed a lifetime.

'What did you say?' It was very slow and deliberate.

'I said I—'

'I heard you. You don't know where Lizzie lives,' she whispered. 'So where were you over Christmas? Was you round Peggy's? It ain't that far away, so why didn't you come home?'

'If you give me a chance to explain.'

'*Explain?* Dad's dead, and Mum's been locked up, and you want a chance to explain!' Iris was screaming at Ellie.

'Please Iris, listen.'

Her sister banged the table with her clenched fist. 'I dunno how you can sit there so bloody calm. Mum was right, you are a selfish cow.' Iris put her head on her hands and wept.

'Please, Iris, let me explain.'

Iris looked up, her eyes full of hate. 'Dad's dead, and Mum's been locked away somewhere, and you sit there trying to explain why you stayed round Peggy's all over Christmas,' she repeated hysterically.

'I wasn't—'

Iris jumped up. 'I'm going to bed. I ain't gonner stay here and listen to any more of your lies.'

The kitchen door was slammed shut. Ellie too found herself crying. What was going to happen to them? She had to explain everything to Iris. She would never leave her. But how were they going to manage? And would Iris ever forgive her?

Ellie opened her puffy eyes. What time was it? It was still dark outside. The gaslamp, however, was alight but turned down very low. Ellie then remembered doing that last night. She hadn't wanted to go up to bed, so all night she had sat in the chair going over and over their problems. Sometimes, when she did manage to doze off, she woke in a terrible state after having a bad dream.

Now every part of her body hurt; she couldn't move. Ellie cocked her head. What was that noise coming from the scullery? 'Iris, Iris, is that you?' she called fearfully.

Something being crashed down onto the wooden draining board was the only answer she got.

'You all right, Iris?' called Ellie.

There was no reply.

Ellie shivered. The fire was out. 'I'll go round to work first thing and tell them I won't be in, then I'll see what I can do today. Is it still snowing?' she asked.

Again only silence.

Ellie sighed heavily. What could she do to help make amends?

Iris, who was dressed and ready for work, came hurrying through the kitchen.

'Iris, please listen to me, we've got a lot to discuss.'

But Iris didn't stop.

Ellie felt weak, frightened her legs would give way as she struggled into the scullery. A wash might help her to think straight. Leaning against the sink she let the cold water run over her hands. Her thoughts went to Leonard's wonderful kitchen with a gas stove. He didn't have to wait for the fire before they could have a cup of tea. What would he say when he heard what had happened? She sighed, and said out loud, 'I suppose he'll blame me as well for not letting him come home with me to explain to Mum.' Once again her tears fell. She was feeling very sorry for herself.

'Oh, so you've turned up then? Where the bloody hell 'ave you been these last few days?' Peggy, who was busy polishing the glass counter, looked very angry when Ellie pushed open the door to the tea room.

As Ellie got a little closer she stopped polishing and gasped. 'Bloody hell! You look like you've been hit be a truck.' She rushed round the counter, took Ellie's arm and gently guided her towards a chair. 'What 'appened? Who did this to you?'

'Me mum.'

'Yer mum?' Peggy sank into the chair next to Ellie. 'That woman's a bloody menace, she should be locked away.'

Ellie began to cry.

'I'm sorry, love – but she shouldn't be allowed to do things like this. D'yer know I was worried about you when you didn't come in to work, but I never guessed . . . Was this because you was with . . .?'

Ellie nodded.

'I'm ever so sorry, Ellie. I should 'ave come round to find out where you was.'

'Peggy. Me mum's been locked away.'

'A good thing too if you ask me.'

'It wasn't for hitting me, it was for killing me dad.'

Peggy put her hand to her mouth and her face drained of colour. 'Oh Ellie,' she gasped. 'Yer mum killed yer dad? Ellie, what can I say?'

Ellie fumbled for her handkerchief. 'It's all my fault.'

'That's as may be, but to kill someone . . .'

'It was an accident,' she sobbed.

'How did it happen?'

'Well, when I got home and told me mum I'd been to Lizzie's, she wanted her address.'

'And you couldn't give it to 'er.'

Ellie shook her head. 'No,' she croaked. She went on to tell her about what had happened, and how she had finished up in hospital. Peggy's eyes grew wider and wider.

'I don't believe it,' she whispered when Ellie stopped to wipe her eyes. 'I just don't believe it.'

The bakery door opened and Mr Jenkins strode angrily across the floor.

Ellie kept her head down.

'What's going on here? Miss Walsh, I trust you have a perfectly good excuse for not turning up for work these past three days?'

Peggy was on her feet, her face like thunder. 'Harry, before you start leading off I think you ought to hear what Ellie has to say.'

Mr Jenkins was clearly taken aback at Peggy's familiarity; he was even more so when he saw Ellie's bruised and swollen face.

'My dear, what happened?' he gasped.

'You'd better sit down,' said Peggy abruptly.

He did as he was told, and Ellie went through her story once again.

When she'd finished, Mr Jenkins said in a shocked voice, 'My dear, what a terrible thing. Your mother murdering your father. What's going to happen to her?'

'She didn't murder 'im,' shouted Ellie, confused at his statement. 'It was an accident.'

Mr Jenkins leant back in the chair and put his fingertips together. 'Ah yes. But will the authorities see it like that?'

Ellie was bewildered. It had never occurred to her or Iris that their mother could be had up for murder. Ellie screwed her handkerchief into a tight ball. 'If . . . if they do say it's murder . . . could she be hanged?' she croaked.

'You will have to wait till the trial.'

'A trial?' whispered Ellie.

Peggy gave Mr Jenkins a filthy look. 'But surely not if it was an accident?'

'I'm only saying what might happen.'

Ellie looked from one to the other. To her this conversation wasn't real. They were talking about her mother being hanged for murder. For murdering her father, and it was all her fault.

She struggled to her feet and gathered up her handbag. 'I've got to go to the police station. I've got to find out if . . .'

'Good luck,' said Peggy. 'Don't worry about work.' She looked at Mr Jenkins. 'We'll manage.'

'I must take me little bit of money for me fares.'

'What money?' asked Mr Jenkins.

'Ellie keeps her tips here,' said Peggy. 'I'll get 'em for yer. Let us know how you get on. Oh, I nearly forgot. Mr Kent popped in the other evening just as we were closing, said something about taking you to the club tonight, as it's New Year's Eve. Funny now, thinking about it, 'e did look worried and he asked for your address.'

'Did you give it to him?' asked Ellie eagerly.

'No, I told him I didn't know where you lived, I thought that was best.'

Ellie could have cried. 'If 'e ever comes back again—' she stopped. Would he want to see her like this? 'Don't matter.'

'When 'e does come in I'll tell him what's 'appened.'

'No. No don't. I'll write to him,' she lied. She needed time to work out her future. That's if she had one.

'OK, please yerself.' Peggy kissed her cheek. 'Look after yerself, love,' she said with genuine affection.

With her two shillings safely in her bag Ellie left the tea room and made her way to the police station. On the bus she felt utterly miserable. She thought about the club and the good time they would all be having tonight. Was it only a week ago she'd been happy beyond words? Would she ever see Leonard again? He had been in the tea room to see her, and he had asked about her and wanted her address. He'd said he wanted to take her out again; but would he now? Tomorrow was the start of a new year, but what did it hold for her?

'You'll have to wait and see the sergeant,' said the young policeman when Ellie asked where her mother was being held. 'He'll be out in a jiffy.'

Ellie sat on the hard wooden seat that ran along the brown painted wall.

'You look like you've been in the wars,' he laughed. 'Had a row with yer boyfriend?'

Ellie turned away and ignored him. She hadn't the strength for polite conversation.

'This way, Miss Walsh,' said the sergeant, opening a door and stepping to one side.

He sat behind a desk and smiled. 'You look a bit better now.'

'Was it you who . . .?'

'I came to your house. Sad business this.'

'Sergeant, where's our mum?'

'She was taken to Greenwich, there's a special kind of hospital there for those . . .' He picked up a pencil.

'Can we go and see her?'

'I don't think it would be wise just yet. Besides, I don't think she would recognize you. She didn't even know who your sister was when we took her away. No, I think it's best if you leave it for a bit. I'll give you the address and you could write and ask them how she is and when it would be suitable to see her.'

Ellie swallowed hard. 'What about Dad?' she whispered.

The sergeant sat back. 'Did your mother have any insurance policies?'

'No.'

'I don't think you and your sister have got enough money to give him a proper funeral then, have you?'

Ellie shook her head.

'I'm afraid it will have to be a pauper's grave. Don't worry about it. It will all be taken care of.'

The sergeant was about to stand up when Ellie quickly asked, 'Will Mum be had up for murder?'

He slumped back down in his chair. 'There will have to be an inquest of course, but I think we can safely say that it was an accident. And besides, as I said before, your mother, unfortunately, is in no fit state to be questioned.' He sat forward. 'What sparked it all off?'

'Me,' said Ellie sadly.

'You?'

'I didn't come home over Christmas, and when I got indoors Mum started hitting me, and it just got out of hand.'

'Well at least you and your sister's stories match. Now you go on home. Try not to worry too much.'

As Ellie left the police station she thought that was easier said than done. Her worries weren't just going to go away. She had Iris to think of: and what about her mother? How would they manage when she came home? It was all her fault; this guilt was something she would have to carry with her to her grave.

Chapter 21

After lighting the fire and putting the fish and chips she'd bought for her and Iris's tea into the oven, Ellie sank wearily into the armchair and closed her eyes. She was pleased to be home. Getting around had been very tiring.

Her thoughts went to Leonard. She would have to get in touch with him. Peggy said he'd looked worried. She let a slight smile lift her swollen face. She had to see him again, but not just yet, not till her face healed.

A loud knocking on the front door quickly brought her to her senses. Had Leonard found out where she lived? she wondered as she hurried along the passage. Had he come to see her?

'Molly,' she gasped disappointedly, as she eagerly opened the door. 'What do you want?' Ellie's tone was far from friendly.

'Don't like this weather, it's perishing out 'ere. Thought I'd wait till you got your fire going before I popped along. You gonner let me in or yer gonner make me stand on yer doorstep for ever?'

'What d'you want to come in for? So you can gloat over what's 'appened?' Ellie was angry.

Molly stood her ground. 'No I ain't come to gloat, as you call it, I come ter see if you wanted any help.'

'We don't want help from the likes of you.'

'Yer did the other day. 'Sides, who else yer got then?'

Ellie slowly shook her head. 'Don't know.' She stood to

221

one side as Molly pushed past her.

'See you go past me window, so I gave it a while before I popped in.'

Ellie really didn't want her in the house. She was probably only looking for something to gossip about, as if she didn't have enough about the Walshes to keep her going for months to come. But it didn't seem she had much choice.

'Yer look a bit better than when I saw you last.' Molly plonked herself at the table.

That statement made Ellie feel very guilty for being so unfriendly. 'I should thank you for helping Iris.'

'Don't worry about that. See you've got the kettle on; how about a cuppa then? Been ter see yer mum? How is she?'

'I don't know,' she whispered. 'They wouldn't let me go and see 'er.'

'Mind you, she didn't look too good when they carted 'er away. All that hollering and hooting.'

Part of Ellie wanted to throw her out. What did she want? Could she really be any help?

As if reading her mind, Molly added, 'I know everybody thinks I'm a nosy old cow, but I can only pass on a bit of me wisdom for those that wants it.' She sat up straight and looked Ellie in the eye. 'You've got a rough time in front of yer, girl, and you're gonner need all the 'elp you can get.'

Ellie was confused. Should she talk to this woman whom they had always feared? But she *had* come to Iris's aid when she'd needed her.

'So, if you want a shoulder to cry on,' Molly went on, 'remember I'm always 'ere.'

Ellie began filling the teapot, shuddering at the thought of crying on Molly's grubby shoulder. But she had to confide in someone – though surely not Dirty Molly? Ellie, her back to Molly, took the cups from the dresser, trying to hide the tears welling in her eyes. 'What will they do to Mum? They won't hang her for murdering Dad, will they?' she asked quietly.

'Course not. The doctor could see it was an accident. 'Sides, yer mum was in such a state when they took your dad away. She thought 'e was still alive and tried to stop 'em.' Molly shook her head. 'Very sad affair. You'll 'ave to tell yer sisters.'

'I don't know where they live.'

'What? You must 'ave seen 'em since they left home?'

'No.' Ellie sat at the table.

'What about going round to where they work?'

'They left there months ago.'

'Don't nobody know where they could be?'

Ellie shook her head. 'One of the women at the factory said they'd moved over the water. I can't afford to go there looking for them. I thought at one time Dolly was back over this way, I saw her coat in the pawn shop, but it was Mum what pawned it. I just wouldn't know where to start to look for 'em.' Ellie sniffed, feeling even more vulnerable and lonely. 'What we going to do?'

Molly poured out the tea. 'Dunno. You would 'ave thought they'd try and see you and Iris. They know where you work, don't they?'

Ellie nodded. 'They was very angry with Mum.'

Molly sighed. 'That's as may be. But hate's a terrible thing. You should always make the most of your family. Never know when yer gonner need 'em.'

'Is there only you and your sister?' Ellie asked casually.

'Yes. First yer gotter see about yer dad's funeral,' she said, quickly changing the subject.

Ellie was intrigued; she would have liked to know more about Molly, but she just said, 'The police said that was taken care of.'

'That's all right then. D'you know where yer mum is?' Molly picked up her cup and, putting her elbows on the table, began slurping her tea.

'Greenwich. I've got her address.'

'Well sit down and write to the matron. She'll be able to give you more news, then you and Iris can go and see her.'

'Me and Iris have had a row,' she said softly.

'What over?'

'She blames . . .' Ellie suddenly stopped. She wasn't going to tell Molly why her mother had been so insanely angry.

'She'll be all right tonight, you wait and see. She's 'ad a nasty shock, and she's gotter blame someone.' She looked at the clock. 'I better be orf, me sister's got me tea ready be now. Now remember, I'll always be ready to listen. And don't forgit to write that letter.'

'I won't.' Ellie walked up the passage and closed the front door behind her.

When she was back in the kitchen, Ellie settled herself down in the chair again, and closed her eyes. Iris should be home any minute. Molly was a funny old dear. Did she mean well, or was she just being nosy?

Ellie looked up. Her mother was standing over her, grinning. Her father was on his knees pleading for his life. He slumped on the floor. A hangman wearing his mask suddenly pushed open the kitchen door and grabbed her mother. Ellie screamed and screamed. The sound was echoing round and round her head.

Ellie woke to find tears running down her face. She wiped them away with sweaty palms. Her mouth was dry, and she felt sick.

She looked up at the clock. Iris should have been home an hour ago. Ellie was overcome with panic. Had Iris left her? Was she now all alone?

The front door slammed shut, and after wiping her eyes, Ellie opened the kitchen door. 'You're late. Everythink all right?'

Iris threw her bag onto a chair. 'I went round one of the girls from work's house, to see her mum.' Iris took off her hat and coat. 'She takes in lodgers.'

Ellie slumped back into the armchair. 'You ain't thinking of leaving me, are you? You ain't gonner leave me on me own?'

Iris sat at the table. 'Well I ain't staying 'ere with you.'

'Why?'

''Cos it's your fault Dad's dead and Mum's finished up in a loony bin.'

Ellie sat back. She didn't have any fight left in her. 'If that's what you want I can't stop you. I've got fish and chips for tea. I'll put it on a plate.'

They had their tea in silence.

'I went to the police station,' said Ellie as they stood in the scullery washing up.

'Where's Mum?'

'At Greenwich. The policeman gave me the address. I've got to write.'

'Can't we go and see her?'

'He didn't think it was very wise just yet. He reckons we should wait till she's settled in a bit more.'

'Is that so?'

'He also said not to worry about Dad, as that was all being taken care of. He'll let us know when the inquest will be and when Dad will be . . .' Ellie had to stop; she was so upset she couldn't say the word, and she wasn't going to tell Iris how worried she was after Mr Jenkins said their mother could be charged with murder, even though the policeman had tried to put her mind at rest over that. 'Molly came and asked us—'

'Dirty Molly's been 'ere?'

'Yes.'

'And you let 'er in?'

'Yes. You didn't mind when she helped you with—'

'That was different.'

'Well, I didn't know who to turn to. She was very kind, worried about Mum.'

Iris laughed, it was a hard cynical laugh. 'I bet she was. And you gave her lots of other juicy bits of information she can chew over.'

'No.'

Iris wiped her hands on the towel behind the door and walked away.

Ellie knew she had to tell her about Leonard; but would she listen?

'Are you really thinking of leaving me?' Ellie asked tentatively as they sat in front of the fire.

Iris didn't answer.

Ellie looked round the room. 'There ain't a lot of anythink left here now, but whatever you want you can take.'

'Ta.'

'I won't be able to manage on me own, so I'll have to look for—'

'That ain't my fault.'

'Iris. Please give me a chance to explain what happened over Christmas.'

'Is this more lies to keep me 'ere?'

'No it ain't.'

'How can I be sure?'

Ellie shrugged her shoulders. 'That's something you will have to make up your own mind about. I didn't tell Mum where I was going because she would have stopped me, and if it hadn't been for the snow I would have been home.'

Iris glanced at Ellie, her face full of curiosity.

'I met this man. He comes into the tea room once a month. He took me to see the Al Jolson film. He's ever so nice.'

Iris sat forward. 'That was ages ago, what's that to do with—?'

Ellie raised her hand. 'Just let me finish. A while back he took me to his club, he's a pianist in a band.'

Iris's eyes grew wide. 'A club? What sort of club?'

'They dance and play music.'

'But why you? You ain't exactly – well, is he married?'

Ellie shook her head. 'I went to the club again on Christmas Eve, and stayed too late to get a bus.'

'Where's this 'ere club then?'

'The West End.'

'The West End,' repeated Iris. 'You could 'ave come on the underground.'

'I know, but the snow was very thick and I didn't fancy that long walk from the station. 'Sides, I didn't want to.'

'So where did you stay?'

Ellie looked down at her hands. 'At his flat.'

'His flat? 'E's got his own flat? Was you on yer own?'

Ellie didn't answer.

'Where did you sleep, in 'is bed?' asked Iris in a soft voice.

Ellie nodded. 'Yes.'

Iris stood up. 'Did you . . .?' Without waiting for an answer she went on, 'Why didn't you come home on Christmas Day?'

'I couldn't. There's nothing running.'

'What about Boxing Day? You could 'ave come 'ome then.'

'I didn't want to. 'Sides, I thought I might just as well get hung for a sheep as for a lamb.'

'I'm not surprised you didn't want Mum to know, you would 'ave got a bloody good—' She stopped. 'He must be very nice.'

Ellie didn't answer.

'Was 'e worth it?'

Still Ellie remained silent.

'You couldn't win, could you?' Iris said, with surprising sympathy.

Tears ran down Ellie's face. 'I never thought . . . If only I'd told the truth perhaps Dad would still be 'ere.'

Iris plonked herself down on the chair. 'Yer, but it might 'ave been you laying in the morgue.'

They were very quiet for a while.

'You seeing 'im again?' asked Iris, turning the poker over and over.

'Don't know.'

'Would he let you move in with 'im?'

'Don't think so. 'Sides, it's too far to go backwards and forwards to work.'

'Oh,' said Iris. 'I'll make a cup of tea.' She took the kettle into the scullery to fill it. 'Is he good-looking?' she asked, walking back in.

'Not bad.'

'How old is he?'

'A bit older than me.' Ellie wasn't going to let on just yet that he was twenty years older than her.

'Would 'e marry you?'

'I don't think so, I hardly know him.'

'Yer, but you let 'im . . . you know.'

Ellie blushed. 'Yes I did.'

Iris was sitting on the edge of her chair. 'What was it like?'

Ellie didn't want to answer her. It was too personal, and something she only wanted to share with Leonard. 'You should see your face,' she laughed at her sister's wide-eyed expression. It was the first time she had laughed in days, and gradually her laughter turned to tears, and her body was racked with sobs.

Iris put a comforting arm round her sister.

'Oh Iris, what we gonner do?'

'We're gonner 'ave this cup of tea then go to bed.'

Ellie tried to smile through her tears. 'Please don't leave me.'

Iris didn't answer.

The hangman, a big powerful man, was dragging her mother away. Ellie screamed and screamed and tried to fight him off. He hit her and she fell to the floor. 'Leave her be. Leave her alone. It's my fault me dad's dead. You've got to hang me.'

'Ellie, stop it. Stop it. It's all right, it's me.'

Ellie opened her eyes. She held Iris tight and sobbed into her shoulder.

'Shhh, you've had a bad dream.'

Ellie gently cried. 'How long are these dreams going to go on?'

'I don't know,' Iris replied. 'You was shouting somethink about a hangman. Ellie, you don't think Mum could be hanged, do you?'

Ellie sniffed and wiped her nose with the back of her hand. 'No, course not. Come on, let's get some sleep. It's a new year tomorrow; 1928's got to be better.'

'I hope so.' Iris went to turn over. 'Ellie, they couldn't say Mum *murdered* Dad, could they?'

'No course not, it was an accident. You saw that.'

'Yes, but it's only my word.'

Ellie propped herself up. 'What're you saying?'

'D'you think the police believed me?'

'Why shouldn't they? The doctor saw it as well.'

'Yes, so 'e did.' Iris turned over.

For a long while Ellie lay awake listening to Iris gently breathing. Her thoughts went to Leonard. She should be with him at his club. She should be laughing and enjoying herself. Was he missing her? What did the new year have in store for all of them – and especially for their mother?

Chapter 22

The following Friday morning was wet and cold. Ellie read the newspapers' placards as they waited in silence for a bus to take her and Iris to the cemetery. 'The Thames overflows. Many feared drowned,' said the thick black letters, but it didn't register; nothing registered. Ellie felt numb.

In the cemetery, the two sisters were the only people watching the workmen lower their father's cheap wooden coffin into the ground. It didn't have any brass handles and the mounds around them had no headstones, though some did have a simple home-made wooden cross to show where a loved one was buried. There was no priest to give their father a blessing. The only sound was the gentle thud of wet sticky mud hitting the coffin. The snow was beginning to thaw, and the ground had become very waterlogged.

Ellie's chilblains were hurting and itching. Every year she had them but this year they were worse than ever. She bent down and scratched them yet again.

Last Wednesday, much to Ellie's relief, the inquest had brought in a verdict of accidental death.

Now it was all over. Their father had gone. They placed a small bunch of flowers on the brown mound.

'Iris, should we see about getting Dad a cross or something so that we know which grave is his?'

'We can't afford anything like that. Besides, I don't suppose we'll ever come back here.'

Ellie began wandering round and picking up stones.

'What're you doing?' asked Iris.

'I'm just going to mark his grave with a few stones. I'd like to put them in the shape of a cross.'

At first Iris stood watching her sister, but after a while she too looked for stones.

Ellie stood back. The wet stones shone out from the brown earth like bright eyes.

'Come on, let's go,' said Iris.

At the bus stop once again, Ellie pulled her scarf tighter at her throat. They were going their separate ways to work.

'I'll see you at home tonight,' said Ellie when her bus came in sight.

'I'll be a bit late.' Iris fiddled with her handbag.

'Why, where you going?'

'Just out. 'Ere's your bus,' she said stepping to one side to let Ellie get on.

Ellie sat on the bus, her mind going over the past week. She felt weary with the burden of her guilt. Would Iris ever forgive her? She was still very angry with her and would hardly talk to her, but was that because she herself was feeling guilty about leaving her? The strain was beginning to get Ellie down. How long could this go on? They still hadn't had an answer to the letter she sent to the matron of the home their mother was in. Perhaps they would get one before the weekend, then they could go and see their mother. If she came home, now it had been proved their father's death was accidental, that might make Iris feel a little better towards Ellie. If she was thinking of leaving home, it might help her to change her mind.

Ellie looked out of the window as the bus trundled along. Everywhere seemed dirty and grey. Ellie knew they had many problems in front of them. How could they afford the rent, on their money? What about coal and food? What if their mother did come home; who would look after her? And if Iris did leave home, could she afford to live in lodgings? Ellie felt so miserable and alone. What had happened to Leonard? She had been back at work all week, and every night had hoped he would be outside the tea room to see how she was. She should never have spent all that money on a new frock; she would have to pawn it now.

'How did it go?' asked Peggy when Ellie walked in.

'All right, I s'pose. I ain't ever been to a funeral before. Oh Peg. It's awful watching 'em put the coffin in the ground.' A tear ran down her face. 'Me dad's in the ground, and it's cold and wet. He'd still be alive if it wasn't for me.'

Peggy put a comforting arm round her shoulders. 'Now come on, you can't spend your life fretting about it, what's done's done, and you can't bring him back.'

Ellie's tears flowed. 'I don't want to go in the ground,' she sobbed. 'I don't want the worms—'

'Don't talk like that. Now come on, put your uniform on and do some work, it'll take yer mind off it.'

Ellie did as she was told, although her heart wasn't in it.

That night Iris didn't mention leaving home, so Ellie was hopeful that the idea might have all blown over.

On Saturday morning as they were getting ready for work, Ellie received a letter from the matron of the hospital telling her that their mother was still settling down and having treatment and it wasn't advisable to see her this week.

Ellie passed the letter to Iris, who asked, 'So when we gonner see 'er then?'

'I don't know. I'll write again and ask if we can go next Sunday. I'll also ask when she's coming out.'

Iris threw the letter onto the table. 'I don't want 'er to come out.'

'What?' said Ellie, shocked.

''Ave you honestly thought about it? What if she ain't all there? Who's gonner look after 'er? Feed 'er, and take 'er to the lav? You gonner give up work to do it? And what would we live on? Go on, answer me that.' Tears were streaming down Iris's angry face. 'All 'cos you wanted a bit of fun. You didn't think of the consequences, did you? And how many lives you'd ruin.'

Ellie felt sick. It *was* her fault. What if her mother did come home? She knew Iris was right; who would look after her? If only she could turn the clock back to Christmas Eve. If only she knew where Lizzie and Dolly lived. They would help.

'Iris, I can only say I'm sorry. I never wanted this to happen, I never wanted Dad to die.' Ellie broke down. She laid her head on the table and wept. 'Please tell me. What am I gonner do?'

Iris sat next to her. 'Yer, well, Mum's always been a bit nutty . . .' She suddenly stopped. 'Ellie,' she whispered, 'you don't think . . .?'

Ellie raised her tearstained face. 'What?'

Iris's face was ashen. 'You don't think it could be passed on?'

Ellie wiped her face with the back of her hand. 'What, you mean, like, hereditary?'

Iris nodded.

'Dunno. Ain't never thought about that. We don't know nothink about her mum and dad.'

'She's never told us about any of her relations, or if she had any brothers or sisters.'

'Nobody's ever been to see us. She's never told us anythink. How did she end up like she is? We never did find out if Dad was in the army, or what went on with Mum and Mrs Andrews.'

'Mrs Andrews? What was that about?' asked Iris, wide-eyed. 'I don't know nothink about that.'

'Don't really know, just that Mum was flaming when she thought I was seeing Terry Andrews, and Dirty Molly told me Terry's mum and our mum had a fight in the square.'

'No! Does Dirty Molly know what it was over?'

'I don't know.'

'Couldn't we find out?'

'I'd 'ave to ask Dirty Molly up here.'

'Yer,' said Iris thoughtfully. 'S'pose you would.'

'Look at the time,' said Ellie. 'I've got to go.'

'We'll talk about this tonight,' said Iris.

As Ellie walked to work her mind was going over what Iris had said. Could their mother's madness be hereditary? Could they inherit it? And would Dirty Molly tell them what had happened all those years ago? If of course she knew.

Ellie was surprised when Leonard Kent walked in. In all the confusion of the past two weeks, she had forgotten it was his Saturday to come into the tea room.

'Hallo Ellie,' he whispered as she took his hat and coat. 'We have got to talk.' He gently touched her face. 'Did your mother do this?'

'It's a lot better now,' she said, quickly pulling away.

'I tried to get your address from Miss Swan, but she refused to give it to me. I was very worried about you, more so when I found you hadn't been to work.' He sat in his usual chair and picked up the menu. 'I was hoping you would have written to me.'

'I ain't got your address,' said Ellie quietly. 'Your usual, sir?'

'Yes please. I'll be outside at six when you finish.'

He took a long while over his tea and scone, and every time Ellie looked across at him he smiled. She wanted to run over to him, hold him and cry on his shoulder. She felt safe with him.

When he left there was a shilling under the plate. Ellie smiled.

Ellie hadn't told Peggy Leonard would be waiting outside at six. She didn't want him to come in, she wanted to see him on her own; she wanted to tell him all that had happened without any interruptions or comments. She had no idea quite how Leonard would take her news.

★ ★ ★

'Ellie, my dear Ellie,' said Leonard, gathering her into his arms as soon as she stepped out of the shop door. 'Why didn't you let me take you home? Your mother wouldn't have done this to you if I'd been there.' He gently kissed her still slightly bruised cheek. 'You've got to leave her. You can't stay there.'

Ellie pushed him away. 'Can we go somewhere and talk?'

'Of course. There's a pub round the corner, we can sit in there.' He took her arm.

The warmth from the pub fire was comforting, and for the first time in weeks Ellie felt relaxed.

Leonard put the drinks on the table. 'One ginger beer,' he said, pushing a glass towards her. 'Now, you'd better tell me what happened.'

Ellie sat back and told him the full story. He didn't interrupt. When she stopped to wipe her tears away he leaned forward and whispered, 'I'm so sorry, so very sorry. But you mustn't blame yourself for your father's death.'

'But if I'd—'

'If only you had let me take you home.' He ran his fingers through his thick, sandy-coloured hair. 'What are you going to do? How are you going to manage?'

Ellie played with her glass. 'I don't know. Iris is talking about moving out. If she does, I don't know how I'm gonner pay the rent . . .' She stopped as her voice began to break.

'That's one problem that is easily solved. You must come and live with me.'

'I can't.'

'Why not? If you sister's moving out, what is there to stop you?'

'I . . . I can't move in with you. If me mum comes out of hospital, I'll have to look after her.'

'Do you think she will come out?'

Ellie hung her head. 'Don't know.'

'It's likely she won't – at least for some time. You must think of yourself. You must come and live with me.'

She suddenly thought about the madness that might be in her blood. She had to have time to think – to think of an excuse. 'I couldn't come over the water every day to work; I couldn't afford the fare and pay you.'

'Is that all that would stop you?'

'I love my job.'

'Yes I know. But you can't live on your own. Besides, I'm very fond of you, and I would love to have you share my home.'

Ellie blushed and quickly cast her eyes down. Was he asking her to marry him? 'Thank you,' she said. 'But we must wait and see what's going to happen to Mum first.'

'Of course, but you will think about it?'

She nodded.

'Look, I'll give you my address, and you can write and let me know what's happening. Give me your address, and when I'm over this way again I'll come and see you when you're at home.'

'That would be nice.'

'I'd come over tomorrow but unfortunately I have to meet someone, and I can't put him off. What about next Sunday?' he said enthusiastically.

'Yes, that's . . . no, no. I've just remembered we might be going to see me mum then.'

He looked at his watch. 'I'm sorry, Ellie, but I really must go.' He finished his drink. 'I'll walk you to your tram.'

Ellie gathered up her handbag. 'Thanks. I'll write and let you know what's going to happen.'

As her tram came trundling into view Leonard took her in his arms and gently kissed her full on the mouth. 'Take care, my dear.'

She waved goodbye through the window. She felt happy for the first time since this nightmare had started. Was her future now being taken care of? Leonard said she could go and live with him. Did he want to marry her? Although she would be sad at leaving Peggy and the tea room, perhaps she could find a job in the West End. They might even pay better. But what if madness *was* in the family?

She couldn't even think about this brand new life until she put her mind at rest. She had to get to the hospital soon to find out. The doctor must know.

The gaslight was burning in the passage, so Ellie knew Iris was home. She was glad about that; the fire should be alight, and the kettle on.

'You look pleased with yourself,' said Iris when Ellie walked into the kitchen.

'Leonard came in today, and gave me a shilling tip, that's why.' Ellie wasn't going to tell her just yet that if their mother didn't come home she didn't mind if Iris left, as she had made up her mind to move in with Leonard.

'I've got a couple of sausages from the butcher near the shop, and a bit of veg as well,' said Iris. 'The bloke in the greengrocers let me buy just a couple of potatoes.'

'I'll get the frying pan,' said Ellie.

All evening Ellie waited for Iris to tell her about moving away. In the end she couldn't contain herself any longer. 'Did you see that girl's mum about moving in with her?'

Iris looked uncomfortable. 'Yes.'

'So when you going?'

'You sound eager to get rid of me. Why's that? What's this boyfriend of yours been saying to you?'

'Nothink.'

'She's going to let me know at the end of the week, if you must know. The lodger she's got now is leaving then.'

'Oh. So you've made up your mind then. What if Mum comes home?'

Iris turned her head away. 'I'll let you know then.'

'Thank you, but don't bother to put yourself out too much, will you,' said Ellie angrily.

'Why? If Mum don't come out, what difference will it make to you if I go or stay?'

'What difference? What difference?' Ellie was on her feet. 'I'll tell you what difference it'll make. First of all, if you go I've got to find somewhere to live, and if you decide to stay we've got to work out if we can afford the rent on this place or should look for something cheaper. So when you feel like it perhaps you'll let me know.' Ellie stormed out of the room and went upstairs.

She flung herself on the bed and cried. Were her hopes and dreams of only a few hours ago slipping away? She wanted to live with Leonard, but she knew she had a duty to look after Iris and her mother.

Chapter 23

All week Ellie had been hoping for a letter from the matron of the home telling them they could visit their mother; and all week, as Ellie passed Dirty Molly's, she felt tempted to knock and ask her to come up and see her and Iris so that perhaps they could find out something about their mother and father's past; but something always seemed to hold her back. Perhaps deep down she didn't really want to know.

Leonard was true to his word and wrote Ellie a long letter telling her about his pupils and the boys in the band, and said when she felt well enough she must come to the club again. He also wrote that if their mother wasn't coming home and Iris was going to leave her, she should seriously think about moving in with him; but he never mentioned anything about them getting married.

It was Saturday, and as she was hurrying home her thoughts were full of Iris. Was she going to see the woman about renting a room tonight? Iris had been very evasive about it all week. Did she really want to go? Poor Iris, like her, she too must be in a quandary.

Ellie had her head down against the wind that was blowing fit to bust. She looked up and suddenly realized she was on a collision course with Terry Andrews.

'Steady on there, Ellie,' he said, taking her arm to stop her falling.

She felt her heart miss a beat as he held on to her.

'It's a bit rough out 'ere ternight. Ellie, me and Mum was

241

ever so sorry to 'ear about your dad, and Mum said your mum's in hospital. Is she getting better?'

'Yes thanks, Terry,' she croaked. She wasn't going to go into any details. 'Your mum all right?'

'Not too bad. How are you and your sister managing?'

'All right.' She was touched that he sounded concerned.

'Look, I know we ain't got much, but if you need anything, just pop over and we'll try to help out.'

'Thanks Terry, that's really kind of you.'

''S'all right. I'd best be off.' He went to move away, but Ellie caught his arm.

'Terry, you working yet?'

'Only a bit 'ere and there at the moment, but I'm hoping to start a proper job soon.'

'That's good, I'm really pleased for you. Where will you be working then?'

He smiled. 'I've bin doing a bit for that new garage in Rotherhithe New Road, and the gaffer's talking about taking me on full time.'

'Oh Terry, that's really good news.' She wanted to throw her arms round his neck and kiss him.

'Look, I really must go.' He quickly moved on, leaving Ellie alone.

Ellie slowly continued across the square. She felt mixed up; he still made her heart jump whenever she saw him. Her feelings towards Terry were so very different to what she thought of Leonard. Was that because she had known Terry all her life and they came from the same background? Or was it because he was more her age and not so worldly as Leonard? What would Terry say if he knew she had slept with a man? Would he mind if . . .? She quickly dismissed any idea of going out with Terry; he had made it perfectly clear the last time they spoke that he didn't want any commitment. Besides, he couldn't offer her what Leonard could.

Ellie's head was soon full of other thoughts. Mrs Andrews

let out a room. Could they do that? That would help with the rent, and might be the answer to their problem. 'I'll discuss it with Iris tonight, and if she agrees, I could pop over and ask Mrs Andrews how she goes about it,' said Ellie to herself, and her step was lighter as she walked on.

Ellie pushed open the front door and was pleased to find a letter from the matron on the doormat. In it she told them they could come to the home next Sunday to see their mother for just a short while. But they mustn't expect too much.

'What does she mean, we mustn't expect too much?' asked Iris when she got home and Ellie handed her the letter.

'Dunno. We'll just have to wait and see tomorrow. Did you have anythink planned?' asked Ellie nonchalantly, secretly praying she wouldn't be telling her she was moving out.

'No.'

'Iris, I've been wondering. If Mum comes home and we've got to stay here, perhaps we could take in a lodger like Mrs Andrews does.'

'What? Where would they sleep?'

'Dunno, but we could think of something. It's just a thought.'

'Who would cook and clean for 'em?'

'We'll have to see what Mum's like first. But I thought you might stay if Mum comes home. After all, we've got to look after her.'

'We?'

'Well, she is your mum as well.'

'S'pose so. Anyway, let's wait and see what she's like tomorrow, shall we? Then we'll talk about me staying or . . . Let's wait.'

The following morning they made their way to Greenwich. They had carefully added their money together to pay the week's rent and the fares.

'I'm glad Mr Jenkins lets me have some things cheap,' said Ellie cheerfully as they stood at the bus stop, 'otherwise we might starve.'

Iris didn't answer. She looked troubled.

'You all right?' asked Ellie for the fourth time that morning.

'I told you, yes. Now don't keep on.'

'Just asked, that's all. I think this is our bus.'

The conductor gave them a funny look when they asked to be put down at the hospital. 'You be careful in there, gels.' After looking up and down the aisle he leaned forward and said close to their faces, ''Eard there's a right load o' loonies in there.'

'We're just going to see an old neighbour,' said Ellie quickly. 'She fell down the stairs.'

He gave them their tickets. 'That's all right then.'

After a while he told them which road to take, and they walked silently to the large grey building, set back from the road, that seemed to loom out of the damp grey day.

When they reached the door Iris suddenly grabbed hold of Ellie's hand; she was shaking.

'What's wrong?' asked Ellie.

Iris stopped. 'I don't know . . . I don't know if I want to see her.'

'But you must, we've come all this way.' Ellie took Iris in her arms and held her close. 'Once we see her it will be all right. The first time's got to be the worst.'

'What if she asks about Dad?' Tears were rolling down Iris's cheeks.

'We'll think of somethink. Now come on, dry your eyes.'

'Ain't you worried?' sniffed Iris. 'What if she starts leading off again?'

'That's what the nurses are there for, now come on.'

Ellie too felt very apprehensive, but she wasn't going to show it in front of Iris. In many ways she was more worried that they could be taking their mother home with them. She rang the bell.

A key was turned in the lock and a rosy-faced nurse opened the door.

'We've come to see our mum. Ruby Walsh.'

'You have to see Matron first,' said the nurse. 'Follow me.'

They followed the young woman, and Iris, screwing up her nose, squeezed Ellie's hand.

Strong disinfectant must have been used to hide the smell of dried pee, but it wasn't very successful.

'Go with the nurse,' said the matron after they'd made themselves known to her. 'But remember what I said in my letter: you mustn't expect too much.'

'This way,' said the young nurse.

Ellie froze as a long moaning sound filled the white-tiled corridor. 'What's that noise?' she asked as they followed the nurse.

'Just one of the inmates. Don't worry about it.'

Ellie thought Iris would break her hand, she was gripping it so tight.

'Don't you call them patients?' asked Ellie quietly.

'Some are. But most of them are here for the rest of their lives, poor things. They're not really ill, it's just that their families don't want them.'

Ellie was amazed at this young woman dismissing the plight of some of these people so readily.

An old man shuffled past them and smiled. Ellie could see something was wrong but couldn't put her finger on it.

'Mr Low,' shouted the nurse. 'Go and put them back at once.'

Mr Low nodded and smiled again.

'He will keep taking other people's false teeth if they leave them in a glass, and he goes round wearing them on top of his own,' said the nurse quite unperturbed. 'It can create such a lot of problems at mealtimes, as we can spend so much time searching for false teeth.'

It was then that Ellie realized what was odd about the

man's smile. She wanted to laugh.

'Your mother is in that room.' The nurse pointed to a door. 'She shares with another woman, Lena. Don't take any notice of what Lena tells you. She says we hurt her, but we don't; she's always falling over, and then blames us for her bruises.' She stood to one side.

Both Ellie and Iris stood for a moment trying to pluck up courage to push open the door.

The nurse did it for them.

They stood in the doorway and looked around the small room. It had just the bare essentials: two beds, two chairs, and a table.

Ellie's mother was sitting at the table with her back to them. She appeared to be staring at a blank wall.

Another small scraggy-faced woman was sitting on one of the wrought-iron beds, her dark piercing eyes like shiny buttons. Her grey hair was pulled back into a bun, emphasizing her pointed, ferret-like features. She was wearing a frock that Ellie knew belonged to her mother. It was much too big for her and hung in great folds from her skinny, hunched shoulders, and she had it pulled up above her knees exposing her short thin legs, encased in thick, brown lisle stockings. She wasn't wearing shoes and the stockings were wrinkled and didn't seem to have any visible means of support. For a few seconds Ellie watched fascinated as she dangled her legs over the bed, swinging them backwards and forwards. She looked almost as if she was waiting for the stockings to fly off.

''Allo gels,' she said cheerfully. 'Come on in. We don't get many visitors, do we Ruby?'

Ruby Walsh didn't move.

''Allo Mum,' said Iris, as they slowly moved into the room.

'That yer mum?' asked Lena. 'I 'ad a mum once, don't know where she's gorn.'

Ellie gave Lena a slight smile and moved closer to her

mother. 'Mum, it's me, Ellie.'

'Ellie, that's a pretty name,' said Lena, swinging her legs faster. 'My name's Florence. Florence Nightingale. I was a nurse.'

'That's nice,' said Ellie.

Iris stood beside the table, while Ellie sat in the other chair.

Ellie took her mother's hand.

Ruby Walsh suddenly turned her head and pulled her hand away, her eyes wide open, darting from Ellie to Iris.

'Mum, it's me, Iris.'

Lena clapped her hands excitedly. 'Iris. That's a pretty name. My name's Joan. Joan of Arc. D'yer know they tried to burn me once.'

Ellie wanted to laugh. How many names did Lena think she had? She must have been educated at some time to know about all these people.

'How d'yer feel, Mum?' asked Iris.

'I ain't yer mum. Go away. Ain't never seen yer before.' Ruby Walsh went and stood in the corner with her back to them.

'Don't you remember me, Mum?' Ellie said, appalled.

'Ain't ever bin married, so go on, shove off.' She pushed Ellie away and flapped her hands in her face.

'I ain't old enough to get married,' said Lena. 'And I don't think me mum would let me.'

Ellie wanted to scream at this pathetic old woman. She wanted her to go away and let them try and talk to their mother in peace.

'Don't you remember me?' asked Iris.

'No, should I?' Ruby Walsh still had her face to the wall. 'Can you 'ear these silly cows, Mum, they think I'm their mother. Never got married, did I. No Mum, don't 'it me. I'm sorry.' Ruby Walsh slid to the floor and put her hands over her head. 'Mum, no don't, please Mum, don't 'it me,' she cried.

Ellie and Iris stood looking at her. Both had tears streaming from their eyes. This used to be their mother.

Lena sat watching them, her dark eyes flitting from one to the other. She slid off the bed and moved closer to them. 'She thinks it's her mum what hits her, but it ain't, it's these so-called nurses. Look what they done ter me.' She lifted up her frock and showed them large purple bruises on her skinny white thighs.

Ellie and Iris gasped, not only at the bruises but because she didn't have any drawers on.

Slowly they began to walk away. Iris was sobbing and Ellie took her arm.

'Let's go and see the matron, she might be able to give us some hope.'

A woman ran past them screaming, her eyes full of fear. 'Don't let him catch me,' she cried out, grabbing Ellie's arm. But there was no one chasing her.

'It's all right,' said Ellie.

'No it ain't. Quick, come with me. I know where we can hide.'

'You go,' said Ellie softly. 'We'll catch you up.'

The woman ran on. At the corner she beckoned for them to follow her, but they turned and walked away.

Ellie thought if she stayed here for very long, she too would be running around screaming.

'I told you not to expect too much,' said the matron, when they'd found their way to her office.

'But our mum didn't know us,' said Iris.

'Has your mother ever been violent before?'

'No,' said Ellie quickly. 'Why?'

'She appears to have been beaten at some time in her life, and that could be the reason she fights back.'

'Does she know Dad's dead?' asked Iris quietly.

'No, she doesn't know her own name, and she certainly doesn't know she was married.'

'Will she ever get better?' asked Ellie.

'One day her memory may come back, but we mustn't bank on it.'

'How long will she stay here?' asked Ellie.

'In this hospital? Could be quite a while. We have to wait and see what progress she makes,' came the reply.

Ellie coughed and tried to speak but the words stuck in her throat. 'Lena's got a lot of bruises.'

Matron smiled. 'She's been showing you them?'

Ellie nodded.

'You mustn't take what she says too seriously. She does throw herself about at times.' Matron stood up. 'Now I must get on. Do come and see me any time you visit your mother.'

'Please,' croaked Ellie. 'Please. Could you tell us. Is what's wrong with Mum . . . could it be in the family?'

The matron looked at them long and hard. 'We don't think so. Your mother has had a shock. Something happened, and part of her brain has switched off. Now come on, no more tears. You don't have anything of that sort to worry about.'

Ellie began to cry deep, loud sobs.

The matron hurried round her desk and put a comforting arm round her shoulders. 'There, there. You mustn't upset yourself, it wasn't your fault.'

'It was. It was,' cried Ellie. 'It was my fault. Now me mum will always be . . .' She picked up her handbag and ran from the room.

Outside Iris grabbed her. A nurse was swiftly on their heels.

'Matron wants to talk to you,' she said.

Slowly they followed the nurse back in.

'Bring the girls a cup of tea, nurse.' She turned to Ellie and Iris. 'Sit down,' she said sternly. 'Now I know you have both had a shock, but you mustn't blame yourselves. This condition could have been brought on by anything, and the fact your father was accidentally killed seems to have triggered it off.'

The nurse gave them the tea.

'Thank you,' said Matron. 'As I was saying. You must not blame yourselves. You both have your lives in front of you, and you mustn't be burdened with guilt.' She leaned forward and smiled. 'Now finish your tea and go home and start a new life.'

Outside the two sisters sat on the wall and cried, oblivious to the cold drizzle that surrounded them.

After a while their tears subsided.

Iris blew her nose. 'Why didn't you tell her that Mum had been vicious before? What about that time she nearly killed Dolly?'

'What good would it have done?' sniffed Ellie. 'Come on, let's go home. I only hope I don't finish up in a nut house.'

'She did say we ain't got nothing to worry about,' said Iris. 'Ellie, do you think they do hit 'em at that place?'

'I don't know. Some of 'em must be hard to handle.'

'S'pose so.'

Ellie also worried about that, but at that moment she had so many other problems on her mind, not only about her mother, but the rent, coal and everything else. How will it all end? she thought in despair.

Ellie was on her knees blowing into the grate trying to get the wood to light. 'We should 'ave brought this wood indoors, it's too damp to light.' She threw the matches onto the floor.

Iris was sitting at the table. 'What we gonner do?'

'Keep trying till we get it to—'

Iris began to cry. 'I don't mean the fire; I mean what we, you and me, what we gonner do?'

Ellie sat next to her. 'I don't know,' she said softly. 'I honestly don't know.'

Iris looked up, her face pale and tearstained. 'I think we should have a talk.'

Ellie nodded. 'We've got a lot to talk about, and I think we need to clear the air.'

Iris nodded and wiped her eyes.

A sharp banging on the front door's knocker caused them both to sit up.

'I bet I know who that is,' said Ellie rising from her chair. 'I saw her looking out of her window as we walked past. Perhaps we might get a few answers to our questions.' She moved towards the door.

'That's supposing she knows something,' said Iris.

'As there's no one to dispute it, she might make it all up,' said Ellie as she walked up the passage.

Chapter 24

''Allo gel. Just popped along to see how yer mother is. You did go ter see her, didn't yer?'

Ellie nodded and stood to one side to let Molly bustle through, knowing she wouldn't be kept talking on the doorstep.

''Allo Iris,' said Molly, hobbling into the kitchen. 'Ain't you got that bleeding fire alight yet?'

'The wood was wet,' said Ellie.

'It's bloody cold in 'ere. I'll just 'ave to keep me coat on.' Molly settled herself at the table. 'Well, how was yer mother? She coming home?'

'No,' said Ellie, standing behind Molly and shaking her head sharply at Iris. She didn't want her telling Molly too much.

'Well, how is she then?' asked Molly in an irritated tone.

Ellie sat beside her. 'She ain't too good. The matron said she don't know when she'll be home.'

'That's a shame. Was she upset about yer dad?'

Ellie knew she had to be very guarded about what she told her. 'She don't remember much just yet, the hospital said she's still in shock.'

'She will be. It's only natural. It'll all come back, give her time.'

'Molly,' said Ellie casually. 'Did you know much about our mum and dad? When did they first move 'ere?'

Molly smiled. 'Dunno. Must'a been before the war,

253

before me and me sister moved 'ere anyway. Don't know where they came from.' She paused. 'Me and yer mum could never see eye to eye. I think yer dad must'a been injured at some time, it might 'ave been in the war.'

Both Iris and Ellie looked surprised. 'Why? What makes you say that?' asked Iris. 'Dad never talked about being in the war.'

'I don't remember much about the war. I certainly don't remember Dad wearing a uniform. He did go away, but I thought it was to work,' added Ellie with a puzzled look on her face. 'I wonder why he didn't tell us.'

'I overheard him telling someone something about the guns,' said Molly. 'I don't forget much.' She touched her temple. 'Stores it all up 'ere. If you ask me, I think it was a bit o' shell shock.'

'Who was he talking to?' asked Ellie earnestly.

'Don't remember.'

'Was it me mum?' Ellie wanted to smile. So much for her storing all the so-called information she picked up.

'No. Don't think so. Anyway they was already living 'ere, before me and me sister moved into the square. It was in the war – after we both come out of hospital. One of those Zeppelins bombed us, you know.'

Both Ellie and Iris's eyes were wide open, and Ellie asked, 'You was bombed? Where was that?'

'Not round this way, bloody Germans.' Molly looked angry. 'That's why I sit under the tree when I can, don't like ter be shut in. Makes me all nervy.' She twiddled with her fingers. 'Don't know why I'm telling you all this. I only come up to see how yer mother was.'

'Don't stop,' said Iris eagerly. 'So why do you sit outside?'

Molly's eyes misted over. 'I ain't as daft as everyone thinks.' She took a handkerchief from her coat pocket and dabbed at her moist eyes. Her voice softened. 'Yer see, I know what it's like to lose yer mum and dad. I was holding me mum's hand all the while we was buried under the house. It finished up just a bloody great pile of rubble.'

Ellie took in a sharp breath. 'You was buried under rubble? That must 'ave been awful.'

'It was. I couldn't move, pinned down be a rafter. I lay holding me poor mum's hand for hours. I tried talking to her, but she just lay beside me getting colder and colder. Me sister was outside, and she wasn't too bad.' Molly looked as if she had gone off into a dream. 'Me mum 'ad been dead for hours before we was finally rescued and me dad had been killed outright. So yer see, I ain't all that daft, just don't like to be shut in. Being buried alive 'as that effect on yer. Don't really like talking about it, so I don't know why I'm telling you all this.' She regained her composure and straightened her shoulders. 'Now, get the fire going and get yerselves a cuppa, and remember if I can help, just give us a knock.' She stood up. 'I'll see meself out.'

Ellie and Iris sat looking at the kitchen door after she left.

'I don't believe it,' said Ellie. 'All these years we thought she was just a silly old woman, and she'd been through all that. It must 'ave been awful.'

'Makes you feel a bit guilty the way we used to take the mickey out of her when we was kids,' said Iris sadly. 'Wonder why her and her sister never got married.'

'Could be their men friends got killed in the war.'

'Don't see a lot of her sister,' said Iris.

Ellie was still thinking of other things. 'I wonder if Dad *was* in the war?'

'We'll never know now.'

'If only we still saw Lizzie and Dolly, they would know.'

'Fat chance of ever seeing them again.' Iris looked angry. 'We could do with 'em here, now.' She stood up and banged her chair under the table.

'And we never got round to asking Molly what the fight with Mum and Terry's mum was all about,' said Ellie.

'Didn't seem very important after what she's been through.'

'No, I suppose not.'

'I've got a feeling we'll be seeing a lot more of Molly after this,' said Iris.

'I wonder why we always called her Dirty Molly?' asked Ellie.

'Well she does pong a bit in the summer, and so does her dog.'

Ellie smiled. 'Yes she does, I'm glad she never brought it in here.' Ellie got on her knees in front of the empty grate. 'Better have another go at this fire, otherwise we ain't gonner get a cuppa tonight.'

Soon the fire was crackling away and the kettle's lid jumping up and down.

'I'll make the tea and you put those cakes Mr Jenkins gave me yesterday on a plate, they shouldn't be stale yet,' said Ellie. 'It ain't much, but it's better than nothing.'

Iris did as she was told.

When they were both sitting at the table Ellie asked, 'Are you going to leave now Mum ain't coming home?' Her thoughts were on Leonard.

Iris looked at the tea leaves in the bottom of her cup. 'Ellie, that woman wants seven and six a week for the room and food. I can't afford that, that's all I earn all week, I'd 'ave nothing left to spend.' She looked up. 'D'you think we could stay 'ere?'

Ellie couldn't answer her. She had been hoping Iris would say she was off, so that Ellie could have gone to live with Leonard.

'Ellie. Did you 'ear what I said?'

'Yes.'

'Well, what d'you think, could we manage to stay here?' Iris suddenly sounded cheerful.

'I don't know.' Ellie looked straight at her. 'You've changed your tune quickly. Only the other day you couldn't wait to get away from me, now you want to stay – why?'

Iris looked uncomfortable. 'When I saw Mum, I realized

we've only got each other now. Well, I dunno, I think we ought to try and make a go of it.'

'I don't know. I don't know if we can afford to stay here.'

'What if we found somewhere cheaper? We could stay together then, couldn't we?'

Ellie looked at Iris. She was right, they did only have each other, and they would have to manage as best as they could. After all it was her fault they were on their own, and she had to go along with Iris, she had to look after her. Much to Ellie's sorrow, any ideas of living with Leonard had to disappear.

'We will have to sit and work out what we have to spend, and then see if we can manage.'

'What about if we took a lodger,' asked Iris eagerly, 'like you said?' She was smiling for the first time in days.

'We wouldn't be able to feed them, and I doubt if we'd get enough. No, let's wait and see how we manage.'

'Pity we ain't got nothing to pawn,' said Iris.

'I've got the frock and shoes I bought for that club's do I went to on Christmas Eve.'

'You 'ave? What's it like, did it look nice?'

Ellie nodded.

'It's a shame you've got to pawn it. Still, perhaps when we're in the money you'll be able to get them out again.'

Ellie smiled weakly. She knew that would never be. And Iris hadn't even tried to talk her out of pawning the dress. Ellie knew that to do so would be to lose the last link she would have with Leonard's club. She could never go there in her scruffy clothes. But this situation had been brought about by her selfishness and she couldn't send Iris away, not now. Iris needed her.

Ellie wrote and told Leonard that Iris had decided to stay, quashing any ideas of her moving in with him. He wrote back that he was very disappointed.

As Ellie read his letter a tear ran down her face. Not as

disappointed as me, she said to herself. He also said he still wanted to take her out. She wrote back and told him that was out of the question now. She didn't want to tell him she had nothing to wear. Dolly's frock, and the pretty one she'd bought for Christmas, and the silver shoes, had been pawned, but she couldn't bring herself to pawn her lovely nightgown. Perhaps deep down she was hoping that one day she would be sharing Leonard's bed again.

Although money was very tight Ellie and Iris found they could just about manage. They looked for rooms, but most of them were dirty and smelt of dried pee. The walls were usually dotted with red stains, where previous lodgers had squashed the army of bedbugs that had crept out of the cracked lathe-and-plaster walls, or from under peeling paper. The landladies wanted almost as much rent as they were paying now. Nearly all the women who were letting the rooms looked dirty, and smelled, and the thought of them cooking their meals made them shudder.

Mr Jenkins was kind; although he told Ellie he couldn't give her the rise she asked for, he always baked a few extra sausage rolls, and when he baked bread always made a misshapen loaf for her. He told her it was just in case Mr Cole came in and counted them, and found he had given a good loaf away. Iris would stop at the shops near the market on her way home from work and get the veg from a man who, as it was the end of the day, sold them off cheap. Sometimes Molly would give them a bowl of soup her sister had made, saying she'd made too much. Day by day, the two sisters survived.

Winter was at long last giving way to spring. Ellie and Iris had only been to see their mother once more, and the response had been exactly the same. It upset them for days, often provoking them into argument, so they decided not to waste their money on going to see her for a while. Matron said she would write and tell them if there was any change.

Leonard came into the tea room for his usual once a month tea and scone, and always left her a shilling. Ellie would look at him with longing in her heart. How near she had been to living like a lady. In all his letters he told her how much he wanted to take her out again, but she always declined. What was the point? She couldn't go with him, she didn't have any decent clothes. He also told her his door was always open if she ever changed her mind. She never answered his letters as quickly as she used to now; there wasn't that much to say.

One Friday Ellie was putting the rent, gas and coal money into little bags as usual. She sighed. 'If only we could do something at home, or find another job in the evenings, or Sundays.'

'I was talking to John . . .'

'Who's John?' asked Ellie.

'He's the man in the greengrocers. I've seen him lots of times; he always used to laugh and take the mickey out of me when I had to scrabble round the back of the stalls for Mum.'

'That wasn't very nice of him.'

'He said if I didn't work on Saturdays he would let me work there with 'im.'

Ellie looked at her. 'Is it his shop?'

'No, it's his dad's.'

'How old is this John?'

'Dunno, about twenty.'

'Is he good-looking?'

'Yer, a bit.'

'Iris Walsh, you ain't thinking of going out with 'im, are you?'

'Dunno,' she said loftily.

Ellie looked at her little sister. She had grown up very quickly – mentally and physically. She was now a tall, striking blonde, with large blue eyes. If she had the right clothes to wear she would certainly turn heads. It must make her feel very resentful, working with lovely frocks and not being able to afford one.

'Would you mind?' Iris asked.

Ellie quickly turned away. She couldn't escape the knowledge that it was her fault. Every now and again she was filled with remorse. Would this feeling ever leave her?

'Ellie, I said, would you mind?'

'No, course not.' She smiled. 'You'd better wait for him to ask you first though.'

Iris smiled. 'He has, and I'm going to the pictures with him on Saturday. Is that all right?'

'Course. It'll make a nice change for you. Anything's got to be better than sitting in here night after night.' Ellie sighed. 'I wish I was going out.'

'Why don't you ask your Mr What's-'is-name?'

'Ain't got nothing to wear.'

Iris put her arm round Ellie. 'I'm sure something good's gonner happen soon.'

Iris was beaming when she came home from the pictures on Saturday night. 'He's ever so nice. I'm glad I managed to persuade Mum to get me a new coat, well secondhand new, before all—' She stopped. 'Well, you know.'

Ellie nodded. Iris did look nice when she went to work, and, like Ellie, once at work she had her uniform, so that didn't put her apart from the rest of the girls in the store. 'Well, you seeing him again?'

'Course, in the shop.'

'No, daft, I mean is he taking you out again?'

'Don't know. But I'll see him on Monday.'

Every Saturday after that Iris went to the pictures with John. Ellie felt even more lonely. Iris had John, and Peggy had Mr Jenkins. Her job was still the highlight of her life, and the only time she felt smart was when she was wearing her uniform. If only she had something nice to wear she could go to Leonard's club on a Saturday. She threw the book she was reading on the table. Would living in this poverty ever end?

She went and sat in her father's chair. Had he really been in the army? If so, what did he go through, and why did he never talk about it? If only she could turn the clock back, she would ask him all sorts of questions. And what about her grandparents? They must have had some, but why had they never been mentioned? They would never know now.

And what about poor Molly, being buried alive and holding her dead mother's hand? These Germans must be very wicked people. And was Leonard German? He said his parents lived there. Her eyes became heavy and once again she was being chased by the hangman. And again she screamed and woke herself up.

Every Friday evening the two girls sat and counted out their money.

'It's just as bad as giving Mum our wage packets,' said Iris good humouredly.

'I know; at least then I could keep any tips. Never mind, we'll get by.' Ellie tried to sound lighthearted, but deep down she knew how hard it was getting to make ends meet every week.

Their first priority was the rent, that had to be paid; then after the gas and coal money was taken out they could think about buying food. The rent book was always left on the inside windowsill; the man would lift the window, take the money and put the rent book back. Ellie never bothered to check it, as their rent man had been the same one for as long as she could remember.

This Friday it had been pleasant weather, the day warm with the promise of a long and eagerly awaited summer. Ellie wandered into the empty front room, but despite the sun still shining it felt bleak and cold. She went over to the windowsill to place the money in the book for next week's rent and to her surprise she found a letter inside. It was from the landlord, Mr Cole, informing them that their rent was going up by one shilling a week. She looked at the date; it was going up this week. She felt sick. How could they afford another shilling a week? She hurried back into the kitchen.

'Iris, what we gonner do? That Mr Cole's gone and put our rent up.'

'What?'

'Our rent, it's gone up by a shilling a week.'

'We can't afford that.'

'We must. We've got to find it somehow, otherwise he'll throw us out.'

Iris looked at Ellie. 'We just about manage now.' Tears sprang to her eyes. 'I'm fed up with living like this; not having any nice clothes, and sometimes not even having much to eat.' She thumped the table. 'I'm sick of it, sick of it.'

Ellie went to put her arm round her young sister's shoulder but she was brushed away.

'I'm so sorry, Iris.'

Iris's sobs filled the kitchen. 'If only Mum was 'ere.'

'We didn't 'ave much when Mum was here, so I don't know . . .'

Iris lifted her tearstained face. 'I know we didn't have much, but we didn't have to come home to a cold house every night, and we didn't have to wait till the fire was alight before we could have a cuppa tea, and we didn't have to clean out the grate and get the wood and do our washing and . . .' Her tears fell once more.

Ellie once again felt the heavy burden of guilt weighing her down. She sat at the table. 'You're right, we can't go on like this. I'll go over and ask Mrs Andrews if she can help us find a lodger or something.'

Chapter 25

As Ellie closed the front door behind her, her thoughts were suddenly full of Mrs Collins and the day she had been thrown out of her house.

"Allo gel, all right then?' called Molly as Ellie crossed the square.

'Yes thanks.' Ellie hesitated. Since finding out about Molly's reason for sitting under the tree she had felt more kindly towards her. Ellie went over and sat next to her. 'Molly, has your rent gone up?'

'Yer. That greedy bugger's put 'em all up, and some of the other property he owns as well, so the rent man told me. Will you and your sister be able to manage it?'

'Don't know, don't think so. I'm just going over to ask Mrs Andrews about getting a lodger.'

'You wanner be careful about that, gel. Could get a very nasty character in, and you'd have hell's own job to get 'em out. Two nice young gels like you on their own.' She took a sharp breath. 'Could be very nasty.'

'Perhaps we could get a woman. We've got to do something if we wanner stay here.'

'That's true. You could end up with a nice young lady, I s'pose. I see Mrs Andrews 'as got one now. 'Ere, she might 'ave a friend who's looking for a room.'

'I hope so. We've got to do something. I was thinking about Mrs Collins.'

'Nasty business that was. I often wondered what 'appened

to 'em; nice little widder woman she was. That sort always finish up with problems. And that cow's son Cole ain't got no feelings.'

'That's what I'm worried about.'

'You go and 'ave a word with that Mrs Andrews, she might be able to help yer.'

Ellie smiled. 'Thanks Molly. I'll go and see her right away.'

She gently banged the shiny knocker. Everything about the house looked so clean. Although it seemed Ellie had known Mrs Andrews and Terry all her life, she had never been inside the house.

''Allo Ellie,' said Mrs Andrews, her small features lighting up. 'This is a nice surprise. What can I do for you? I was so very sorry to hear about yer mum and dad. How's your mum taking it?'

'Not too bad. We don't see her very often because of the fares.'

'Where is she?'

'Greenwich.'

Mrs Andrews' expression changed; she looked concerned. 'Not in that hospital for . . . I know that one.' She stopped.

'You do?' asked Ellie with surprise.

Mrs Andrews quickly recovered her smile. 'It was a while ago, used to know someone who was there. Will your mum be in there long?'

'Don't know.'

'Anyway, what can I do for you?'

'I really want some advice.'

'You'd better come in.'

Ellie didn't know what to expect when she walked in, as there was no Mr Andrews, and Terry always seemed to be out of work. So the smell of cooking and the neat and tidy kitchen, with just the bare essentials, took her unawares.

'Sit yourself down. Now, how can I help you?'

'You know Mr Cole has just put up all the rents?'

'Only too well. I'll have to charge me lodger another shilling a week at least to cover it. Go on, sit yourself down.'

Ellie sat at the table, that was covered with a dark green chenille cloth. 'That's what I wanted to know about. How do you go about getting a lodger?'

'Most of 'em come recommended. Usually have men, but this time I've got a very nice young lady.' Her pleasant face broke into a smile, lighting up her pale blue eyes. Terry didn't look like his mother at all, he was dark. Mrs Andrews went on, 'She works in Rotherhithe New Road, so she don't 'ave far to go. She should be home soon. I 'ave to give 'em tea and breakfast, do their washing and clean their room. Could you do all that?'

Ellie shook her head. 'We ain't even got any proper sheets.'

'They must have good clean linen, otherwise they don't stay five minutes.'

'What if we only charged 'em a few shillings?'

'Then I'm afraid you'd get all the roughs, and two young girls alone in the house, well, that ain't very good.'

Ellie knew she looked despondent. 'What we gonner do?'

'If only I'd known you was having a job to manage. I thought, with both of you in good jobs – pity you didn't say before, you and your sister could have moved in here with us. But then there's yer mum to think about. You've got to keep the house on for her. When's she coming out of . . .?'

'Don't know.' Ellie felt even more miserable. To think she and Iris could have stayed in this clean house, and been waited on, and perhaps even had a few pence a week over to go out or buy clothes. 'How long is your young lady staying?'

'Miss Jones. Wouldn't like to say.' She leaned forward. 'Think she's got a soft spot for my Terry – so anything could happen.' She gave Ellie a knowing look.

Ellie wanted to die. She had never thought that anyone

265

else would be interested in Terry. 'Is Terry working?' she croaked.

'Yes, he's in the garage, works full time now. He's very lucky, and the boss has really taken a shine to 'im. Miss Jones works there as well, she's in the office. That's how she knew I let rooms.'

'I'm so glad for him; he's wanted a proper job for a long while.'

'Yes. Things are getting better for us all the while. I'm sorry they're not for you and your sister, though. But if I hear of anyone, anyone who is all right that is, I'll let you know.'

The sound of laughter came from the passage.

'Here's Terry and Miss Jones now.'

The kitchen door flew open and a tall young woman walked in. She was wearing a neat little beige straw cloche hat, and a pretty floral frock. Her long legs were covered in silk stockings, and beige shoes completed the picture. She was lovely.

''Allo Ellie,' said Terry coming into the kitchen behind her. 'What you doing 'ere? Don't ever see you over 'ere.' He was wearing greasy overalls and had a dirty face. He smiled and turned to the young woman. 'This is Ellie, a neighbour. Ellie, meet Joyce.'

She held out her gloved hand. 'Pleased, I'm sure.'

'Hallo.' Ellie took the limp hand and quickly shook it. She turned to Terry. 'Your mum said you've got a job now?'

'Yer, things are really looking up.' He looked very happy.

'I'm pleased for you.' That's all Ellie could think of saying and quickly added, 'I'd better be going.'

'If I hear anything I'll send Terry over,' said Mrs Andrews.

'Thank you.'

'But, be careful who you take in, won't you?'

'Yes, yes thank you.'

Ellie rushed across the square, so that Molly wouldn't see

the tears filling her eyes. But why should she care about Terry? She had been with Leonard, and would live with him if she could. She was cross with herself for being silly and jealous. Would she ever really get Terry out of her thoughts?

'Well,' said Iris, when Ellie got in. 'What'd she say?'

'She reckons we have to cook and clean for 'em if we want a decent rent.'

'Oh,' said Iris. 'We can't do that, not and go to work as well.'

'No I know. She's got a girl staying there now, and Mrs Andrews said if she'd known we were looking for rooms we could 'ave stayed there.' Ellie sat at the table.

'That would 'ave been nice.'

'But she also said we should keep the house on for when Mum comes out.'

Iris sat next to her. 'D'you think she will ever come out?'

Ellie shrugged. 'Don't know. Iris, what we gonner do? Mr Jenkins can't give me a rise; what about your boss?'

'We only get 'em on our birthdays.'

'We can't go on like this.'

'I'm ever so sorry for going off at you like that,' Iris said sheepishly.

'That's all right. It's hard for us to manage, and keep a sense of humour,' said Ellie sadly.

'Perhaps something will turn up.'

Ellie sighed. 'I don't know what; it'll 'ave to be a miracle, I reckon.'

'Don't forget I'm going to the pictures with John tomorrow night, so don't worry about getting me anythink to eat.'

'I'd like to meet this 'ere John,' Ellie said more brightly.

'Can't bring him home to tea, can I?'

Ellie grinned. 'Perhaps one day; that's if you ain't chucked 'im be then.'

'Can't do that, we'd never have any veg if I did.'

'It's a sorry state of affairs when you only go out with a bloke 'cos he can provide us with cheap veg.' Ellie laughed, but it was a sad, halfhearted laugh. 'You'll have me looking for a good-looking butcher next.'

'Now that's not a bad idea.' Iris looked serious. 'But it ain't just his veg I like, I like 'im as well.'

Ellie looked at her. 'Remember I'm your next of kin, so if you're thinking of getting married, me gel, I'll have to sign you away.'

Iris laughed. 'I ain't that serious.'

The following morning as soon as Ellie got to work she told Peggy of her problems.

'I didn't tell you that Mr Jenkins had his rent put up as we wasn't sure if it was just the shops that Mr Cole had put up,' said Peggy. 'Mr Jenkins is very worried about it; he said he can't raise his prices to cover it. Mr Cole's bloody greedy.'

'I don't know what me and Iris are gonner do. I did go and ask Mrs Andrews about letting a room, but I don't think we can as we ain't got much. We ain't got many bedclothes, or crocks, and we'd 'ave to feed 'em.' Ellie sat at a table. 'It would be nice if we could go and live with someone, but as Mrs Andrews said we've got to think about when Mum comes out.'

'Will she ever come out?'

'Don't know.' Ellie sighed and stood up. 'Better get on with it.'

All day her mind was on her problem. If only it was Leonard's day to come in. Perhaps she could ask his advice. She would write to him tonight.

At the end of the day, as they were clearing away, Peggy looked out through the open door. 'Hope it's gonner be a nice day tomorrow.'

'Why?' asked Ellie. 'You doing anything special?'

Peggy looked at the bakery door and grinned. 'Me and Mr Jenkins are going to the seaside for the day.'

'Lucky old you. I ain't ever seen the sea. It must be really nice to see the sand and . . . Where you going then?'

'To see one of his cousins down near Margate.'

'That'll be nice. Have a good time, see you Monday.' Ellie left the tea room with her thoughts. Peggy, Mr Jenkins and Terry; they all seemed to have a purpose in life now, but what did she have?

On Sunday Ellie woke to a warm and sunny morning, and after finishing her few chores decided to go for a walk. She wandered round the park, and was walking the long way home past the asylum when she looked through the gates and to her surprise saw Terry walking towards her. She didn't run and hide this time, as she wanted to know why, if he was working full time, did he bother with coming to this place on a Sunday?

'Hallo, Terry,' she said as he pushed open the gate. 'Didn't think you'd still be coming here to work.'

He looked taken aback. ''Allo Ellie,' he said, shutting the large black gate behind him. 'What you doing round 'ere?'

'Just been out for a walk. What you doing in there?' She inclined her head towards the asylum. 'Didn't think you'd still be working in there.'

''Er, just like to keep the job on, keep me 'and in like, yer never know, might need it again one day. You on yer way 'ome?' Although he looked anxious he sounded happy and carefree.

She nodded, and for once didn't know what to say.

He fell in step with her and began whistling.

'You sound happy.'

'Yer, well I've got a decent job and me mum's got a nice lodger, not like some of the surly stuck up buggers we've had at times, and yes, I think I can honestly say that for the first time in me life, I'm happy.'

'Miss Jones seems nice.'

'Yes she is, very nice.'

'You and her, you know, walking out together?'

He laughed. 'Course not. Don't think she'd 'ave me anyway.'

He didn't say *he* didn't want to go out with Miss Jones. He'd been quite different towards Ellie when she'd wanted him to go out with *her*. Perhaps after all he did only see her as a mate.

Ellie felt her heart break. What else could go wrong? Their rent had been put up and she wasn't going to live with Leonard, and now it seemed Terry would be courting Miss Jones if he got the chance.

With Terry whistling at her side, she continued the journey home in silence.

'Did you have a nice time yesterday?' Ellie asked Peggy as soon as she got into work.

Peggy looked vague. 'Yes, yes we did.'

'The weather was nice. Whereabouts did you go?'

'I told you, Margate.'

'Oh yes, did you see Mr Jenkins' cousin?'

'Yes.'

'Is that it, that all you gonner tell me?'

'We had a very nice day.'

Mr Jenkins came out of the bakery. 'Good morning, Miss Walsh,' he said smiling. 'I trust Miss Swan has told you the good news?'

Ellie shook her head. 'What good news?'

'You'd better sit down, Ellie,' said Peggy seriously. She looked at Mr Jenkins. 'Me and Harry are gonner get married.'

Ellie jumped up and threw her arms round Peggy's neck. 'Oh Peg, I'm so pleased for you. When's the big day?'

'August.'

'August?' repeated Ellie. 'But that's only two months away. What'd your mum have to say about it, is she pleased?'

Peggy blushed and looked at Mr Jenkins. 'Yes, yes she's pleased.'

'I'll get back to work,' said Mr Jenkins quickly, moving away.

'Ellie, it ain't 'cos . . . 'Cos I ain't.' Her face turned an even deeper shade of red. 'Mum don't mind me getting married, but . . .' Peggy looked ill at ease. 'She don't like the idea of moving.'

'You won't be that far away; just round the corner.'

'Ellie, yer better sit down.'

Ellie looked at her quizzically and did as she was told.

Peggy sat next to her and played with the corner of the tablecloth, quickly folding and unfolding it. 'Ellie,' she said slowly, 'you see I ain't just moving round the corner. We're going to Margate; we're gonner open up our own tea shop there.'

Ellie gasped, she felt the wind had been knocked out of her. She didn't speak. They were going away. Her mind was racing – her job, what about her job?

Peggy was still talking, but now she was sounding a lot more confident and happier. 'Me mum ain't keen, but we told her it would be nice near the seaside, and she'd have her own room, and she could help us out when we get busy in the summer. You should see it, Ellie. It's so pretty and upstairs has got so many rooms . . .' She stopped. 'What's wrong?'

Ellie had a tear running down her face. 'I'm really happy for you, Peggy. But what's gonner happen to the tea shop? What about me job?'

Peggy quickly averted her eyes. 'We're both really sorry about that. I know things ain't been all that good for you just lately, but I'm sure everythink will work out, you wait and see.'

'Will Mr Cole get a new baker?'

'Don't know.'

'What did Mr Cole say about it?'

'Harry ain't told him yet. I don't think he'll be all that pleased, mind.'

Ellie was devastated. The one thing in her life she was sure of was her job, her wonderful job that had kept her sane all this time – and it was slipping away. What did the future hold for her and Iris now? Peggy said she hoped things would work out for her, but Ellie couldn't see how. She knew now that she had reached rock bottom.

Chapter 26

Ellie had lit the fire and was sitting at the table waiting for Iris to come home from work. She felt so miserable. What was going to happen to them? She would have to write and tell Leonard. If the tea room was going to close down she would no longer be seeing him once a month. Everything was beginning to get too much. What would Iris say about her being out of work? Jobs were very hard to get; what could she do? If only she'd been able to go to high school then perhaps she could have been a secretary, like Miss Jones.

'Hope you've got the kettle on,' said Iris, breezing into the kitchen. 'Cheer up. Not had any luck with a lodger yet, then?'

Ellie shook her head.

'Got some nice veg. John's ever so kind, I didn't have to pay for any of this. He said it was to keep me sweet so he could ask me out. Ain't that nice . . .? Ellie, what's wrong?'

Ellie brushed away a tear. She was so happy for Iris. She didn't want to have to bring her back down to earth. 'Iris, Peggy and Mr Jenkins are getting married.'

'Wow. That's one way of getting cheap labour, I suppose.' She laughed. 'When?'

'August.'

'August? That's a bit quick. She ain't, you know?' Iris gave her a knowing smile.

'No. It's because they're moving.'

'Moving? What, giving up the tea room?'

Ellie nodded.

'Where they moving to?' Iris sat at the table. She suddenly looked worried.

'Margate.'

'Margate. That's miles away. What about your job? What about the tea room, who's gonner take it . . .? Oh no.'

Ellie sighed deeply. 'We can't manage on your money alone; you'll have to find somewhere to live.'

'But what about you?'

'Don't worry about me, you just look after yourself. I suppose I could always ask Peggy to take me with her.' She gave her sister a lopsided grin.

'Would they?' asked Iris eagerly. 'Would they take you?'

'I shouldn't think so for one minute. They've got her mother to worry about, so they don't need another mouth to feed.'

'Ellie, if I did find somewhere, would your Mr What's-'is-name let you move in with him?'

'I don't know.'

'Well you wouldn't have to worry about getting back over this way to go to work now, would you?'

'No.'

'That's settled then. I find a cheap room somewhere and you move in with your fancy man.'

'We looked for cheap rooms before, remember, and all we found was filthy dirty places you wouldn't keep a cat in.'

'Most of 'em did 'ave cats, and dogs and mice, and bugs too.'

'All right, so where do you think you could get a cheap place?'

'I'm going to ask John. They've lived there for years and know all sorts of people.'

'You make it sound very easy.'

'It could be. Well at least we've got – what, two months – to get it sorted out.'

Ellie half smiled. Iris was trying so hard to be practical, but where would she find a cheap room? Ellie shuddered to think what her sister might be reduced to. And was it fair that she would have to live in with someone she didn't know, while Ellie was going to be in comparative luxury? That's if Leonard still wanted her. Once more, guilt flooded Ellie's mind.

As if reading Ellie's thoughts, Iris said, 'If you do stay with him, you'll have to try and stop having these bad dreams.'

'I still wake up thinking the hangman's going to get me.'

'I know, I can hear you shouting.'

'I wish there was something I could do.'

'What, to stop yourself dreaming?'

'No. To look after you.'

Ellie was very surprised when the following Wednesday Leonard was waiting outside the tea room.

'Ellie, I got your letter and I just had to see you,' he said urgently. 'Let's go along to Lyons.'

She was speechless as he took her arm and propelled her along the road.

Inside Lyons they gave their order to a waitress.

'Are you sure you don't want anything to eat?'

She would have dearly loved to say yes, but decided against that. 'No, a cup of tea will be just fine. I'm sorry if my letter . . .'

He took her hand. 'You must come and live with me. You haven't any excuses now. You don't have to come over here to work, not if they are moving away.'

'But what about my sister?' She pulled her hand away, and keeping her eyes down said, 'I can't leave her. It was all my fault, I must look after Iris.'

'It was also my fault. I should have come home with you, or at least made sure you got home on Christmas Day.'

'But I wanted to stay with you.'

'I know, and I wanted you to stay.'

They sat back while the waitress put the tray on the table.

'What am I going to do?' she asked, as tears silently ran down her cheeks.

'Move in with me. Please, dry your eyes.' He handed her his handkerchief.

'I can't. I must help Iris.'

Leonard poured the tea into the cups. 'There has to be a way round this. Give me time to work something out.'

'Why did you come over here tonight?'

'I was helping a pupil who's working for the end of term exam.'

She was a little disappointed at that remark: he hadn't come over just to see her after all. But perhaps he had only got her letter this morning – and at least he had come to see her, and was trying to help with her problems. Her mind was wandering. With her elbows on the table she sipped her tea. She would dearly love to move in with him, but she would have to find a job. If only Iris could find somewhere nice. If only Miss Jones would move out she could live with Terry and his mum. Suddenly she found herself comparing Leonard with Terry. If only it was Terry who had a home for her. But no, she knew she wanted to be with Leonard.

'Ellie, are you listening to me?'

'Sorry. I was thinking about Iris,' she lied.

'Well I'm sure we will be able to work something out. Would you like some more tea?'

'No thank you.'

'Look, I must go; playing in the club tonight.'

'Yes, of course.' She stood up. 'Thank you for coming to see me.'

Outside he took her face in his hands. 'You have been through such a lot. You look tired. We must put the sparkle back into those lovely eyes.' He tenderly kissed her mouth. 'Bye, Ellie Walsh.'

'Bye, Leonard Kent,' she said softly as he went in the opposite direction to her.

During the rest of the week Peggy and Mr Jenkins told Ellie all about the tea room they were going to rent. It seemed they had been planning the move for a very long while, and had just been waiting for the right property to come along.

'That's why when Mr Cole came in that time and looked round, we thought he'd found out we'd been looking,' said Peggy.

Ellie listened, but really couldn't work up much enthusiasm for their plans. She was losing her job, the job she loved so much. Mr Jenkins told her he would give her excellent references, but that wouldn't help her to get work in the middle of a Depression.

Ellie was in bed when Iris came home on Saturday night. She now slept in her parents' bed, as her nightmares had been keeping Iris awake. As usual she lay on her back going over and over their problems. This week they could just about afford the extra rent – but what about next week?

Iris poked her head round the door. 'You asleep?'

'No.' Ellie sat up.

As Iris sat on the end of the bed the glow from the gaslight in the passage surrounded her head like a golden halo. 'I think I've got the answer to our prayers.'

'Don't tell me you've persuaded John to marry you and whisk you away to some foreign island.'

'Don't talk daft. Tonight we didn't fancy the pictures so we went to the pub with his mum and dad. They're ever so nice.'

'Iris, you ain't old enough to go in a pub.'

'They sat me in a corner and they all huddled round me. 'Sides, they know the landlord. A lot of their friends was there, they're a smashing bunch and we had a lot of laughs. Anyway, they asked where I worked and, well to cut a long story short, I told 'em we was worried about our rent going up and we couldn't—'

Ellie banged the bed in anger. 'Iris, you didn't tell 'em all our business, did you? You didn't tell 'em all about Mum and Dad?'

'Grant me with a bit of common. I told 'em me dad was dead and me mum was in hospital and she's never coming out 'cos she's very ill. They felt ever so sorry for me.'

'I bet they did. It must'a been better than going to the pictures for 'em.'

'Don't be like that. Anyway, Mrs Day, that's John's mum, she's got a friend who lets rooms, and they are ever so reasonable, and ever so nice.'

'Did you go and see 'em?'

'Well no, it was too late. But Mrs Day reckons there's room for you there as well, and I'm sure one of the shops would find you some work. It might not pay much, but she only wants six bob a week all found, so that can't be bad.'

A tear gradually slipped down Ellie's cheek. Her little sister was now looking after *her*. 'What does John have to say about all this?'

'He reckons it's a good idea, and Mrs Marsh, well, Bessie as she likes to be called, is a very good friend of the family, and she's a good cook. He said she will look after us all right. We can go and look at the room tomorrow if you like.'

'That sounds a good idea.'

'Well I'm off to bed now, see you in the morning.' Iris trotted off cheerily to bed.

Ellie's head was full of thoughts as she lay down. Iris had found a home and a family: six shillings a week all found. Iris would have good food and not have to worry about washing and chores, and she would be able to save a bit. Could this be a turning point in their lives? If she did move in with Leonard she would never lose contact with Iris, not like Dolly and Lizzie. If only she knew where they were – but would they help them? And if she did move in with

Leonard would she still want to go to work? She wanted to be independent, and not a kept woman. That thought brought a smile to her face, but it quickly vanished when she realized he hadn't mentioned anything about getting married. And she would also be leaving Elmleigh. But what did it have to offer? She was losing her job: Peggy and Mr Jenkins were starting a new life; Iris was starting a new life, and Terry had Miss Jones. She turned over. 'And I should be happy at starting a new life,' she said to herself.

On Sunday morning they went off to Rotherhithe New Road to look at the room Mrs Marsh was letting. First of all Ellie was introduced to John Day. He was a good-looking, tall young man with striking blue eyes and a mop of light brown hair.

''Allo Ellie. Heard a lot about you.'

Ellie was taken aback. 'I haven't heard much about you.'

'Ain't much to tell, and I ain't got nothing to hide. Come and meet me mum.'

Mrs Day was a plump woman with laughing blue eyes, who seemed to be permanently smiling. ''Allo love. Iris said you was the good-looking one in the family, and she was right. Mind you, she's a bit of a stunner herself. I said to my John, you better hang on to 'er, otherwise yer gonner lose her.' She nudged Ellie's arm with her elbow. 'Think 'e's had his eye on her fer years.'

'Oh Mum,' said John blushing.

Ellie laughed.

'We used to watch her skip past the shop and pick up all the mouldies after the stalls moved off.'

'I didn't know that,' said Iris.

'Always was a pretty little thing,' said Mrs Day. 'Now look at her, turned out to be a real beauty.'

Iris was blushing and laughing.

An older man walked in. ''Allo gel, I'm the old man,' he said to Ellie. A thick leather belt held up his trousers, which was just as well as his braces were dangling round his waist. He had a mischievous twinkle in his blue eyes. 'Now you've met the lot of us, that is except me other boy, but 'e's married and moved orf to Essex. Works in a car factory, silly sod.'

'Tom Day, watch yer language in front of these nice young ladies, and pull yer braces up.'

'Sorry love,' he said to his wife, laughing, and doing as he was told.

'Come on,' said John. 'I'll take you both round to see Bessie.'

'Ellie – I can call you Ellie?' asked Mrs Day.

Ellie nodded. 'Of course.'

'Bessie will look after you both. Her place is spotless, you can eat yer dinner off the floor.'

'Why's that? Ain't she got no plates?' laughed Mr Day.

'Trust you to say somethink daft like that.' Mrs Day tutted and turned to Ellie and Iris. 'She's a widder woman, lorst her old man a few years back, didn't 'ave any kids. Her old man left her quite comfortable, but she likes company. That's why she takes in people, she says it gives her a reason to cook an' all. She's ever such a good cook. You're lucky, I think her lodger's just moving out; she don't 'ave any trouble letting. I think you'll be all right round there. Anyway, pop back and let us know.'

'Thank you. We will, Mrs Day,' said Ellie.

'Call me Ada, everyone else does.'

Outside John led the way. 'Me mum and dad ain't bad. Mind you, you should hear 'em when they has a row. Half the street can hear 'em, but it ain't nothink to worry about, they think the world of each other really.' John's long stride was causing the girls to break into a trot now and again.

'Slow down a bit, John,' said Iris. 'We've only got little legs.'

He grinned. 'Sorry gels. They might only be little, but they're very shapely.'

Iris gave him a playful push. 'Oh you.'

'I'll walk a bit slower.'

Ellie looked up at him. How she envied him his genuine love for his family. It would be wonderful for Iris if she too could find happiness and love with this close-knit bunch of people. 'Is your brother older than you?' she asked.

'Yer, but only by a couple of years. He's married to a nice gel. Mum was a bit upset when they moved away, but 'e's not cut out to work in a shop. Mind you, when they start a family me mum'll be over there like a shot. Don't reckon we'll see much of her then.' He laughed. 'That is, till the old man drags her back 'ere.'

Ellie glanced at Iris. She was beaming with happiness.

'Right, 'ere we are.' John knocked on a door that fronted right onto the pavement. It was quickly opened and a youngish, round-faced woman stood there and smiled. ''Allo, you must be Ellie and Iris. Come on in. 'Allo John, how's yer mum?'

He snatched off his cap. 'She's all right, Bessie.'

'Would you like a cuppa tea?' Bessie asked as they tramped down the passage behind her. The lovely smell of cooking filled the air, causing Ellie's stomach to rumble.

'Yes please,' said Iris and Ellie together.

'Sit yourselves down,' she said when they entered the kitchen.

Ellie and Iris looked around at this neat, tidy room. The brass fender gleamed and the fireplace with its little china ornaments on the shelf above shone. The grate was white as snow and everything was orderly and clean.

Bessie put a tray on the table that was covered with a crisp, well starched white cloth. On the tray were cups and saucers, a sugar bowl and a jug of milk. 'Kettle won't be long, had it on a low gas all ready for you.' She smiled a warm smile, and Ellie knew Iris would be happy here.

'I don't know if Ada told you, but I normally only take one guest. At the moment I already have a lady, she's at church. Prefer ladies, they ain't so much trouble. But she's going at the end of the week, so if you don't mind sharing the double bed, I will take you both.'

'It might only be Iris,' said Ellie. 'I might be staying with a friend.'

'That'll be nice for you. Where does she live?'

Ellie could feel herself blushing. 'Over the water, the West End.'

'That's nice.'

'Ellie's got to get herself a job as well,' said Iris quickly, looking at John. 'The tea room where she works might be closing.'

'Oh that's a shame. Why's that?' asked Bessie.

'They're moving to Margate.'

'Margate's ever so nice, have you ever been there?'

'No,' said Ellie.

'Me late husband took me there.' She had a faraway look in her eyes. 'We went there for our honeymoon. Now, if you've finished your tea, we'll go upstairs and you can take a look at the room. Ada told you I charge six shillings a week, didn't she?'

They both nodded.

When Bessie pushed open the bedroom door Ellie almost gasped out loud. The room was bright and well furnished, with a dressing table that had a mirror. There was a wardrobe as well as the large double bed, the lace curtain was spotless, and the flowery curtains were gently blowing in the breeze. Ellie heard Iris take in a breath.

'This is lovely,' she said walking into the room. She twirled round. 'It really is lovely.' Her face was wearing the broadest grin Ellie had ever seen.

'I'll do any bits of washing you'd like me to. I don't provide a midday meal, only on Sundays.'

'It smells very nice,' said Ellie.

'I do like cooking,' said Bessie as they went downstairs to where John was waiting.

'I'll take it,' said Iris. 'When shall I move in?'

'Well, you can please yourself, but it won't be too long, will it?'

Iris shook her head.

'I'll help you bring all your stuff round,' said John.

'I ain't got that much,' said Iris.

'As soon as I find out about my friend,' said Ellie, 'Iris will let John know. Is that all right?'

'Course.' She opened the front door. 'Give yer mum me best, John.'

'Will do, Bessie. Bye.'

As soon as they were round the corner Iris stopped and, throwing her arms round John's neck, kissed his cheek loudly.

He grinned and rubbed his cheek. 'What was that for?'

'For getting me that room.' Suddenly her face crumpled.

'What's wrong?' he asked anxiously.

'I'm so happy I want to cry.'

'I'm happy too,' he said gently.

Ellie felt pleased for Iris; she was going to be really looked after by Bessie, and with John and a happy-go-lucky family like the Days taking her under their wing, Baby Iris would at long last find true happiness.

But what about her? Would living with Leonard work out as well as she was hoping?

Chapter 27

As they walked home Iris was full of her new room. 'I'm going to have a dressing table with a mirror, and a wardrobe. Ellie, I can't believe it.'

Ellie laughed. 'I remember when you carried on 'cos Dolly and Lizzie wouldn't let you have a whole drawer to yourself in their dressing table.'

'That was a real old bit of junk, but it did look nice in our room.'

'I was always disappointed it didn't have a mirror.'

'I'll have a mirror,' said Iris grinning. 'I'll even let you look in it if you want to.'

'Thank you very much.' Ellie laughed and knew that, like her, Iris was almost delirious with joy.

'I really can't believe this is happening to me, and all for six shillings a week. I wish you was coming as well.'

'What, and have me sharing your bed and keeping you awake with me bad dreams?'

'You are sure about going and living with What's-'is-name?'

'Don't keep calling him What's-'is-name. I told you, his name's Leonard.'

'Is he very old?'

'A bit.'

'You sure you're doing the right thing?'

'Dunno.'

'You don't *sound* too sure.'

'Well, it's a big step.'

'You can always stay with me if it don't work out. What do you think of John?'

'I like him, and his mum and dad. Wish our mum and dad had been a bit like them.'

'That would have been nice. What about Mum?'

'I'll write and tell the matron we're moving.'

'Ellie, what will happen if Mum gets better and wants to come home?'

'I don't know.' Ellie too was very worried about that. 'We'll just have to cross that bridge if and when we come to it.'

'We'll never find out where Lizzie and Dolly live now, will we?'

'Not if we move away. But that was up to them. I think they were selfish not to keep in touch.'

'Ellie,' said Iris softly. 'You'll keep in touch with me? You'll come and see me sometimes, won't you?'

'Course I will.'

'When shall we move?'

'I'm going to ask Mr Jenkins if I can leave this Saturday. I know I won't be giving him proper notice, but if we move out on Sunday we don't have to pay any more rent. That way you'll have the money for your first week's rent.'

'What about Mum's furniture? I know it ain't much, but we might be able to get a couple of bob for it.'

'I reckon a rag-and-bone man's our best bet. Trouble is, being at work all day we don't see one.'

'What about Molly?'

'S'pose we could ask her, but it will mean coming back to Elmleigh.'

'I'll ask John tomorrow; he might know someone who might be able to help. To think, I'll be able to start saving for some new clothes.'

'I hope I can get a job. I tell you, Iris, wearing a brand new frock is really wonderful.'

'Just touching 'em in the shop's lovely.' Iris slowed her step down. 'Ellie, I know I shouldn't say this, but with Mum being away and that, well, in some ways we're going to start to have a good life now, ain't we?'

'I hope so. Although I still feel very guilty about it.'

Iris put her arm through Ellie's. 'You mustn't. Let's get home and start to sort out the few bits we've got.'

When they turned into Elmleigh, Molly was sitting on the seat.

''Allo gels,' she yelled out. 'You look pleased with yourselves, come and sit down for a bit.'

'Ellie, you gonner tell her?' said Iris quietly, before Molly could hear.

'Not just yet, wait till after the rent man calls,' whispered Ellie.

They sat beside Molly.

'Been to see your mum?' she asked.

'No, we've been out.'

'Oh. Anywhere special?' asked Molly eyeing them suspiciously.

'No, not really,' said Ellie. 'Just fancied a walk, that's all. Molly, when does the rag-and-bone man come round?'

'Every Friday. Why, you got something to sell?'

'We don't think Mum will be back, so we thought we might sell their bed.'

'That's a good idea. Mind you, you ain't got a lot left in there to chuck out now, 'ave you?'

'No,' said Ellie. 'But even if we only got a few shillings . . .'

Molly laughed. 'Don't think you'll get a few shillings; pence, more like it. Old Tinker ain't all that generous with his money.'

Ellie felt Iris stiffen. 'Still, a few pence will buy a bit of tea and sugar,' she said quickly.

'Course it will, love. You both finding it a struggle?'

'A bit,' said Ellie.

'Whatever you do, try not to get behind with yer rent,

otherwise old Cole'll 'ave you out on the street before you can look round, and he'll keep any bits of furniture you leave behind. Him and that Tinker bloke are like that.' She crossed her fingers.

Iris looked at Ellie. 'Come on, let's go and sort out a few bits we might be able to get rid of.'

'I'll always let 'im in for you if yer like.'

'Thanks Molly,' said Ellie as they walked away.

'I'll ask John if he can help, but if not Molly can see that bloke,' said Iris when they were out of earshot.

'I don't think she'd let that Tinker get away with too much,' said Ellie. Somehow in Molly she knew they'd got a real friend.

'Does Mr Cole know you're going?' Ellie asked Peggy on Monday morning when once again Peggy was telling her about their plans.

'No, not yet.'

'D'you think he'll find someone else to take over the tea room?'

'Don't know.'

'Peggy, do you think Mr Jenkins will let me leave this Saturday?'

'What, leave early?'

'No.' Ellie carried on polishing. 'Leave for good.'

Peggy quickly looked up from the cabinet she was wiping out. 'Why? You got another job?'

'No. But Iris has got a room and Leonard said I could move in with him, and if we go this week we won't have to find another week's rent.'

'You could still come here to work.'

'But it would take a lot of my money in fares.' Ellie was upset at Peggy's answer. 'Besides, if Mr Cole came in and found me working here after we'd left without telling him, and sneaking off owing him a week's rent, well . . .'

'He don't know where you live.'

'I bet he does. If not he would soon find out.'

'Don't talk daft. What if later on this Leonard don't want you?'

Ellie stiffened. 'Why? What do you mean?'

'Well, he is an old man, and he might get fed up with you after a while.'

'He ain't that old.' Ellie got cross with Peggy when she kept on about Leonard's age, more so now she was marrying Mr Jenkins. ''Sides, I ain't got much choice, have I? No job and no home.'

'No, s'pose not,' said Peggy gravely. 'But he still ain't asked you to marry him, has he?'

'I don't know that I would even if he did ask me,' Ellie replied loftily.

'Well at least you'd 'ave some sort of security.'

Ellie didn't have an answer to that, so she asked, 'Would you mind asking Mr Jenkins about me leaving on Saturday?'

Peggy didn't reply, she just went into the bakery.

Ellie couldn't understand Peggy's attitude. She had always been so kind and helpful, but lately she had changed. Did she resent her going to live with Leonard? And what if she *was* angry with her leaving so soon? When they left, she would be out of work.

Ellie was busy polishing when Peggy came out. 'Well?'

'He ain't very pleased, you wanting to go without notice, but he said you can.'

'Thanks Peg. If you give me your new address I'll write to you.'

Peggy smiled. 'That'll be nice.'

Ellie didn't like to ask if he was going to stop her a week's wages. She would wait till Friday to worry about that. The most important thing on her mind now was waiting for Leonard's answer to the letter she had just sent telling him of their plans.

All week Iris and Ellie gathered together the few bits they

wanted to keep. The rest they put in a pile in the passage ready for Fred, the man John was coming with on Sunday. They were pleased he was going to take both beds as well. Leonard had written that he would also be over, to help Ellie carry her few belongings.

Ellie and Iris were up very early on Sunday morning, giggling like a couple of schoolgirls. Today was a big day in their lives. John was the first to arrive, along with his mate Fred. When they pulled up they were quickly surrounded by a bunch of kids. They were still loading the van when Leonard knocked on the door.

'It's open,' yelled Iris. 'Oh 'allo,' she said when Leonard walked into the empty house. 'You must be . . . Ellie's out in the yard.'

'I thought it was you,' said Ellie, coming back into the kitchen. 'Everything seems to echo now. You've met me sister?'

'Yes,' said Leonard.

'Did you have a job finding us?'

'No, no, not at all.'

'Right, that's it, gels,' said Fred. 'I'll give you a pound for the lot, how's that suit yer?'

'A pound?' said Iris, her eyes shining. 'That's great. Have you got two ten-shilling notes?'

'Course, love. 'Ere yer go then.' He handed Iris the money, and she quickly passed one of the notes to Ellie.

'Thanks, Fred,' said John. 'I'll see you back at home a bit later. You ready then, Iris?'

Iris looked sad. 'Yes. We can walk with you to the bus stop, can't we?' she asked Ellie.

Ellie nodded.

'We'll wait outside,' said Leonard.

'Yer,' said John.

Iris let her tears fall as she flung herself at Ellie. Ellie too was crying and they stood locked together.

'You will write, promise?' sobbed Iris.

290

'Yes, and I'll come to see you.'

Iris dabbed at her eyes. 'You sure you're going to be all right with him?'

Ellie nodded. 'He's very nice, you wait till you get to know him.'

They stood at the door of the kitchen and looked around. It was empty and sad-looking, and for a few moments neither spoke. They both knew of each other's thoughts and memories.

'Come on, dry your eyes,' said Ellie. 'Remember, this is the start of a new life.'

Together they walked out into the sunshine.

'Good luck, gels,' shouted Molly. 'If yer ever round this way come and see us.'

Ellie nodded.

At the corner of Elmleigh, Ellie stood and turned. This had been their home for as long as they could remember, but there was nothing left to keep them here now.

She turned and walked away.

Nobody spoke as all four walked on. At the bus stop Ellie and Iris hugged each other. Leonard kissed Iris's cheek and said he hoped to meet her again soon.

Ellie kissed John's cheek. 'You will take care of her, won't you?' she whispered. 'She's all I've got now.'

'Course I will,' he said softly.

On the bus Ellie looked out of the window.

'Is everything all right?' asked Leonard.

Ellie nodded.

'I like your sister, she's very pretty, and her young man seems a nice friendly chap.'

'I bet John put some money towards that stuff his mate took.'

'Why? What makes you say that?'

'You didn't see it. It was a right load of rubbish. The few pots and pans we had had holes in, and we'd stuffed bits of

291

rag in 'em to try and stop the water coming out. There was chipped cups and plates, and even the curtains were falling to pieces when we took them down. The whole lot was only worth a few bob.'

'That was kind of him, then, to help out. Come on, cheer up, that's all behind you now. You and your sister are starting a new life.' He squeezed her hand. 'And I hope they are going to be as happy as we are.'

Ellie's thoughts went to yesterday. Mr Jenkins and Peggy had surprised her when he gave her an extra week's wages, and Peggy had given her a clock. She said it was to remind Ellie of her every time she looked at it. They both hugged her and wished her well. Peggy was tearful, and said she was so very sad to see her go.

Tears rose behind Ellie's eyes, but she quickly blinked them back. She looked down at her handbag; inside was her two weeks' wages, and the ten-shilling note she'd got from Fred. She had never had so much money, and for the first time in her life she felt rich. She couldn't wait to spend it on new clothes. 'But I've got to find a job,' she suddenly said out loud.

'Well you can worry about that tomorrow,' said Leonard.

She smiled.

'That's what I like to see, that lovely smile. You know, it was your smile that first bowled me over.'

She held on to his arm. 'Thank you for taking me in.'

He laughed.

Ellie's thoughts went back to Peggy. Was she right? He had never mentioned anything about them getting married. But at this moment she didn't care. Her dream had come true: she was going to live with him.

Chapter 28

'Take your coat off. I'll make a cup of tea,' said Leonard as soon as they walked into his flat.

Ellie sat on the sofa clutching close to her the two paper bags that held all her worldly possessions. She couldn't believe it. She was really going to live here with Leonard. She looked round the room remembering the last time she'd sat here. Was it just six months ago? If only she could turn the clock back to Christmas. Her father had been alive then, and her mother sane. She tried to think about how happy she and Iris were now, but her thoughts kept returning to her parents.

'Your sister Iris is a pretty girl, and she seemed happy enough,' said Leonard walking into the lounge with a tray.

'She's gonner stay with a nice woman, and I think her and John . . . well, we'll have to wait and see about that.'

'You haven't taken your coat off.'

'I was just sitting here wishing I could turn the clock back.'

He sat next to her. 'You will never be able to do that. Most of us have done things in our lives we regret, and wish had never happened, but Ellie, that's the past now, and you are young and you must get on with your life.'

All the emotion of the past months suddenly became too much for her and the sobs burst out. Leonard put his arm round her and held her close. She buried her head in his shoulder, wetting his shirt with her tears. He didn't speak, he just gently kissed her face and neck, and made soothing noises.

Gradually the tears and sobs subsided. She lifted her head and he kissed her mouth long and hard, then, taking her hand, led her into the bedroom. The tea remained on the tray, and grew cold.

The club didn't open on Sunday or Monday nights, so after their meal they sat and talked. He told her where to shop, and some of the interesting places nearby she could visit.

That night as she lay in his arms Ellie's feelings were mixed. She loved being here with him, but when she thought how she'd brought this about, that heavy burden of guilt was all around her once more. She was pleased Iris was happy, but the thought of her mother in that dreadful place upset her. And because of her, her father was dead.

She drifted off to sleep, but suddenly she screamed. The hangman was shaking her. 'Stop it,' he shouted as she tried to run away. Her screams filled her ears. 'Stop it, Ellie, please stop, it's me.'

She opened her eyes. 'I'm sorry,' she cried, holding on to Leonard.

'My poor darling, you're having bad dreams. You're safe here with me.'

Her face was wet with tears and perspiration, her heart beating so fast she thought it would burst. 'I'm sorry,' she whimpered again. Would she ever be rid of this guilt?

He put his arms round her. 'I will never let any demons take you away.'

During the following week, while Leonard was teaching, Ellie spent most of the day going round the shops and markets. She wanted new clothes, but cringed at the prices in the shops. At the market she bought two frocks for five shillings each, and after a bit of haggling managed to get a summer coat for seven and six. Then she bought new vests, knickers and stockings. She had never had money to spend like this, and she was enjoying every moment of it. She knew getting a job with so many people out of work was going to be difficult, and if she was to look for a position here in the West End she would have to look right.

All week when Leonard went to the club he repeatedly asked Ellie to go with him, and although the evenings were lonely while he was working, she had reluctantly to refuse, as at the moment she didn't have anything suitable to wear, and she wasn't going to waste her money on a frock for the club. She did wonder if the lovely frock and silver shoes she had for Christmas were still in the pawnbrokers; perhaps one day she could go and find out. No; her first priority was getting a job.

Leonard had laughed when she told him she wanted to pay her way, and told her not to worry about it. But she was determined to be independent. Although she loved being here with him, and knew she would never want to leave, Peggy's warning often came back to her, and deep down she wasn't too sure of what the future held in store for her, for marriage was still never mentioned.

When she got home from shopping Ellie would proudly show Leonard her latest buys. He said he liked her taste.

At the end of the week she felt confident enough in her new clothes to go out and look for a job. Armed with her glowing references from Mr Jenkins, and after several disappointments, she finally found a position in the tea room of a large department store, Beaumonts.

'It's ever so posh,' she told Leonard when he got home. 'And I'm to get a pound a week, that's more than I was getting, and the lady said we get good tips.'

He looked up from his writing. 'That's nice.'

'I'll put the kettle on,' she said, going into the kitchen. She leaned against the sink. Thought you might have shown a bit more interest, she said under her breath.

Taking the tray into the lounge she sat on the sofa. 'Could

we go over and see Iris on Sunday so that I can tell her about me new job?'

'My, my new job.'

'Sorry. My new job. Well can we?'

He put his pen on the table. 'Why not?'

Ellie smiled. Now with a job to go to she wouldn't feel so lonely when Leonard was out teaching.

Leonard sat back in the chair. 'Now, tell me about this job.'

Ellie went into great detail about the store, and the hours she would have to work. 'It's quite posh, and the girls look a bit stuck up. The uniform is a bit like the one I wore before. I'm ever so nervous about it, but I reckon I'll be all right.'

'I'm sure you will,' he said kindly, and went back to his writing.

On Sunday, it was well into the afternoon before they left to visit Iris. Ellie had been looking at the clock and getting agitated, but Leonard was busy with some papers, and it seemed that every time she spoke he asked her to be quiet, and he didn't want to be interrupted.

'Please, Ellie, we will go when I'm ready, but I must finish these today.'

Ellie sat on the sofa and patiently waited.

'Ellie.' Iris, her pale blue eyes sparkling, threw her arms round her sister's neck when they at last walked into the Days' kitchen.

'You look ever so well,' said Ellie, noticing how flushed and happy she looked.

'So do you. How did you know I was round here?'

'Mrs Marsh told us.'

'Sit yourselves down,' said Mrs Day. 'Fancy a cuppa?'

Ellie looked at Leonard, waiting for him to answer. 'Yes please,' he said.

'You look ever so nice,' said Iris. 'I like your coat.'

'I like your frock. Everything all right?'

Iris nodded. 'I've spent all that money on new clothes.'

'So have I,' giggled Ellie. 'What about your room, is it all right?'

'Bessie's been ever so good to me, and so 'ave Ada and Tom.'

'And what about me?' said John grinning. 'I'm the one what takes you out.'

Iris smiled. 'And not forgetting John of course. You got a job yet?'

Ellie nodded. 'I start on Monday, in the tea rooms in Beaumonts.'

'That should be nice,' said Mrs Day walking in from the scullery with a tray. 'Nice shop, I gets all me curtains from them. Would you and your young man like to stay and 'ave a bit of tea with us?'

'I don't know.' Ellie didn't like to make the decision, so she looked at Leonard, again hoping he would say yes.

'If you're sure we won't be in the way,' he said, 'and please call me Leonard.'

Ellie wanted to throw her arms round his neck, she was so happy.

'Don't 'e talk nice,' said Mrs Day. 'Iris said you play in a band, that right?'

'Yes, a dance band, and I teach music, that's my first love.'

Mrs Day handed him a cup of tea. 'Fancy that, a teacher. We ain't ever 'ad a teacher here fer tea before, 'ave we Tom?'

Tom Day wandered into the kitchen with his braces dangling round his waist, looking very bleary-eyed. 'No. Wonder what they taste like, 'ope you ain't tough. Don't reckon they're as good as shrimps and winkles though.'

'Tom, behave yourself. Don't take no notice of 'im, silly s— old fool. 'E's just got up, likes a little doze on Sunday afternoons.'

'Well I 'ave to be up early every day of the week so I reckon I deserve a bit of a rest.'

'Pull yer braces up,' said his wife, tutting loudly. 'Always has ter 'ave his braces hanging down. One of these days yer trousers are gonner fall down.' She turned to Leonard. 'Hope you like shrimps and winkles?'

Iris nudged Ellie who was also grinning.

'Yes, I do,' answered Leonard.

'That's good, 'cos that's what we've got for tea, and a bit of home-made cake.'

'That sounds very nice.'

'We like to go up the pub for a drink Sunday night. Would you fancy coming with us?' Tom asked Leonard.

Ellie crossed her fingers, and secretly prayed he would say yes.

'I don't see why not, we've got nothing to hurry home for. Only Ellie's job in the morning.'

'We won't stay that late as I 'ave to be at the Garden by three.'

'The Garden?' queried Leonard.

'Covent Garden.'

'At three in the morning?' asked Leonard.

'Yer, that's if you want the best stuff.'

'I'm just about getting home from the club then.'

'Funny old world, ain't it. Still, we all has to work funny hours for a crust, don't we? 'Ere,' said Tom. 'D'yer mind if I calls yer Len? Leonard's a bit of a mouthful fer me.'

'Not at all,' he said smiling.

Ellie sat at the table aware that she was surrounded by people who had a genuine love for each other. In many ways she envied Iris; to be part of this loving family must be wonderful.

Later that evening they trooped up to the Days' local, the Red Lion. They pushed open the door, and were greeted with friendly waves and shouts. The place was noisy and full of smoke, someone was bashing away on an old out-of-tune upright piano, and a few old dears sitting holding on to their glasses were singing.

'What d'yer drink, Len?' asked Tom Day. 'I'm a bitter man meself, so's me boy; the old girl likes a drop o' stout. What about you two girls?'

'I'll have a shandy,' said Iris.

'Me too,' said Ellie.

'I'll have a bitter,' said Leonard.

'I'll give yer 'and, Dad,' said John, giving Iris a wink.

''Spect you're only used to champagne,' said Mrs Day to Leonard as she sat herself down.

'No, not really.'

'I like champagne,' said Ellie.

'When did you taste champagne?' asked Iris.

'At Christmas at the club Leonard plays at.'

'Was it nice?' asked Iris.

'It's all bubbly, and it tickles your nose.'

'What d'yer play in the band?' Tom Day asked Leonard as he put the drinks on the table.

'The piano.'

'The piano, that's nice,' said Ada taking the froth off the top of her stout. 'And you give lessons as well?' she asked.

'Yes.'

'Wish we had a piano, always fancied getting up in 'ere and giving 'em all a tune.'

'You'll 'ave ter get on this joanna sometime,' said Tom. 'We could do with a bit o' class round 'ere.'

Ellie noted Leonard didn't answer, he only gave them a slight smile.

'You should have been here last night,' said Iris. 'We was having a right old time. A real knees up.'

'That sounds really good,' said Ellie enthusiastically. 'But Leonard has to work on Saturday.'

'Pr'aps you could come over on yer own one Sat'day,' said Mrs Day.

'I will have to work till quite late.'

'So do I,' said Iris.

'You don't have to rush home. I'm sure you could always

stay with Iris, I know Bessie wouldn't mind,' said Mrs Day.

Ellie smiled. 'That would be nice.'

'It's something you'll have to think about, Ellie,' said Leonard.

As the evening wore on Tom began singing, and when John sat beside Iris, Ellie could see the love in their eyes. She noticed the way they looked at each other and the gentle way they touched each other, and wondered how long it would be before they were talking about getting married. What a wedding that would be, with the Days! Ellie smiled at Iris; she knew things could only get better for her young sister.

At home and in bed, Ellie snuggled up to Leonard. 'Thank you for taking me out tonight.'

'It was my pleasure. I could see you were enjoying yourself. The Days seem to be pleasant enough people.'

To Ellie they were wonderful; but would Leonard like to be in their company for very long?

'Could we go again next Sunday?'

'I won't make any promises.' He hesitated. 'I may have some work to do. But if we were to go, I certainly hope they wouldn't expect me to play their old broken-down piano.'

'I'll tell Iris to tell 'em.'

'Ellie, if you would really like to go over there one Saturday, I wouldn't stop you.'

'Thanks. It would be nice.'

Would he be willing to go there again next Sunday? Ellie wondered. Well, she would have to wait and see. A lot could happen between now and next Sunday, and the new job tomorrow was the first thing she had to face.

Chapter 29

The following morning, long before Leonard was awake, Ellie slipped out of bed. In the bathroom she took extra care when getting dressed as she wanted to look smart.

'You're up early,' he said, sitting up and rubbing the sleep from his eyes as he watched her put the tray of tea and biscuits on the bedside table. 'And I must say you look very nice. But you would look a lot better without that slice of toast in your mouth.'

She waved the toast in the air and twirled round in front of him. 'I'm going now, as I don't wanner be late on my first day.'

'Good luck.'

'Thanks.' She kissed him lightly on the cheek, and left.

She felt like skipping all the way to the store. Everything was going to be wonderful. She had a job and was living with Leonard, and Iris was happy living with Bessie and having John to look after her. She thought about the Days and what a nice, easygoing family they were. If only . . . The smile quickly disappeared from her face when she remembered her own family. But, she told herself, there was nothing she could do about the past, and she let her thoughts drift to her new job.

When she had been accepted for work in Beaumonts tea rooms, she had been told to go into the store through the staff entrance, which was located round the back in a dirty alley. It was forbidden to go through the front doors once

301

you became staff. As she approached the rear of the large building, the slight breeze blew paper and other rubbish round and round in circles. A small group of young women giggled and made their way through the scruffy door and up the stairs. The back stairs were gloomy and dark, and the excited voices of girls relating their weekend activities, and their clattering footsteps, echoed on the concrete stairs. She had also been told to go to the staffroom where there would be a time clock to clock into the store, and a Mrs Moss would give her a uniform.

The staffroom was full of chattering girls, some already in uniform. Ellie was to learn later that some of the girls lived in a hostel nearby, which was run by the store for their staff.

'Excuse me,' she said to a girl wearing a uniform that looked like a waitress's. 'Where can I find Mrs Moss?'

'Over there, the one in the navy frock sitting at the desk.'

As Ellie made her way over to Mrs Moss, she stood up. She was a tall, imposing woman who wore her grey hair pulled back into a tight bun. Her half glasses were perched on the end of her nose, and her long pearls were knotted, the knot resting on her ample bosom.

'Excuse me,' said Ellie again. 'I'm Ellie Walsh.'

Mrs Moss looked over her half glasses at Ellie, and sniffed. It was almost as if she had a bad smell under her long beaked nose.

'I've to see you about a uniform,' continued Ellie.

'What department?'

'The tea rooms.'

'Your name?' Mrs Moss scanned the papers she was holding.

'Elenore Walsh.'

'Follow me.'

Ellie fell in behind her as she walked swiftly across the room. She was aware of other girls looking at her as she passed them, but nobody gave her a welcoming smile.

'Have you clocked in?' asked Mrs Moss over her shoulder.

'No,' said Ellie. 'Not yet.'

Mrs Moss suddenly stopped, and Ellie was so close behind she thought she was going to tread all over her.

'You had better do that first. Come with me.' She turned and Ellie walked behind her once again.

They stood before the large clock.

'Do you know what to do?'

'Yes,' said Ellie weakly. She'd had to clock in when she'd worked at the factory.

'Very well, look for your card. They are in alphabetical order. Quickly girl, we haven't got all day.'

Ellie found the card with her name on, put it in the machine, pulled down the handle, took it out and put it to the other side. Mr Jenkins' tea room hadn't been like this.

'Now follow me.' Mrs Moss went over to a large cupboard that lined one wall. On a thick silver chain round her waist were a bunch of keys that jangled as she walked, giving the girls time to stop their conversation and continue with whatever they should be doing.

She unlocked one of the cupboard's many doors and looked Ellie up and down. She gathered various items of clothing, and giving them to Ellie said, 'These should fit. Put them on, then come and see me. You can leave your things on the benches.'

Gradually the staffroom began to empty. Ellie quickly took off her frock and put the black one on. She tied the pretty white apron round her waist and put on the white headband. She then went over to Mrs Moss.

'Very nice. Turn round. I see you have cleaned your shoes, that's very good.'

Ellie did as she was told, pleased her shoes were presentable.

'You have to look after your own uniform, and keep it clean. Take it home at weekends and wash it. Once a year we provide you with another, but if you need another before then through wanton use, you must replace it yourself.

Now, show me your hands. You must keep them clean at all times. Customers don't want to be served by girls with dirty hands.'

Ellie held out her hands and Mrs Moss turned them over. 'They're fine. Now be off with you, and report to Miss Penn.'

Ellie knew the tea rooms were on the top floor of the four-storey building. 'Do I use the lift to get to—?'

Before she could finish she thought Mrs Moss was going to explode. Her face turned scarlet and she shouted, 'The lift! The lift! None of the staff are allowed to use the lift. Whenever you move from one floor to the other you use the back stairs at all times.'

Out on the concrete stairs once more, Ellie stood and laughed. What a lot she had to tell Leonard and Iris. Iris had never said she had to go through all this, but then Iris worked for a small, family-run store, not a big one like this; and this was the West End after all. But what a lot of fuss over putting a tray of tea things on a table. Wouldn't Peggy have a laugh. As she made her way up to the tea rooms, Ellie wondered if she would like it here, after all. But then the money was good, and once she knew the ropes perhaps it wouldn't be so bad.

She pushed open a door, and found herself in the kitchen, surrounded by the loud clatter of crocks.

'You the new girl?' asked a tall dark-haired girl about Ellie's age.

'Yes.'

'Go and see Miss Penn, she'll tell you which is your station.'

'Where will . . .?'

'She's by the till. Dark hair. She don't wear a headband.'

'Thank you.'

In the plush tea room with beautiful chandeliers hanging from the high ceiling, Ellie walked silently along the deep red carpet runners that edged the highly polished wooden floor. The tables were covered with crisp white tablecloths, and the carpet led to Miss Penn.

'You must be Miss Walsh?' said Miss Penn, looking up from her books.

Ellie nodded.

'There are four young ladies here, and you each have your own station. Follow me.'

Once again Ellie found she was trotting behind someone. They walked to the far end of the room. 'This is your station. As the other girls leave, you will find you will move nearer the door, and that will mean you get more people sitting at your tables and of course more tips. You will be busy sometimes, but not as often as those near the door. But that doesn't mean to say you can slouch around. You must be on your toes and look pleasant, but not too pleasant, at all times. This will give you time to learn your trade and wait on tables efficiently. Now, go into the kitchen and find out where everything is; and by the way, you have to pay for any breakages.'

Ellie felt devastated. Learn how to wait on tables? She was beginning to wonder if she really wanted to stay here.

For the rest of the day she found her way around. She carefully checked all the cutlery and condiments at her station, which was a large mahogany desk with a cupboard underneath. Nobody spoke to her; in fact the other girls didn't even seem to notice her. At seven o'clock it was time to leave. She had hardly any customers, and certainly no tips. This wasn't what she wanted; her feet hurt and she felt miserable; but she knew she had to stick it out. Jobs were very hard to get.

Leonard was home before Ellie. As soon as she sat down she took off her shoes and related all the day's happenings, and he sat and listened.

'So it won't be so bad when I get nearer the door and have more customers. But they seem a bit stuck up, and I can't see us having a laugh like me and Peggy did.'

'You know, you don't really have to go out to work.'

'Yes I do. I couldn't sit around here all day, and expect you to feed me.'

'You are such a silly little thing.'

She looked at him. 'I ain't silly.'

'I didn't mean it that way. I love you being here, and I would be just as happy even if you didn't go to work.'

She looked down at her fingers. If he offered to marry her that would be different. 'I must go to work.' She was thinking of the week before when Mrs Tomms the cleaning woman had come, and the way she'd looked her up and down. 'I like to earn a bit of money 'cos I like to buy clothes.'

'Of course you do. But isn't there anything else you can do?'

'No. If only I could 'ave gone to high school, perhaps I could 'ave been a secretary.'

'Is that what you would like?'

She nodded.

'But you don't have to go to high school.'

'Yes you do. I ain't got any certificates, and they don't even look at you if you ain't got any certificates.'

'No, I suppose they don't.'

'With so many people out of work, the clever ones always get the best jobs.'

'Yes, you could be right.'

'Could we go and see Iris on Sunday? I've got to tell her all about me—' She quickly looked at him. 'My job.'

'I should think so, but we mustn't make a habit of it.'

'Oh I won't. It's just that I . . .' She stopped. 'I want to tell her, that's all.'

He smiled. 'Of course you do.'

'Thanks.' She kissed his cheek.

For the rest of the week Ellie's working days were the same.

She felt very lonely, and sad that she hadn't made a friend to talk to, but as Leonard told her, it was early days. She missed Peggy and wondered how they were managing without her. She also missed Iris and was longing for Sunday when she could tell her about her week. But at night when Leonard held her in his arms and made love to her all her fears vanished.

On Sunday afternoon they were once again in Mrs Day's kitchen.

'Thought you might be over,' she said, after kissing Ellie's cheek. ''Ope you're gonner stay for a bit o' tea; got in more than enough for you both.'

Ellie looked at Leonard, who smiled and shrugged his shoulders.

Ellie and Iris sat in the corner and chatted on almost non-stop. Their giggles caused Leonard, who was sitting with John, to look up. John was trying to engage him in a deep conversation, but Ellie noted Leonard didn't look too thrilled about it. Ellie told Iris all about her job, and although she tried to make it sound interesting, the fact that she wasn't that happy there still came over. 'But I've got to stick it out.'

'Well it can only get better,' said Iris. 'Pity our place don't have a tea room; you could 'ave worked there.'

'That would have meant coming back over here every day. No, it'll be all right when I get used to it.'

'You coming up the pub after tea?'

'Dunno, I'll 'ave to see what Leonard says.'

'Are you, you know, all right with him?'

Ellie nodded. 'Course.'

'I wish you could come over here on a Saturday, we really do 'ave a lot of fun. I'm ever so glad I met John. His mum and dad treat me like one of them, and it's lovely to be part of a happy family.' Iris smiled contentedly.

'D'you think you and him will, you know, get married one day?'

Iris blushed. 'Wouldn't be at all surprised.'

'You're very lucky.' Ellie suddenly stopped. Iris wasn't lucky; she'd lost two of her sisters through no fault of her own, her mum was in an asylum, and her dad was dead. Ellie gently patted her hand. 'But you deserve it,' she added softly.

'By the way I've got meself a new frock, it's pale blue and ever so nice,' said Iris, quickly changing the subject. 'I'm gonner wear it on me birthday. We're going to have a party up the pub next Sat'day. You are gonner come?'

'I don't know. You'll have to show me your frock when we come over again.'

'Look, if you're not going to Len's club on Saturday why don't you come over here for the evening? If you didn't want to go home you could always stay the night with me. What d'yer say?'

'I don't think he would like that. 'Sides, I don't finish work till nine on Saturdays.'

'Neither do I. Oh come on, after all it will be me birthday party.'

'But your birthday isn't till the Wednesday.'

'I know, but they have to get up early every morning so we decided Saturday would be the best day. You could come straight from work. What d'yer say?'

'I don't know.'

Iris glanced across at Leonard then back to Ellie. 'Well it's up to you.'

'I expect I'll be going to his club soon. I was hoping to get meself a dance frock next week, but I forgot they keeps a week in hand.'

'OK, please yourself. But remember, the invite is always there. Now I'd better help Mrs D get the tea.'

Ellie sat for a few moments reflecting on what Iris had said. She would like to come over here one Saturday, and Iris's birthday would give her a good excuse, but would Leonard mind? She would ask him when they got home and find out what his reaction would be.

★ ★ ★

Leonard looked up from his papers. 'Well I'm not so sure,' he said when Ellie asked if he'd mind if she went over and stayed with Iris next Saturday. 'Why can't you come to the club with me?'

'I told you why. I ain't got the right sorta frock, and I'd feel a bit out of it. 'Sides, it's Iris's birthday party. I should be able to get a new frock the week after next, then I can come with you.'

'Come here.'

Ellie stood in front of him. She felt like a child standing in front of the teacher.

He gently touched her cheek and she felt a ripple of excitement travel over her.

'Well, OK this time, but don't stay all day on Sunday. I don't want to come over and get you.'

Ellie threw her arms round his neck. 'Thanks. I promise I'll behave me— myself.'

He grinned. 'I'll look forward to taking you to the club again.'

'And I shall look forward to coming with you.'

Chapter 30

Standing at the bus stop, Ellie felt very excited at the thought of going out with Iris and the Days. She had written and told her she would be coming over and staying the night. She smiled to herself. Who'd have thought a year ago that she would be pleased she was going to see Iris? Such a lot had happened to them since Christmas. Ellie shuddered despite the warmth of the evening as she recalled the last time she had stayed out all night.

She quickly banished those thoughts; tonight she was going to enjoy herself. It would help make up for the sad feeling she'd had earlier in the week when she had had to write and refuse the invitation to Peggy and Mr Jenkins' wedding in August. She wouldn't be allowed time off work just for a wedding. Ellie remembered going to see Lizzie married; Mr Jenkins had let her have time off for that.

In her letter Peggy had told her all about the frock she was going to wear. It was to be a church wedding, and a cousin of Mr Jenkins was going to be her bridesmaid, with a pink frock. Ellie read the letter over and over again, wishing she could find some way of going to see them. Peggy also told her about the new tea room in Margate, and how much her mother was looking forward to going there now. Lucky Peggy, Ellie said to herself.

Ellie's hand had hardly left the knocker of the Days' front door when it flew open and Iris was hugging her.

'Ellie. I saw you out of the front room window. I'm ever

so pleased you could come. John, John, look, it's Ellie.'

'I like your frock,' said Ellie as Iris dragged her into the kitchen.

''Allo love,' said Mrs Day, holding out her arms in a welcoming gesture. 'Don't bother taking yer cardi orf as we're just going. Tom's gorn already. You staying with Iris ternight?'

Ellie nodded. 'That's if Bessie don't mind.'

'Course she don't,' said Mrs Day, taking Ellie's arm and almost bodily whisking her out of the house and along the road.

The pub was only on the corner, and as they approached Ellie could hear someone playing the piano. She couldn't imagine Leonard playing like that. He had told Ellie that a piano was an instrument that had to be loved and tenderly caressed. When he played something classical, as he called it, he closed his eyes and looked like he was being transported into another world.

In the pub a man was pounding the piano keys with gusto, causing the beer in the glass on top to slosh from side to side.

'What yer 'aving, gel?' asked Mr Day, catching sight of them as soon as they walked in.

'I'll have a shandy please,' said Ellie.

Iris tucked her arm through Ellie's. 'I'm ever so glad you came tonight. I know it ain't the same as What's-'is-name's club, but we do enjoy ourselves.'

'I can see that.'

For the remainder of the evening Ellie laughed and sang. She even got up and did a knees up with Iris and Mrs Day. They were such a happy crowd, and all too soon the landlord was calling time.

'Come back for a bite of supper,' said Mrs Day when they finished their drinks. 'It ain't much, but a bit o' bread and cheese and pickles goes down a treat at this time o' night.'

Ellie was looking forward to that.

After they finished supper John walked them back to Bessie's. Ellie felt a pang of envy when John put his arm round her sister. She wanted Leonard to be here with her. When they reached the front door Iris pulled the key through the letter box and opened the door. John gently kissed Ellie's cheek before clasping Iris in his strong arms. Ellie walked inside.

'I'm still up, girls,' called Bessie from the kitchen. 'D'yer fancy something to eat?'

'No thanks,' said Ellie. 'Mrs Day made us a sandwich. You don't mind me staying the night, do you?' Ellie sat at the table.

'No love, course not. It's nice to see sisters getting on.'

Iris, her face flushed, pushed open the kitchen door. ''Allo Bessie. You still up?'

'Just wanted to finish off these curtains. Did you enjoy yourselves tonight?'

'I should say so.'

'What about you, Ellie?' asked Bessie.

Ellie beamed. 'I had a lovely time.'

'They're a good crowd those Days.'

'I'm ready for bed,' said Iris.

'So am I,' said Ellie. 'It's been a long day.'

'I hope you don't still have those rotten nightmares,' said Iris as they got undressed.

'They're not so bad now I've got someone to cuddle up to.'

Iris began giggling when they finally settled down in the large double bed.

'What's so funny?' asked Ellie.

'I was just thinking. I 'ope you don't start cuddling me, expecting me to be Leonard.'

'Daft 'aporth.'

'Mind you in that nightie no wonder he has his wicked way with you. Is that the one he bought you?'

'Smashing, ain't it?'

'I should say so. I'll have to get one and see if I can't get John into bed with me.'

'Iris Walsh, you're nothing but a hussy.'

'I know, but it takes one to know one.' She laughed and quickly put her hand over her mouth to stop the noise. She propped herself up on one elbow. 'Ellie, d'yer mind living in sin with him?'

Ellie was taken aback. She hadn't thought about it being sin. 'Well . . . I . . .'

'Has he asked you to marry him yet?'

'I don't think he will. I think he's worried about the age difference.'

'Well yer, he is a bit old. Ellie, what's it like? You know . . .?' Iris gave her a nudge.

Ellie smiled, pleased it was dark and Iris couldn't see the grin on her face. 'Well if it's with the right man, it's very nice.'

Iris sat up. 'Is that it, just very nice?'

'What d'you want me to say? "You get swept along on a sea of passion, and nothing else matters except being with the one you love"?'

'Oh er,' giggled Iris. 'Sounds like you read too many penny dreadfuls.'

'Come on, turn over and let's get some sleep.' Ellie didn't want to tell her that what she had been saying was the truth.

'Ellie,' whispered Iris. 'Ain't you worried about having a baby?'

'No, Leonard is very considerate about that sort of thing.'

'Ellie?'

'Now what is it?'

'I've been wondering about Mum.'

Ellie was suddenly wide awake. 'What made you . . .?' She didn't know what to say.

'I was wondering,' Iris repeated, 'how she is. Have you heard from the matron?'

'No. I would have told you if I had. Now let's get some sleep.'

'I suppose she's all right?'

'I would think so. We could always go and see her, you know.'

Iris didn't answer.

'If you like, I'll make some arrangements. Now go to sleep.'

'Goodnight,' said Iris.

Ellie lay awake. She was filled with guilt again, but this time it was because she hadn't written to the matron telling her that she had moved. I must do that as soon as I get back, she said to herself.

The following morning Ellie said her goodbyes to Bessie and the Days. She felt a little reluctant to leave them. She held Iris close. 'Happy birthday for next Wednesday.'

'Thanks for that lovely brush and comb set.'

'Well at least you've got a dressing table to put it on,' said Ellie. 'When Peggy gave me mine I had to keep it in the box. I'd better be going.'

Iris kissed her.

As Ellie walked away she couldn't remember ever having enjoyed herself or laughed so much as she had last night. Although she loved being with Leonard, he didn't laugh as much as the Days. But then he was different in so many ways. So worldly and sophisticated.

She banged on his front door. She didn't have her own key, and she began to grow anxious when he didn't answer. She banged again, much harder this time. Where was he?

'When I was cleaning the car I saw him go out,' called the man upstairs from his window.

'Did he say if he was going to be long?' asked Ellie.

'Didn't ask,' came the reply.

Ellie was starting to get angry. He didn't want her to stay all day at the Days', and yet he wasn't at home when she did get back. Was he doing this on purpose? Was he trying to make a point? She sat on the stone steps and leaned her head against the wall. The warm sun was comforting. Where could he have gone? Why didn't he leave a note on the door, or the key under the mat, or with the man upstairs?

'Ellie. I very nearly fell over you. How long have you been sitting there?'

Ellie opened her eyes and stared up at Leonard. She scrambled to her feet. 'Since this morning.' Her mouth felt dry and she shivered. The sun had gone down behind the tall houses and left the basement in shadow. 'Why wasn't you at home? Where yer been?'

He put his key in the lock. 'Out. I've been out. I didn't expect you back just yet, I thought you might have at least stayed for lunch, or whatever they have. I daresay you'd like a cup of tea?' He closed the front door behind her.

Ellie was disappointed at his welcome. She'd expected him to take her in his arms and tell her how much he'd missed her. 'Did you go anywhere nice?' she asked, hoping to find out more.

'Only for a drink with an old pal of mine.'

'That's nice. Is he from the club?'

'No.'

Ellie wanted to ask more, but she could see he was being very guarded.

During the evening she tried to tell him about the pub, the singsong, and the way the man played the piano, but he didn't appear to take much interest in her conversation. He looked worried as he played his sorrowful music, his brow furrowed as though deep in thought.

'Is something wrong?' she asked.

'No.'

'Are you cross with me because I stayed with Iris last night?'

'No of course not, you can do what you like, I'm not your keeper.'

She wanted to go to him, but he seemed distant.

All evening Leonard played the piano. They were soft haunting tunes, and Ellie knew he didn't like to be disturbed when he played this type of music, and it made her feel sad. Was this because of her? But surely he would have told her. Who was this person he had gone for a drink with, and why wouldn't he tell her who he was?

At nine she got up and went to the bathroom to get ready for bed. She couldn't believe two evenings could be so completely different. She loved Leonard and hoped when they were in each other's arms he would tell her what was troubling him.

They didn't make love that night, and the following morning Ellie woke with a start. Leonard's side of the bed was empty. He never got up very early! She hurried out of the bedroom. He was leaning against the sink and holding a cup with both hands, a faraway look on his face.

She rushed over to him. 'Leonard, what's wrong?'

'Nothing.'

'Why are you up so early?'

'I couldn't sleep.'

'Why? What's bothering you?'

'Nothing. By the way, Mrs Tomms comes today, so could you make sure you pick up all your stockings and things.'

'I normally do. Why? What's she been saying?'

'Nothing really, it's just that she doesn't like tidying up after you.'

That remark made Ellie angry. 'She doesn't tidy up after me. Besides, I ain't got that much to keep tidy.'

'Haven't.'

'Haven't, ain't, does it matter?'

'It matters to me.'

Ellie left the kitchen with tears streaming down her face. They were having their first row. She got herself dressed and, shouting out her goodbye, left.

For the rest of the day she felt miserable, and the fact that nobody spoke to her in the store didn't help. She couldn't wait for seven to come.

All the way home her thoughts were churning over. Would her job always be like this? Was Leonard still angry with her? Would he want her to leave? What was worrying him? 'I should have been more understanding; after all, he was always kind to me through all my troubles,' she said under her breath.

Going down the basement steps, she approached the front door with a great deal of trepidation. Did he still want her to live with him? Fear gripped her. What if he threw her out, where would she go? She lifted the knocker.

The door was already open, she gently pushed it and tentatively walked in. The smell of something good cooking filled the air.

'Ellie, oh Ellie.' Leonard rushed up to her and pulled her into his arms. 'My dear, I'm so sorry.' He kissed her upturned face.

Ellie held him tight. Why had she ever doubted him?

'I've done a special treat, a sort of I'm-sorry meal,' he said, helping her off with her coat.

She laughed, with joy and relief. 'It's me that should be sorry for going off out like that this morning.'

'Nonsense. Come and sit down.'

They finished their meal. 'Thank you,' said Ellie. 'That was really lovely. Now are you going to tell me what was worrying you last night?'

Leonard gathered the plates together. 'It's nothing to concern your pretty little head with,' he said dismissively. 'Now tell me about Saturday, and what kind of day you had today.'

'I told you last night, but you wasn't listening.'

'Yes, I'm very sorry about that.'

Ellie knew she couldn't push that subject any longer, so

she settled down and told him about Saturday again. This time he was more attentive. 'And as far as today went, it was just the same and as boring as last week.'

'It'll get better, I'm sure. Come on, let's go to bed.'

Ellie smiled. As far as she was concerned, it was getting better already.

Chapter 31

The following morning Ellie walked into the bedroom as usual with Leonard's cup of tea.

'Thank you,' he said, then, reaching out and holding her hand, he waved a crisp pound note at her.

Ellie stood staring. 'What's that for?' she asked.

'For you to buy yourself a new dress, so you can come to the club on Saturday,' he said, pressing it into her hand.

'I can't take this,' she whispered, giving it back to him.

'And why not?'

'Well I can't. It's, well, it's another week's wages for me. No, it ain't, isn't right.'

'Call it a birthday gift.'

She laughed. 'But my birthday isn't till February.'

'Well just say it's a present from me to you because I want you to spend Saturday evenings with me.'

She leaned across the bed and threw her arms round his neck. 'Are you sure?'

'Of course.'

'Thank you. I'm so lucky to have someone like you to look after me.'

'Go on, off with you, before I make you come back to bed. Then you'll be late for work.'

Ellie giggled and ran out of the bedroom. A whole pound to spend on a new frock! She didn't know if she was allowed staff discount, but she would find out today.

Miss Penn told her they were allowed to shop before the

store opened, so she arrived early the following morning and chose a frock.

'That's lovely,' said Leonard as she twirled round in front of him that evening.

'Just think, I've got a new frock from a West End store. Thank you, thank you, thank you.' She covered his face with kisses. 'I'm so pleased I'm coming with you to the club again,' she said enthusiastically.

He laughed. 'You're such a sweet little thing.'

Ellie hurried home on Saturday to get ready. Leonard had to leave before her as she didn't finish work in time to go with him, and he had left the front-door key under the mat.

She felt very grown up as she walked up the steps to the club on her own. She even gave Ben, the doorman, a beaming smile.

'Will Greta and May be there?' she had asked Leonard the night before.

'Don't think so. The boys move about quite a lot, they're not regulars.'

He had also told her her usual table would be waiting for her. 'Do you think you'll be all right?' he had asked.

'I should think so.'

Ellie grinned to herself; she had liked the sound of 'your usual table'. She gave Leonard a little wave as she made her way to the table near the band, but was surprised to see so few people here tonight. She hadn't sat down before the waiter was at her side.

'Drink?' he asked.

'I'll have a port and lemon,' she said confidently. Mrs Day had told her to order that; she said it was nice.

Gazing round the room she remembered the last time she had been here, on Christmas Eve. It had been lively and exciting then, and she had been drinking champagne. Tonight was different, and she wasn't going to let her memory linger on what had happened after that night.

Gradually, as the evening progressed, more and more people arrived. When the band struck up with the latest tunes the atmosphere improved, and she clapped enthusiastically after every number.

'Mind if I sit down for a moment?'

Ellie looked up at the man Leonard had called Curly many weeks ago.

'See he's brought you here again.' He inclined his head towards the band and Ellie noted the look of disapproval on Leonard's face.

He leaned very close to Ellie and the smell of drink was strong.

'You living with him then?' he said, pulling a chair out from the table and sitting down.

Ellie bristled. 'I don't think that is any of your business.'

'You ain't the first, you know.'

'Don't suppose I am.' She cast her eyes down, unable to look him in the face. Panic was beating in her chest. What was he going to tell her? Was her Leonard married?

Curly leant forward and tapped the end of his large cigar into the ashtray, then he sat back. 'And I suppose you know all about what he got up to in the war?'

'No I don't, and I'm not interested.'

Curly laughed. 'I was in the war, and I ain't got any time for these bloody Germans.'

'He isn't German.'

'That's what he told yer? S'pose he ain't, not now.'

Ellie didn't want to argue with this man, and although she was intrigued about Leonard's past she didn't want him to tell her something she would rather not hear. 'If you'll excuse me, I'm going to powder my nose.' Ellie walked away. She was shaking with anger, but couldn't believe how self-confidently she had acted. In the powder room she sat looking in the mirror. Should she have tried to find out if Leonard had ever been married? No, whatever Leonard had done before she met him was his affair, and none of her business. Besides, he had told her he wasn't married, so that should be enough. Ellie leaned forward and put some lipstick on. Anyway, the war had been over for a long while now, so why were people still harping on about it?

As they walked home Ellie began telling Leonard what Curly had said. 'Who is Curly?' she asked.

'He's a club member now. Don't know that much about him really.'

'He seems to know a lot about you.'

'Well, he was on the staff at one time, and you know how men talk, especially when they've had a few drinks after the club closes.'

Ellie snuggled up close to him. 'Did you have a girl staying with you?'

'Yes, I did have a young woman staying with me for a short while some time ago, but she left.'

Ellie stiffened. 'Did you love her?' she asked quietly, dreading the answer.

He laughed. 'Good lord no. She was my cousin's daughter; she came over here after the war to study.'

'She's German as well then?' she said brightly.

'No – well, not by birth anyway.'

'Don't you hear from any of your family now?'

He opened the front door. 'I'll put the kettle on.'

Ellie yawned. 'I'm really very tired. Would you mind if I went to bed?'

'No of course not.' He kissed her cheek. 'I'll try not to wake you.'

She smiled to herself. If he was going to make love to her she didn't mind one bit if he woke her.

Ellie was thrilled when a few weeks later she managed to buy another frock, and throughout the summer she went to the club every Saturday night. Even though she had asked Leonard many times, they had only been to see Iris on just one other Sunday since Ellie had gone there alone. Although they had made him very welcome, Ellie knew he didn't really like going out with the Days.

'Can we go and see Iris today?' asked Ellie after lunch.

'No, I've got to go out.'

'Oh,' said Ellie pulling a face. 'Will you be out very long?'

'Couldn't say.'

'Can I come with you?'

'No, I'm sorry, it's strictly business.' Leonard was stuffing papers into his briefcase.

Ellie plonked herself on the sofa. 'You went out on so-called business last Sunday. I get fed up here on me own.'

'My own. My. My.' His voice was raised and Ellie looked at him in bewilderment. 'How many times do I have to tell you about that? I'm surprised they haven't picked you up at the store over the way you speak sometimes.'

'Don't talk to anybody, do I.'

'Now come on, don't sulk.' His voice had softened. 'I'm sorry. Why don't you go and see your sister on your own? You don't really need to drag me along.'

Ellie face lit up. 'Could I? Would you mind?'

'Of course not.'

'You will leave the key under the mat, won't you?' she asked, remembering the last time she had been to see Iris on her own.

'Of course I will.'

Ellie could have jumped for joy. She grabbed her coat. 'I'll see you later. I won't stop for tea.'

Ellie knocked on Bessie's front door.

'Hallo love.'

'Is Iris in?'

'She's upstairs tidying her room. Fancy a cuppa?'

'Yes please.'

'I'll yell up when it's ready.'

'Ellie,' said Iris when she opened the door. 'This is a

lovely surprise. Where's Len?' she asked, looking over Ellie's shoulder.

'He had to meet this man. I think it's something about some piano lessons.'

'You don't sound very convinced.'

'It ain't nothing to do with me what he does.'

'Hark at you. You sound very grumpy.'

'I'm all right. What about you?'

'We had a smashing time up the pub last night. Oh Ellie, I never thought I could enjoy meself so much. You should try and get over again one Sat'day.'

'I go to the club with Leonard now I've got a few new frocks,' she said without much enthusiasm.

'What's it like over there? I'd love to go one night, it must be ever so exciting.'

Ellie smiled. 'Yes it is.' She didn't have the heart to tell her that some nights she would dearly love to change places with her. The music was great, but sitting every Saturday night on her own, not talking to anyone, was a little bit dull.

'Pr'aps one night me and John could come over.'

'That'd be nice,' said Ellie enthusiastically. 'I'll ask Leonard if you have to be a member.'

'By the way, guess who came in the pub last night?'

Ellie shook her head.

'Terry Andrews and this Joyce girl. She's ever so nice.'

'I know, I've met her.'

'She had this lovely coat on, and he looked really smart.'

Ellie didn't know why, but she bristled. 'Did you talk to them?' she asked curtly.

'Yes, but they only stayed a short while. Another couple joined them and they went off. He was saying he's got a good job now, and with Joyce being their lodger, things are really working out for them. He asked about you. I told him you had a good job over the water and that you was living with—'

'You didn't go and tell him I was living with a man,' interrupted Ellie. 'Did you?'

'Why? Was that wrong?'

Ellie slowly shook her head. 'It's just that I don't like everybody knowing my business.'

'Well it's the truth, and I didn't see what harm it would do; after all, you ain't gonner go out with him, not now.'

'No,' said Ellie sadly.

'How's the job?'

'Not bad. I've still got the same work station. D'you know, some of those women have been there for years, so it looks as if I'm never gonner get any nearer the door.'

Iris laughed. 'With a bit of luck one of 'em might drop dead, then you'll move along the line.'

'Dunno if I want to stay there that long.'

'Ellie, you don't sound very happy. Is Len treating you all right?' There was genuine concern in Iris's voice.

She nodded. 'Course. It's just that I don't have so many laughs as I did when I was working with Peggy, and most evenings Leonard is at the club. I'm just being silly.'

Iris looked at her sister. 'I want you to be happy.'

'I am,' she said smiling.

Iris continued folding her clean washing and putting it in her drawer. Bessie called up the stairs to tell them the tea was ready.

'By the way, have you heard any more from that matron?' asked Iris.

'No, I just had the one letter after I wrote to say we'd moved. I told you it was only to say there was no change in Mum. Iris, I wouldn't mind going to see Dad's grave sometime. Would you fancy coming with me?'

'Dunno. What's there to see? Just a pile of earth. Why d'you wanner go?'

'I don't know. Perhaps we could put a cross or something on it, just to let people know his name.'

'Dunno about that. 'Sides, it ain't as though anyone else will ever go there, is it?'

'No, s'pose not.'

Iris linked her arm through Ellie's. 'Now come on, let's go down and have that cup of tea, before you get too morbid.'

All the way home Ellie was getting cross with herself. She should be more than content. She was living with Leonard, and had money to spend. Iris was happy living with Bessie, and she had plenty of friends in the Days. Even Terry was happy with his new job and his girlfriend. She sighed, and gazed out of the bus window.

Amongst the people ambling along the pavement, a young woman hurrying in the opposite direction to the bus caught Ellie's eye. Ellie sat up; there was something familiar about her. She peered out of the window. It was Lizzie. Her Lizzie. Ellie jumped to her feet and rang the bell.

'The next stop's a bit further on, love. I thought you was going to—' said the conductor.

'I've just seen me sister,' she said joyfully.

The bus seemed to take forever to reach the next stop. Ellie quickly leapt off the platform and ran back. The pavement was hard beneath her feet. She couldn't see Lizzie, people were blocking her view and she had to jump out of their way. Her every step jarred her bones, she was beginning to get breathless. Her heart was beating fast and her side hurt. She had a stitch. Please, don't let me miss her, don't let her go down a side street, Ellie panted to herself.

Suddenly there in front of her was Lizzie, wearing a lovely coat and hat, and talking to a very good-looking young man, not her husband. Ellie stood for a few moments deciding what to do. They appeared to be in deep conversation.

'Lizzie. Lizzie,' she called.

Lizzie turned and the colour drained from her face. 'Ellie. What're you doing here?'

Ellie ran up to her and threw her arms round her neck. 'Oh Lizzie,' she cried, tears streaming down her face.

Lizzie stood perfectly still, her arms at her sides. She was totally unemotional.

'Such a lot has happened since you and Dolly left home.' The man Lizzie had been talking to cleared his throat.

'Look, Dave, I'll see you this evening.' Lizzie quickly stood back, without introducing him to Ellie.

'OK.' He smiled and touched his trilby, and kissing Lizzie's cheek turned and walked away.

'Who was that?' asked Ellie, wiping her eyes.

'Just some bloke I know. Now, what's all this about?'

'Is there somewhere we can talk? Do you live near here?'

'No,' she said abruptly.

'What about Dolly?'

'Don't see her now. She's married, you know?'

'I guessed as much. Does she live near here?'

'No. Look, there's a pub up the road, it's got a snug so we won't look out of place in there.' Lizzie began to move away.

'You don't seem very pleased to see me,' said Ellie when they had settled in a seat in a far corner of the snug bar.

'Well, it's a bit of a shock.' She inclined her head towards the bar. 'Look at those old tarts giving us the once over, they're worried we might go out on their patch.'

'What for?'

'Ellie, you're still as bloody naive as ever.' She took a packet of cigarettes from her handbag and offered Ellie one.

Ellie shook her head.

'Well, what you doing round this neck of the woods, and what's been 'appening to the rest of the Walshes?' Lizzie lit her cigarette, and screwed up her eyes against the smoke.

Ellie looked at her. Her face was heavy with make up, and her mouth was set in a hard line as she blew the smoke high into the air.

'Dad's dead.' Ellie stopped and waited for a reaction.

'That's a shame. What'd 'e die of? It wasn't bloody hard work, I bet,' laughed Lizzie.

'Mum killed him,' said Ellie softly.

'What?' exploded Lizzie.

The women at the bar looked over at them.

Lizzie leant forward. 'What, murdered him? I ain't read nothing in the papers about that. How did she manage to do that?'

'It was an accident. She hit him and he banged his head on the fender.'

'She's doing time now, I suppose. Serves her right.' Lizzie grinned.

'No, she's in an asylum.'

'What?' said Lizzie again, but a little quieter this time. 'She's in a loony bin? Well, that's a right turn up for the book, and if you ask me, it's no more than she bloody well deserves. Always said she was a barmy cow.'

'Ain't you sorry about Mum and Dad?'

'Not really. She deserves all she gets.'

'What about Dad? Don't you wanner see his grave?'

'No.'

Ellie was upset that Lizzie wasn't interested in their family's affairs. 'Don't you wanner know how it happened?'

'Not really.'

Ellie looked at her.

'Well go on then, if you must.'

Very briefly Ellie told her that she and her mother had had an argument, and when she went to hit her she missed and hit her father, and it had unbalanced her mother's mind.

'Well, I suppose she's in the right place.'

The conversation lapsed. 'Me and Iris found it very hard to manage.'

'I expect you did. Here, I hope you ain't come over here to find me for a hand-out?'

Ellie shook her head.

'By the way, how is dear little Baby Iris these days?'

'She's all right, she works in a store.'

'You still at the tea shop?'

'No, they moved to Margate. I work in a big store now.'

'Which one?'

'Beaumonts.'

'That's nice, do you get discount on the goods?'

Ellie nodded.

'I'll have to pop in sometime and have a look round.'

Ellie was getting angry with Lizzie. 'Do you ever see Dolly?'

'No, ain't seen her for months, she's got very frumpy since she got married. Wouldn't be surprised if she ain't got armful of kids before long.'

'I'd like to see her again. D'you know where she lives?'

'No, she moved away.' Lizzie aggressively tapped the end of her cigarette into the ashtray. 'Tom had the opportunity to move Essex way. We don't bother to write, didn't see eye to eye after I left Ern.'

'You left your husband?'

'Yer, he got very boring. A bit of a drag.'

'Who was that bloke you was talking to?'

'Mind yer own business.'

'Sorry.'

'Don't look like that. 'E's just a friend. Trouble is he's married so we have to be careful.'

Ellie looked long and carefully at her sister. She was so hard and full of herself. 'Why didn't you or Dolly get in touch with us after you left? You knew where I worked. You could have come to see me.'

'Didn't see much point. We wanted to get as far away as we could from that place. Elmleigh Square.' She sniffed. 'Wouldn't be seen dead back at that place now. You still living there?'

'No. Iris is in lodgings in Rotherhithe New Road, and I'm . . .' Ellie didn't want to tell her about Leonard. 'I'm living at the store's hostel.'

'That's nice.'

'Can I see you again?' asked Ellie.

'Why? We ain't got nothing to talk about.'

'Wouldn't you like to see Iris again?'

'Not really.'

Ellie was beginning to get upset. 'Would your Ernie know where Tom and Dolly moved to?'

'Na. Don't ever see him, since I moved out, and I heard he moved with the job again, so you can't go chasing him round there.'

'Where do you live?'

Lizzie viciously crushed the end of her cigarette in the ashtray. 'You're asking a bloody lot of questions.'

Ellie began to raise her voice. 'I ain't seen you for months. I tell you our dad's dead and Mum's in a home and you ain't a bit interested, and you won't tell me nothing about you.'

'Keep your voice down. Ain't much to tell. I left Ernie, moved to a smaller place, got meself a good job, and I'm having a good time, so what else d'yer wanner know?'

Ellie knew she wasn't going to get anywhere with Lizzie. She picked up her handbag. 'Well at least I know how you feel about us. If you do ever hear from Dolly, could you come to Beaumonts and let me know?'

'Don't think I'll ever hear from her. We had a mighty big row when I left Ern.'

Ellie stood up. 'Bye Lizzie.' She walked out of the door knowing she would never see either of her older sisters again.

'Me and Iris must always keep in touch,' she whispered to herself. 'She's all I've got now.'

Chapter 32

Ellie walked along in a dream, her mind churning. Her two older sisters didn't want to know anything about the family. Lizzie wasn't the least bit concerned that her dad was dead and her mother in an asylum. It was as if they had never existed. Would Dolly be upset if *she* knew about their mother and father? Why was Lizzie so hard? Ellie was angry. All these past months she had tried to find her sisters, and all the time they hadn't wanted anything to do with them. Ellie continued to walk. She didn't know where she was going; she didn't know this area that well.

When a bus pulled up at the stop beside her, she automatically got on.

'Where to, love?' asked the conductor as she sat down.

'I'm sorry?'

'I asked yer where yer going.'

'Oh, I don't know. What number's this bus?'

The conductor raised his eyes to the ceiling. 'It's a number 22, and we go past the cemetery, and then on to . . .'

'The cemetery, please.' Ellie's eyes filled with tears.

'I'm sorry, love. Yer just lorst someone?'

She nodded. 'My sister.'

He gave her her ticket and patted her shoulder. 'Time heals, girl,' he said sympathetically. 'Time heals.'

Ellie looked out of the window. She wasn't sure if this bus was going to the cemetery her father was buried in, but she did know there weren't that many round here, and they were quiet, peaceful places that would give her time to think.

'Cemetery, love,' said the conductor softly as the bus came to a stop. 'Keep yer pecker up, love,' he called after her as the bus pulled away.

She was pleased when she caught sight of the large black wrought-iron ornamental gates; it *was* the one her father was buried in. She made her way past the towering monuments, shrines for former loved ones. Angels looked down on her; huge lichen-covered crosses rose from the ground, bearing the names of those dear departed, though time and weather had long since eroded the letters away. She walked past grey headstones that over the years had shifted, and were now leaning at dangerous and drunken angles. Her feet crunched on the gravel path as she moved towards the far corner. The paupers' corner. No huge crosses, stone monuments or angels towered above these grass-covered mounds.

Ellie stopped and looked around. Which one belonged to her father? Where was he? Every mound looked the same. What about the small cross of pebbles, which on that sad morning she had carefully arranged on the top of his mound? All the tiny hillocks were overgrown, all covered with long grass. A few simple wooden crosses still stood. She began to search, carefully at first, then in desperation, rushing from one mound to another. But it was all in vain. She sat on the grass and cried, her body racked with pain and sorrow. She cried for her father, her mother, Lizzie, Dolly and most of all, for herself.

Ellie finally raised her head. She felt exhausted. The sun was slowly going down behind the houses. She shivered. How long had she been sitting there? She had to get home. Home to Leonard. Her Leonard.

Outside the cemetery gates she glanced at a man selling pathetic-looking bunches of flowers; another, with a sad face, had a tray of matches hanging round his drooping shoulders. Times were very hard and these men would be facing another cold, bleak winter very soon.

Despite her puffy eyes she managed a slight smile. At least she had a job, even though she wasn't that happy there. She was getting a wage, not like a lot of people who were out of work, and she had a nice home to go to; and best of all she had Leonard, who she knew really cared for her.

'You're late. I thought you said you—' Leonard stopped when he saw Ellie's face. 'What's happened? Ellie, what's wrong?'

She rushed up to him and threw herself into his arms.

He gently kissed her wet cheek. 'My God, whatever's happened?'

'I saw Lizzie.'

'Your sister Lizzie? Where?' He pushed her from him and looked into her face. 'Was she at Iris's?'

'No. I don't know where it was, I was on the bus,' she sobbed. 'And I got off and we went to a pub and we talked. Oh Leonard, she wasn't a bit sorry about Mum and Dad, and she's left her husband, and she don't know where Dolly is, and—'

He put his arm round her shoulders and led her to the sofa. 'Come and sit down. I'll make a cup of tea and then you can tell me all about it.'

Ellie let herself be led.

In the kitchenette Leonard filled the kettle. His thoughts were on the meeting he'd had earlier in the afternoon. Why did this have to happen today? He wanted to tell her about it, but it wasn't fair to give her any more bad news just yet. No, it would have to be shelved for a few days. Poor Ellie.

He sat quietly listening to all Ellie had to say.

'I'll have to go and tell Iris,' she said when she finished. 'She'll be ever so angry with Lizzie. I can't believe she'd be like that.' Ellie blew her nose.

'Do you think she will come in to Beaumonts?' Leonard asked.

'Don't think so. I don't think she ever wants to see me again.'

'Well I shouldn't worry about her any more. What say we go to the pictures tonight? We haven't been for ages.'

Ellie smiled. 'I'd like that.'

Despite her meeting with Lizzie, Ellie was very cheerful and determined to be happy at work.

On Thursday morning when she took Leonard his cup of tea, she asked, 'Would you mind if I went to see Iris on Saturday?'

'I thought you would rather go on Sunday; you get more time to chat then.'

'Well I . . .'

'If you leave it till Sunday I'll come with you.'

'Would you?' Ellie smiled and kissed him. 'Thank you. I'm so lucky.' She sat on the bed. 'I wish I didn't have to go to work. I wish I could stay here all day with you.'

'I told you, you don't have to . . .' He stopped. 'Anyway I'm not here all day, I have to be off later too.'

'I know, it's just that we don't have a lot of time together.'

'We have all day Sunday and Monday evenings. Now come on, be off with you.'

She kissed him and left. As she walked to work she pondered on the fact that he hadn't told her to give up work, as he normally did when she said she was fed up. Marriage was never mentioned. Was he getting tired of her now? Was this why he wanted her to work? Would she have to look after herself one day?

Saturday evening Ellie walked into the club, sat at her table and ordered her port and lemon.

She looked round at some of the now-familiar faces. One or two gave her a slight nod. They all knew she belonged to

336

the piano player. She sat fiddling with her glass, and tapping her foot in time to the music.

'Hallo there.'

She looked up and froze. It was Curly.

'You look very nice tonight.'

She shot a glance at Leonard; his face was full of anger. 'Thank you,' she whispered, dreading him sitting at her table.

He leant on the back of her chair but made no attempt to sit down. 'Got a couple of drinks waiting for me, but that gentleman over there said he'd like to buy you a drink, so I thought I'd better come over and find out what yer poison is.'

Ellie looked across the dimly lit room and gasped when she saw who it was. 'I'd rather he didn't.'

'Why? Old Cole's a good bloke, and got a few bob. If you like old men, you might do better with him than old Piano Pete up there.'

'No, no thank you.'

'He ain't gonner like it.'

'I'm sorry.'

Curly strolled back to the table Mr Cole and his party were sitting at.

Ellie tried hard not to look at them, but out of the corner of her eye she watched them talking and looking in her direction. She knew he was a regular. Most times when she'd seen him he'd been too interested in his young, pretty companions to notice her. But she had been dreading bumping into him. Did he know who she was? And did he know she hadn't given him her last week's rent? She began to get worried. Why had he picked on her?

He stood up and began weaving his way towards her.

Ellie knew it was pointless rushing to the ladies. No, she was safer here, with Leonard keeping his eye on her.

'I was very disappointed when you wouldn't have a drink with me, young lady.' Mr Cole pulled out a chair and sat at her table. 'You look so alone sitting here week after week; I was only trying to be polite.'

She had kept her head down; now she looked up and opened her mouth to speak, but he carried on.

'I realize you're with old Len up there, but I know he don't mind me talking to you. Besides, d'you know, I'm sure we've met before. Never forget a pretty face.' He threw his head back and laughed out loud. 'I know where it was – it was the tea room, you used to work there. I bet I'm right.' Without waiting for an answer he went on. 'Mind you, you look a bit different in that frock with that fancy thing in your hair.'

Ellie touched the diamanté hair slide. She was very proud of it. How dare he call it a 'thing'?

He squinted and cast his eyes over her. 'I was bloody wild about old Jenkins going.' He waved his hand at the waiter. 'Now come on girl, what yer having?'

'Nothing, thank you.'

He turned to the waiter. 'Get whatever she drinks, and I'll have me usual. Now, I've forgotten your name.'

'Ellie,' she whispered. She wanted to say Miss Walsh, to keep it on a very impersonal level, but guessed he might remember her surname, and connect it with the unpaid rent.

'Ellie, my, that's a pretty name for a pretty young thing.' He sat back. 'D'you know, I remember I came in just after you'd had your hair cut.' He leaned forward. 'Bet you never thought I'd remember that, but like I said, I never forget a pretty face.'

The waiter put the drinks on the table.

'So, where you working now? Or is he looking after you?' He inclined his head towards the band.

'I work in the West End,' she said softly.

'That's nice. So where're you living?'

'I live with Leonard.'

'Oh yes,' he smirked. 'So I've been told.'

The way he said it for some reason made Ellie feel suddenly dirty.

He looked into his glass and slowly swirled the whisky round and round. 'Didn't you use to live near the tea room?'

'Not too far away,' she croaked.

'I own a lot of property round that way, so if he ever throws you out and you're looking for somewhere to stay, I can always put something very nice your way.'

Ellie wanted to laugh. What did he have that was very nice? Everything he owned around Rotherhithe was falling down. 'Thank you,' she said, biting her tongue.

When the band began playing their signature tune, the couples left the dance floor for the short interval.

Mr Cole looked at the band. 'I'd better be off. Don't want old Len shouting his head off.'

Ellie was surprised at that statement; she had thought Mr Cole never worried about anybody.

Leonard quickly left the stage and sat beside her. 'What did he want?'

'He said he remembered me from the tea room.'

'Is that all?'

'He bought me a drink. I didn't want him to.'

'Oh, is that all?' repeated Leonard.

Ellie nodded. There wasn't any point in telling him the rest of the conversation.

Chapter 33

Iris was very angry when, on the following day, Ellie told her in detail the conversation she'd had with Lizzie.

'I can believe that. Always knew Lizzie was selfish. Well I never want to see her again,' Iris said aggressively.

'Don't suppose we ever will.'

'Only if she goes into Beaumonts,' said Leonard.

'D'you think she will?' asked Iris.

'No,' said Ellie. 'I don't think we'll ever see her again.'

'Well we won't miss her,' said Iris.

'Iris, when I left her I went to the cemetery to try to find Dad's grave.'

'You didn't tell me that,' said Leonard.

'There wasn't a lot to tell. I couldn't find it.'

'Well,' said Iris, 'don't see the point in keep upsetting yourself. After all what's done's done, and we can't turn the clock back.'

Ellie only wished she could. Iris clearly didn't want to talk about their parents, for she carried on talking to John, totally dismissing the subject. Ellie didn't see any reason to tell her about the conversation she'd had with Mr Cole; Iris wouldn't be interested in that, either.

Sunday evening wasn't any different to the others Ellie had shared with the Days, and once again when they were in the pub she laughed and sang along with them. Leonard didn't volunteer to play the piano, and thankfully Mr Day didn't push him to. All evening Ellie kept her eye on the door in case Terry should walk in with his young lady. She was ready to introduce Leonard to him, just to show Terry she hadn't wasted her time waiting for him.

Leonard was very quiet on the bus home, and Ellie was afraid he was cross with her for going to see her sister. But after all he had suggested it, she said to herself as, putting her arm through his, she snuggled up to him. He looked down at her, smiled, and patted her hand. All her fears quickly disappeared.

Today had been more boring than usual, Ellie thought as she left the store for home. All day it had been misty and the few people that had ventured out were well wrapped up against the damp. They hadn't lingered very long over their coffee. Now the weather had worsened. The buses had stopped running and there were very few people on the streets. The fog was thick and swirling; a yellow glow hung round the hissing gas lamps, the noise loud and eerie in the empty streets. Ellie's footsteps echoed on the pavement. She longed to be indoors in front of the lovely warm fire, with a mouthwatering smell coming from the kitchen. She loved Monday evenings. Leonard would be home and they could sit and talk, and he would play those haunting tunes. Then when they went to bed . . . She smiled, pulled her scarf tighter round her and shuddered with excitement.

'It's a terrible night out there,' she said, walking in and taking her coat off. She now had her own key.

Leonard was sitting in front of the fire, toying with the poker and staring into the dancing flames. He didn't jump up to take her coat, or kiss her.

'Dinner smells good. Are you all right?' she added quietly.

'Yes, yes, sorry, I was miles away then.'

'So I could see,' said Ellie apprehensively.

Leonard quickly kissed her cheek. 'Dinner's ready, sit yourself down.'

Ellie did as she was told.

There wasn't the usual laughter and conversation at the table. He did ask if she had been busy, and she asked him what he had been doing with himself.

'I had to go out.'

'More difficult pupils?' she asked, noting his mood.

'No,' he said pushing his empty plate away.

'That was lovely, thank you.' She made a move to kiss him, but he backed away.

'Ellie, you had better sit on the sofa. I have something to tell you.'

Ellie froze. She knew by his tone it was going to be something bad.

He came and sat next to her, and took hold of her hand. 'I don't really know where to begin. I'm very fond of you, and . . .'

Ellie wanted to cry. What was he going to say? Was he married, or was he . . . She couldn't think.

'Ellie, as you know, I used to live in Germany. I never told you much about myself, as at the time I didn't think it mattered, but for these past few weeks I've had a visitor, and . . .'

Ellie stared at him. It must be his wife, flashed across her mind.

He cleared his throat. 'I'd better start at the very beginning otherwise it won't make any sense. You see, my parents are – were – English and my father's profession took them to Germany. I was educated in England, but was back in Germany when the war broke out. I managed to get out and was interned here.' He looked at her. 'You do know what I mean, don't you?'

She shook her head.

'I was put in a camp because my parents were still in Germany.'

'Is that what that Curly was on about?'

'Yes, he found that out when my cousin's daughter came over here.'

'She was the one who stayed with you?'

'Yes, I took her to the club and she went out with Curly a few times.'

'You didn't tell me that.'

'I didn't see the point. Anyway it doesn't matter now. At the time I asked her if she knew anything about my parents, as I hadn't heard from them for a number of years. She said she would ask her father, who was still living over there. I also wrote to him a few times, but never received an answer. I thought many times that I would go and try to find them, but the years passed. I had a good job and my teaching, and then I met you.'

Ellie thought she would cry with relief. He hadn't gone because of her. He must love her.

'But over these last few weeks things have changed.'

Ellie felt she had turned to stone. She couldn't move.

'You see, someone has told me that my cousin did find out about my parents. Unfortunately they have both passed away now.'

Ellie took his hand. 'I'm ever so sorry.'

He gave her hand a pat. 'The reason my cousin didn't reply to my letters was that he is living in their house. Well to get to the point, my parents were German sympathizers, and quite wealthy, and it seems that they have left a considerable amount of money and property, and this friend suggests I should go and try to claim my inheritance.'

'Oh Leonard, that's wonderful. Will you be very rich?'

'My friend seems to think so.'

'So when are you going?'

'Next week.'

'Next week?'

'I don't think I should wait for much longer. It will be

difficult as it is to get it sorted out after all this time.'

'Will you be away for very long?'

'I don't know.'

Ellie hesitated before she asked, 'Did you want me to come with you?' She said it softly, desperately wishing the answer would be yes. She would love to go abroad – to see the sea, to be with Leonard in a new country. He interrupted her racing thoughts.

'No, I'm sorry. You see, I don't know how long I shall be away.'

Ellie sat back deflated. 'What about me? Where can I go?' she asked, full of fear.

He looked surprised. 'You can stay here of course.'

'I can still live here?'

'Of course. I want you to be here when I return.'

'But what about . . .'

'Look, I'll pay a month's rent in advance; and you do have your own income.'

Was this why he hadn't said anything about her giving up her job? He must have known about this weeks ago, and there was still no mention of getting married.

'During that month,' he continued, 'I'll be able to find out what's happening, and then, well who knows.'

'I won't see you for a whole month.'

He kissed her cheek. 'I know, but think of the good time we'll have when I get back.'

She smiled, but her heart was heavy. 'When are you going?'

'Sunday.'

'Sunday? As soon as that?'

'Yes. Once it's settled I'll be back.'

When Ellie pushed open the front door the following Saturday she felt suddenly desolate. There in the doorway was Leonard's case ready for him to take in the morning.

'Hallo,' he said, rushing to greet her. 'I've done us a very special meal, and we can spend the evening together.'

'It seems funny having you home on a Saturday,' she said sadly.

'Yes, I must admit it feels rather odd to me. But if you ever want to go to the club, don't hesitate. I've sorted it out and left money to cover any drinks you might want.'

'I wouldn't go on my own.'

'But you're always on your own.'

She smiled. 'But I've always got you looking after me.'

He held her close. 'I love that smile. Look, why don't you take Iris and John one Saturday night? You'll be able to sign them in. I'm sure they'd like it.'

'I suppose I could. But you're only away for a few weeks, and then you'll be back and we can . . .' She hesitated. Would it be the same? What if he was a rich man – would he still come back? And would he still want her to live with him? And if he didn't get his inheritance, would he still want her?

'Right, time to dish up.'

Ellie sat at the table, feeling upset. Why, just as she was happy, did another problem come her way? 'This is lovely,' she said, trying to do the delicious meal justice, despite the fact that every mouthful was a job to swallow. She didn't want to upset him after all the trouble he'd gone to, or to spoil their last evening together.

In the week that followed Ellie felt really down in the dumps. She had no one to talk to at work, and she hated coming home to a cold and empty flat. She felt as miserable as the weather. She missed Leonard so much, and the warmth of the flat, and his cooking. The only thing she had to look forward to was that on Saturday she was going to spend the night with Iris.

On Saturday she had a long letter from Leonard in which he told her how much Germany had changed since he had last been there. He was going to see his cousin on Friday so he should have more news next week.

She held his letter close to her. 'He should know if he is a rich man by now,' she said out loud. She looked at the letter again. 'I hope he doesn't get a lot of money, because then he might not want me.'

That evening the greeting from the Days was the same as usual, and once more Ellie was laughing and enjoying herself.

'You don't have to go home in the morning, you know,' said Bessie when they returned to the house. 'I can give you a bit of dinner, always got plenty.'

Ellie's face lit up. 'Can I? I'll pay you.'

Bessie laughed. 'Don't worry about that this week, but if you're going to do it a few times then I'm sure we can come to some arrangement.'

'Thanks, Bessie.'

When they were settling down in bed Ellie asked her sister, 'Iris, you don't mind me staying, do you?'

'Course not. Now let's get some sleep.'

Ellie turned over. For the first time in a week, she had someone to talk to, and to cook her a meal. It was so warm and cosy and homely here. She sighed. She could understand Iris being happy living here, and at this moment she could enjoy it as well. Then Leonard filled her thoughts. That brought a smile to her face. 'Please, come back to me soon,' she whispered.

All week she waited for a letter, but none arrived, and on Saturday she was back with Iris. For the next two weeks life took on the same pattern. But she grew worried that she hadn't heard from Leonard. He had been gone three weeks now, and next week the rent was due. She had enough money saved for a few weeks' rent, but after that . . . Panic seized her. What if he didn't come back? She couldn't manage his rent, and food, and pay Mrs Tomms. He hadn't given her an address, as he was moving from the hotel, so she couldn't write to him. What was happening over there? Why didn't he write?

On Monday she rushed to the door when a letter plopped on the mat. 'I knew you wouldn't let me down,' she cried, but was filled with disappointment when she saw it wasn't from Leonard. It was from the matron of the home their mother was in. It was very short, and Ellie's eyes, full of fear, quickly scanned the page.

Dear Miss Walsh,
   I am writing to inform you that there has been a slight improvement in your mother.

'Oh no,' groaned Ellie out loud. 'Don't say she's coming home.'

The doctors have decided that she is fit enough to be moved to another hospital.

Ellie sank into a chair.

I will be able to let you have more details in a few days; in the meantime, if you would like to come and visit your mother, I am sure you will be very pleased with her progress.
   I remain your obedient servant,
   Edith Tennet
   Matron

Ellie read the letter over and over again. She and Iris would have to go and see her on Sunday, just in case they sent her miles away.

The following day her long-awaited letter from Leonard arrived. It was full of apologies for not getting in touch before. He had seen his cousin and there were a great many problems. He didn't think he would be home for a few weeks. He went on to say that he had met some of his old friends, and that he was staying at a Frau Muller's house. At last she had an address to write to. She had so much to tell him.

Chapter 34

It was Saturday, and Ellie was going to spend another weekend with her sister. She told her about the letter she'd had from the matron and was stunned at Iris's attitude.

'I'm sorry, Ellie, but I ain't gonner go to see her,' she announced, 'and that's that.'

'But why not?'

'I don't like that place, it stinks.'

Ellie was beginning to get angry. 'I don't like it either, but it's the least we can do. If they move Mum miles away we might not see her for years – or ever again,' she added softly.

'I said I ain't going and that's that.'

Ellie plonked herself on the bed. 'First you didn't want to go to Dad's grave, now you don't want to go and see Mum. You're no better than Lizzie.'

'Don't say that.' Tears welled up in Iris's eyes. 'I don't wanner see Mum 'cos she ain't our mum now, she's just a silly old woman.'

Ellie put her arms round her sister's heaving shoulders. 'I'm sorry, it's just that I think we should go.'

'I ain't, and you can't make me.'

'No, I know.' Ellie sighed. She knew it was pointless arguing with her. 'I'll go on my own in the morning. I'll tell Bessie not to bother about dinner.'

That evening in the pub wasn't as happy for Ellie as the others had been, although the Days tried hard to cheer her up. In many ways she wished she hadn't bothered to come.

★ ★ ★

Ellie was very apprehensive as she made her way once again to the asylum. She wished Iris was with her. What would her mother be like? What were the improvements the matron had mentioned? Would her mother recognize her, and remember that dreadful night? And most of all, would she go mad at seeing Ellie again, and blame her for her husband's death?

Ellie shuddered as she walked up the long path. Today was cold and damp, a typical November day. Christmas was next month. Christmas. Such a lot had happened in just a year. Her thoughts went to Peggy and Mr Jenkins. The only letter she'd had from them was to tell her everything was just fine, and they were really happy. Ellie remembered the decorations in the tea room. A slight smile lifted her cold, pinched face. She would buy some and put them up in the flat. That'd please Leonard, she said to herself. They'd have the best Christmas ever, even if he didn't get any inheritance.

'Miss Walsh,' said the nurse. 'If you just wait here I'll see if Matron is free.' She swept almost silently away.

Ellie sat down on a wooden bench. The sound of groaning and screaming suddenly filled the long narrow corridor, and shouts of 'I ain't going, I ain't going' made Ellie cringe.

I couldn't work in a place like this, she said to herself, looking around at the cold, white-tiled walls. It would drive me mad.

'Matron will see you. You do know where to find her, don't you?' said the nurse, who seemed to appear out of nowhere.

Ellie nodded.

Matron was sitting behind her desk. Her back was very straight and Ellie wondered what sort of stays she wore, and how long it took her to do up all the hooks and eyes.

'Miss Walsh, please take a seat.'

Ellie did as she was told. She clutched her handbag to her, almost afraid to hear whatever Matron was about to tell her.

'I assume you got my letter?'

Ellie nodded.

'Well I'm very sorry, but I'm afraid you've had a wasted journey.'

Ellie let out the breath she had been holding. 'But where's me mum? She ain't . . .?'

'No, no, my dear. Please, don't upset yourself, she's fine. It's just that we had transport going to another institution and the doctor thought it would be a good idea to send your mother.'

'Where's she gone?'

Matron smiled. 'I think you'll be pleased to know she's gone to the home in Southwark Park, which I understand is near to where you used to live.'

Ellie nodded. Her mouth dropped open. 'Me mum's back in Rotherhithe?'

'Yes, I thought you'd be pleased about that. You do know where it is, don't you?'

Again Ellie nodded.

'Good. Now I'm afraid I am rather busy.'

'Oh yes. Thanks.' Ellie quickly left the room, and the awful smell of carbolic that filled the air in there. Let's hope the other one smells a bit better, she thought. She suddenly smiled, wondering if Terry still worked there. It would be nice talking to him again and finding out how Molly was. She could even go and see her after she'd been to see her mum. For the first time since Leonard had gone away Ellie's step had a spring in it.

Ellie wrote to tell Iris about their mother being moved back to Rotherhithe. She also told her that she wasn't going to be over on Saturday night. She had intended to suggest that on Sunday they could go and see their mother, but decided against it. She would go on her own, just to find out how Mum was.

On Sunday afternoon Ellie looked out of the window. The rain was beating down onto the basement steps, then gurgling into the drain. She moved away from the window and sat in front of the warm and comforting fire. Although she was almost ready to go out, she held back, reluctant to get a soaking. Then a knock on the door startled her. She jumped up. Had Leonard come home? Why didn't he use his key? She threw open the door.

'Iris. John.' She looked quickly from one to the other. 'What's wrong?'

'Nothink's wrong. You gonner let us in? It's bucketing down out there.'

Ellie opened the door wide and stood to one side.

Iris laughed as she shook her umbrella out of the door. 'You should see the look on your face. Who you expecting, then?'

'No one . . . Well, not you two anyway. I'll take your wet things into the bathroom, and for Gawd's sake don't make a mess otherwise Mrs Tomms will have me guts for garters.'

'Don't know why you still bother about her.'

'Can't do much, can I, she's Leonard's.'

'Did he pay her before he left?'

'I expect so. Anyway, what you doing over this way?'

'When I got your letter I thought you might be a bit miffed 'cos I wouldn't go and see Mum, so I thought I'd come and let you make us a cuppa. We can't stay long.'

'Oh,' said Ellie. 'I was going to see Mum this afternoon. Don't suppose you want to come with me?'

'No,' was the curt reply.

'I shouldn't if I was you, Ellie,' said John. 'It ain't nice out there, you'd soon be soaked through.'

'Perhaps you're right. I'll put the kettle on.'

'Ellie.' John gave a nervous cough and looked at Iris. 'I ain't told Iris this. I thought it best to come over, 'cos of where your mum is, before you go there.'

Ellie looked at him. 'Why?'

John's face was very red. 'I don't think you've heard about what they do there, in that place your mum's in?'

Ellie sat down. 'No, I ain't.'

John was very uneasy. 'It's only a rumour, mind.'

'Well get on with it,' said Iris, her eyes wide.

'They do say they do experiments on people.'

Ellie gasped and put her hand to her mouth. 'What sort?'

'Drill holes in their heads.'

'What?' screamed Iris, looking dumbfounded. 'Who told you that?'

'Someone who came in the shop. They said they shave their heads first, so they can mark where they want to drill.'

'I don't believe it,' said Ellie. 'Terry Andrews works there, I'll ask him. They wouldn't be allowed to do something like that, would they?'

'Dunno.'

All three sat very quiet. Ellie felt sick at the thought of someone drilling a hole in her mother's head. 'I'm going to see her next Sunday. Do you want to come?'

Iris shook her head. 'I couldn't. What if they . . .?'

Ellie jumped up. 'That's it, make me feel worse.'

'Ellie, I'm sorry.' John looked decidedly unhappy. 'I shouldn't have said anything. It just came out.'

'It ain't your fault, John. I'll have to go next week and find out for meself, but thanks for warning me.' Ellie gave him a smile.

'This is a very nice place,' said Iris looking around and trying to ease the situation. 'No wonder you didn't want to go back to Elmleigh.' She stood up. 'This is a lovely piano, but different to the pub's.' She ran her hands over the well polished walnut wood, then tried to lift the lid. 'It's locked.'

'Leonard always keeps it locked.'

'Why's that?'

'Don't know. I've never asked.'

'Have you got the key?'

'No, he keeps it on his keyring.'

Iris laughed. 'Here, you don't reckon he's worried in case that Mrs Tomms has a knees up when you're out?'

'I shouldn't think so, she's a bit of a misery.'

'Well, it seems funny to me. Can we have a nose round?'

'Course.' Ellie took them to see the kitchen.

'It's a bit small. What if you finish up with a load of kids?'

Ellie didn't have an answer. 'You wait till you see the bathroom.'

'Wow. This is really great. And look at that bath. You're ever so lucky, Ellie, to find a bloke like Len to look after you.'

Ellie smiled. 'Yes I am, and I'll be glad when he's back.'

'Have you heard when that's likely to be?' asked John.

'No.'

'What's in that room?' asked Iris.

'It's me bedroom.'

Iris giggled. 'Well go on then, open the door.'

Ellie really didn't want anybody to see their very private domain. But she didn't have any choice when Iris impatiently pushed open the door.

'This is a bit of all right. Mind you, can't say I'd have picked that colour bedspread.'

'Remember this is Leonard's flat.'

'Yer, now where's that tea?'

Ellie went to the kitchen. She didn't want them here while Leonard was away. She felt they were intruding. She carried the tray of tea things back into the living room.

'This is a far cry from Elmleigh,' said Iris, leaning back on the sofa. 'Seems we've both done all right.'

'Ellie, Iris thought that perhaps we could come over to Len's club next Sat'day. What d'you think?' John looked uncomfortable as he sat on the edge of the sofa.

'Yes, why not? Now you know where we live you can come here, and it's not too far away, we can walk it.'

'It'll be nice to go somewhere different for a change,' said Iris.

Ellie looked at Iris. It seemed she was getting fed up with the usual routine. 'I thought you liked going to the pub?'

'We do, but we thought it'd be nice to do something a bit different.'

'Is it very expensive?' asked John.

'Don't know, I ain't ever had to pay.'

Iris put her arm through John's. 'Don't worry about it.'

After they left, Ellie sat and wrote another long letter to Leonard, even though she hadn't had a reply to her last one. She told him her mother was now back in Rotherhithe, and that Iris and John were going with her to the club next Saturday. She also told him how much she missed him, and couldn't wait for him to come home.

Another uneventful week passed, with no letters from Leonard. Ellie sighed; all week she had tried to put out of her thoughts what John had told them about the home. It must be only a rumour. If only she'd had the time to go and see Terry, he might know.

Iris and John would be arriving soon. She really didn't want to go to the club without Leonard. She smiled, remembering how once it had been the most important thing in her life. Now, without him playing the piano, it wouldn't be the same.

The doorman touched his hat and greeted them with a smile.

Iris nudged Ellie and giggled. 'Cor, it makes yer feel ever so important, don't it?'

Ellie only smiled.

'I love yer frock,' said Iris. 'Makes yer look ever so grown up.'

'And you look very nice too, Iris. That blue certainly suits you.'

Beside Iris she suddenly did feel very grown up and sophisticated.

The band were playing a slow tune when they walked in, and couples were locked in each other's arms. Ellie felt sad when she looked up and saw another man seated at the piano. 'This is me table,' she said as they carefully made their way towards it.

As usual the waiter was at her side almost immediately. 'Good evening, miss, nice to see you back again. I trust Mr Kent is well?'

'Yes thank you. John, what're you drinking?'

John nervously ran his fingers round the inside of his stiff white collar. 'Dunno. What d'you normally drink?'

'I'll have a port and lemon,' said Ellie.

'So will I,' said Iris, trying to sound confident.

'You don't have a beer, be any chance, do you?'

'Certainly.'

'Wow Ellie,' said Iris. 'This is a really smashing place. Look at the way that silver ball up there makes little arrows of coloured lights dance round the room. No wonder you didn't want to come home that Christmas.'

Ellie quickly took in a breath. She didn't want to be reminded of last year. 'Do you dance, John?'

'No. Got two left feet. Do you?'

'No.'

'Don't any of these old men ever ask you?' asked Iris, still squirming around in her seat in wonder.

'No. They all know I'm with Leonard.'

'Well you ain't tonight, so who knows, tonight could be your lucky night, Miss Walsh.' Iris laughed.

'I can't dance, so it wouldn't be very lucky for them if I was to get asked. Why don't you and John have a go?'

'We might make fools of ourselves,' said John.

'Come on John, let's have a go,' Iris giggled.

The band struck up with a fast tune.

'What's that they're doing?' asked John.

'It's called the Charleston.'

'I ain't getting up for this,' said John, leaning back in his chair. 'Look at 'em kicking their legs about, I'd probably end up falling arse over tip.'

Ellie laughed. Perhaps it had been a good idea to come here after all.

As the evening wore on Ellie could see John and Iris were enjoying themselves; they even got up and danced, but just the waltzes. If only Leonard was here, her evening would be complete. She closed her eyes and let the music drift over her.

'Would you like to dance, Ellie?'

She quickly opened her eyes. 'Mr Cole.'

'Your young man's not been here lately. Someone told me he's gone back to Germany. Not for good, I hope?'

'No, he should be back soon.'

'Well in that case, I think you and me could have a little dance without him glaring down on us. What d'you say?'

'I don't dance.'

'Well it's high time you learnt, young lady. Come on, on your feet.'

'I don't—'

'I'm not going to take no for an answer.' He took her arm and roughly pulled her to her feet.

Ellie quickly glanced at Iris, but she was too busy dreaming in John's arms.

Mr Cole held her very close. She could feel his hand hot and sticky on her back through her thin frock. His legs pushed against hers, making her move in the right direction.

'There, that ain't so bad now, is it?' he said, turning his head towards her, sending wafts of whisky into her face.

She didn't answer, and caught sight of Iris's grinning face as they passed them.

Ellie could feel Mr Cole's hot breath on her neck. His weight was making him pant. The music seemed to go on and on for ever.

At last he was leading her back to her seat. 'Thank you, my dear.'

Iris and John also returned.

'And may I ask who is this charming young lady?'

'My sister. Iris, this is Mr Cole.'

Iris quickly took a breath.

He held up his hands. 'Please, call me Bernard. Iris, I'm very pleased to meet you. And you, sir, are?'

'John. You're the Mr Cole what owns—'

'Mr Cole, sorry Bernard, owns a lot of property round Rotherhithe way. He owned the tea room where I used to work.' Ellie had to interrupt, and she knew her voice was high and unnatural, but she was terrified John or Iris would let him know they knew who he was.

'Can I get you good people a drink?'

'No thank you,' said Ellie quickly. 'I think we'll have to be going soon.'

'Ellie, could I speak to you for just a moment?' His tone was forceful.

Ellie looked at Iris. Fear was mounting inside her. Did he know who she was? He seemed to know everything. Was he going to ask about the unpaid rent?

He took her arm and led her away to one of the plush seats that lined the walls. They were dark, secluded seats.

They sat down.

'Ellie, I know Len's away, and I've heard through the grapevine that he ain't coming back.'

Ellie gasped. 'He is. Who told you that?'

'It doesn't matter.'

She jumped up. 'It does matter, it matters to me. Who told you these lies?' She quickly looked across at Iris. John made to stand up, but Iris put a restraining hand on his arm.

'Sit down, girl,' said Bernard Cole. 'You see, I know more about you than you think.'

Ellie sat down and closed her eyes. What did he know?

What was he going to say? She felt sick.

'I don't suppose you earn a lot of money, and if he ain't gonner be around to pay the rent, well, have you thought about how you're gonner manage?'

She sat up straight. 'I don't know where you've got the idea that Leonard isn't coming back home from, but I can tell you you've got it all wrong. Now if you don't mind I'm going back to my sister.' She stood up.

'Just a minute.' He took out his wallet. 'I like you, gel, and I could make you very happy. Take this ten-bob note and get them a drink.' He inclined his head towards Iris and John who were watching their every move.

'No thank you.'

He waved the ten-shilling note at her. 'Come on, don't be such a silly little cow. If you don't want it I'm sure that young man could do with a drink.' He forced the money into her hand.

Tears welled up in her eyes. She wanted to get away from him. She would never come here again without Leonard.

'Now, here's my card. Remember, if you ever want a friend to talk to, I'm always ready to listen, and if you ever want a roof over your head, I'm sure we could come to some sort of arrangement.' He smirked. 'And that could be very beneficial to both of us.' He stood up and faced her. 'I could get very fond of you, young lady.' He took hold of the tops of her arms and, pulling her close, kissed her hard on the mouth.

Ellie felt she was going to be ill. He let her go and reeling back she rubbed her mouth with the back of her hand. She was trembling with anger. Without a word she turned and walked over to Iris.

'What'd he say? What'd he want?' asked Iris eagerly.

Without looking back Ellie picked up her handbag and rammed the money in it. Tears were stinging her eyes. 'Come on, we're going.'

'But Ellie, why?'

'I'll tell you later.'

Outside the cold, biting wind took their breath away.

'You going on the bus?' asked Ellie. 'Or would you rather come back to Leonard's?'

'No, thanks all the same,' said John. 'We'll catch the bus. It was a nice evening. Certainly different from any place I've ever been to.'

'Ellie, you gonner tell me what all that with Mr Cole was about? He kissed you. What did you let him do that for?'

'I didn't let him.'

'You could have fooled me.'

'He told me he didn't think Leonard was ever coming back and he as good as offered me a home in with him.'

'But ain't he married?' asked John.

'Yes.'

'The dirty old sod.'

'Ellie, you ain't gonner go with him if Len don't come back, are you?'

'What d'you take me for? I can't stand the man.'

'Does he know we owe him a week's rent?'

'I don't know,' said Ellie. She tried not to show it, but deep down she was very worried, and not only about Mr Cole and the rent. What if her Leonard didn't come back? Then there was her mother . . . All her worries seemed to be crowding round her once more.

Chapter 35

Despite the miserable weather, Ellie knew she had to visit her mother. As she walked quickly through the park she remembered how she had tried to stop Terry and talk to him when she saw him coming out of the asylum. At the time she had desperately wanted to go out with him. Did he still work here, now he had a good job at the garage? All the times she had been to the pub with Iris and the Days, he had never come in with his Miss Jones. She had to see him, to find out more about this place. She shuddered at the thought of someone drilling a hole in your head. Did they really do those terrible things to people?

The asylum had a long gravel path and Ellie approached the large red-brick building very apprehensively. What was her mother like after all these months? What would she find? What if her mother's hair had been shaved off? Ellie wished she was on her way home.

When she reached the door she lifted the ring of the black knocker. It was so heavy it almost fell out of her cold hand. It banged against the thick oak door. Ellie heard bolts being drawn.

'Yes?' A greyhaired old man opened the door just wide enough to poke his head round.

'My mother has been moved to this . . . here, and I've come to see her.' Ellie wanted to giggle with relief. At least *he* had hair!

'Just a minute.' He went to shut the door, but changed his mind. 'What's 'er name?'

'Ruby Walsh.'

He closed the door and Ellie heard the bolt being shot.

This is more like prison, she thought. Perhaps they don't like people knowing what goes on in here. How could Terry work in a place like this? The cold was intense, and she stood stamping her feet.

The bolt was drawn again, and this time the door was opened by a young nurse. 'Come in. I'm sorry about that: I'm afraid old Charlie is a bit over-cautious. He won't let anyone in he's not sure of. Who have you come to see?'

'My mother. Ruby Walsh.'

'Follow me.'

Ellie followed the nurse into the large hall. It was sparsely furnished, but a beautiful wide staircase stretched in front of her. On either side was a corridor.

'If you wait here I'll find out if she's in a fit state to receive visitors. Please, take a seat.'

Ellie wanted to stop her before she moved away. What did she mean, in a fit state? What had they done to her?

She sat on one of the benches and looked around in amazement. This place was so different from the other home. People said that this house once belonged to a very wealthy family, and the owner went mad in the war. He had nurses and the like to look after him, and when he died his wife couldn't bear to live in it so she gave the building to the people who had looked after him, on the understanding they used it for other soldiers who went mad. She thought it must have been very lovely in its day; she could almost imagine the fine furniture, carpets and wonderful paintings. The tall ornamental ceilings must have had beautiful chandeliers hanging from them at one time.

She would never have believed such a beautiful house was behind that forbidding door. Did they do experiments, like John said? She wondered again. In all the years she had lived in Elmleigh she had never heard about that. Did they drill holes in people's heads? Perhaps it was only a rumour from one of John's silly customers who had nothing better to talk about. If they had shaved her mother's head, then she would know for certain.

'Would you like to come this way?' said the nurse, interrupting her thoughts. 'We are not sure how she is going to react to seeing you.'

'Is she all right?' asked Ellie, her palms sweating with fear and anticipation. Would she be wearing a hat?

'She just sits quietly.'

'I hope I don't upset her too—' Ellie stopped, she didn't want the nurse to know she had been the cause of her mother's breakdown in the first place.

'That's something we will have to see. She's in the conservatory.'

The nurse led her through a large room and out into a room made completely of glass. It was bright, airy and warm, so different from that other home. Tables and easy chairs were dotted all around; men and women were sitting chatting or quietly reading, though some were just sitting staring into space. But the atmosphere felt relaxed. As Ellie got a little closer she could see that a few men were in wheelchairs. The nurse went to the far side and there, sitting all alone, gazing out on to the garden, was her mother.

Tears steadily spilled from Ellie's eyes. Her mother looked a lot thinner and they had cut her hair, but it hadn't been shaved. The nurse gently touched her shoulder, and when she turned she had a vacant look on her face.

'Mrs Walsh, your daughter's here.'

Ruby Walsh looked at Ellie, her blue eyes dull and lifeless, her face pale.

'Hallo, Mum, how are you?'

Ruby Walsh grabbed the arms of the chair. Her knuckles turned white. Her eyes looked up pleadingly at the nurse. 'I ain't gotter daughter,' she whispered. 'Me mum won't let me git married.' She began to cry.

Tears streamed down Ellie's face. She wanted to throw her arms round her mother's neck and beg her forgiveness.

'There, there, don't cry.' The nurse patted her hand. 'There must be some mistake. I'll bring you a cup of tea.' The nurse beckoned for Ellie to follow her.

Ellie dabbed her eyes. 'Will she ever remember?'

'I'll take you along to see Sister. She will be able to tell you more.'

Once again Ellie followed the nurse. At the door she stopped and looked across at her mother. She had gone back to gazing out of the window.

'Please sit down,' said the sister, who was sitting at a desk. She began leafing through some papers in front of her.

Ellie was still in awe at her surroundings. She coughed.

'Is something bothering you?'

Ellie nodded. 'We always thought you did terrible things to people in here.'

'We have heard the rumours. Let me assure you this is not an experimental hospital. This place is for people who have nowhere to go. That is what the owner wants.'

Ellie half smiled. 'I didn't know this was such a lovely place. We always thought you only came in here 'cos you was barmy, but those people look . . .'

The sister smiled. 'We had so many soldiers with shell shock and other injuries that they decided this would be of better use as a convalescent home.'

'Oh. It's very nice.'

Sister looked back at the papers. 'Now, about your mother. We have a few patients like her who have had breakdowns and are not dangerous, and when we get a spare bed we try to move them here.'

Ellie began to relax. 'When I think of the times Mum threatened *us* with being sent away.'

The sister smiled and held up her hand. 'Please, don't

run away with the idea that all mental institutions are like this. As far as I'm aware this one is very exceptional, and was only possible because of our kind benefactor.'

'Will Mum ever get better?'

'I'm afraid the doctors don't hold out much hope. Something must have happened to your mother when she was a child, and she has clearly reverted to her traumatic past.'

'Could *we* get it? Could me and me sisters go barmy?'

'No.'

'Will she ever remember us?'

'We don't think so.'

Ellie sat back. She felt deflated.

'You can call any time you are round this way. We don't have strict rules.'

'Will it be worth it?' asked Ellie sadly.

'I couldn't say. But if you want to reassure yourself that she is all right, and doesn't have any holes in her head,' the sister smiled, 'then from your point of view, it's a good idea. We will leave that up to you.'

'Why was me mum sent here and not kept in that dreadful place in Greenwich?'

'As I said, she's one of the lucky ones. Remember, you can call at any time.'

As Ellie walked away down the drive, she wasn't sure how she felt. The home certainly didn't seem to have fulfilled her fears. When she saw Terry again she would ask him if what the sister had said about how caring it was was true.

It was getting dark and the rain was being whipped up by the biting wind. She felt cold, and decided not to go and see Molly today. Perhaps she would call on her the next time she came to see her mother. But goodness only knew when that would be; after all, would it really be worth it? Somehow, though, Ellie couldn't see herself walking away from her mother for ever. She guessed she'd be back.

It was the beginning of December. There still hadn't been

any answer to the many letters she had written to Leonard, and every day Ellie was getting more and more worried. So far she had managed to pay the rent on the flat, but her savings were dwindling fast and if she didn't hear from him soon she didn't know how she would manage.

It was Monday, and when she got in from work her eyes alighted on a piece of folded paper leaning against the clock. She was laughing and crying at the same time. He was home, her Leonard had come back.

But the writing wasn't his. It was from Mrs Tomms, telling her she would no longer be cleaning as she hadn't been paid for the last two weeks. There was an address, if Leonard wanted her to come back when he got home. Ellie sat down and brushed her tears away with her gloved hand. What was wrong? Why hadn't he written?

She needed to talk to someone. On Saturday she would go over to Iris and stay the night. Then on Sunday she would visit her mother and Molly.

The following morning Ellie was in the kitchen when she heard a letter drop onto the mat. She hurried to the door and picking it up was overjoyed to see Leonard's handwriting. She tore at the envelope. Please say you're coming home soon, she pleaded silently. A folded piece of white paper fluttered to the floor. Ellie bent down and picked it up. She gasped in amazement. It was a five-pound note. Although she had never seen one close to, she knew what it was. She had never touched a five-pound note before. Why had he sent her all this money? She began to panic. What was it for? She fingered it for a moment, then carefully read the letter.

My very dear Ellie,

This has been a very interesting time in my life. I do apologize for the delay in answering your letters, but I can assure you that you are never out of my thoughts.

However, since returning to Germany I can easily

understand my parents' enthusiasm for the German way of life. Now I am older, I too find it totally absorbing, and fully agree with many of their radical and forward-thinking ideas.

You will be pleased to hear I will be getting the family home and all my inheritance, though unfortunately it is going to be a long drawn out legal process. I may even have to become a German citizen, but that is in the distant future.

I am sending you five pounds, which should take care of the next six weeks' rent. After that I may well be able to tell you of my plans. It might mean my staying in Germany. I will not be back in time for Christmas, so take care of yourself. I'm sure you will enjoy being in your sister's, and the Days', company over the festive season.

Don't worry about me, Frau Muller is taking very good care of me. We were good friends many years ago.

There will be a parcel for you nearer Christmas, and just in case I don't get an opportunity to write to you again, I will take this one to wish you a very happy Christmas

All my fondest love,
Leonard
XXX

Ellie reread the letter several times. She sat and stared at the paper. He wasn't coming home for Christmas. He might stay in Germany for ever. He didn't say he loved her and missed her, not in the true sense. And who was this Frau Muller?

Her world was falling apart. How could everything that had been so good, go wrong? What would she do without him? She didn't want to be here without him. If he stayed in Germany where would she live?

She was utterly miserable. She put the five-pound note behind the clock on the mantelpiece, and noticed the time. She should be on her way to work, but what was the point?

She took the letter and went back to bed.

Chapter 36

A loud banging on the knocker woke Ellie from her fitful doze. Who could it be? It wasn't Mrs Tomms' morning; besides, she'd left. She looked at the clock: it was half past two. Ellie, catching sight of her red eyes and bedraggled look in the mirror, pulled Leonard's dressing gown round her and shuffled to the door.

She opened it slightly and peered round. A man wearing a brown tweed suit and a black bowler hat stood there.

'Is Mr Kent at home, miss?'

'No. I'm sorry.' She went to shut the door but the man had his foot there, stopping it.

'Where is he?' He gently fingered his thick moustache.

'Abroad. Would you kindly remove your foot.'

'I ain't moving till I've got me money.'

'Money? What money?' asked Ellie in alarm.

'Payments on the piano.'

'What payments?'

'Mr Kent is buying that joanna on the nut and bolt, and 'e ain't kept up the payments, so . . . If I don't get me money, I takes the piano, it's as simple as that.'

Ellie was shaken. What could she do? She had had no idea his precious piano wasn't paid for.

'The boss 'as sent numerous letters, but ain't had any answers, or money.'

Ellie could see in her mind's eye all the letters on the mantelpiece that were addressed to Leonard.

371

'Well, do I send the van round?'

'No, no. How much does he owe?'

'To date, three pounds seven and six.'

'What? I haven't got that.'

'Well, I'll—'

'No, wait just a minute,' said Ellie interrupting him. 'Wait here.' She tried to close the door but his foot was still there.

'No funny stuff, young lady.' He bent his head closer. 'Remember, I ain't just been born into this job.'

'No. I'll get the money.'

'It's surprising how many people manage to find the money when threatened,' he said nastily.

'I should have gone to work,' she mumbled to herself, going to the fireplace. She pushed the letters to one side, and took the large white five-pound note from behind the clock. Well, that's the rent money gone.

On the doorstep, the man took the money out of her hand. 'A fiver, eh?' He grinned. 'I told yer you could find it if you looked. Ta.'

'What about the change?'

'I'll hang on to that, it'll cover the next few weeks. That way we don't have to bother you till after Christmas, so at least you'll be able to have a singsong. You'd better tell Mr Kent, if we don't get paid then, we take the joanna. Nice meeting yer. Bye.'

She'd have to go to work now, if only to find the rent, she thought dully. She picked up the envelopes from the mantelpiece and studied them. They looked as if they were all bills. 'Leonard, you must know about the money you owe,' she said out loud. She froze when she saw some from the same people. What other debts did he have? How many more men would be banging on the door? How could he do this to her? Angrily, she decided to write to him right away. There were so many questions she had to ask.

★ ★ ★

The next morning when Ellie walked into the tea room Miss Penn almost jumped on her.

'Miss Walsh,' she called. 'Come here.'

Ellie walked over to her; she knew what was coming.

'And where were you yesterday, Miss Walsh?'

Ellie wanted to tell her the truth, that she had stayed in bed because she was miserable, but decided against that. 'I wasn't feeling very well,' she whimpered.

'I hope it isn't anything catching?' Miss Penn took a step back.

'No, just a few aches and pains.'

'Well, see it doesn't happen again. I don't like being shorthanded.'

Ellie wanted to smile. She didn't think anyone would even have noticed she was missing, stuck up at the far end of the room.

'You do know, of course, that you will be stopped a day's pay?'

Ellie nodded. 'Yes, I know.'

'Right, be off with you.'

Ellie walked to her station. She wished she had come to work yesterday; not only had she lost a day's pay, but she had had to hand over that money to the piano man. It hadn't been one of her better days. She smiled. In some ways, though, it had been worth staying in bed and wallowing in her own misery. Nobody had disturbed her or told her to buck up. She'd just lain there all day, and cried, and felt very sorry for herself. It had done her good, in a way.

By Sunday, Ellie was tossing up what to do. She didn't really want to see Iris, as she knew all that had happened would come out. No, she would wait till she heard from Leonard, and got some answers to her questions. She knew she had to get out, but where could she go that didn't cost money? She didn't want to see her mother, but she did want company. How much did she have to spend?

She sat on the bed and counted out her money. First of all, she had to put aside a pound for rent. She began to get angry. 'I'm no better off now than when I lived in Elmleigh, having to watch what I spend, and worry about coal and gas and food, with only my money coming in.' She threw her handbag across the room. 'Damn you, Leonard,' she shouted. 'Why didn't you think of me? Why couldn't you take me to Germany . . .?' She stopped. How much would it cost to go there?

She hurriedly picked up her bag and added up all the money she had. She caught sight of her evening bag. She'd never spent the ten shillings Mr Cole gave her. Ellie tipped the contents of the bag on to the bed. There was the ten-shilling note, and his card. She read the card. What if Leonard wasn't coming back? What if she couldn't afford to go to Germany? She certainly couldn't afford to stay here, but where could she go? She could always live with Iris, but how long would they remain friends if that was to happen? Thoughtfully, she tapped her teeth with Mr Cole's card.

It was then she decided to go and see Molly. She needed someone to talk to.

Elmleigh looked cold and drab when she turned into the square. The tree's branches were bare. What would have happened to her by next spring, when the leaves would be that wonderful fresh bright green? Where would she be?

Ellie wasn't surprised to see Molly sitting in her window, but she was surprised at Molly's pallor. She gave her a wave and knocked on the door.

Molly's sister opened it. 'Hallo?' she said. 'You're one of the Walsh girls.'

'Ask her to come in,' yelled Molly from the front room.

''Allo gel,' said Molly, her face lighting up when Ellie came up to her. 'It's good to see yer.'

'You all right?' asked Ellie.

'Not too bad, touch of bronchitis.'

'It's sitting outside in all weathers. I've told her for years, time and time again I've said it, but will she listen, oh no, not our clever Molly.'

'Wynn, go and make a cuppa.'

Molly's sister left the room.

'She does go on. Now, what brings you round these parts?'

'Just needed some company.'

'That's really nice of yer to think of me. You sure you ain't got another reason?'

'What d'you mean?'

'Where's this bloke of yours then? You 'ad a row?'

Ellie laughed. 'No, he's had to go to Germany.' She quickly remembered Molly's feelings about the Germans. 'He had to go there on business.'

'You sure?' Molly said searchingly.

Ellie nodded.

'Well, just ser long as it's not monkey business, then you're all right. How's yer sister?'

'She's fine. Lives with a very nice lady, Bessie Marsh, and she's going out with John Day.'

'Don't know no Bessie Marsh. Is that the Days what own the greengrocers in Rotherhithe New Road?'

Ellie nodded.

'Nice family that, she couldn't do better than to get in with that lot. Now what about you? Where you living?'

'Over the West End.'

'West End, eh. Oh very posh. You happy?'

'Yes. I work in Beaumonts.'

'That's nice.'

Wynn came in with a tray of tea things. 'I'll just get the pot.'

Ellie quickly looked at the door. 'Molly, is it very expensive to go abroad?'

'Should think so. You have to get a passport.'

'Where would you get that from?'

'Dunno. Should think the town hall would be able to tell you all that. I know you have to have a photo on it.'

'Would it cost much?'

'Dunno. Then there's the boat. Where're you thinking of going? Not to Germany, I hope.'

'No. I thought if Leonard had to go to say, France, I'd like to go with him.'

'You must be in the money then.'

Wynn came back carrying the teapot. 'Who's in the money?' she asked.

'Ellie here, she's thinking of going to France with her bloke.'

'How lovely. It'll cost a fair bit. Your young man must have a lot of money.'

'Not really a lot, but he is comfortable.'

'You ain't getting married then?' asked Molly.

Ellie blushed. 'Not just yet.'

'Don't let him keep yer dangling, gel, make sure you get that ring on yer finger.' Molly nodded and gave her a knowing look.

'How's your mum?' asked Molly's sister.

'She's not too bad. She's been moved to Southwark Park.'

'You been inside?' asked Wynn, pouring out the tea and handing Ellie a cup. 'I've heard it used to be very grand when that family lived in it.'

'Course she 'as, yer daft 'aporth. She's been to see her mum.'

'Sugar's there if you want it,' said Wynn, giving Molly a filthy look.

'It hasn't got any nice furniture in there,' said Ellie, trying to change the subject. 'The rooms are very tall, though, and must have been really lovely once.'

Wynn bent forward. 'A lot of soldiers went there after the war. Years ago I wanted to be a nurse, I could have helped look after them, but our parents were against it at the time, then Mum got . . . Didn't seem to be a lot of point after that.' She rubbed her left knee as if in pain.

Ellie fidgeted. 'Did you ever hear that they did, you know, experiments in there?'

'Did hear some rumours years ago, but that Mrs Andrews told us they *was* only rumours.'

Ellie sat up. 'How did she know?'

'Think one of her lodgers had a mate in there. He was in the war, so she said. Don't think you've got anythink to worry about.'

Ellie felt happier about that. She looked at the two sisters. They were so different. She had never spoken to Wynn before. She was the older by far, but Molly looked much scruffier and weaker, and she didn't speak as well as her sister.

Molly must have been reading her thoughts, for she said, 'Wynn went to a posh school. I was a bit of a rebel and ran away.'

Ellie giggled. Yes, she could see that Molly must have been a rebel in her time.

'Have you been to see your mother today?' asked Wynn.

'No.' Ellie finished her tea. 'I was coming over to visit Iris, and I thought I'd pop along to see you, just to find out how you're getting along.'

Molly looked at her quizzically. 'That's nice.'

'I must be going, I expect I'll have a bit of tea round there. Oh by the way, who's living in our house now?'

'Don't see a lot of 'em.'

'No, but we hear their kids,' said Wynn.

'I'll be able to find out more when the weather improves,' said Molly grinning. 'The old rent man told me you'd scarpered, owing a week's rent. Bet old Cole ain't none too happy about that.'

'You won't tell him you've seen me, will you?' asked Ellie.

'Course not. Mind you, I don't think Cole would know who you was. Anyway we've got a new chap now. Wally's retired; he said it was through ill health, but I've got a feeling Cole sacked 'im. It's a young chap now, very good-looking. I dunno how long he'll last, though, if he don't chase some of 'em for the rent. Old Cole won't be standing for too much of that.' Molly laughed. 'Wouldn't be surprised if some of the so-called ladies round here don't pay this young lad in kind, the way he comes round the square all red-faced and panting.'

'Molly,' said Wynn in disgust. 'Trust you to come out with something like that.'

Ellie was grinning as she got up. 'I really must go.'

Outside she stood and looked at her old house. Memories came flooding back, and she couldn't really remember any of them being good ones.

Ellie decided to go home. She didn't see any point in going round to see Iris. She knew she wasn't very good company at the moment.

She sat on the bus and wondered about her future. What should she do? Where could she go? She suddenly felt very lonely. She was alone. Christmas was in four weeks. A year ago she was happy, her father was alive, and her mother knew who she was. Then, all through her own selfishness, everything changed. Now only Iris seemed to have a purpose in life. Why had Leonard let her down? Would he come back to England? Deep down Ellie wasn't really sure; and after Molly had told her she would have to get a passport, and have a photo on it, which must all cost money, she knew she wouldn't be joining him.

Chapter 37

All week Ellie pondered on whether or not to go to the club on her own on Saturday. If Mr Cole was there perhaps she could be nice to him, and find out what she would have to do to stay in one of his houses. She shuddered at the thought of it. Why did Leonard make her come down to this? She was still waiting for an answer to her last letter.

It was cold and drizzly on Saturday as Ellie travelled home from work. She had made up her mind to go to the club. She need only be amiable to Bernard Cole, if he was there; she didn't have to fawn over him. Then she could see what the outcome would be. She wasn't happy about it, but what other choice did she have?

Her spirits were lifted when she saw on the doorstep the parcel Leonard had promised her. She rushed in, and without bothering to take her coat off, tore at the paper. There was a letter, a nightdress case and an embroidered handkerchief. When she saw there was also ten one-pound notes, she knew the worst. She let them flutter to the floor and sat on the sofa.

After reading the letter she sat back deflated. He wasn't coming home. Frieda Muller was a widow, and he was going to marry her. Ellie moaned out loud. She couldn't believe it. Her dreams, her hopes. She tried to re-read the letter; had she read it right? But she couldn't see the words, they were blurred through her tears.

'Leonard, how could you do this to me?' She wiped her

eyes. 'Why didn't you want to marry me? I could have made you happy.'

The letter went on. 'I expect this news will come as a bit of a shock to you. I'm sorry about that, I was fond of you even though we were from such very different backgrounds. We had fun together, and after all we had no serious commitment to each other. You are young and pretty, and will soon find someone to take my place.'

He went on to say the ten pounds was to pay any outstanding bills. Frieda had made the handkerchief. Ellie quickly threw that into the empty fireplace. He asked her forgiveness for not returning home, and said that in some ways he was sorry about how things had worked out, but Germany was his home now. She could have anything in the flat she wanted, and could stay there if she could afford it. He even suggested Iris came and lived with her. Ellie felt her world had ended.

Two hours later she was still sitting with her coat on staring at the letter. She looked up at the clock. It was too late to go to the club now. Besides, she wasn't really in the mood to be nice to anybody.

All that night she tossed and turned trying to work out her future. She longed for Leonard to be beside her, needed his arms round her to comfort her.

Would Bernard Cole want her, now she was available? She knew deep down she didn't want him, but at the moment she couldn't see what other option she had.

When at last she woke her head was aching and her eyes were smarting. She felt exhausted. She knew she had to tell someone, and decided to go and see Iris.

'Hallo Ellie. You're early,' said Bessie. 'I think Iris is up. You all right?'

'Yes thanks.'

'You look a bit peaky. You gonner stop for a bit of dinner?'

'Would that be all right?'

Bessie smiled. 'Course. Love to have you.'

This has got to be the answer, Ellie thought. She could move in here, though she was still not sure she wanted to share with Iris. And what about a job? She wouldn't want to go back and forth to the West End every day. She really didn't like her job, but with work so scarce what else could she do?

'You don't look very happy,' said Iris when Ellie walked in.

'I'm not very happy,' said Ellie, plonking herself on the bed.

'Here, watch it, I've just made that.' She smoothed out the bedspread.

Is this what sharing would be like? thought Ellie.

'So, what's wrong?'

'Leonard ain't coming back to England.'

'What?' Iris too plonked herself down on the bed.

'He's going to stay in Germany, and,' Ellie hung her head, 'he's gonner get married.'

'What?' screamed Iris again. 'Who to?'

'A woman he knows in Germany.'

'That's a bit quick, ain't it?'

'It seems he knew her before.'

'How long have you known about this?'

'I got a letter yesterday.'

'The bloody two-timing sod.' Iris stood up. 'Sorry about that. D'you know, I always thought there was something funny going on; well, you know, him not wanting to marry you. Has he known this tart very long?'

'Yes. He knew her when he lived over there before the war.'

'That was years ago! So has he been carrying a torch for her all this time?'

Ellie shrugged her shoulders. 'Don't know.'

'Why's he waited so long to go back to her then?'

'He's been left some money, and he had to go back to claim it, and he met up with her again.'

Iris sat back down. 'Ain't she ever got married?'

'Yes, and it's just my luck that she's a widow.'

Iris took hold of Ellie's hand. 'I'm really sorry. You don't have much luck with your life, do you?'

Tears rolled down Ellie's cheek. 'What am I gonner do? I can't afford the rent on the flat, and a man came last Monday to take the piano away.'

'Wasn't you at work?'

'No, I didn't feel too good.'

'You all right now?'

Ellie nodded.

'And what d'you mean, came to take the piano away?'

'He'd got it on hire purchase, and was behind with the payments. He'd sent me some money for the rent, so I used that to pay the man. If I'd known then Leonard wasn't coming back I would have let him take it away.'

Iris sat very quietly.

'What am I gonner do, Iris?'

'First of all you'll have to move, you can't afford to keep a place like that on.'

'I was thinking about asking Mr Cole if . . . You remember what he said.'

'What?' yelled Iris. 'You ain't gonner do nothink like that. Ellie, that makes you no better than a street tart. There's got to be something better.'

'Well go on then, tell me what?' Ellie had thought about the hostel Beaumonts had for its staff, but she knew she was going to leave that job as soon as it was at all possible.

'You'll have to come here and stay with me, won't you. It'll be a bit cramped, but anything's gotter be better than having old Cole running his dirty hands all over you. You'll have to travel backwards and forwards to work though.'

'S'pose so. When can I move in?'

'After dinner we'll go down and ask John if he can

borrow the van. Do you owe any rent?'

Ellie nodded. 'Two weeks.'

'In that case, you can do another runner. After all, the rent book's in his name.'

For the first time in days Ellie let just the hint of a smile lift her face.

'Oh Ellie, love, I'm really sorry,' said Ada Day when she finished listening to the story.

'That's the trouble with these educated blokes, they think they can ride roughshod over the likes of us,' said Tom.

'Look, Ellie, when d'you want me to bring the van over?' asked John.

'Don't know. I ain't got that much.'

'Good job for that, it'll be a bit cramped in Bessie's,' said Iris.

Ellie could see Iris really wasn't that pleased about the arrangements, but Bessie had welcomed her with open arms. 'Would next Sunday be all right?' she asked John.

'Don't see why not. Be better if we get you moved before Christmas.'

'Thanks.'

Tom Day scratched his head. 'You said he told you you can take anythink you like?'

'Yes,' said Ellie.

'And you've got that in writing?'

'Yes.'

'And you said that piano's a good one?'

'It's a real cracker,' said John. 'Why, Dad, what you got in mind?'

A broad grin spread across his father's face. 'D'you know, I reckon we could find a buyer for it at this time o' year.'

'Oh, but it's not mine to sell!' cried Ellie.

'It might not be yours, but well, someone's gonner make a pretty penny or two out of it. If the shop takes it back they'll re-sell it.'

'I know, but . . .'

'Well I reckon you deserve a bit of cash back after all he had from you,' said Iris.

Ellie blushed. Whatever Leonard had had, including herself, she had given it more than willingly. 'I don't know,' she said softly.

'Now, Tom Day, don't you start encouraging this young lady into bad habits,' said his wife. 'Don't you listen to him, love. Come on, the lot of yer, let's get this 'ere table laid for a bit of tea, otherwise it'll be chucking out time before we get to the pub.'

Tom Day smiled. 'I'll have a word with Tosh in the pub. He might know what it's worth, and you never know, he might even have a punter lined up.'

Ellie felt very uneasy at the thought of selling Leonard's precious piano. But if she wasn't living there, how would the shop get in to take it away?

In the pub, despite all her worries, Ellie enjoyed the music and laughter and was sorry when it had to end.

'D'you want to stay here for the night?' asked Iris.

'No, thanks all the same, but I've got to collect me uniform. Will you be coming with John on Sunday?' Ellie asked her.

'I should say so. Want to see what's lying around that flat. Might find a few bits and bobs that'll come in useful.'

No you won't, Ellie wanted to cry out. Everything in the flat belongs to Leonard! But she knew it would be of no use. He had gone from her life, and wasn't coming back. Why worry on his behalf?

'See you Sunday,' said Ellie as she made her way home. As she sat on the bus she thought how she called it home, but without Leonard it was just an empty shell. She looked out of the window. The shops were decorated for Christmas. Why did these things always seem to happen at this time of the year? Last year she'd been happy at the thought of going out with Leonard, and working in the tea room with Peggy and Mr Jenkins. The year before, Lizzie had been going to marry Ernie. Now everything seemed to be falling apart. Lizzie wasn't with Ern, she didn't know where Dolly was, and, apart from what had happened to her mother and father, she had lost Leonard. Did the Walshes have a curse on them? She didn't want to move in with Iris, although they got on better now than they had ever done. Would it all end and the rows start again?

Sunday was a bright, clear day, but very cold. Ellie was pleased that John arrived early.

'Got a few helpers,' he said, walking in with Iris close on his heels. Tom Day followed.

'I've got my bits packed,' said Ellie.

'That all you got?' asked Iris.

'Yes.'

'Mind if I look round? Oh, guess what?' said Iris, looking in the cupboards. 'John's mum was telling me that Terry come in the shop yesterday, and you'll never believe it.'

Ellie stopped tidying up and looked at Iris.

'You know he works in that garage near the shop? Well, he was saying – this is nice,' she said, picking up an ashtray. 'Can I have it?'

Ellie nodded. She wanted to scream at her to get on with it. What had Terry told them? 'What was you saying about Terry?' She tried to sound as nonchalant as she could.

'Oh yes. Poor old Molly's dead.'

Ellie sank down onto the sofa. 'Molly's dead?'

'Seems she had a heart attack.'

'But I only saw her the Sunday before last and—'

Anger was suddenly written over Iris's face. 'You saw her the Sunday before last? You come over to Rotherhithe and didn't come to see us?'

'No, I know. I was going to see Mum, but changed me mind.'

'So, why didn't you come and see us then?'

'Don't know.' Ellie wasn't going to tell her she didn't

want to see them as she had been feeling too miserable. 'Poor old Molly. Do you know when the funeral is?'

'Don't think Terry said.'

'Got a buyer for the old joanna, girl,' said Tom Day. 'Let's have a look at it.' He walked over to the piano. 'Nice bit o' wood.'

'It's locked,' said Ellie, half hoping that would make him think again. She didn't like the idea of stealing the piano.

'Not to worry, we can still get it open. Got a knife?'

Iris rushed into the kitchen and was back almost at once. 'Ta, gel.' With a quick snap the lid was open. Tom ran his hands over the keys. 'It's got a lovely sound. Pity we couldn't find a better home for it.'

'Where's it going?' asked Ellie.

'The pub. The landlord said he'd give you a tenner.'

Ellie knew it was worth a great deal more than that, but at this moment it didn't matter. Other things were on her mind. Molly was dead. Her friend had gone. How many more losses would she have to cope with?

The flat had been virtually stripped. All day the van had been back and forth taking the larger items away. Ellie felt sad and guilty as she climbed in the van for the last journey. This had been Leonard's home, and for the past year she had enjoyed all its comforts with him.

'I'll give you a couple of quid for the sofa,' said Tom. 'That'll do for the old girl's Christmas box.'

John laughed. 'Reckon Mum'll really like that, Dad. Mind you, I dunno what we're gonner do with all the other stuff – any ideas, Ellie?'

'No, not really. I could ask Bessie if she wants anything.'

'Don't worry about it, gel,' said Tom. 'I know a couple of blokes that'll buy any bits orf yer, and I'll make sure you get a good price for 'em.'

'You're certainly well off now,' said Iris. 'What, it must be close on twenty-five pounds.'

'What yer gonner do with it then, gel?' asked Tom.

'Don't know.' Ellie clutched her handbag.

'You know, you've nearly got enough to start your own business.'

'I couldn't do anythink like that.'

'Why not?'

'Don't know nothink.'

'Leave it out, Dad. It's Ellie's money, and she can do what she likes with it.'

Ellie looked out of the van's window. The sky had turned grey. Her thoughts went to Molly. Poor Molly. She couldn't believe she had gone, all the years she had known her. She had to go and see her sister, but not today. She felt cold and tired and she also felt very unhappy. For the first time in her life she had a lot of money, but it didn't warm her heart or bring her any comfort. All she wanted now was for someone to love her.

Chapter 38

That evening, when they were in the pub, Ellie was surprised at how quickly the contents of Leonard's home were dispersed. It seemed Tom Day had plenty of acquaintances willing to part with their money when they saw the quality of the goods he had to offer. Although Ellie and Iris had kept back some items, it still upset her to see so many of the things she'd liked being sold. But she knew she couldn't keep them, so what was the point in getting upset? Besides, the money would come in handy.

Ellie looked across at the piano. It was causing a great deal of interest, and Tosh the landlord was very proud of his new possession. How long will it look like that, though? thought Ellie. Soon beer would be spilt over it, and cigarettes left to burn the well-polished walnut veneer. To Ellie, the tone sounded wrong in a pub. She wanted to remember the nights Leonard played those wonderful haunting tunes.

'Come on, gel, drink up,' said Tom, invading her thoughts. 'It'll soon be closing time.'

For Ellie that couldn't come soon enough. She felt lost and, even though she was surrounded by so many well-meaning people, alone.

'You ain't half got a lot of frocks,' said Iris, pushing the clothes to one side and squeezing her own frock into the wardrobe. 'Some of 'em are a bit posh.'

'I bought those to wear at the club. I had to look a bit near the mark.'

'Well you won't be going there again, so I reckon you could put some in a bag and take 'em down the pawn shop.'

'I don't want to do that,' cried Ellie. 'And I don't want them all screwed up.'

'Well, my things are getting screwed up. We'll worry about it tomorrow, but I still think you ought to put some of 'em away.'

Iris hadn't changed; she still had to have the last word!

'What time you gotter get up?' asked Iris as they climbed into bed.

'What time do you get up?'

'Seven, but you'll have to go out before me.'

'I ain't going to work tomorrow. I'm leaving that place.'

'But Ellie, your money ain't gonner last for ever.'

'I know. I've got a few jobs to do, then I'm gonner look for somewhere else.'

They both lay quiet for a while, then Iris asked, 'Ellie, do you still have those nightmares?'

'No. Come on, let's get to sleep, it's been a long day.'

Ellie lay awake for hours. Although she was tired sleep wouldn't come. She didn't want to go back to Beaumonts, but as Iris said her money wouldn't last for ever. Tomorrow she would see Wynn and find out when Molly's funeral was going to be, then she would go and buy Christmas presents. That should cheer her up.

Ellie hesitated before she knocked on the door. The front room curtains weren't drawn. Everybody drew the front room curtains when there'd been a death. Was Molly laid out in the front room? Ellie knocked.

'Come in. It's Ellie, ain't it?' Wynn looked pleased to see her when she opened the door.

Ellie nodded. 'I was ever so upset to hear about Molly.' They walked down the passage into the kitchen. Ellie quickly glanced at the front room door; it was closed.

Wynn sniffed. 'Sit yourself down. It was a bit of a shock, our Molly going like that. D'you fancy a cuppa?'

'Please, if it ain't too much trouble.'

'Ain't any trouble, glad of the company.' She shook the kettle that stood on the gleaming range. 'There's enough water in here for us. There was me, worried about her bronchitis, and it was her heart what took her in the end.'

'I liked Molly,' said Ellie, half expecting to be invited into the front room to see her.

Wynn smiled. 'I know all the kids used to take the mickey out of her, and she could be a bit funny at times, but she wasn't a bad old stick,' she said with affection.

Ellie found it difficult to talk to Wynn and was grateful when tea and biscuits were put in front of her. There were long pauses in the conversation. 'When's Molly's funeral?' asked Ellie.

Wynn looked surprised. 'It was last Friday. Didn't you know?'

Ellie gasped and shook her head. 'I only heard about it yesterday. When did she . . .?'

'A week ago. Last Sunday.'

'I'm ever so sorry. I would have got some flowers.'

'Don't waste your money on flowers, love. Molly wouldn't want that.'

'Where's she buried?'

'Nunhead. Is your dad there?'

Ellie shook her head. 'No.' She didn't want to tell her that he was in a pauper's grave.

Wynn rubbed her left knee.

'You all right?' asked Ellie, pleased at the diversion.

'It's me arthritis, plays me up something rotten.'

'Can't the doctor help?'

'No. Don't trust doctors. Ain't you supposed to be at work?'

'No. I wasn't feeling well, then I decided to come and find out . . .'

Wynn smiled. 'That was very kind of you. I hope you feel better soon.'

'I'm all right really. I'd better be going. I'll call in again.'

'Thanks, love, I'd like that.'

All the years she had lived in Elmleigh, and Ellie had never spoken to Wynn before. 'She's not a bad old dear,' said Ellie to herself. She was upset that she'd missed Molly's funeral. Ellie stood for a moment or two and looked round Elmleigh; there were so few people left in the square that she knew.

'What you been doing with yourself today?' asked Iris as they sat down to the delicious meal Bessie put in front of them.

'I went to see Molly's sister. I thought I'd go to her funeral, but she was buried on Friday. She died last Sunday.'

'I know, didn't I tell you that?' said Iris, stuffing potatoes in her mouth.

'No you didn't. Why not?'

'Didn't think it was that important. Didn't think you'd wanner go to her funeral. Bessie's a smashing cook, ain't she?'

'Yes,' said Ellie sadly.

'You going to work tomorrow?'

'S'pose I'd better.' Ellie knew, however, that she'd be in for another ticking off.

Ellie was right, she did get a telling off, and was told that if it hadn't been Christmas, their busiest time, she would have been sacked. But she didn't care.

All week she went backwards and forwards to work, not knowing what she really wanted. Some evenings on her way to Bessie's she did some shopping and halfheartedly looked for a job. She even wandered into Days' greengrocers, hoping they might find her something to do.

'I'm gonner see Mum tomorrow,' said Ellie on Saturday, as she and Iris were getting ready to go to the pub.

'Well don't ask me to come with you. Have you seen my scarf, I left it on—'

'I put it away.'

Iris tutted. 'Can't find anythink now you've moved in, you're always tidying up. Why can't you leave my things where I leave 'em?'

'It makes the place look untidy.'

'Just leave my things be,' said Iris angrily.

Iris didn't bother to try to hide the fact that she wasn't too pleased about Ellie staying with her now.

In the pub the paperchains and the mistletoe hanging from the ceiling were causing a great deal of excitement; a lot of the old men couldn't wait to get any female, young or old, under it, and the ribald remarks were always accompanied with plenty of laughter. Next Tuesday was Christmas Day.

'Bet you're really glad you're gonner be with Iris this Christmas,' said Mrs Day.

'Yes I am.' Deep down Ellie wished she was spending it with Leonard.

'You are coming up on Christmas Day, ain't yer? We 'ave lots of laughs.' She patted Ellie's hand. 'Do you know, you two are like the daughters I never had.'

Ellie smiled at her. She knew they would try to make her happy. 'It's nice to be part of a family.'

As usual the singing, the jokes and laughter went on till Tosh threw them out. Ellie knew she *should* be happy here.

'You sure you won't come with me?' asked Ellie, as she was preparing to visit her mother.

'I told you no, so don't keep on.'

'You do like the cardigan I got Mum for Christmas, don't you?'

'Yes.' Iris raised her eyes to the ceiling.

'I best be going,' said Ellie, picking up her coat. 'See you later.'

'Bye,' said Iris, her tone one of relief.

Half an hour later, Ellie was being taken to the conservatory where her mother sat, exactly where Ellie had left her the last time she had been here, staring out at the garden. It was grey and cold outside, but in here it was warm and cosy. They had paperchains draped round the room, and a large tree stood in the corner.

'If that's a present for your mother, you can leave it under the tree,' said the nurse. 'Has it got her name on?'

Ellie nodded. 'Shall I put it there?'

'If you like. Would you like a cup of tea?'

'If it's no trouble.'

The nurse moved away.

Ellie sat near to her mother but didn't speak to her. It was strange to sit next to this silent woman who had spent so many years shouting at her. When the nurse brought the tea Ruby Walsh turned and looked at Ellie, her eyes still with that faraway look. Ellie smiled at her, but she quickly turned away.

For over an hour Ellie sat and observed her mother. She was happy when one of the other patients came and spoke to her, telling her how much he was looking forward to going home for Christmas.

'You're going home?' Ellie asked.

'Only for a short break. Me wife can't cope with me full time, not with the kids an' all. I 'ave these funny turns, see.'

'Still, it will be nice to go home.'

'Yer.' He moved on.

Ellie stood up. Her mother quickly turned and looked at her. Was there a spark of life in those sad eyes? Ellie smiled and said goodbye; there was no point in upsetting her by trying to tell her who she was.

★ ★ ★

Ellie stood outside the sister's office for a moment, wondering if she should go in. The door opened and the sister asked, 'Did you want to see me, Miss Walsh?'

Ellie hesitated. 'I'm not sure, but me mum . . .' She stopped. Was she just clutching at straws? 'I thought me mum looked a bit better.'

'Yes, we noticed she did take some interest when the men were putting up the paperchains. But I think it was just because of all the noise they were making. Some of them are worse than children.' She smiled. 'Are we going to see you on Christmas Day?'

'I don't know.'

'We have a carol service in the morning, then Father Christmas comes in the afternoon. If you can make it you will be very welcome.'

'Thank you.'

Ellie walked slowly down the gravel drive. What if her mother was to get better and wanted to come home? Where would home be? She pushed open the large black gates. She would have to get a house.

'Ellie! Ellie Walsh!'

She turned. 'Terry,' she whispered as Terry Andrews rushed towards her.

'What're you doing here?' he asked, closing the gate behind her. 'Is your mum in there?' He flicked his thumb over his shoulder.

She nodded. 'I didn't think you still worked here.'

'You're looking well.'

Ellie was taken aback. Normally he was prepared to run a mile rather than talk to her.

'You know poor old Molly's dead?'

'Yes, Iris told me.'

'Shame that, she wasn't a bad old girl. Me mum was very upset, she always got on all right with her.'

Ellie couldn't believe this was the same Terry. He seemed

self-assured and happy, and willing to chat to her, just like he did when they were kids.

'You're living over the water, ain't yer?'

'No, not now.'

'I thought Iris said . . .'

'I was, but, well, it's a long story. I'm staying with Iris now. You still at the garage?'

'Yer.'

'You look well.'

'D'you know, Ellie, I ain't been this happy for years.'

'Why's that?' Ellie asked.

'Well me new job for one thing. Even got a Christmas bonus.'

'And what about Miss Jones?' she asked tentatively. 'She still with you?'

'Yer.'

Ellie didn't want to ask any more questions. For some reason she felt hurt. Iris had John and Terry had Joyce Jones. 'Iris said she saw you in the pub a while back.'

'Yer. We popped in there when we was on our way out. Do you go in there now?'

Ellie nodded.

'Might look you up one Sat'day.'

'That'd be nice.' They got to where Ellie knew they would have to part company. 'It's nice to see you again, Terry.'

'And it's nice to see you again. Take care.'

Ellie watched him walk away with a confident swagger. Was it her imagination, or did he seem genuinely glad to see her?

Chapter 39

Ellie felt pleased as she made her way to Bessie's. Although she had been very busy at work, and felt weary, the tips tucked away in her handbag were comforting. Come the new year she would be looking for another job and, with the money she already had, she knew that for a few weeks she could afford to look after herself.

She threw herself on the bed.

'Hurry and get yourself ready, they're waiting for us up the pub.' Iris peered in the mirror and ran her little finger over her lipstick.

'I'm tired.'

'A couple of drinks and you'll soon be fine.'

Ellie slowly stirred herself.

'You've got two days to recover, now get a move on.'

Ellie smiled. Two days away from Beaumonts. Two days to actually talk to people.

It was Christmas Eve, and Ellie wasn't going to dwell on what had happened a year ago. She knew that in the Days' company there would be plenty of laughter. As soon as they walked in the pub they were welcomed with open arms. All evening she sang and laughed and, pushing last year from her mind, relaxed and enjoyed herself.

'I might go and see Mum tomorrow afternoon,' said Ellie as they jumped into bed.

'I'm glad Bessie puts the hot water bottle in here. It's nice, ain't it? Mum didn't do things like that for us, did she?' Iris ignored Ellie's statement.

Ellie moved her feet around till she managed to get one foot on the stone ginger-beer bottle that was full of hot water.

'Don't take up all of it,' said Iris, kicking out.

'Ow, that hurt. Did you hear what I said about seeing Mum?'

'Yes. And I ain't going. I've got John a great big jigsaw puzzle and I'd rather stay in his house and do that.'

'Please yourself.'

Iris wedged herself up on one elbow. 'Ellie, I don't know why you keep bothering to go and see her, she don't know you, and you only keep upsetting yourself.' She flung herself back on the pillow. 'Now go to sleep before Father Christmas gets here,' she giggled.

Ellie too laughed. 'Daft 'aporth.'

Christmas morning; Ellie sat up. It was light outside. She could hear Bessie singing downstairs. She looked at the bottom of the bed. Two lumpy stockings were hanging there.

She grinned and nudged Iris.

'Stop it,' came a muffled voice thick with sleep.

'Iris, look. Sit up.'

'Why, what's the—' She too peered at the bottom of the bed. 'What's those?'

'Father Christmas has been,' said Ellie, laughing and scrambling down the bed to retrieve them.

Iris also began laughing as she tipped the contents of the stocking out on the bed and began pulling at the wrapping paper round the strange-shaped objects. 'Bessie's wonderful. See, I told you he would come.' Iris had tears running down her face. 'Look, I've got an orange.'

'So have I, and look, a pair of stockings and a bar of chocolate.'

Iris sniffed. 'I ain't ever had a stocking before,' she said softly.

Ellie put her arm round her sister's shoulders, unable to speak. This was going to be a wonderful Christmas for them both, and she must think of the future not the past. 'Did you get Bessie a present?' she asked, swallowing hard.

'Yes, did you?'

Ellie nodded. 'Come on, let's give her them.'

They rushed downstairs, and with lots of laughter and hugs, they exchanged presents.

Later, when they had finished breakfast, they hurried along to the Days, and once more laughter, kisses, hugs and presents were exchanged, then it was time for Christmas dinner.

'You still gonner see Mum this afternoon?' asked Iris.

'Yes. I might stay there for tea, so don't worry if I'm late getting back.'

Ellie smiled at the men and the few women who were sitting around wearing paper hats. Her mother was in the same place, and even the green crêpe paper hat didn't lift her sad expression. Her eyes still had that faraway look. Iris was right. Why did she bother to come and see her? Ellie knew why; her conscience troubled her, and it always would.

She had had a cup of tea and was making her way to the kitchen to return her cup and saucer when she could have sworn she saw Terry Andrews disappear into a room off the corridor. What was he doing here on Christmas afternoon? Surely he didn't have to work on Christmas Day? And what about Joyce Jones and his mother – he wouldn't leave them, not today?

Ellie's heart skipped a beat and she hurried along the corridor. The door to the room he'd gone into was closed. She stood for a moment or two, deciding whether or not to knock.

The door opened.

'I'll tell 'em, Mum.' Terry came out and almost knocked Ellie over. 'Ellie!'

'Hallo,' she stuttered.

'What's happening?' asked Mrs Andrews coming to the door. 'Why, 'allo Ellie. Terry said your mum was in here.' Mrs Andrews pulled the door to. Ellie couldn't see into the room.

Ellie was speechless, she knew her mouth had fallen open. What were they doing here?

'Have you been to see your mum? Is she all right?' asked Mrs Andrews.

Ellie nodded.

'Half a mo, Ellie, I've just got to get a nurse.' Terry moved swiftly along the corridor.

'Who have you come to see?' croaked Ellie.

'We'll be going home in a tick. You ready to go yet?'

Again Ellie nodded.

'When the nurse comes we'll be off. We can all walk home together if you like,' Mrs Andrews said.

Ellie couldn't believe it. Why wouldn't she tell her who she'd come to see?

The sound of a man coughing sent Mrs Andrews scurrying back into the room. She left the door ajar. Ellie couldn't see much, just a small pile of blankets with the top of a head showing. Mrs Andrews leant over and, making gentle soothing noises, ran her hands over the tousled head.

Terry and a nurse came back.

'I'll give him an injection now,' said the nurse, walking into the room and closing the door, leaving Ellie outside.

It was a few minutes before Terry came out. 'Sorry about that.'

'Terry, who is it?' asked Ellie.

'Me dad.'

'Your dad?' she replied, her eyes wide open. 'But I . . .'

Terry looked ill at ease. He glanced at the door. 'It's a long story. We'd better wait till we're outside before I tell you.'

The nurse left the room, and Terry went back in, closing the door behind him.

Ellie was dumbfounded. Terry's dad was alive. Everyone had always thought his mum was a widow. Ellie suddenly realized she was still holding her cup and saucer. She hurried back to the kitchen and then on to the conservatory where she had left her handbag. For some unknown reason she felt very happy and, unthinking, kissed her mother's cheek. Even the lack of response didn't dampen her feelings.

Terry and his mother were walking along when Ellie caught up with them.

'I must say you're looking very well, Ellie,' said Mrs Andrews.

Ellie smiled. She knew her cheeks were glowing, but she couldn't explain why. She felt excited, and somehow there seemed to be an air of expectancy about her.

'Terry here was saying you're living back in Rotherhithe; staying where your sister lives.'

'Yes. Bessie's very nice.'

'I'm pleased. Your nice young man's gone away then?'

'Yes.'

'Mum,' said Terry. 'Leave it out.'

'Sorry about that.'

'How do you . . .?' Ellie was amazed.

'I goes into Days' for Mum's veg, and I often ask after you and Iris.'

'You do?'

'You've had a bit of a rough time of it, one way and another,' said Mrs Andrews. 'Shame about poor old Molly.'

'Yes, I went to see her sister last week.'

'Did you now, that was kind of you. She's not a bad old girl, likes to keep herself to herself. Mind you she's gonner miss Molly and all the gossip. Not that we get a lot round Elmleigh now. Don't know many folk, and since you Walshes have gone . . .'

'Give it a rest, Ma.'

She smiled and pulled up her coat collar. 'Sorry. I do go on sometimes. This wind's a bit parky, be glad to get back home. D'you fancy coming in for a cup of tea?'

'That'd be nice.' Ellie thought Mrs Andrews appeared nervous and jumpy.

'You can have a bit of me Christmas cake as well.'

'Mum makes a lovely cake. Could keep the blokes at the garage more than happy with that; that's if she'd let 'em have any cake.'

'Go on with you.' She gently pushed Terry.

Ellie wanted to ask about his dad, but it didn't seem right, not at the moment. When they reached their door, Ellie asked, 'Is Miss Jones indoors?'

'No, she's gorn home for Christmas.'

'Oh, where's that then?'

'Kent somewhere,' said Mrs Andrews. 'Terry, take Ellie's coat while I give this fire a poke, then we can have a cuppa. Banked it up with all the peelings; that kept it in while we were out, and the kettle's nearly on the boil. Don't go out much these days, only to do a bit of shopping. You're working over the water then, so Terry said.'

'Yes, Beaumonts.' Ellie was amazed at how much the Days must have told him about her.

'That's nice.'

The kettle's lid was soon bobbing up and down.

'I'll see to the tea, you take Ellie in the front room. The fire's alight in there.'

Ellie was surprised when she walked into the front room. Most people round here never had it furnished, but this one looked warm and cosy.

'Mum likes to keep this nice,' he said, obviously noting her expression. 'When we used to have a lot of lodgers coming and going they used this room if they had any studying to do. Sit down.'

Ellie sat on the edge of the dark green Rexine sofa.

'Ellie, I'm ever so glad to see you. I suppose I ought to tell you what we was doing at that place.'

'I always thought you worked there.'

'Yer, I let most people think that.'

'Look, Terry, you don't have to tell me, not if it's very personal.'

'No, I want you to know.' He ran his fingers through his dark hair and sat next to her.

Ellie felt apprehensive. What was coming?

'It goes back a long way. I was only a small kid when we moved here, but—'

The door opened and Mrs Andrews came in with a tray loaded with tea things and a cake. 'Don't mind me.' She sat down.

'I was just telling Ellie about Dad.'

'I won't interrupt,' said Mrs Andrews, pouring out the tea.

'My dad was in the army during the war, and he was up at the front, fighting.'

'I'll put some more water in the pot.' Mrs Andrews left the room.

'Terry, what about your mum? Should you be telling me all this?'

'I want to, Ellie.' He looked embarrassed. 'As a matter of fact, I've wanted to tell you for a long while.'

'You have? Why?'

'I'll be coming to that. You see, when me mum told me he was still alive, and in a mental home, I very nearly went mad. At first I was angry with her for keeping the truth from me, but then she explained that kids blab, and before long everybody would have known. She'd had to wait till I was older.'

Ellie tenderly touched his arm. 'It must have been a shock for you.'

'Yes, yes it was.'

'I can understand her not wanting everyone to know. I feel the same way.'

'When I went to see him he didn't know who I was, but I dunno, I felt I had to visit him, just in case.'

'I know, I feel the same way about me mum. Did your mum visit him?'

'Not fer years. She said she couldn't bear to see him like that, not after the kind of man he'd been, but now . . . He ain't got long.'

'Oh Terry, I'm really sorry.'

He patted her hand. 'You know what it's like to . . . You've had more than your fair share of unhappiness.'

She smiled.

'My dad was a gunner in the war, and it seems he suffered from shell shock, and, well. At first they thought he was swinging the lead, and they made his life hell. In the end it sent him right round the bend. But you see, I didn't know that till a while back. Mum kept that very quiet.'

'You didn't know your dad was alive?'

'No. It was only when I found a letter from the home. I know I shouldn't have read it, but, well.' He smiled. 'You know what a nosy lot us kids are.'

Ellie nodded.

'When she first talked to me about him, and about him being in the loony bin, I thought it must be hereditary. So, you see, I was always afraid to get fond of anyone, just in case I finished up the same way.'

Ellie wanted to throw her arms round him; she wanted to hug him and hold him close. Instead she said very softly, 'I know how you felt. Why did your mother tell everyone she was a widow?'

'She thought that was best when we moved here. That was till she bumped into your dad.'

'My dad?' exploded Ellie. 'What's my dad got to do . . .?'

'Your dad was also in the army.'

'I didn't know that.'

'Well it seems it was only for a short while. He was with my dad when he was sent to the hospital.'

'What was wrong with my dad?'

'Don't know. Something to do with his heart, so Mum said.'

'Your mum knows about my dad?'

'Yer, that's what the fight was about.'

'What, the fight between my mum and yours?'

'Yes.'

Ellie's eyes grew wider and wider. 'Quick, go and get your mum, I want to know all of this.'

Terry opened the door. 'Mum, come in here.'

Mrs Andrews came in.

Ellie jumped up. 'Please Mrs Andrews, tell me about me mum and dad. I've been trying to find out for ages, but now we don't see Lizzie and Dolly, and Molly's gone, I ain't got no one to ask.'

'Sit yourself down, love. I didn't realize it was that important to you.'

'Well, when Mum was put away, I thought, a bit like Terry I suppose, I thought we could finish up round the bend.'

'Oh, you poor dear. I know what Terry went through till I told him the truth. What is it you want to know?'

'Why did my mum hate my dad so? Was it to do with the war?'

'No, I don't think so. It was just a collection of things, I think. You see, your dad had a bit of a funny heart. He was only in the army a few weeks be all accounts. I think he was worried about going to work, because of his heart.' She stopped and poured out more tea. 'My Tone was in the army right at the beginning, and in a lot of the fighting.'

'I told Ellie that, and that he had shell shock.'

'Well after a lot of trouble they finally decided that my Tone wasn't in a fit state to be a soldier and they sent him to a hospital. Your dad was there at the time, and when he found out we lived in the same square he came to see me and told me my Tone was being sent to Greenwich.'

'That's where Mum was.'

'I know. A couple of times your dad come with me to visit Tone.'

'If only we'd known,' said Ellie, sighing sadly.

'Your mum saw us talking and walking together, and I think she must 'ave got hold of the wrong end of the stick. I was having a baby; I fell pregnant just as Tone went into the army. Well, your mum didn't think I had a husband, and when I started to show she must 'ave put two and two together and thought – You see, by then I'd told everybody I was a widow woman. Didn't want 'em to know me old man was in the loony bin even if it was because of the war. Well one day she starts shouting and waving her arms about, and calling me all sorts of names. I started to walk away and she hit me. Molly tried to stop her. Your mum was like a mad woman.' She looked up guiltily. 'I'm sorry, I shouldn't have said that.'

'What happened then?' asked Ellie, her eyes wide.

'I fell over, and your mother started kicking me, and, well, me baby was born dead.'

Ellie gasped. 'My mum did that? You poor thing.' Ellie knew what it was like to be on the end of her mother's boot. 'I bet you hated me mum after that.'

'It might not 'ave been her fault, losing the baby I mean. But we wasn't exactly bosom pals, before or after.'

'No wonder she never liked me talking to Terry.'

'I think it did play on her conscience a bit.' Mrs Andrews sniffed and wiped her nose. 'Shouldn't have told you all that, not on Christmas Day. Now come on, cheer up.'

Ellie could see the memory was very painful.

'I'm sorry, Ellie,' said Terry. 'I've wanted you to know about this for a long while.'

'Why?'

'I'll just pop out and fill the kettle,' said Mrs Andrews. 'Would you like to stay for a bit of tea, Ellie?'

'I don't know.'

'Well, think about it.' Mrs Andrews left them alone.

'Terry, why did you want to tell me about this?'

'When Mum told me Dad was still alive, I knew I had to go and see him. When you saw me at the home, I was visiting him. I let you think I was working there 'cos, like me mum, I was ashamed of me dad, and the stigma. Then one day I got really upset. The day you asked me to go out. I was angry with Mum and Dad; then she told me all about him . . .'

'Why did she leave it so long?'

'Dunno. Think she'd got herself in too deep through telling every one she was a widow. She couldn't suddenly produce a husband, could she?'

'No. Is your dad very ill?'

'Yer. He don't know us.'

'I'm very sorry, I know what that's like.'

'Last year, when I found out about me dad being shell shocked, so it couldn't be hereditary, like, I wanted to ask you out. But then I heard you'd gone off with that bloke.' He bent his head and fiddled with his fingers. 'I shouldn't say this, but I'm very fond of you, Ellie. Always have been. I know I should have said something before, but I was afraid; then I lost you. You moved away and Molly told me you was living with some bloke.'

Ellie thought her heart would burst. 'But what about Miss Jones? I thought . . .'

'She's only a lodger, and she won't be here for much longer.'

'Why's that?'

'She's getting married in the spring, and moving back to Kent.'

'But I thought Iris said you was taking her out?'

'No.' He laughed. 'I did once, when Iris saw me in the pub, but that was only to meet her boyfriend and his sister; they were up here to see the sights.'

Ellie began to laugh. 'And I got all upset over it.'

'You did?' His face lit up. 'I'm sorry, I should have . . . But all the years, even when we was kids, I liked you. I used to get so wild when you asked me to go out with you. I couldn't say yes, I didn't have any money; then I was worried that I might finish up like me dad. When me mum told me why me dad was like that, I very nearly did go mad. And it was too late, you'd moved away.' He pulled at his shirt cuffs.

'Terry, it was me who put our names on the elm tree.'

'Always thought it was. I wish you still felt that way about me.'

She wanted to throw her arms round his neck and cover his face with kisses, but instead she whispered softly, 'I've always been very fond of you.'

'But what about your bloke?'

'He's left me. He's gonner get married.'

'What?' Terry jumped to his feet. 'He's been two-timing you? The dirty rotten— where is he? I'll sort him out.'

'He's gone away.'

Terry sat down.

'Please, Terry, please don't think I'm saying all this just because I'm . . . I do love you, and I think I always have, even when I was with Leonard.' She suddenly stopped. 'Would it worry you that I've . . . you know, with another man?'

'I must admit it did make me bloody angry at first, but when I found out about your mum, and what had happened, I could understand you wanting to get away from home. Ellie, tell me the truth, did you love him?'

'I thought I did, but I think I mistook love for gratitude. I was so happy to be in his world. When he took me away from . . . the life we led, I thought it was love, but deep down I missed this kind of life, and the people. I know I've always loved you, Terry. And I know this is where I belong.' Tears ran down her face. 'Now all I've got to do is find a job I like, then everything will be wonderful.'

'I thought you liked it at Beaumonts?'

'I hate it. Terry, if Miss Jones is moving out later on, do you think your mum would have me as a lodger?'

'I don't see why not, but what about Iris?'

'She don't want me living with her. We'll soon be at loggerheads again if we stay together for very long.'

Terry put his arm round her shoulder. 'This is certainly turning out to be the best Christmas I've ever had.'

'And if I get a new job it could be the start of a brand new life that we can share.'

Terry sat forward. 'I'd like that. Say, you was always very bright at school, and you passed a scholarship – what if I ask me boss if you could take over Joyce's job?'

'What, in an office? Would you?'

'Yer, why not.'

'I'd love that.'

Terry took her in his arms and kissed her long and hard. Ellie knew she had found everything she had been looking for. And just like the tree in Elmleigh Square, come the spring, she too would burst forth, the tree with its bright new leaves, and Ellie with her new life.

If you enjoyed this book here is a selection of other bestselling titles from Headline

LIVERPOOL LAMPLIGHT	Lyn Andrews	£5.99 ☐
A MERSEY DUET	Anne Baker	£5.99 ☐
THE SATURDAY GIRL	Tessa Barclay	£5.99 ☐
DOWN MILLDYKE WAY	Harry Bowling	£5.99 ☐
PORTHELLIS	Gloria Cook	£5.99 ☐
A TIME FOR US	Josephine Cox	£5.99 ☐
YESTERDAY'S FRIENDS	Pamela Evans	£5.99 ☐
RETURN TO MOONDANCE	Anne Goring	£5.99 ☐
SWEET ROSIE O'GRADY	Joan Jonker	£5.99 ☐
THE SILENT WAR	Victor Pemberton	£5.99 ☐
KITTY RAINBOW	Wendy Robertson	£5.99 ☐
ELLIE OF ELMLEIGH SQUARE	Dee Williams	£5.99 ☐

Headline books are available at your local bookshop or newsagent. Alternatively, books can be ordered direct from the publisher. Just tick the titles you want and fill in the form below. Prices and availability subject to change without notice.

Buy four books from the selection above and get free postage and packaging and delivery within 48 hours. Just send a cheque or postal order made payable to Bookpoint Ltd to the value of the total cover price of the four books. Alternatively, if you wish to buy fewer than four books the following postage and packaging applies:

UK and BFPO £4.30 for one book; £6.30 for two books; £8.30 for three books.

Overseas and Eire: £4.80 for one book; £7.10 for 2 or 3 books (surface mail)

Please enclose a cheque or postal order made payable to *Bookpoint Limited*, and send to: Headline Publishing Ltd, 39 Milton Park, Abingdon, OXON OX14 4TD, UK.
Email Address: orders@bookpoint.co.uk

If you would prefer to pay by credit card, our call team would be delighted to take your order by telephone. Our direct line 01235 400 414 (lines open 9.00 am–6.00 pm Monday to Saturday 24 hour message answering service). Alternatively you can send a fax on 01235 400 454.

Name ....

Address ....

....

....

If you would prefer to pay by credit card, please complete:
Please debit my Visa/Access/Diner's Card/American Express (delete as applicable) card number:

Signature .... Expiry Date ....